C.A. James was born in Spalding and sets her novels in evocative Fenland countryside of South Lincolnshire. e works as a bookseller, researcher and teacher. She a lifelong fascination with crime fiction and its history. e is also a well-established non-fiction writer, under a separate name.

Christina James

In the Family

SALT

CROMER

PUBLISHED BY SALT PUBLISHING
12 Norwich Road, Cromer, Norfolk NR27 0AX United Kingdom

Salt Publishing 2012

Printed in Great Britain by Clays Ltd, St Ives plc

Typeset in Paperback 9/10

ISBN 978 1 907773 24 2 paperback

1 3 5 7 9 8 6 4 2

To the real James

CHAPTER ONE

It was bitterly cold on the A1 slip-road. Joel Carson, although wrapped in a council workman's donkey-jacket (the kind with lime-green shoulder inserts) and wearing an oversized pair of protective gloves, was frozen. Long tendrils of hair had escaped from his beanie hat, and were being whipped against his cheek in stringy strands. His nose was running, and, as he was unable to remove the gloves because his fingers had lost all feeling, he was wiping it at surreptitious intervals on the knitted cuff of his sleeve. He was one of a gang of four, three 'work experience' school leavers including himself and Marvin, a gangling black man in his twenties who had just been promoted to supervisor.

Joel had promised his mother that he would stick it out for the whole six months, and he would keep his promise. After that, he had no intention of working for the council or for anyone else. He had friends who made a living from street trading of various kinds and he intended to join them. He scowled at Marvin as he turned away from shouting some order to the little group about clearing the weeds as well as the rubbish. Joel hated Marvin, partly because of his bossy and unreasonable way of 'managing' his subordinates, but mainly because he was a sham. He knew that before his sudden rise from the ranks Marvin had been just as reluctant to do the thankless manual work as he was himself. Well, let him lord it over them. He was welcome to be a tin-pot motorway maintenance gang boss if he wanted. Joel wanted out. He squatted down on his haunches beside a bush, which was as far out of the wind as he could get, and, flinging the heavy gloves to the ground, lit a cigarette. He cupped its fragile glow in a cradle that he made with the frozen fingers of both hands. When he thought that it was properly alight, he took a long drag, drawing the smoke deep into his lungs.

The paltry contentment that he managed to extract from this action was short-lived. He was totally unprepared for the sudden sharp pain when a huge hand smote the back of his head, but it was a sensation that he recognised instantaneously. A 'good clip' to the back of the head had been his father's favourite form of chastisement, and therefore one that he particularly loathed. Caught off balance, he fell face first into the mud, and then scrambled to his feet to turn on Marvin. He landed a punch on Marvin's jaw and Marvin hit him back. Nick and Pete, the other two workers, downed tools to watch.

Marvin head-butted Joel and Joel kicked him viciously on the shins. Marvin responded with a rugby-type tackle and then both were rolling in the mud. Joel lost his temper, slapping Marvin's face repeatedly and shouting, "You bastard!" through gritted teeth. Marvin was the lither, and, rolling free, stood and hauled Joel to his feet before knocking him down again. Dazed, Joel fell to his knees on a pile of filthy old rags.

"Get up!" Marvin shouted. "Get up, you little shit!" He stood towering over Joel, his face twisted with hatred. "Get up, I said!"

Suddenly, Joel was not listening, nor did he now want to continue the fight. Transfixed, he pointed to something poking up from the matted knot of rags.

"Marvin," he said in a low voice, "what do you think that is?"

Marvin peered down into the mud-churned mess.

"Jesus Christ!" he said. "It's a finger-bone: a finger bone with a ring still on it."

Five hours later, Detective Inspector Tim Yates had had a tent set up over the remains on the bleak roadside verge and had just arrived at the scene himself, having been called out from an evening at home with his wife of eighteen months, Katrin. The council workmen were still there, crammed into a police car on the hard shoulder. The A1 had been closed from the exit before the discovery – which was adjacent to the body – to the one after it.

Night had fallen and if possible it was even colder and more desolate than it had been earlier in the day. Tim's spirits were not dampened, however, though he thought with a pang of the quiet dinner that he and Katrin had promised themselves. Not for the first time, he congratulated himself on his luck in having a wife like her – one who not only did not complain about the more uncivilised aspects of his job, but who actually understood them. Katrin had never been a police officer herself, but for the past several years she had worked as a police researcher and this had allowed her insights into the nature of police work which made her wryly accepting of the many disturbances to her private life that being married to a policeman created.

Tim had only been standing on the hard shoulder for a few minutes, but he was already soaked. Unwisely, he had brought no hat, and his thick, reddish hair was now plastered to his head. Thrusting his hands deep into his pockets and hunching his shoulders against the cold, he climbed up the slippery bank and poked his head into the SOCO's tent.

"Have you found anything else?"

"It looks as if there is a complete skeleton here – more or less, anyway. There are some bones missing, but they could have been disturbed by animals – or we will find them lower down in the soil." Patti Gardner beamed up at him. He was aware that she had long had a crush on him which they both recognised to be hopeless, though he had encouraged it in a half-hearted way before he had met Katrin.

"Male or female?"

"We can't say for certain – we need to carry out some lab tests to be sure – but judging from the remnants of clothing, and the ring that was found on the finger-bone, the remains are almost certainly female."

"How long has she been here?"

"Again, it is difficult to say. I hope that the fabrics that we're finding with the body will give us an accurate idea, once they're analysed. From the general decay of both the remains and the fabrics, I'd say they've been here for at least twenty years; but as you know it is always hard to tell in these cases. You might be able to find out when that stretch of road was turned into motorway, or the last time that tree planting work was carried out on the verges. It would help to narrow down the timeframe a little."

Tim nodded and thanked her. He walked over to the police car, which was crammed to bursting with two policemen and the four council workers. There was a noxious smell of damp meeting none-too-clean clothes, with other less obviously identifiable odours whose nature he preferred not to consider too closely.

The policeman sitting in the driver's seat made to get out of the car.

"It's all right – stay where you are, Constable . . . ?"

"Wright, sir. And this is PC Chakrabati."

Tim nodded at them, then craned his neck so that he could see the faces of the council workers.

"I'm afraid I'm going to have to ask you to accompany us to the station. It's impossible for us to interview you here without everyone getting soaked. Two of you can come with me in my car, and two of you can stay with Constable Wright. If you need to contact anyone, you can either do it now or from the station."

Marvin spoke first. He seemed excitable, and keen to exert his authority.

"I will come with you, Detective. It was me who found the bones. I'm in charge of the gang – Detective."

"I found the bones, you evil great scumbag," a voice cut in.

Tim peered further into the car. A skinny youth was glaring ferociously at the black man.

"There are no prizes for being the person who found them," said Tim, amused. "It isn't a treasure trove. No doubt you can each tell us your version of events when we get to the station. You" – he spoke to the skinny youth – "had better stay with Constable Wright, since you clearly don't see eye-to-eye with – what's your name?"

"Marvin Thomas, Detective"

". . . with Marvin. What's *your* name?"

"Joel Carson," Joel muttered sulkily.

"Well, Joel, you stay with Constable Wright, and you" – he pointed at Pete – "come with Marvin and me."

CHAPTER TWO

Mine has been a drab sort of life. There were many great things I could have done – I had the brain for it – and yet I have not fulfilled a single one of them. I could make many excuses, including that I had a very plausible desire to escape into ordinariness from my extraordinarily nasty childhood. But the truth is that I am lazy: bone idle. I always take the line of least resistance. Well, almost always.

As I look around my flat, I realise that I, aged fifty, should be living somewhere better; and certainly that it should be cleaner. Peter is adamant about the latter. No doubt he will make changes in that respect, in his emphatic energetic way.

It is because of Peter that I am in rather a pensive mood today. It is nearly thirty years since I lived under the same roof with another person, and then I had no choice. I got a place of my own as soon as I could afford it. And although I have had girlfriends and, eventually, boyfriends, I never wanted to share my home with them. I even preferred not to share my bed, if some alternative solution could be found. But although I have resisted all the little voices telling me that I am meant to be an island, somehow ever since I met him I have known that one day I would be compelled to ask Peter to live with me. He is moving in tomorrow.

In one sense I am rather astounded that he has accepted the offer. Peter is very upper class and superlatively fastidious. He went to Winchester and then to Peterhouse. His collars and cuffs are always snow-white and starched. I think that he has read almost every worthwhile novel written in the English language (though, not to do myself down, I might add that I have read quite a few myself) and certainly all of the even passable poetry. Yet he jumped at the chance! Any port in a storm, I suppose. I happen to know that his lease was about to expire and that his ancient tough Mummy had not come up with the renewal money as he had expected. But I like to think – am certain, in fact – that there is more to it than that. Little by little, Peter has become the love of my life; and I think that he feels the same way about me.

That doesn't mean that I am not scared – it would be no exaggeration to say terrified – however. I don't know what it will be like living with Peter. He has so much energy, and is so decided in his views, that I may not be able to cope. He has already said that he wants to move the furniture around (apparently he is regarded as extremely proficient at rearranging the contents of rooms) and to re-hang the pictures. I think that I can bear this as long as he doesn't start throwing things away. I have been living surrounded by the same possessions – with virtually no additions – for almost one third of a century. It is not their value or their appearance that concerns me, but their ingrainedness – they are part of me. Peter must appreciate that. But I'm sure that he does. He can be very sensitive.

I feel guilty about Elspeth. She's my cat. She's fifteen, and not used to strangers. She's met Peter once or twice and seems to like him well enough. I do hope that she won't be unhappy.

I'm not sure what people at work will say when they know about us. Most of the younger ones have guessed that I'm gay – though bisexual would be a more accurate term – but there are still one or two people who remember that I went out with Kathryn Sheppard for a while. They will be confused. But I'm certainly not going to worry about what they think. I'm much more concerned about how things will work out with

Peter. Poor Kathryn. I haven't thought about her for ages.

I must tidy up in a minute. Peter is coming to supper, but not to stay the night. He said that it would help him if I could cook for him, as he is very busy packing his things. When we have eaten, he will return to his own flat for the last time and carry on packing. When we eat together, I usually cook. Peter is a much better cook, but often I don't have the ingredients for the sort of food he prepares. All those exotic oils and herbs. I expect he will be bringing them here now; or if not we will buy some. It's all very exciting, really.

I'd better move the sofa and clean under it before he arrives. The last time he moved it, he was disgusted by the fluff and pieces of biscuit he found there. I suppose it was rather nasty. I think I'll cook chicken Caesar salad tonight. Peter likes that, though he wishes that I wouldn't use Cardini's dressing. He says that he makes his own, from eggs just put in boiling water for a minute and extra virgin oil. I must say I like Cardini's. No doubt Peter is right, and it's the sugar they put in it that attracts me. I don't pretend to have as fine a palate as he does.

The windows could do with a clean, too. It's a while since the last window-cleaner left the area and I haven't managed to find another one. I must ask the girl who lives downstairs if she knows someone. Or perhaps I'll just leave it to Peter. He'll be sure to know what to do.

I can hear footsteps in the corridor outside – he is probably here already and I haven't done a thing – no cleaning or cooking! I know he will be annoyed. Dear God, I wish he could understand how *afraid* I am. When I feel like this, I am quite paralysed – unable to lift a little finger or do anything at all. Not anything. My mind goes blank. Even sitting still exhausts me.

CHAPTER THREE

It was a sultry afternoon in late July. The housekeeper's daughter was playing in the drive. She scooped the gravel into two small heaps, creating a bald patch of earth just in front of her feet. Despite the heat, she was wearing heavy lace-up shoes. She could feel her feet sweating inside them, bruising her white socks with the stain of black polish. She swiped at the gravel, suddenly hot and irritable. Hobnailed boots came crunching across the sweep towards her, but she did not look up. She knew from the way that he walked that it was Mr. Sam.

The boots halted when they reached her. Still she did not look up, though she could see the coarse grey boots and his legs. She knew that it was rude not to look at him. She did not care.

"Little Miss Tirzah," he said. It was a joke. She didn't know why he called her by that name, but when he was playing with her he always did. Normally, she did not mind, but today she scowled and bent her head lower.

"Hey, little miss," he said, bending down and taking her chin in his hand, so that she had to look to one side to avoid his gaze. "I've told thee before about raking up the gravel – leave it lying flat, or you might cause an accident. And at very least I'll have yon gardener after me!"

He pointed to where John Horsley stood, his stern meagre figure bent over his hoe as he coaxed weeds out of the rose

9

beds. She knew that this was a joke too – that John Horsley, like everyone else, took orders from Mr. Sam – but still she did not oblige him with a smile.

"What's the matter, Missy," he continued, looking kindly on her. "Don't you have anything to do? No-one to play with, is that it?"

She shook her head. Her hair was dark and dead straight, cut by her mother into a severe bob with a short fringe. She looked at him directly now, and he saw that there were tears welling up in her light hazel eyes. He put his arm around her shoulder.

"Nay," he said. "What is it, child?"

"There's a dead bird," she said. The tears were coursing down her cheeks now.

"Well, birds do die – like all of us. Where did you find it? Show it to me."

She jumped to her feet, her red-and-white gingham dress twirling outwards to expose chubby knees above her rather thickset legs. Sam himself stood up more slowly. She took his hand and led him round the edge of the lawn to the greenhouse. Among a heap of broken flowerpots there lay a large dead crow. It looked as if it had been festering for some time: its underside had been ripped open, perhaps by a fox or by some other wild bird, and its entrails hung out in purplish ropes, alive with white maggots.

"I want to have a funeral," she announced.

He was suddenly concerned. Looking at the bird, he realised that it could not have fallen where it lay by chance. It must have been moved there.

"Dorothy," he said. "Tell me the truth. Have you touched it?"

She stared at him boldly, and for a fraction too long.

"No, Mr. Sam," she said, shaking her head.

"Are you sure? Because it's important. If you've touched it, it could make you ill; and I should have to send you in to your mother to wash your hands in disinfectant and change your clothes."

"No," she said. "I didn't touch it."

He kissed her briefly on her forehead.

"That's all right, then. Wait here while I fetch a spade – and don't touch it now."

He brought a light spade from the greenhouse, and dug a shallow hole under the yew hedge. Then he lifted the dead crow carefully on to the spade and flipped it into the hole, shovelling the loose earth back on top and tamping it down with his boots.

"There," he said. "We have had the funeral. You can put a stone on it to mark the spot if you want to."

She nodded, and was walking away from him when she changed her mind, turned and ran back to him, and gave him a hug, clumsily, because he was still carrying the spade. He chuckled.

"That's more like my Tirzah," he said.

Later her mother called her in to tea. It was scrambled eggs with Marmite toast, normally her favourite, and a meal that she had pleaded for earlier in the day. However, she could eat only a few mouthfuls, and even her cup of tea seemed to rise up in her throat and choke her. Eliza was annoyed.

"Mrs. Frear gave me those eggs especially for you. If you don't eat them, you won't go out again today."

She went to the room that they shared and lay down on her bed. She shut her eyes and fell into an uneasy sleep. When she awoke, the daylight was fading and she was vaguely aware that Eliza was in the room preparing for bed. She had changed into her floor-length nightdress and had knelt by the bed to pray. She did not seem to notice that Dorothy had not washed or changed out of her daytime clothes. Dorothy turned over and slept again.

The next time that she awoke, she could see the dawn breaking outside the window and hear the cowman whistling to the small herd of cows to come down the field to the dairy for milking. She was very hot. She tried to sit up, but she felt terribly weak and slumped sideways against the pillow. Her sore throat raged. She was afraid to wake her mother, but desperate for water. At night, there was always a glass of water on her mother's bedside table. She swung both legs over the side of the bed and planted her feet firmly on her rag rug. The she tried to stand. She was aware of herself falling, as if into a bright light, and felt her head take a sharp knock against the side of the bed as she fell. She thought that she heard the thud of her own body as it hit the floor.

She did not know how many hours or days later she gained consciousness. She was barely awake and could only see through a grey blur. Her limbs felt dead and heavy. Her throat was horribly sore and there was a nasty taste in her mouth. Her tongue was furred and felt as though it were blistered. When she breathed, she made a whistling sound and each intake of breath gave a stab of pain to her neck – not the putrid, pervasive soreness of her throat, but a sharper, cleaner pang, as if someone had just twisted a razor there. Through the gummy lids of half-closed eyes, she could make out a figure huddled at the end of the bed, head tied in a triangular scarf. It was her mother, weeping. She drifted back into sleep, hot and uncomfortable.

It seemed only a moment or two later that she was again awake and being raised in the bed. She struggled feebly – it hurt too much to be pulled about – and was reprimanded sharply by her mother's voice.

"Be gentle with her, Mrs. Drake," said someone with kindly authority. "She has a long convalescence in front of her yet – her arms and legs will feel sore and you can expect her to be very lethargic. Now, Dorothy, I need to get you into a sitting position so that I can look at your throat. I'm afraid it will hurt a little – we have had to make an incision and put a little silver tube inside it, because you were finding it hard to breathe."

His hands were cool and deft, but when he touched her neck the pain was dreadful. She made no sound, but the tears welled up in her eyes.

"Good girl," he said, placing her gently back on the pillow. "I shall leave it in for a few more days," he added, speaking over his shoulder in a brisker tone. "Then she must come to the cottage hospital to have it removed. It is too risky to try to do it here. Keep her in bed in the meantime."

"Yes, Doctor. Thank you," said her mother reverently. "May she have visitors? I mean just from the house. Mr. Sam is anxious to see her."

"If he only stays for a few minutes, and doesn't overtire her. I don't think that there can be any risk to him of infection now."

Her mother brought him one of the china ewers from their room, and poured out hot water into an enamel bowl. He washed his hands with some ceremony and took the towel of Indian linen from her slowly. He was looking at her intently. Despite the ridiculous scarf, she was looking very handsome. She was not unaware of her good looks.

"You're a good mother, Eliza." he said. "Dorothy, you're a lucky girl to have so many people care for you. We'll soon have you running around again."

At his praise, her mother bridled with pride. "Say thank-you to the doctor, Dorothy," she said.

Dorothy raised her head and managed to croak thank-you as he departed. It hurt her to speak. She felt indignant: it was clear that she should have been the centre of attention during his visit, but already her leading-lady role was being stolen from her by her mother.

Mr. Sam came in and sat on a chair by the bed. He was carrying a jar containing a little posy of wild flowers.

"Eh, Tirzah," he said. "I've brought you a bit of the summer, since you can't go outside. Aye, but you're a bad lass. You told me that you hadn't touched yon crow and doctor says you must have. He says that's probably how you got the diphtheria. Your poor mother has been beside herself with grief. Lord only knows what she'd have done if . . ."

"Don't, Father," her mother cut in, but indulgently – her voice carried none of its habitual harsh edge when she spoke to him. Only she and Mrs. Kitty and his two sons were allowed to call him "Father". "The child has suffered enough, and she'll know not to try to deceive us again." She cast Dorothy a baleful look while Mr. Sam was searching in his sleeve for a handkerchief.

CHAPTER FOUR

Inspector Tim Yates considered himself to be an ordinary man, of average intelligence for a graduate. He was also happy, and comfortable with himself. He had no hang-ups about his middle-class upbringing, excellent education, sexual proclivities or even his red hair. He was proud of his job, and saw no need to apologise for it. He did not use it as an excuse for being moody, gloomy or unduly introspective, and indeed he was none of these things. His ordinary disposition was equable, if not sunny. Nor did he think that his zest for life made him bumptious, unfeeling, loud or overproud of his achievements, or that it had turned him into the sort of male who aggressively proclaims himself to be a 'regular bloke'.

Tim was six feet one inch tall, with a (reasonably) athletic physique which he kept (reasonably) in shape by cycling as often as he could. He was not interested in developing a six-pack, abhorred team games and contact sports (though he was good at building teams at work), drank with a moderation that only occasionally crept to excessive levels because he was enjoying himself so much that he had lost count of the units and ate moderately healthy food which was high in vegetable content (though in Tim's book this included chips).

As well as the red hair – which to be more accurate was a resonant shade of auburn – Tim had eyes the colour of clear jade and a fair but not effeminate complexion. His hands were slender and delicate, and gave away his sensitivity. On the other hand, his feet were massive, and his friends joked that it was because of them that he had been born to be a 'Plod'.

When he had graduated Tim had chosen a career in the police force purely because he thought it would be interesting. He had not agonised over the decision, nor had he made it, unlike so many of his colleagues, because he had been thwarted in his first choice of occupation. He went into policing with his eyes open and was under no illusions about how frustrating, harrowing or tedious it could be on occasion, nor about the intrusions and interruptions that it would cause in his personal life.

If there was one area in which Tim showed himself to be a little too idealistic and starry-eyed, it was in the parallel fascination which he felt for the probing of and general study of the criminal mind. There was more than a little of the psychologist manqué within him. This created in him a tendency to project elaborate motives and sophisticated thought processes upon the most brutal and basic of thugs. Fortunately for his own credibility, the early fulfilment of his ambition to lead a murder squad had meant that this outlook had not led him into professional blunder. To his own satisfaction at least, he had proved that all but the most straightforward of murderers – and these tended also to be the most violent – had suffered some trauma in their past which had forged kinks and flaws in their psyches, or exhibited the symptoms of one or more of the recognised classifiable psychological disorders. That the more cynical and hard-bitten old-stagers among his colleagues sometimes observed that the criminal in question was taking him for a ride seldom abashed him. He believed that this in itself was a symptom of deviant behaviour. The trick lay in spotting the deviance.

Tim's greatest leisure pursuits were cycling and literature. He devoured books of all kinds, especially works on modern history, current affairs and fiction. Although he read modern 'literary' authors, his favourite genre was undoubtedly crime fiction. He maintained an affectionate regard for the creations of many post-war crime writers, whilst at the same time considering that the portrayals of their mostly tortured policeman protagonists were more far-fetched than the extravagant plots in which they usually found themselves.

Tim had met Katrin when he was attending a crime statistics seminar at a police college. It was an event that he had signed up for with reluctance, pushed into it by his boss, Superintendant Thornton, who had said that he needed to have an overview of criminal patterns in order to be a good copper. In principle, he knew that this was correct, and he was the last person to denigrate putting a bit of cerebral gloss on police work. But he had envisaged that in practice this would mean spending a whole day in the company of mostly middle-aged men, being lectured to by another middle-aged man on trends of criminal activity in certain geographical regions, government targets for the apprehending of various types of criminal and how police forces were or were not meeting them, and, more abstrusely and yawningly boring (he knew because he had had to attend lectures on it while he was training), lots of econometrics charts tracing the relationship of national prosperity – or the lack of it – to rises and falls in criminal behaviour.

When he arrived to register for the seminar, the police college itself had been a pleasant surprise. He had imagined a grim Gothic building made of red brick, perhaps a former Victorian workhouse or 'place of correction'. He had attended other courses in buildings like the latter; he did not doubt that they had been chosen by the organisers of the training programmes to prove how serious their schemes of work were, and how earnest their students; and to dispel any suspicions that the latter were being treated to a 'jolly', by making the surroundings as gloomy and uncomfortable as possible. Some seminars even took place in Methodist centres where the sale of alcohol was forbidden. However,

Bagden Hall – despite its unpromising name – had turned out to be an elegant neo-Palladian mansion with a double sweep leading to its porticoed doors. It proved also to have a marbled hall when eventually he had entered to register himself. The lecture rooms, all leading off a kind of minstrels' gallery on the first floor, were airy and spacious, and fitted with sophisticated media suites for the presentations. The bedrooms were equally luxurious – his own had a four-poster bed with tester – and a peek into the dining-room revealed tables gleaming with damask cloths and lead crystal glasses. There was also a small bar. He thought perhaps that he would be able to stand two days in this place very well indeed.

Nevertheless, his first day there had been pretty soporific. As he had predicted to himself, most of those attending were over forty, and most of the lecturers closer to sixty than fifty. They had presented graphs and pie charts until his mind blanked and he felt himself drifting into sleep. The final presentation of that first day was even on statistics about statistics: the lecturer, who was not a police officer, but an economist from a local university, had droned on about how much the crime statistics influenced police work and the economy in general. As if, thought Tim, the average copper – or even the exceptional ones privileged to attend this seminar – were motivated by such considerations. He began to dread dinner and the evening which stretched ahead, despite the luxurious room, and even more the prospect of another full day of the same sort of stuff tomorrow. He told himself sternly not to relieve his ennui by having too much to drink. He knew that a day sitting through more presentations – and, even worse, taking part in group exercises – would be the more excruciating if accompanied by a hangover. Taking heed of his own words of wisdom, he resolved not to join his fellow delegates in the bar before dinner, but to retire to his room for an hour to make some phone calls and check e-mails.

He had just resisted the blandishments of the red-faced man with greasy silver hair who had been sitting next to him all afternoon to accompany him for a drink – no great temptation there – and was crossing the reception area to take the lift to his room, when the main door opened and a dark-haired young woman struggled in with a huge shocking pink suitcase. Appraising her upwards from her shapely legs to her neat figure, glossy dark hair and beautiful grey eyes, Tim felt his chivalrous instincts kicking in quite precipitately. He noticed that the man and woman who had been stationed at the reception desk when he had himself arrived had disappeared. Perhaps they were not expecting any more arrivals so late in the day. At any rate, it was clear that the offer of help with luggage which he had himself received would not be available to the young woman, which was very satisfactory from his point of view.

"Can I help you with that?" he had asked.

She had not answered him, but had dropped the heavy case, which she had been lugging along by means of a sort of rigid strap – the suitcase was fitted with two tiny wheels which were obviously inadequate when the case was full – and lifted her hands with the palms towards him, at the same time raising both eyebrows and turning down her mouth in mock helplessness and anguish. Tim had been fascinated: it was the sort of expression he had seen illustrated in pictures of nineteenth century pierrots, but he had never actually witnessed anyone replicating it in life. He took his hands out of his pockets and sauntered over to her as casually as he could, holding out his right hand when he reached her.

"Tim Yates," he said. The fingers that grasped his were long and slender, and very cold. Close up, her skin was flawless, and pale olive in colour.

"Katrin Schuster," she said. "Could you possibly carry this for me over to the reception desk? The wheels on it are quite useless, and it keeps on tipping over." She was wearing a black silk blouse with a cream-coloured scarf, which looked as if it might also be of silk, wound round her neck and a pencil skirt, with a short fake fur jacket which was obviously not keeping her warm. Her shoes, stilettos with, he guessed, four-inch heels, were totally impractical. He noted this last point with approval. He saw plenty of women wearing 'sensible' shoes every day of the week.

"Of course," he said, taking the case by the handle, and lifting it with more difficulty than he had expected – what had she got in there? "But reception seems to have packed up for the day. Perhaps you'd care to sit down," – he gestured at two giant Chesterfield sofas which had been placed at right angles to each other between the door and the receptionists' desks – "while I go and find somebody. I've been here all day, so I stand a better chance than you do of spotting someone who might be able to help," he added quickly, worried in case she thought he was patronising her.

She didn't seem at all perturbed by the suggestion. "Thank you," she said, obediently doing as he said. She crossed one leg gracefully over the other and rummaged in her bag, before stopping suddenly.

"Damn!" she said. "I've just remembered that I gave up smoking last week. Pity. This is just the sort of day on which you need a cigarette. I don't suppose that you . . . ?"

"Unfortunately not," said Tim. "I don't smoke. But in any case . . ." he gestured at the No Smoking sign on the wall. She shrugged.

"Much better for me not to."

He nodded agreement.

"Are you here for the statistics seminar?" he asked. "Because if you are, I admire your cleverness in getting out of the first day. It has been deadly dull – and that's putting it mildly."

"I have come for it: but not as one of the delegates. I'm one of the speakers."

"Oops, sorry!" said Tim. He felt his face grow red.

"Oh, it's OK," she said, with a grin. "I had nothing to do with designing it, and I'm certainly not a statistician. I think that I was brought in for a bit of light relief. I've got the pre-lunch slot tomorrow, as well, so no doubt no-one will bother to listen to me – they'll all be thinking about taking a break, if not actually disappearing into the bar."

"Well, I shall certainly listen to you. What are you going to talk about?"

"You should have asked that first, before you promised to listen! You can't have looked at the schedule for tomorrow, either, though admittedly my name doesn't appear on it; one of my colleagues was supposed to be giving the presentation, but she's gone down with 'flu. I got a call on my way back from the airport, which is why I wasn't here earlier, and also why I've brought so much luggage with me." She glanced ruefully at the shocking pink monster.

"You mean you're still supposed to be on holiday today?"

"Yes. First day back tomorrow. But being here will beat sitting at my desk checking up on hundreds of e-mails."

"I wouldn't be too certain about that," said Tim.

"If it's as boring as you say, I may just stay in my room and check the e-mails there, except when it's my turn to speak."

"It's not that bad," said Tim quickly, regretting for the second time in five minutes that he had let his tongue run away with him. "You could give it a try the course delegates might amuse you. I've never seen such a stereotypical set of coppers."

"I'm used to coppers," she said. "I work with them all the time. I wouldn't be able to identify a stereotype, though; most of the ones I work with have individual quirks. But you're right: I do find meeting them interesting. If the people here aren't brain-dead from all those statistics, I'm sure they'll be interesting to talk to. You are, after all."

Tim felt both put down and flattered, all in one go. He was curious, as well.

"You still haven't told me what you do. Do you work with coppers all of the time, or is it only part of your job? Are you a psychologist – or a psychiatrist?"

"Nothing so glamorous, I'm afraid. I'm a police researcher.

I expect you've met quite a few like me. We dig up the background information to serious cases and sometimes recommend expert witnesses. We aren't always treated seriously, as a matter of fact. I think that's partly why Commander Rawlinson asked my colleague to speak – to make you all appreciate how much we can help you if we're allowed to. I may even throw in a few stats to prove it," she added mischievously.

"I can honestly say that I appreciate everyone who helps me and my team, or becomes part of my team," said Tim. It sounded a little pompous, but it was true. He had little time for hierarchy or bogus professional pride. "But I can equally honestly say, I've never worked with anyone remotely like you." He said it in a bantering way, but she could see that he was in earnest. She laughed again, almost a schoolgirl giggle.

At that moment, the old man whom the receptionist had earlier referred to as the 'concierge' belatedly put in an appearance. He was a man of about sixty, whose face had apparently been set habitually in such a morose expression that its skin now fell naturally into deep sad grooves; his drooping, badly-cut greying hair and moustache gave him the look of Lewis Carroll's walrus. Nevertheless, he managed a small smile in her direction, which was more than he had vouchsafed to Tim earlier.

"Can I help you, Miss?" he enquired, surveying the huge suitcase. "Are you here for the conference, or just visiting?" He eyed Tim askance, as if to indicate that he knew that Tim was trying to lead the woman astray. He consulted a piece of paper that had been sellotaped to the reception desk.

"I'm Katrin Schuster. I'm one of the speakers tomorrow, but you won't find my name on your list. I'm standing in for a colleague, whose name should be on it: Louise Thresher."

The concierge ran his forefinger down the list with painful slowness. How difficult could it be? Tim thought impatiently. There were only about thirty people on the course, lecturers included.

"Ah, yes. Ms Thresher. Room 307. Could you just fill in this sheet – for security purposes? You only need to give us your name and address. We don't use most of the boxes on this form."

Katrin smiled and nodded, writing her name and address on the form with a considerable flourish before she handed it back to him. He took it from her and scrutinised it, then turned back to his list and carefully crossed out 'Louise Thresher' many times, so that the words were entirely illegible, before printing her name above the black block of ink that he had created.

"Can I carry your case up for you, Miss?"

"I'll do that!" said Tim, with alacrity. The concierge looked at him with venomous watery eyes, as if he had made an improper suggestion.

"Are you quite happy with that, Miss?" As Tim joked much later, he might just as well have said, "We don't want no shenanigans going on here."

She nodded, obviously trying not to laugh. Tim heard the roar of voices in the bar get suddenly louder and guessed that dinner was about to be served. He vowed to get Katrin Schuster out of the reception area before his new colleagues clapped eyes on her. He fervently hoped that, by the time she had sorted out her belongings, she would have missed dinner and given him the excuse to take her somewhere else. He seized the case again and loped up the two flights of stairs as fast as he could without actually running. Katrin followed more slowly. The concierge watched, irradiating disapproval.

"Wow," said Tim, when she had unlocked the door and he had hefted the case over the threshold. "You've got a suite. How did you manage that?"

She shrugged.

"Speaker's privilege, I guess." She wandered around the room a little. "Do come in – since I don't have to invite you into my bedroom in order to offer hospitality, I'm sure we would be behaving with perfect decorum. Sitting-rooms are only for sitting in, after all. Ah, that's what I was looking for," she added, moving over to a huge ornate sideboard which stood against the interior wall and swooping on a decanter which had been set on it. "Complimentary sherry. I was told that this would be here. There's some complimentary fruit somewhere, too." She lifted the bottle. "Would you like some?"

"Sherry's not really my kind of . . . oh, what the hell, it's better than going down to the bar, and no point in looking a gift horse, etc. Yes, please."

She poured sherry into two of the tulip glasses that had been arranged on a tray with the decanter, and handed one of them to him. He took a gingerly sip of the pale yellow liquid. Fortunately, it was a dry sherry, so at least drinkable.

"Sit down for a minute, if you've got time," she added. She grinned. Tim realised that he was behaving with adolescent gaucheness. He had not felt so tongue-tied since he was fourteen. His earlier attempt at sang-froid had evaporated. He nodded and sat obediently. She sat down beside him, not too close, but in a companionable way. She chattered on about her holiday and her plans once she got back to work, while he listened and responded. By the time they were on their second glass of sherry, his uneasiness had vanished and he was mimicking Superintendant Thornton to a very appreciative listener. She kept on giggling until they were both laughing uncontrollably.

"Goodness!" she said suddenly, looking at her watch. "Dinner's started. We'll either have to go in late or miss it – and I'm starving."

Within five minutes of having first spoken to her, Tim had had no intention of escorting her to the police delegates' dinner at Bagden Hall. He did not even pretend that he was annoyed at having missed it.

"Did you see any restaurants when you were riding here in the taxi?" he asked.

"I think that there was a gastropub in the last village

before you reach here from the station," she said. "A place called Frensham, or something like it."

"Fancy going to suss it out?" he said. "My treat." He stood up and offered her his arm. "Or, to put it another way, 'I'd be delighted if you'd do me the honour of accepting my invitation to dinner, Miss Schuster'."

She giggled again.

"Give me a couple of minutes," she said, kicking off the stilettos. "I've been travelling since the crack of dawn today. I just need to freshen up a bit."

She disappeared back into the tiny lobby that led to her sitting-room. He heard her lugging the big suitcase into the bedroom, and decided that it would be indelicate to offer to help. He remained seated on her yellow sofa, idly flicking through an advertising brochure for Bagden Hall, until she returned. She'd been more than a couple of minutes, but still pretty swift, he thought, admiringly. Now she was wearing skinny jeans and a white polo sweater, and carrying the fur jacket. Her jeans were tucked into knee-high boots. Tim smiled approval. He decided not to risk complimenting her verbally.

"Next step," he said, "is for us each to sneak out of here without being observed. "I'll go first, then you won't have to stand around in the cold. You follow in a few minutes. My car's a BMW that's seen better days. It's dark blue. I'll bring it round from the car park and wait just the other side of the main entrance, at the top of the sweep."

Ten minutes later they were driving into Frensham. They found the pub immediately. It was called The Queen's Head and it stood right next to the road. Its sign, painted in primary colours, depicted a female head in a Tudor headdress – perhaps intended to represent that of one of Henry VIII's wives– lying severed on the ground, the neck ruff and the jewelled band holding the headdress still, improbably, in place. A square placard tacked underneath it proclaimed 'Gourmet meals served daily. Local specialities. 12.30 – 2.00

and 6.30 – 8.30. Tim glanced at his watch. It was a few minutes after eight o'clock. It looked as if they would be lucky.

They laughed about their first dinner together many times afterwards. Inside, The Queen's Head turned out to be a 'spit and sawdust' establishment with wall-to-wall football blaring from an outsize TV, which was being watched by half a dozen or so locals standing at the bar. No-one appeared to be eating. However, the landlord – a balding man with a huge gut – assured them that he was still serving food, and brought grubby menus. There was steak and chips, curry and chips or steak and kidney pie and chips.

"Gourmet in every case," said Tim, smiling ruefully. "Do you want to risk it?"

"Why not?" Katrin had smiled back. "The worst that can happen is that we both have to bunk off tomorrow because we've gone down with food poisoning. I'll try the pie – it's less likely to have been made on the premises than the other things." Tim afterwards said that he had loved her from this moment on, for her wonderfully enterprising attitude. Most of the girls that he knew would have thrown a tantrum at this point.

Two pies duly arrived, each accompanied by pale greasy chips and bright green frozen peas. The vegetables proved to be inedible, but the pies were passable, especially when washed down with the real ale which was The Queen's Head's only redeeming feature. Katrin was probably right about their provenance. Despite the questionable food, the evening passed like a dream. They talked about each other, their jobs, their interests, their families. Tim felt as if he had never known anyone so well or cared for anyone so much.

Outside in the car park, they paused and kissed. And kissed some more. When finally they reached Bagden Hall again – just before its ridiculous curfew of 11 p.m., after which all the doors were locked – it took all his powers of self-restraint not to follow her up the broad staircase to her suite of rooms once more, instead of turning past reception to his own room at the end of the ground floor corridor. Afterwards, she had said that she was disappointed that he had been so circumspect. However, it had enabled her to manage a reasonable night's sleep and then get up early to do some work.

The next day, she delivered an engaging talk, having spent most of the morning in her room preparing it. The old lags all vied with each other to sit with her at lunch, so that it was mid-afternoon by the time Tim got the chance to speak to her again. The seminar was almost over by then and people were preparing to depart. He gave her a lift to the station, where they exchanged telephone numbers and e-mail addresses. He was convinced that they would meet again, and soon, but nevertheless he was overcome with an overpowering sense of sadness – of the transience of all truly pleasurable things – as he drove home.

"Learn anything useful from that seminar?" asked Superintendant Thornton.

"Yes, sir," said Tim. "I found out what a big help police researchers can be."

"Funny you should say that, because I've been thinking of advertising for one. Perhaps you could help me draft the jd."

CHAPTER FIVE

It was a glowering February morning and dawn had just broken, although it was well after 8 a.m. It was three days after the discovery of the skeleton, and Tim Yates, sanguine as he normally was, was beginning to get annoyed that he had still received no results from either the pathologist or the National DNA Database. Katrin had already left for work, and he himself – characteristically, for time-keeping was not his strong point – was in danger of being late for his first team briefing on the case. He reflected angrily that there wasn't much point in a team briefing unless they could identify the victim – although he knew that he was being unreasonable, especially with regard to the database, as the probable date of death made it unlikely that they would find a match. The only clues that they had to go on were some shreds of fabric, which a forensic analyst had already dated 'with reasonable accuracy' as having been manufactured in the early 1970s, the ring, and the plastic Red Indian. Juliet Armstrong was investigating the likely provenance of this and she had given him to understand that she had made progress. Otherwise, nothing.

He decided to call Juliet on his cellphone. He knew that she would already be at the police station, setting things up for the meeting. Juliet was nothing if not efficient and, although her painstaking attention to bureaucratic detail sometimes irritated him, he would be the first to acknowledge the value of this in a team whose other members all shunned 'the paperwork'.

"Juliet? It's me. Have we heard anything back from the pathologist or the DNA database yet?"

"Good morning, sir. No – you asked me that question yesterday afternoon. I chased them both then and they said that they would pull the stops out. I'm hoping we might get something today."

"I'm on my way in now. If we don't have anything by the time I get there, I shall call them myself and give them a rocket. I should like to know what they think we mean when we say something is urgent."

"As you wish, sir. I suppose they can be forgiven for thinking that work on what we believe to be an old crime is not quite on a par with some of their other jobs. The skeleton has probably been by the side of the dual carriageway for thirty-odd years, after all."

"That's not the point, it's . . . forget it. I'm on my way."

Tim's bad mood had not abated when he reached HQ. When he entered the incident room, he found the investigation team – such as it was, for it consisted of only three officers besides himself – assembled. As he knew she would have done, Juliet Armstrong had written what information they had collected so far on the glass screen and stuck several photographs of the remains of the skeleton from different angles at the top of it. Tim immediately felt brighter. He poured himself coffee from the insulated jug and took one of the seats at the circular table.

"Good morning, everyone," he said. "Thank you, Juliet, for getting everything ready. You're an inspiration, as usual."

Juliet blushed. She was rather a dumpy woman in her early thirties, with poor skin. She wore heavy, black-framed spectacles and seemed to be unable to control her thick black corkscrew curls. He saw Andy Carstairs, Juliet's counterpart and exact contemporary, smother a grin, and realised that he might have pushed his praise too far. The last thing that he wanted to do was to humiliate her. He moved swiftly into the briefing.

"Let's begin by summarising what we already have. At approximately four-thirty p.m. last Monday afternoon – just as it was getting dark – a skeleton was found by workmen on the reservation of the southbound carriageway of the A1. It appears to have been there a long time. All that was found with it were some fragments of blue cloth, some metal circlets and hooks and eyes, probably part of a woman's bra, a silver ring of the type that I believe is known as a 'friendship ring' – they are inexpensive and available from shops and boutiques all over the country – and a terracotta-coloured plastic Red Indian. Forensic tests show that the skeleton is that of a young woman, and that she probably died about thirty years ago. Cause of death so far indeterminate. Her exact age cannot be determined, either, but she was probably about twenty-five when she died, and certainly no older than thirty. Andy has been looking up the names of women reported missing in this age group during the period, and come up with five. Andy, tell us what you know." Tim did not add that he had had a conversation with Andy Carstairs on the previous day, which had prompted him to commission a separate piece of research of his own.

Andy Carstairs rose and moved to the glass screen. He indicated a list of names that he had already written there in blue marker pen. Two photographs were stuck alongside them.

"I've looked up missing persons records for the period 1972–1978", he said. "These are the ones that appear to fit. Valerie Stimpson, a mother of two. Disappeared in the Cowbit area in February 1972. She was in her early thirties, but I've included her anyway. The policeman on the case thought that she had been murdered by her husband. We have several photographs. This is the best of them, though it's a bit grainy. Rachel Benyon, a student at Boston College. Reported missing by her parents in September 1972. Friends said that she had run away to the US with her boyfriend when she took fright at the approach of her exams, so the police didn't take it all that seriously. The case is still open, though. She was never traced. She's a bit young for our victim: she was only twenty-two when last seen. Shakira Khan, an Asian shopworker, who lived in Peterborough. She was twenty-five – exactly the right age. We may need forensics to do some more work to see if they give a more accurate picture of the race of the victim. Shakira was reported missing by neighbours in May 1975. Her family were not keen to help with police enquiries and said that a marriage with a cousin had been arranged for her in Pakistan, so she was no longer resident in the UK. Her employers said that she had not handed in her notice, however. I suspect that nowadays the police would have wanted to take it further, but the case was closed after some relatively cursory enquiries. We have no photograph of her. Annie Hart, who was quite a well-known prostitute. She was last seen working her patch in Lincoln in January 1976. It was thought at the time that she may have been one of the Yorkshire Ripper's victims, but Sutcliffe did not confess to having killed her and concealing bodies so well that they couldn't be found was not his usual MO. Obviously, she also lived quite a long way from his usual geographical orbit. We think that she was in her early twenties. There is a photograph, though not a good one, because she was already known to the police. Finally, Kathryn Sheppard, who was reported missing by her mother in the autumn of 1975. It was assumed by the police investigating her disappearance that she had been murdered, because she vanished without a trace.

" I have left Kathryn Sheppard until last, because her disappearance was investigated extensively by the police at the time. As I said, they concluded that she had been murdered, although they never found the body. Her boyfriend was arrested on suspicion of her murder, but the police had to release him for lack of evidence. His name was Charles

Heward. One interesting twist to the case was that a former boyfriend of hers, Hedley Atkins, was the son of Dorothy Atkins, a woman who murdered her mother-in-law. Her case was famous at the time. Dorothy Atkins had been remanded in custody pending her trial at the time of Kathryn Sheppard's disappearance, so she was never regarded as a suspect, though I've discovered that she was allowed temporary bail on several occasions while her defence was being prepared. The police interviewed Hedley Atkins, and reported him as being very co-operative, but it's clear from the notes that the police really thought that either Kathryn had run away or, more probably, that Charles Heward had murdered her. They just couldn't pin it on him."

"Thank you," said Tim. "Let's hope that we're lucky enough to discover that the remains belong to one of these women. I assume that their files contain dental records, etc. Do we have any idea what they were wearing when they disappeared?"

"There are dental reports in some of the files, sir. I've sent them to the pathologist, for comparison with the skull that was found. The Kathryn Sheppard case was also re-opened briefly in 1990, because her mother had preserved some hair and clothing and wanted to have her DNA profiled. The police were encouraging people to undergo DNA profiling voluntarily for the purposes of elimination at the time and they therefore arranged for profiles to be done of several murder victims, as a kind of showcase of how it helped their work. Kathryn Sheppard and Annie Hart were both profiled. Not the other women on my list, unfortunately – either they weren't chosen or there was no suitable DNA material to use. Human tissue that might yield DNA was not routinely collected from crime scenes until the late '80s."

"Obviously we need those results from the DNA service as soon as possible. What about Pathology? Do we have anything from them yet?"

"They've promised a report this afternoon. From what

they've said to me, I don't think it will tell us much, except to confirm what they've already said: that the remains are those of a female adult aged 25 – 30, and have been in the ground about thirty years. But we shall see."

"Get on to them if they haven't sent you anything by the middle of the afternoon. Juliet, you said that you had some information about the fragments of cloth that were found?"

"Yes, sir. We think that it was blue denim-look cotton. It was imported to this country from Asia in great quantities in the seventies and eighties. Some companies in the UK still import it, but not the more reputable ones. The factory that makes it was exposed by an investigative journalist for exploiting child labour, and sales of it here dropped off immediately. They didn't stop completely, though."

"Meaning that the cloth we have could be any age from the period that it was first imported?"

"No, I don't think so. The path lab says that it has probably been in the soil for at least twenty years to have reached that stage of decay, even though it is ordinary cotton and not denim, which would take longer to rot. There was also a fragment of a different type of material which has been sent for further analysis. It looks as if it might be part of a washing instructions label. If so, we might be able to track it back to the retailer who sold the garment."

"Well done. Is there anything else?"

"Nothing yet, but I'm still working on the plastic Red Indian. I've consulted a model expert about it, and he says that he thinks that it was probably a free gift with breakfast cereal. I've had some life-size photographs of it taken, and I'm having them sent to all the main breakfast cereal manufacturers today. If we can get someone to identify it, we might at least be able to narrow down the time of death to the period in which it was distributed."

"Whoever left it there had not necessarily just acquired it," said Andy Carstairs. He knew that he was being ungenerous: it was just that Juliet Armstrong's blue-eyed Goody

Two-Shoes image got on his nerves on occasions like this.

Tim gave him a level look.

"Agreed," he said, "but I'd say that the balance of probabilities would be in favour of such an assumption. And it's one of the few things we have: there's precious little else to go on. Well done, Juliet," he added again.

"What next, sir?" asked Ricky McFadyen. Ricky was a solid detective constable who would probably not make further progress in his career. He offered few opinions on the cases that he worked on and certainly could not be accused of trying to hog the limelight. He was, however, excellent at pursuing a line of enquiry once someone else had set him on the right track.

"We wait for the results," said Tim. "If necessary, we will mount an investigation without knowing the identity of the victim. But it will be a bloody sight easier if we can find out who she was before we go any further."

Tim was about to break up the meeting when Juliet's cellphone rang.

"You'd better take that call," he said, in response to the question in her look. "It might be the laboratory."

Juliet moved away to the window, ostensibly to get better reception, but partly, Tim guessed, because she was nervous at suddenly finding all eyes fixed on her. The conversation which followed was short and intense.

"You're quite sure?" she repeated twice. "Yes, we'd be grateful for a written report. Thank you very much indeed, Professor Salkeld."

She switched off the phone and laid it on the windowsill.

"That was the lab, as you thought, sir," she said. "They say they've got a perfect match. The remains found on the sliproad are those of Kathryn Sheppard. They're going to send us a report, but they say there can be no possible doubt."

Ricky whistled.

"There must be a link with the Dorothy Atkins case. It's too much of a coincidence that Kathryn Sheppard was formerly

Dorothy's son's girlfriend – isn't it? Surely this indicates that Dorothy was a serial killer?"

"It might," Tim agreed. "But there is barely even circumstantial evidence, since Dorothy was probably in custody at the time that Kathryn Sheppard disappeared. We don't know exactly where or how Kathryn died and we're unlikely to find out. And for that matter, we don't know the exact circumstances of Doris Atkins' death, either. Dorothy Atkins consistently refused to say anything about her mother-in-law's murder."

"If Dorothy Atkins did kill Kathryn Sheppard, presumably there is no chance of making an arrest?" said Ricky. "She must have died a long time ago."

"On the contrary," said Tim. "I got Katrin to check out what happened to her after Andy e-mailed me with details of his list of possible victims. He had a bit of a hunch that the dead woman might be Kathryn Sheppard. Dorothy Atkins was sent to Broadmoor, and then eventually released into a care home in Crowland, where she still lives. I think you'd be correct in assuming that we'd be unlikely to get a conviction, given her age: but we owe it to Kathryn Sheppard to find out if she was indeed killed by Dorothy. And of course, if we find evidence that it was Dorothy, that would make her a serial killer, as you say: which means that there might have been other victims as well, ones whose deaths have either not been connected to Dorothy Atkins, or have remained undiscovered."

CHAPTER SIX

Peter has been here for almost one week now. I'm not sure how I feel about it. It is not exactly relaxing having him here – in fact, I feel quite tense almost all of the time. But there are moments of pure – joy? Is that the word? I'm not sure. There are certainly moments of release – and moments of much more shocking vulgarity than I had expected. Peter is quite a dark horse under that civilised veneer!

Can I stand it for ever, though? I discussed this with Peter before we took the plunge and he said that I would not have to if I did not like it; that he would ask me once a month if I wanted him to leave. Things are rarely as cut-and-dried as that, though, are they? One moment I might want him to go, the next moment, to stay. Asking him to leave would be as difficult as asking him to move in was in the first place.

There has been a lot in the news about the skeleton that the police found on the motorway. They haven't identified it yet – or if they have, they are still claiming not to know who it is. Something tells me that it must be Kathryn. I suppose I always knew in my heart of hearts that this would have been what had happened to her: that she would have died violently. She was such a tart. I'm surprised that no-one from work has 'come forward' to volunteer the information that it might be her. People like being busybodies when they have nothing to lose or gain – except five minutes of glory, perhaps. And Kathryn is still remembered there.

In a funny sort of a way, I did love Kathryn. If I could have married anyone, it would have been her. I'm far from certain that she loved me, however. I was very young, but I had made rapid progress since I had joined the company, and I was certainly regarded as one of the movers and shakers of the future. Despite the advantages conferred by her degree – though, to be honest, within the company university degrees were regarded with a certain amount of ambivalence at the time – I'm sure that she saw me as a passport to a glittering career for herself. She paid me in full, though. The sex with her was amazing – far more sensational than anything I have experienced with anyone else, Peter not excepted: even at the time I realised that it was a tragedy that my heart was not in it.

I can see her now, sitting at her desk that first Christmas Eve. We were supposed to be leaving work early, but the phone kept on ringing. She leant across me as I grabbed the receiver and, snatching it away from me, pushed the cradle back down. "There", she said. "That's put a stop to that. Now we can concentrate on indulging in a bit of privacy for a change." She was sitting on my desk, and she leaned right back across my shoulder. She was wearing a vee-necked sweater, and her breasts were swelling against the fabric. It was a pearly sort of colour. Gently I pulled her on to my knee, and she kissed me. I put my hand on one of her breasts, and she did not make me take it away. I went home with her that evening and we made love. Afterwards, I lay in the dark worrying about whether she had noticed how inexperienced I was and it may have been because of this that I did not stay; or maybe I just needed to be on my own. I came home in the early hours, before Christmas had properly begun. In the year that we were together, I never once spent the whole night with her.

She was always very curious about my family, which of course was difficult for me. I did not want to answer her questions, and I certainly had no intention of introducing her to either of my parents. Eventually I agreed that she should

37

meet Bryony. We all met at the White Hart for a drink. She and Bryony hit it off immediately. There was quite a big age gap between them, though not as big as the one between me and Kathryn. But Kathryn and I were both working, while Bryony was planning to go to university a year later than her friends at school, so she must have been nineteen; and Kathryn was twenty-two, and had graduated the year before. She was almost four years older than I was, just as Tirzah was four years older than Ronald.

What is it about girls that makes them stick together in that infuriating way? I had been close to Bryony as a child – we were united against the horrors if our parents' rows – and was now close of course to Kathryn, in the physical sense, anyway. But no sooner had they met than they developed this very intimate relationship which not so much excluded me, as made fun of me: it put me firmly on the outside. They didn't seem to see how much it upset me. It also made me very angry. When I'm upset, I often can't act; but when I'm angry I certainly can.

It was Kathryn's fault, of course. She was that much older: and Bryony looked up to her. Bryony was such a little waif. Her hands were tiny. You could have taken one of them in yours and crushed the bones just by squeezing. Kathryn was quite different: she was buxom and curvy and would have been blowsy and overweight by now. Perhaps dying young is a gift. Never to get old, never to have to compromise, never to be full of the sorts of doubts and fears that have beset me both before and after Peter's arrival.

Bryony was upset when Kathryn and I split up. She seemed to blame me, even though it was obvious that it could not possibly have been my fault. It was in vain that I told her Kathryn's story of meeting Charles Heward on the train. She didn't believe it for a minute; and when I thought about it, neither did I.

It was a Monday. I had not seen Kathryn in private for a few days, because she had spent the weekend with her mother in

Derby. She had taken the day off work and planned to travel back in the afternoon. We had been going to meet friends for dinner. I had left the office early and Kathryn said that when she arrived she would pick up a pineapple and some flowers to take with us and come round to the flat later.

I knew as soon as she knocked on the door that there was something wrong. The fact that she did not use her key should have alerted me, but she could have forgotten it and it was only when I went to let her in that I knew that some-thing unpleasant had happened. She was empty-handed, for one thing; and, for another, there was a kind of stricken look on her face. I realised later that it was simple guilt: but at the time I thought that she was ill, or that someone had dis-tressed her. I went to kiss her, but she dodged me.

"Darling," I said, "are you ill? What is it?"

She remained standing.

"Hedley," she said, "I don't know how to tell you this . . . I might as well come straight out with it . . . I've met someone else."

At first I could not take it in. I thought that she must mean that she'd met a friend and couldn't come to dinner that evening. Then it dawned on me that she was leaving me. I could not understand how she had managed to meet someone so quickly, or where they had met. She had told me in such a clichéd way, too.

"I will try to understand," I said quietly. "But you must see that I've been pitched into the middle of what for me, if not for you, is a crisis, and I'm not sure how to cope. Can you explain to me? Who is it, for God's sake?"

I had started calmly – and in fact, if I were honest with myself, I had begun to tire of Kathryn – or, perhaps more accurately, to realise that she and I were incompatible – but when I thought of her with someone else, it took me all my time not to let her see the rage that she had provoked.

She backed away from me. Perhaps she did see it. It made me want to hit her.

"His name is Charles. I met him on the train when I was going to Derby. I know that it is corny and phoney to say 'love at first sight', but it is the closest I can come to describing it. We were attracted to each other immediately. The journey was over far too soon, so we arranged to meet on Saturday evening for dinner. And – well – you don't want me to spell it out, do you?"

CHAPTER SEVEN

It didn't take Andy Carstairs very long to track down Charles Heward. He had become a very successful corporate lawyer and, latterly, an MP and there were many entries about him on Google. Andy decided to obtain his address and telephone number from the Law Society, as being a more respectable source of information than stuff on the web which might be wrong or out of date. The Law Society was extremely co-operative, once he had faxed a formal request from South Lincolnshire Police, signed by Tim Yates. They faxed back a reply almost immediately. He noted that Charles Heward, QC, ran his office from Gray's Inn: the ultimate address for one of his profession.

He called the number that the Law Society had supplied and was surprised when Charles Heward himself answered. He had been expecting to have to get past a secretary.

"Mr. Heward? This is DC Andrew Carstairs, of South Lincolnshire Police. I wonder if it would be possible to make an appointment to see you. I believe that you may be able to help me with some enquiries that I am making."

"Certainly." The voice at the other end of the line was both confident and ebullient. If, as the child of immigrants, the young Charles Heward had not exactly been a member of the Establishment, his tone certainly proclaimed that he was one now. "Corporate fraud case, is it? I've been asked to help

41

the police with several of those lately. Not usually in your neck of the woods, though."

"No, it isn't a fraud case. I'm investigating a suspected murder. I believe that you knew the victim? Her name was Kathryn Sheppard."

There was a long pause. The next time that Charles Heward spoke, he sounded less confident but angry at the same time.

"The police decided many years ago that I had nothing to do with Kathryn's disappearance. They should never have let it get into the papers that they – absurdly – regarded me as a suspect, even for a short time. It could have ruined my career. I see no point in revisiting all of that now. It was a very distressing period in my life. I know that you police are keen on 'cold cases' these days, but this whole thing has already been resurrected once, and then it got no further than the first time round. There was never even proof that she was murdered, though taking into account the balance of probabilities I'd say that it was likely. She wasn't the kind of girl to just 'disappear', and she had no reason to. But re-opening the case again isn't going to help anyone, least of all her parents, if they're still alive. It's time to let it go."

"I understand how you must be feeling, sir, but we have a good reason for re-opening the case. You see, we have found Kathryn's remains."

There was an even longer pause. When Charles Heward spoke again, he sounded upset.

"Oh, God. Where? And when? How can you be sure that it's her?"

"As I think you may know, her mother insisted that the police had her DNA analysed some years after she disappeared, when DNA results became reliable enough to use for identification purposes. That was when the case was reopened for a second time, as you just mentioned. The police didn't get much further then, in 1990, but the DNA was kept on record. Some workmen found a skeleton by the side of the A1 a few days ago, and we have the DNA match results now. There can be no doubt that the remains are Kathryn's."

"I saw something about the skeleton in the news – I read the article because I knew the area in which it was found, as you will realise – but I didn't make the connection with Kathryn. That puts a different complexion on your request, of course. I will help if I can – though you should know that I co-operated to the best of my ability with the police at the time. Everything that I could contribute then was presumably recorded, and there is little that I can add to it now. In fact, my recollections now are much less likely to be accurate than they were then."

"I understand that, sir, but I'd still like to talk to you about it. There may just be something that you remember now that didn't seem important then."

Charles Heward agreed to see him the next day. Andy caught the train to King's Cross, and then took the tube to Holborn. As he walked round the enclosed square of Gray's Inn, where the raised flowerbeds were being carefully tended by a troop of gardeners dressed in leather aprons, and climbed the corkscrew stairs to Charles Heward's office, he felt as if he'd entered another era. Charles Heward's office itself confirmed the impression. It was the sort of room that he imagined James Boswell had practised from before he gave up the law to become the eighteenth century's foremost literary groupie.

There was no ante-room to the office, and no secretary in evidence, so he knocked on the door which stood ajar to the right of the first landing of the staircase and waited, not sure whether he should enter the room or not. He could hear Charles's deep voice booming from inside, presumably talking to someone on the telephone. However, Charles cut short the conversation in which he was engaged – almost, it seemed, in mid-sentence – when he heard the knock, and shouted 'Come!' The word seemed to reverberate around the walls after it was uttered. Andy smiled. He had seen actors playing the part of public school headmasters use the same curt command, but he had not thought that it had any place in real life, not, at least, in this century.

He pushed open the door. By the time that he had entered the room, Charles Heward had risen to his feet. He came round the side of his desk and extended a huge hand, shooting a snow-white cuff embellished with a heavy gold cufflink as he did so.

"DC Carstairs? I thought it would be you. Sit down, please." He gestured at a spindly Queen Anne sofa that had been placed in front of his desk, and returned to his own massive wooden chair. Andy took in the scene before him and saw that Charles Heward was a tall, bulky black man who was looking very prosperous in his immaculate black suit. The chair creaked under his weight. There was a floor-to-ceiling bookcase fastened to the wall behind him, crammed with outsize legal tomes. For the second time in the space of five minutes, Andy felt that he had walked on to a film set. There was something about the whole room that suggested that Charles Heward had surrounded himself with the grander appurtenances of his profession because they looked right, rather than because he actually needed or had chosen them.

"If you would like tea, we will visit the tea-room eventually. I don't have a secretary. I used to employ one, but I found her more trouble than she was worth. We don't need them now in these days of computers and spell-checkers, do we?" His manner was affable and expansive. As he spoke to Andy, he removed a gold signet ring from his right hand, and rolled it in his palm. It seemed to be a characteristic habit of his – a small outlet, perhaps, for his obviously abundant, restless energy.

"Now," he regarded Andy with sharp eyes. "You say that you have found Kathryn's skeleton. Does it give you any clue about how she died?"

Andy realised that he was trying to take lead in the interview and determined to wrest it back quietly.

"We don't have the results of the tests yet, sir. But you'll realise that I wouldn't have been able to let you know them, anyway. Now, I'd like to go back to the beginning, if you don't mind. Where you were when you first met Kathryn, how you became engaged, that sort of thing."

"I met her on a train. She had been visiting her mother in Derby and she sat next to me when she boarded the train. I'd been at Manchester University for a couple of days at a lawyers' symposium and, instead of travelling straight back to London, I'd decided to make the journey to Peterborough to see a client. The train was held up for some reason – a signalling problem, I think – so we were able to spend a couple of hours talking to each other. I know it sounds corny in a terribly *Brief Encounter* sort of way, but by the end of the journey, we knew that we wanted to be together. We sat in the station café at Peterborough, discussing what we should do. She had a boyfriend and I was actually engaged, but we agreed that we would extricate ourselves from our respective relationships as soon as we could. Kathryn told her boyfriend the next time that she saw him and ended their relationship immediately." He paused, and his face contorted with some emotion: Andy could not decide what. "She was considerably braver about it than I was; it took me a few days to screw up the courage to face my fiancée and her parents. My fiancée was in pupillage in the same law firm that I worked for and her father was a judge. I don't deny that I was worried about the effect that it might have on my career."

"But you went ahead with it?"

"Yes. It turned out to be both easier and harder than I had thought. Easier because Veronica and her family behaved in such a civilised way. Harder because it was obvious how very hurt Veronica was. I'd never quite believed in her love for me up until that moment."

He paused and replaced the ring on his finger.

"After Kathryn's disappearance, I returned to Veronica.

I was grateful that she would take me back; and I've never regretted it. We've been married for almost thirty years."

Andy thought that the way in which Charles Heward delivered this final sentence – almost eulogistically, or in the tone of a parson concluding a sermon – seemed artificial and contrived. He was not surprised that Charles had been a suspect during the original enquiry. There was something about the way he spoke of Kathryn Sheppard that did not convince that he was telling the truth.

"Indeed. As you say, most of the facts that you've been so kind to recount are recorded in the original case notes. Tell me, did you ever meet Hedley Atkins, Kathryn's former boyfriend?"

"Yes – once. Kathryn continued to see his sister – they had become friends, and in fact I met the sister, Bryony, on several occasions. She called round at Kathryn's flat one day when I was there. She didn't stay long and she left when Hedley showed up to collect her. I remember thinking at the time that this was strange: Bryony was a fully-grown adult leaving a friend's flat in a small market town in broad daylight. She hardly needed a chaperone. I thought that she must be in cahoots with Hedley, trying to help him to meet Kathryn again, though I've no idea why either of them might think that this would be useful. Kathryn had just changed jobs – she had been working in the same office as Hedley when she was going out with him, and of course found that hard to bear after their split – so he could no longer see her at work. Anyway, she was civil to him and asked him in for a few moments, so that was when she introduced him to me."

"Did you form an opinion of him?"

"I thought he was weird, to be honest. He was quite a bit younger than Kathryn, though that wasn't obvious: he seemed older than his years. He tried to introduce a few in-jokes to the conversation that included Kathryn and Bryony but excluded me and he clearly resented my presence. That was only to be expected, of course; but I also had the feeling that he wasn't all that concerned about Kathryn, anyway. He seemed much more interested in Bryony – fixated on her, almost."

"Thank you, that's interesting. Is there anything else that you'd like to tell me, that might help this new enquiry?"

Charles Heward had taken off his ring again, and was rolling it around his palm with such fierce energy that he dropped it and it rolled across the floor, coming to rest against the elaborately-carved foot of one of his bookcases. He rose from his chair and bent to retrieve it, surprisingly nimble for such a bulky man. He was still squatting on his haunches, looking up at Andy, when he spoke.

"It probably won't help your enquiry, but there is something that I'd like to tell you. I've had it on my conscience ever since Kathryn vanished, and my wife has had it on hers, too. It seemed vital then to – well, not exactly to deceive, but not to tell the whole story; but the truth seems so much more important now."

Andy held his gaze. "Please continue, sir. May I switch on my tape recorder?"

"I'd rather you didn't; I'd like the information that I'm about to give you to be kept confidential, unless you find later that making it public would help you." He swallowed. "Some time before Kathryn went missing, not afterwards as I told you earlier, and as I maintained at the time, Veronica and I got back together again. I realised that the whole episode with Kathryn had been a mistake, the result of a kind of momentary madness – precipitated, if I am honest, by getting caught up in the glamour of the sort of romantic adventure I had never had before and, I suppose, simple lust. At least, that was true on my side. I think that Kathryn really believed that she had found her soul-mate when she met me." He swallowed again. "Just as when I had left Veronica for Kathryn, now that I was leaving Kathryn for Veronica, I found myself unable to tell Kathryn as soon as I had decided. I don't know why I thought that prolonging the relationship would do any good; I suppose I was just too cowardly to face up to a scene. But she began to get suspicious – our meetings were becoming less and less frequent – and after some weeks I had to tell her. I didn't see her again after I told her. It was a Thursday evening, and she'd just got in from work. She was pretty upset. I didn't contact her over the weekend. As you know, she didn't turn up for work on the Friday after I saw her, or the Monday after that, and eventually her father reported her missing to the police. I told the police that I had last seen her on the Thursday – which was the truth – and of course I had to tell Veronica that as well. Veronica had thought – I suppose I mean, I had led her to believe – that I had broken off with Kathryn some weeks before. When Kathryn disappeared, I told her the truth, and she promised to keep it a secret. Although she was very unhappy about it – she is an extremely honest person – she agreed with me that if it became public knowledge that I had just ditched Kathryn, it would make the police case against me much stronger and, even if I was not charged, that it would affect my career. As you know, I suffered too much adverse publicity as it was."

He stood up slowly and sat down in his chair again. His shoulders sagged, and all the nervy energy that he had exhibited earlier seemed to have drained out of him.

"Poor Kathryn, though. I was truly fond of her. I've never been able to get the idea out of my head that she came to grief because I finished with her."

"I see. Do you mean that you suspect that she had killed herself?"

"Possibly – though I meant it when I said that the balance of probabilities suggested that she was murdered. I think that it is more likely that she either went somewhere that compromised her safety, or sought help from someone who intended her harm."

"Thank you for telling me the truth now, sir. I appreciate it. I will treat the information that you have given me confidentially for the time being, but you will appreciate that I may have to ask you for a formal statement eventually."

Charles Heward nodded. He had taken the ring off again.

As Andy walked away from Gray's Inn later, he wondered if Charles Heward's latest version of his part in the events leading up to Kathryn Sheppard's disappearance was 'the truth, the whole truth, and nothing but the truth'. On the whole, he thought that Charles's story was plausible; but the man was a consummate actor, so how could he tell for sure?

CHAPTER EIGHT

Tim Yates did not know why he had himself decided to interview Hedley Atkins, rather than sending Andy Carstairs, as
he had for the interview with Charles Heward. Perhaps it
was because Hedley was Dorothy Atkins' son. Tim had now
read a great deal about the murder of Doris Atkins and Dorothy's conviction for it, and he found the case both fascinating and unsatisfactory, in about equal measures. If he
were entirely honest, he did not think that either the police
who had handled it or the judge who had presided over the
trial had done a particularly good job. There were too many
loose ends left untied, too many questions left unresolved.
No-one had been able to find a motive for the murder, for
one thing, and Dorothy Atkins had never confessed to it, for
another. The judge had explained away these untidy facts by
describing Dorothy as a 'psychopath', but medical opinion
was divided on whether or not she was insane. It was also
odd that her husband, Ronald Atkins, had been one of the
chief witnesses at the trial, even though he had not been
in the house at the time of the murder; but others who had
certainly been present had barely been questioned at all.
These included Colin Atkins, who was the householder as
well as the shopkeeper, and Doris Atkins' younger brother;
Eliza Atkins, their aged mother; and Hedley Atkins. There
was also a daughter, Bryony Atkins, who gave no statements
and did not appear in court. She had apparently left to take

up a place at Reading University shortly before the murder.

Tim had also read the transcripts of the police interviews that had taken place with Hedley Atkins after the disappearance of Kathryn Sheppard and again when the case was reopened in 1990. Hedley seemed to have been unexceptionably polite and co-operative on these occasions. Tim did not sense from the notes that he had had anything to hide about his relationship with Kathryn. He gave straightforward accounts of the year or so that they had been together and their split. Hedley had described his anger and dismay when Kathryn had left him abruptly for Charles Heward – but these were natural reactions. Tim would have been more suspicious if Hedley had claimed to have taken the break-up calmly. Furthermore, it had happened almost a year before Kathryn's disappearance and there was no record of Hedley having annoyed or intimidated her afterwards. He had said that Kathryn had left the office where they both had worked shortly after she had terminated the relationship and that after that he had only seen her on a handful of occasions. Charles Heward's statements, by contrast, were notably more defensive.

Nevertheless, Hedley would have to be questioned again, now that they had found the skeleton. As far as Tim could deduce, Kathryn Sheppard had only had two serious relationships with men since leaving university, with Hedley Atkins and Charles Heward, and de facto they were both therefore potential suspects. He did not know whether Hedley still lived in Spalding, or had moved away after his mother's imprisonment and his parents' divorce. He could discover no Hedley Atkins in the telephone directory, but examination of the electoral roll revealed someone of that name living in one of the blocks of mansion flats in London Road. This was where Hedley had been living when the case was reopened in 1990. It was an outside chance, but Tim wondered if he still worked for the same employer as well, Maschler's farm machinery. He decided to give it a try.

The voice at the other end of the phone confirmed that Mr. Atkins did still work for the company, but said that he had left for the day. Employees were allowed to work flexi-time and Mr. Atkins usually came in to work at about 8 a.m. and left at 4.30 p.m. Tim asked for his telephone number.

"Hello? Is that Mr. Hedley Atkins?"

"No," said a voice that Tim identified as being male. "It is a *very* close friend of his. I will fetch him for you. Who may I say is calling?" The voice rose higher with every word, until Tim could not be sure that it was not a woman, after all. He also detected some innuendo in the final sentence, though he could not make out its significance.

"Thank you. Please say that it is Inspector Tim Yates, of South Lincolnshire Police."

The voice made no further comment. Tim heard the receiver being laid down carefully. Next he could detect a certain amount of scurrying about and whispering. Tim strained his ears, but could not make out any of the words that were being exchanged, except perhaps the phrase 'some copper' – though he could not be sure even of that. At length, he heard the receiver being picked up again.

"Good evening. This is Hedley Atkins speaking."

"Good evening, Mr. Atkins. Detective Inspector Yates, South Lincolnshire Police. I wonder if I might come to visit you, to discuss some recent developments in a case that I'm working on?"

"What kind of case? Is it something to do with my mother?" Hedley Atkins had sounded cordial at first, but he was more guarded now.

"Not as far as I know. It concerns the disappearance of Kathryn Sheppard. I'm sure that you will remember it: you helped the police with their investigation at the time, and subsequently when their enquiries were reopened fifteen years later."

"Of course I remember it. I must say that I'm surprised that you are still working on it. I had assumed that you had decided not to take it any further, after the second investigation drew a blank."

"Murder cases are rarely closed completely, Mr. Atkins."

"It was never proved that she was murdered though, was it? May I ask what the new developments are?"

"Of course. You may be aware that a skeleton was found at the side of the A1 a few days ago. We now have proof that it is Kathryn Sheppard's."

"Are you certain of that?"

"Quite certain. There can be absolutely no doubt."

"Interesting. I must admit, I wondered whether it was Kathryn when I read about it."

"Indeed? May I come to see you this evening? You will appreciate that we need to follow up all the leads that we have as quickly as possible."

"I'd hardly call myself a 'lead', Inspector. If you've read the notes that were taken during the previous investigations, you will see that I was merely questioned because Kathryn was my girlfriend for a while. In fact, she ditched me for someone else about a year before her disappearance and I rarely saw her after that. But I'm very happy for you to come to see me, if you think I can be of any help."

"Thank you, Mr. Atkins. Shall we say, in half an hour?"

Hedley Atkins was alone when Tim entered his flat some twenty-five minutes later. Hedley shook Tim's hand in a friendly way, and invited him inside. He was a tall, fairly slender man with a slight paunch: his was an athletic body that had been allowed to go to seed. He had a long face with extremely deep-set, brown eyes, and an unflatteringly boyish hairstyle of the pudding-bowl fringe variety.

The flat was quite gloomy and dingily decorated, but immaculately tidy. It had a kind of dilapidated grandeur about it; it was situated in an early Victorian terrace that had been divided up into flats in the 1930s. The ceilings were high and ornately plastered; the sash windows tall and narrow.

There was a tiny kitchen off the entrance vestibule, and, having shown Tim into the sitting-room, Hedley disappeared into it momentarily, emerging again with a kettle, which he held aloft.

"Cup of tea, Inspector?"

"Thank you, that would be kind. Has your friend gone home now?"

"My friend? Oh, you mean Peter. He lives here. He's out at the moment, though."

"I see. I hope I didn't drive him away?"

Hedley Atkins laughed.

"Well, actually, I rather think that you did. He doesn't like policemen, for some reason. I can't think why. He's a perfectly respectable, upstanding citizen, after all."

"I'm sure he is." Tim shrugged. "He's not alone. I'm afraid that quite a lot of people feel intimidated by the police, even if they haven't done anything to break the law. I'm sorry that my visit has inconvenienced him."

Hedley laughed again.

"Oh, I shouldn't feel too sorry for him. He's almost certainly gone to the Punch Bowl. He'll have a good time in there."

Once Tim was ensconced on Hedley's leather Chesterfield with a mug of tea in one hand, he began to talk about Kathryn Sheppard. He found Hedley Atkins cheerful and co-operative. His recollections of the events leading up to Kathryn's disappearance and his account of their time together differed very little from what he had said in his statements to the police in 1975 and 1990. There was one thing puzzling Tim, however. He had decided to ask Hedley about it towards the end of their conversation.

"Mr. Atkins, you said that you did not see Kathryn Sheppard on many occasions after she left her employment at the office in which you also worked soon after she broke off your romance, but that on the occasions on which you did see her, it was in the company of your sister, Bryony. I'm surprised that Bryony wasn't brought in for questioning by the police during either of the investigations into Kathryn's disappearance. Of course I don't hold you responsible for that, nor do I expect you to be able to explain why so little interest was shown in Bryony. It seems to me that she could have been a star witness. So what I would like to ask you is, did your sister ever refer to Kathryn's disappearance when in your company, or speculate what might have happened to her? She must have been upset by it, surely?"

"I'm sure that she was, if she was aware of it. What you need to know, Inspector, is that my sister decided to make a new life for herself after my mother was convicted of killing my grandmother, which was some time before Kathryn disappeared. She changed her name and built a new life for herself, completely away from the family. I was not myself privy to either the identity that she had chosen or her whereabouts, and although we were close as children, I respected her privacy by not trying to find out. She may very well have still been in touch with Kathryn, of course. Only Kathryn herself would have been able to tell you that. I imagine that the police may have tried to locate her, but if they did, they didn't tell me; and from what you say, if they did make such an attempt, they were unsuccessful."

Hedley Atkins delivered this explanation fluently enough, and without any obvious signs of defensiveness or of trying to withhold some part of the truth. Tim wondered if he was imagining the slight hunching of Hedley's shoulders that he thought that he detected as the latter was speaking about Bryony, or the fleeting look of anxiety that seemed briefly to cloud Hedley's expression. On the whole, he thought that he probably was.

CHAPTER NINE

Eliza had two sisters who lived quite near her, Lilian and Louisa. Both were married, Lilian to a painter and decorator and Louisa to a farm foreman, and they each had one son, Dorothy's cousins George and Maurice. Dorothy did not see much of her cousins, because when Lily and Louie came to visit Eliza for one of their regular tea-parties, the boys were invariably left with their fathers, or with neighbours. Dorothy did not understand why, but she did not mind. She herself was never excluded from the tea-parties and, as the only child present, as well as being the only girl of her generation in her mother's family, she was always made much of.

Auntie Lily (her real name, Lilian, was never used) was her favourite. She had had her trials in life – chiefly Uncle Arthur, her husband, who was twelve years older than she, and who, she cheerfully informed everyone, regularly drank them "to the breadline" – but she bore her lot philosophically, and was also a figure of some standing in the community because of her (largely self-taught) nursing skills. Most of the local doctors called upon her to help at births, and she was the nurse in temporary residence at many sick-rooms across the fens, an invaluable asset, since the tiny cottage hospital could only accommodate those acutely ill or close to death.

Auntie Louie was poorer and not as talented. She was also dumpier and less good-looking than either Eliza or Lily, who both had tall angular figures and aristocratic features (Eliza had once been compared to Lady Asquith, and had never forgotten it). Louie had resigned herself to being a labourer's wife, and to mending and making do. She always regarded Dorothy with a faint air of disapproval, though she was kind enough when it came to serving her with slices of pork-pie or cake. It was as if Dorothy were tainted with something that she could not herself help, something which merited disdain but not punishment.

Auntie Lily was a raconteur who liked hinting at mysteries. She would sit Dorothy on her knee and say to her, with meaning, "You ought to have been my little girl." Dorothy did not ask what she meant by this, but she did know that when Lily was in the right frame of mind it was possible to ask her questions about her father. Such questions, when directed at Eliza, were invariably met with a wall of silence, followed by half a day of strictness and snapping. Eliza only referred to Dorothy's father only when she was particularly exasperated with the girl. Then she would say, "You're just like your father," as if that condemned her to turn out badly.

Auntie Lily and Auntie Louie were paying their first visit since Dorothy had recovered from the diphtheria. The special status that the family always accorded to someone who had suffered from a serious illness had therefore yet to run its course. Both had brought her especially nice gifts for her approaching birthday. Lily had dressed a doll for her, and Louie gave her some magic colouring books and a little palette of water colours. She was allowed to have them now, in order to be able to say thank-you properly.

It was a suffocatingly hot day and Eliza had laid a tea-table under the arch of the weeping-willow tree that grew off-centre in Mrs. Frear's rose-garden. Mr. and Mrs. Frear were both away, at an agricultural show. They approved of Eliza's choosing the time of such absences to entertain her sisters.

While Eliza was making the tea, Auntie Lily pulled Dorothy on to her knee and admired her lemon-yellow poplin Sunday

57

dress with the bronze silk smocking on the bodice, which had been made by Eliza herself. Proudly, Dorothy lifted the skirt to show matching knickers with a tiny pocket for her handkerchief. Auntie Louie raised her eyebrows, and Auntie Lily laughed and quickly pulled the skirt back down over the child's knees. Auntie Louie wandered off across the lawn to examine the rose bushes. Dorothy snuggled up to Auntie Lily.

"Auntie," she said, "tell me about my father."

Lily laughed again. She was neither a mischievous nor a hurtful woman, but she had a lively curiosity and she did love a mystery.

"I've told you all that I know, Dorothy. I'm loath to repeat it and I certainly don't want to upset your mother."

"I don't see why she should be upset," said Dorothy rather sulkily.

"'She' is the cat's aunt. You should refer to your mother as 'Mother'."

"All right. I don't see why mother should be upset."

"Well, you see, he treated her rather badly."

"What did he do?"

"He was a chauffeur," said Lily, purposely misunderstanding. "At least, that's what your mother said. She said that he was Sir Gordon MacLean's chauffeur – your mother was working for Sir Gordon and Lady MacLean at the time, as Nanny to their two little girls."

"What was his name?"

"I don't know. Your mother didn't tell me."

"Why didn't she tell you? Didn't you find out when you went to her wedding?"

"I didn't go to her wedding – and then he died, so I did not meet him. He died while you were a baby, so your mother said."

"Well, if she said so, it must be true. I certainly can't remember him and he can't just have disappeared, can he? What did he die of?"

"Malaria, I believe. That's what Sir Gordon told Grannie,

anyway. He had been a soldier in the Great War, and had bouts of illness afterwards. Sir Gordon did hint that he had weakened his constitution in other ways . . ."

"What business was it of Sir Gordon's?"

"Dorothy, that is very rude! Sir Gordon always took a very keen interest in your mother's welfare – and in yours. It is because of Sir Gordon that your mother obtained the position here, as Mr. Frear's housekeeper."

"I like Sir Gordon," said Dorothy. "He always sends me a Christmas present and a birthday present, too."

"Indeed," said Auntie Lily meaningfully. "As I have said, he has your interests at heart."

"Who are you talking about?" asked Eliza sharply as she crossed the grass carrying a wicker and beadwork tray on which she had placed a large brown teapot and hot water and milk jugs.

Auntie Lily knew better than to recount the whole of the conversation.

"I was just telling Dorothy how much you both owe to Sir Gordon," she said blandly.

"Oh, were you?" said Eliza, her voice taut with sarcasm. The subject was dropped. However, Dorothy could see that Auntie Lily's darting mind read a great deal into that one small sentence and the way in which it was said.

CHAPTER TEN

Dorothy believed that she had not been deluded about what the future might hold when she had married Ronald Atkins. After all, she did not love him and did not pretend to herself – and increasingly in the weeks before their marriage, did not pretend to him – that theirs was a grand romance. She thought, therefore, that she was going into it, as she put it, 'with her eyes open'. It was a bargain: she got a husband, he got a wife, and together they would acquire a home which, however humble, would be better than lodging in other people's houses, as they had both been obliged to do all their lives. However, she had been unprepared for two things: the relentless drabness that followed when two people, and subsequently two people and a baby, tried living on a clerk's salary in 1955; and the sheer unnerving monotony of her new existence.

To herself she could admit that she was partially responsible for her plight, marooned as she was with a small child and virtually no money. She had deliberately avoided discussing contraception with Ronald, thinking that at twenty-six it was high time for her to conceive her first child. She had long cherished a dream of what her future as a housewife and mother might look like: it involved living in a warm house scented with flowers both winter and summer, and wearing nice clothes when she met her children at the school gates. She knew women who lived their lives like this: Jayne

Adams, the butcher's wife, for example, who had been one of her contemporaries at school. She did not pause to consider how far removed Ronald's job and income was from that of a butcher ten years his senior who owned a prosperous sausage and pork-pie factory and several shops.

When Bryony had been born, they had not even been living in a house, but in a caravan that had been found for them by Ronald's Uncle Dick. They had saved the deposit for a house, but the post-war building programme was not happening fast enough to supply houses to all who needed them. So they were condemned to the social stigma of 'van' life right at the outset of the marriage.

Dorothy was uncompromising about housework, both in the caravan and later, when after Hedley's birth (to Dorothy's mortification) they were allocated a council house. By this time, all the mortgage deposit money they had originally saved had been spent, first of all on the caravan, and then, after its subsequent sale, on furniture. Despite what Ronald continued to say, there was now no believable likelihood that they would ever own their own house. Women like Jayne had 'home helps'. They may have wielded a hoover upon occasion (since these were desirable items and not owned by everyone: others had to resort to carpet sweepers, tea-leaves and brush-and-dustpan sets), but they certainly eschewed the dirtier menial tasks, such as raking out the fire and cleaning the bathroom with the corrosive Vim powder which was all that was available and would have stripped the skin off their fingers. Eliza had been a housekeeper, not a skivvy, and she would not have dreamt of getting down on her hands and knees to scrub floors or scour a lavatory. Dorothy, who took no pride in this council property – the disgrace of living in it made her despair daily – had no intention of working her fingers to the bone to 'make it nice'. Her definition of house-wife did not equate to cleaning-woman.

Although he had an irascible nature and would lose his temper with frightening regularity, Ronald was curiously dif-

fident when it came to challenging Dorothy about her neglect
of the housework. Invariably fastidious, he would sweep and
polish and dust while Dorothy watched him grimly. Although
she was not prepared to undertake these chores herself,
she regarded it as a personal affront that he had decided to
shoulder them. She would cook, however – very plain food
– until the advent of sixties frozen meals relieved her of this
thankless chore as well. She would wash and iron, the latter
a task which she performed with some pride. She insisted on
doing the shopping, cycling to the market twice a week and
returning with a large canvas shopping bag of fruit, meats,
bread and cakes looped over each handlebar (the groceries
were delivered by Uncle Colin and Ronald grew almost all the
vegetables they ate). She counted every penny of the 'house-
keeping money' (£5) that Ronald handed over each Friday,
and made sure that there was always a little left over to keep
for herself.

Her week was made up of repeating mundane reference
points. Tuesdays and Saturdays were market days. Monday
was wash-day, the nadir of her week, when she was obliged
to slave over the gas copper in the wash-house all day (lunch
on Mondays was always a variation of leftover Sunday joint,
served joylessly with boiled potatoes). Wednesday was the
only day that she got to herself. Thursday was Eliza's day off
from her latest 'situation' as companion to a Mrs. James,
who lived at a gloomy old house called The Laurels in Sut-
terton, and she invariably invited herself to spend the day
with Dorothy. On Sunday Doris came to lunch, and then
stayed to work at her knitting and talk all afternoon until it
was time for tea. Uncle Colin did not accompany her, because
he would not close the shop. On Fridays Ronald came home
early, and 'got under her feet'.

But it was the loss of freedom on Thursdays that Eliza's
visits caused that ignited the deepest fires of resentment in
Dorothy. After Dorothy's marriage, Eliza had changed from
being the severe but doting mother of a self-centred young

woman and had instead assumed the role of hyper-critical matriarch. She could not understand Dorothy's discontent with her lot, and certainly had no sympathy for her aversion to housework. That jealousy played some part in her 'attitude' should have been clear to Dorothy; but Dorothy had a discontented nature, and did not believe that she possessed anything that her mother could envy.

Eliza's routine on Thursdays was identical every week. She would catch the bus into town, do some light shopping, and then make her way to Dorothy's house on the council estate comfortably in time for lunch. On one occasion she had turned up at the parish church day school where Bryony had been enrolled in the reception class, and asked if the girl could be allowed to leave early so that she could accompany her grandmother to her home before lunch. This had caused a furore in the Atkins household, and Eliza was expressly forbidden from attempting such a ploy again. In a rare moment of unity, Dorothy and Ronald had both turned on her and accused her of jeopardising Bryony's future. Eliza, whose own attitude to education was far from cavalier – she was acutely aware that she herself had not had the benefit even of the rudimentary schooling available to most children at the turn of the twentieth century, because her mother was always expecting yet another baby and was therefore dependent on her eldest daughter to stay at home and help – and furthermore, look how she had allowed Dorothy to attend the high school when money had been so short – could not help reflecting that depriving Bryony of a few minutes playing at shop before the bell went was hardly likely to cause permanent damage. But she apologised, and acknowledged that she had been wrong – and even felt secretly glad that Dorothy and Ronald could act in unison when the occasion demanded.

On Eliza's visiting days, they always ate fish. Dorothy was not certain how this had come about, but it was a tradition that she never sought to break. The fish would be followed by a milk pudding or a large jam tart with custard. Very occasionally a treacle tart – Ronald's favourite – would be served instead.

Eliza was not short of airs and graces. She would not hang her coat in the hall with all the other coats, but insisted on folding it carefully, lining outwards, and placing it on Dorothy's and Ronald's bed. She would divest herself of her scarf – usually of chiffon, often mauve or purple in colour – but kept her hat on for the duration of the visit. This had been the custom of the ladies who had visited her employers during her youth, and she was in no doubt that the dictates of good manners demanded that she continue to observe it. Others might let standards slip, but she would not. She would make a point of washing her hands before she came to the table (it appeared that the children were not required to do this), and always fetched herself a glass of water from the kitchen tap before the meal started. She liked to drink out of a vessel known in the household as 'Daddy's beer-glass'. It was the only piece of clear glassware in the place. Drinks for the others were a little hit and miss. If the 'pop man' had visited, the children would have dandelion and burdock or cideapple to drink, served in thick jacquard glasses. Otherwise, they rarely drank with the meal, but would help themselves to orange squash afterwards. Dorothy and Ronald did not drink when they were eating, but invariably partook of a cup of Camp coffee after the plates had been cleared away. To Eliza, 'that stuff' was an abomination and she said so. Asked if she had had enough to eat, she would say, "I have had an elegant sufficiency, thank you," and glare at the children as they slid out of their seats and left the table without asking if they might. Dorothy was usually dispensing tight-lipped sarcasms by this stage. Ronald meanwhile had dispatched his lunch in the quickest possible time and departed for his office with relief. He felt cowed in his own house when his mother-in-law was there.

From Dorothy's point of view, the Thursday afternoons

64

spent with Eliza were better than the mornings. Once the dirty crockery had been cleared away, and Ronald and the children had returned to work and school, there was nothing for Dorothy to do except sit and talk to her mother while Eliza worked at her current piece of embroidery. Occasionally Dorothy would knit, but more often she just chatted. They sometimes broke off their conversation for half an hour to listen to 'Mrs. Dale's Diary' or a serialised play that they had each been following separately all week on the radio. Dorothy felt reasonably at peace on such occasions. No-one required her to do anything other than entertain her mother and make the occasional pot of tea in the little brown earthenware teapot that served two; and listening to Eliza chattering about the doings of her many sisters or her life with Mrs. James was, in fact, quite entertaining. It was only when she came to reflect afterwards on Eliza's taken-for-granted imposition on her time that she felt furious.

That Eliza's death would take place on one of these outwardly tranquil domestic afternoons could not have been predicted by even the most acute observer. Curiously enough, Ronald was the only member of the Atkins family who had not been present when she had died – and even more curiously, Ronald was the person whom the police had interrogated the most thoroughly, for no other apparent reason than that he was the 'head of the household'.

On the day in question, Ronald had arrived home earlier than usual for tea, because he was returning to the factory that evening to conduct a guided tour of the sugar processing plant. It was the last Thursday in October and the start of the tour season. Ronald had been in a good mood: he had just been awarded a pay-rise, the winter tours would also give his wages a further boost and he would not have to sit and talk to Eliza until she set off for the seven o'clock bus because everyone would understand that he had work to do. He rattled his bike over Marine Street, the unmetalled road that skirted the estate, and then jumped off it just before he came in sight of his own gate so that Dorothy would not harangue him about 'racking it up' by taking it over so many muddy ruts and hollows. He was pushing the bike sedately down his own path and about to prop it up against the wall so that he could remove his bicycle clips, when the back door was violently flung open and Bryony rushed out. She would have run past him if he had not quickly ditched the bike and caught her.

"Steady on," he said. "What's the big hurry?"

It was only after he had spoken that he looked properly at her face. It was flour white, her eyes dilated with terror.

"Daddy!" she said, "Daddy! Come quickly! Nana's fallen down the stairs!"

She clung to him, sobbing in a dry sort of way that on later reflection had struck him as rather theatrical – but at that moment he had had no time to think about it. He did notice that Bryony had his mother-in-law's mauve chiffon scarf draped around her shoulders. She seemed not to want to come back into the house with him, but he put his arm firmly around her and led the way. At this point he did not realise that Eliza was dead: Bryony said nothing more, and he asked her no questions.

There was no-one in the kitchen when he entered, though the light was on. He walked straight through into the dining-room, which was also the room in which they sat during winter evenings and where the lights were also burning. The television had been turned on, but the sound was too low to be audible. Hedley was lying on the sofa with one of its yellow-frilled cushions held up against his head, as if he had earache. He did not speak or look up. Ronald let go of Bryony – she ran to the armchair opposite the television and curled up on it, her eyes fixed on the screen – while he continued more hesitantly towards the hall.

The door from the dining-room to the hall opened inwards. Ronald pulled it towards him and almost stumbled over Dorothy, who was kneeling on the brown Marley tiles, her slippered feet pressed under her. She was crouched over Eliza, whose head was lying at a strange angle on the floor. Eliza's legs and the lower half of her body were splayed over the bottom three or four steps of the stairs, and seemed to be almost at right angles to her upper torso. She was still wearing the beige two-piece in which he had seen her at lunch-time, though the skirt had ridden above her knees to reveal Lisle stockings and pale blue directoire knickers. Incongruously, her close-fitting purple velvet hat was still clamped firmly on her head.

Dorothy was just kneeling there, speechless and motionless. She was making no attempt to revive Eliza, to talk to her, or even to feel her pulse.

"Dorothy," he said. "Let me through. Quickly."

She turned to him, and he felt terrified by the look he saw in her eyes. He had thought that she was weak and numb with shock until he looked at her properly and saw the naked malevolence in her gaze. If he had been at all fanciful, he would have described it as evil.

He pushed her to one side, and knelt to take Eliza's pulse.

"Get up, For God's sake," he said to her. "Go round to Harry Daff's and ask if you can call an ambulance."

Dorothy had rearranged herself against the hall wall while he was speaking, her feet drawn up against her chest, her arms wrapped around them. She did not move when he spoke. All the animosity that he had witnessed the moment before seemed to have evaporated and she appeared to have sunk into a kind of trance.

"Bryony!" he shouted in fear and exasperation, "Get round to Mrs. Daff's and ask her to call an ambulance." Harry Daff owned the only telephone in the street, because he worked for the Electricity Board and had to be reachable to be called out if there were emergencies.

He heard Bryony get up and the back door opening and closing. He turned back to Eliza.

He could feel no pulse, either at her wrist or her temple.

The light in the hall was dim, but he could see that her face had turned blue. Her eyelids were half-closed. The look on her face was not peaceful, but he couldn't quite interpret her expression: it could have been one of fear, or pain, or even hatred. Was Eliza capable of hatred? He knew that her daughter was!

"I think that she's gone," he said quietly. "Can you tell me what happened?"

Dorothy had half-buried her head in her knees. She looked up when he spoke, but remained silent.

"Dorothy! Pull yourself together. Tell me what happened. Now!"

"Oh, shut up," she spat at him. "You think you're so wonderful, don't you, coming bursting in here to take charge. What do *you* know, or what can *you* do. She fell. She went upstairs to get her coat and other things and had a funny turn when she was coming out of the bedroom and she fell downstairs. The kids have both fallen down these stairs and not even hurt themselves. She was unlucky."

"Did you see her fall?"

"No. I was in the kitchen, getting the tea ready. I heard a bump – nothing more than that – and then several thuds. Bryony came to fetch me. I found Mother where she is now. Hedley was in there looking at her I think he had been in his room. I sent them both into the dining-room to watch television. That was when you came in. It only happened a few minutes ago."

"Why haven't you got help?"

"I was going to. But I thought I'd wait for you first – I knew you'd be home soon."

"Dorothy, don't you understand that this is an emergency? Isn't it obvious that there isn't time to wait around when someone's dangerously hurt? Let's hope that she died outright. I hope you realise that we'll have to call the police. They'll want statements from you and from the children. There's bound to be an inquest."

Someone rapped the front door knocker.

"Tirzah, it's me, Eileen. Are you all right? I've got Bryony with me. She says that you need an ambulance."

"Eileen, come round to the back door", called Ronald. "Stay there," he said to Dorothy. She did not acknowledge him.

As he hurried through the dining-room, he saw that Hedley was lying in the same unnatural pose on the sofa, staring unseeing at the TV screen. Really, that boy was an oddball – such a little pansy. No backbone at all. God knew where he got his character from.

Eileen – or Bryony – had already opened the back door. They were standing together on the large square of cocoa-nut matting in the kitchen, looking nervous. Eileen was holding Bryony's hand. She was a midget of a woman with permed wispy red hair and very protruding front teeth. According to Dorothy, she was domesticity personified, and spent her days baking, bottling, and making jam and children's clothes. You wouldn't catch Dorothy wasting her life in that way.

"God help us, Ronald, you look terrible." Eileen's demeanour was half compassionate, half avid with undisguised curiosity. "What on earth has happened? I heard the children screaming earlier. Where's Tirzah?"

"She's in the hall. Don't you go in there," he added, as Eileen took two steps towards the living-room. "She's with her mother. The old lady's had an accident – she's fallen downstairs. We think she's dead."

"Have you tried first aid? I'm in St. John's. I may be able to help."

"Yes," said Ronald – afterwards he was not sure why, except that he knew that somehow he had to keep Eileen out of the hall. "No use, I'm afraid. There isn't a pulse. Definitely. Would you mind calling an ambulance for us, and the police?"

"Of course," said Eileen, though something like doubt

flitted across her horsey face. "I'll take Bryony with me, shall I? What about Hedley. Is he all right?"

Ronald shrugged. "He's watching TV. He's all right as far as I know. Strange kid."

Eileen Daff gave him an odd look as she left with Bryony. Bryony was clutching her hand very tight.

By the time the ambulance and the police had arrived, Dorothy was sobbing like any normal, bereaved daughter. At the inquest, the coroner pronounced Eliza's death 'an unfortunate accident'.

CHAPTER ELEVEN

When I was at primary school, a missionary nun came to talk to us. Her name was Sister Hilda. She showed us films of children in Africa singing and studying Maths. She was there herself in most of the footage, wearing a long loose cotton dress and a navy-blue nun's headdress with a wimple. She also wore thick-framed spectacles, and had long uneven teeth. She exactly fitted my idea of what a nun should be like.

Sometimes there was a man with her in the film as well, a monk dressed in a dark rough habit fastened with a cord. He had a long ascetic face. She called him 'Father Anselm'. She explained that Father Anselm was the leader of the mission to which she belonged and that he was part of the active branch of his order. He and the other monks who shared his vocation went out to do good works, to help and educate people everywhere who needed them, at home as well as in places like Africa. There were other monks as well, who belonged to the same order and shared the same beliefs, except that they did not work or mix with people in the world outside their monastery. They devoted themselves exclusively to prayer. The active monks supported them in this, and even looked up to them as being more pious than they were themselves. They prayed all the time and barely spoke to anyone except God. She said that what they were doing was like stoking a furnace, sending up a continuous 'funnel of prayer' to Heaven on behalf of all the rest of us sinners.

I soon got bored with Sister Hilda, especially when she tried to teach us Maths in the way that she had taught the African children, but I was fascinated by the idea of the funnel of prayer. It appeared to be such a good way of sorting things out, without getting involved in any unpleasantness. Instead of confronting problems yourself directly, you could just keep on bombarding God with prayers until he intervened. Her visit to my school had been timely, because I was a shy, nervous child and I had a particular problem that I needed to solve.

Before I say any more, I should like to make it plain that I am not one of those moral degenerates who goes through life continually blaming their parents for their own shortcomings. My childhood was difficult – both my father and my mother had terrible defects – but I do believe that there comes a time in every person's life when they should stop blaming their parents for who they have become and instead accept that they have enough freedom as adults to mould themselves. Philip Larkin may have been right about parents 'fucking you up', but even he broke free; and it has to be said that he did not have a mother like Tirzah. I wonder if he called his mother, Mother? Bryony and I almost invariably called ours Tirzah – though that was not her real name, but one invented by some old man that she knew long before we were born.

Tirzah has always been the big conundrum in my life. She achieved notoriety when I was a very young man by going to prison for killing my grandmother and my relationship with her both prior to this and afterwards was tricky. Yet I was – not exactly – proud of her, but always influenced by her; obsessed with her, even. And it could not be denied that she possessed a profound distinctiveness.

My father was quite different. He was a weak and treacherous little man who liked to keep in with the big bluff farmers for whom he worked and enjoyed boasting about his pitiful possessions to the neighbours. I understood why Tirzah hated him for this; and why she was sickened by his appalling manners. She despised him; and therefore Bryony and I despised him, too.

Like many weak men, my father indulged in a certain amount of casual violence. He would smack me across the face or legs and, although he rarely laid a finger on Bryony, he had still been known on occasion to strike her with the flat of his hand. Far worse were his rages. He would be completing some simple task – such as drying the dishes for my mother – when a chance remark would pitch him into an immediate frenzy. His face would darken and the veins stand out on his forehead, and he would shout a tirade of abuse at anyone within his range – sometimes at my mother, but if either of us was there he would deflect his anger from her and hurl it at us instead. His face became hideously jowly and ugly and he would spit involuntarily as the words came tumbling out. On one of the dish-drying occasions, he threw the tea-towel into the washing-up bowl and swept the cups and saucers that were draining into the sink, where some of them broke treacherously under the soap-suds. Sometimes my mother would retort; sometimes she just fixed him with the stare that told him she despised him. On other occasions she would cry, though when I was older I realised that it was a hard, dry kind of crying, designed perhaps to illustrate what a bastard he was, rather than springing from any real distress.

Usually these daytime outbursts seemed to me to be his fault. In the evenings, however, after Bryony and I had gone to bed, a different kind of row would take place. Although I could not hear every word, I often listened to these arguments as they welled up and ran their course and I could never understand why she precipitated them in the way that she did. They always followed the same pattern. First of all would come her voice, plaintive, nagging, reproaching him for something. He would either reply abruptly, evidently trying to change the subject, or – presumably either because he was in a good mood, or thought she had a point – adopt a wheedling tone and try to pacify her. Neither of these tactics would work. She would carry on, perhaps raising her original grievance again, but always dragging in more and more items to support her argument. She would draw on his past misdemeanours, his general character and his failure to provide the kind of house she would like to live in. Finally she would start on his relatives, especially the three whom we saw most frequently, who lived in the house in Westlode Street (my great-grandmother was still alive at the time of which I speak). This was always the point at which he snapped, and then they would both shout and scream, savaging each other with words until the early hours so that it was impossible for Bryony and me to sleep.

I was desperate to stop these arguments, not because I could not sleep, but because I did not know what was happening downstairs. With the daytime rows, terrible as they were, at least I was there, and I always believed that I had only to stick them out to make sure that nothing irrevocable occurred. In the evenings, I could no longer protect the status quo with my presence. They could have resorted to blows, or one of them might have walked out and made my world collapse, and I would not know and therefore would not be able to stop it. It was out of the question that I should venture downstairs to keep watch after I had been sent to bed, so I had to find another way of coping. Sister Hilda and her funnel of prayer seemed, quite literally, a Godsend.

For several nights I knelt on the floor beside my bed for hours, sending up my prayer funnel to God. I thought of all sorts of ways of asking for His help. I did not ask for it head-on: Sister Hilda had told us that you need to be careful what you ask for, and how you put it to God. So I did not say, 'Please, God, make them stop because it is making me unhappy.' I said things like, 'Please, God, bring peace to this house; let us live in harmony with you and with each other; let us respect your ways.'

It did no good whatsoever. On the sixth night it was particularly cold – we had no heating in the bedrooms. I knelt on the lino in my pyjamas for three hours, for the first hour thinking that perhaps the praying was beginning to work at last, because all was quiet downstairs. Then the shouting started, and it went on and on and on. At first I tried to shut it out. I carried on praying, even saying my prayers out loud, my hands over my ears to drown out the other noise. I got colder and colder: my feet were so cold that I could not feel them, and the goosebumps stood out on my arms where the thin, too-small sleeves of my ancient pyjamas ended just below the elbow. It must have been midnight when I finally gave in and stumbled into bed, clasping my feet in my hands to try to warm them, despair in my heart. The shouting had not stopped. I do not know how long it took me to fall asleep. It seemed like aeons; but I know that when it finally happened, still the shouting had not stopped.

The next morning everyone came down for breakfast, at which I felt somewhat relieved. My mother was sallow and tight-lipped, my father red-eyed as if he had been weeping. I felt tired and sick. My anxiety was so great that I could do nothing; I could barely swallow my tea, certainly not think of eating cereal or the toast doorsteps that my mother had propped against the yellow and brown tea-cosy. Only Bryony seemed to have slept well. She sat at the table now, cheerful and rosy-cheeked, eating Sugar Puffs with the top of the milk. Although I was usually fond of Bryony, at this moment I hated her for her insensitivity.

My mother fixed me with a baleful look.

"What's the matter with you?" she asked dourly.

"Nothing," I said. I looked away from her. "I think I'll go to school early today – there's some homework I need to finish."

"You won't go anywhere until you've had something to eat – will he?" she appealed to my father. He shook his head in half-hearted support of her, but he could not speak. Unlike her, he seemed still to be traumatised by last night's row. The delivery boy passed the window with his newspaper and we listened as it fell to the floor in the hall, the letterbox lid clattering. My father slid away to retrieve it. Grimly, my mother poured out Cornflakes for me. My father returned to the room but not to the table. He stood with his back to the stove, holding the paper up in front of his face.

"What *is* the matter with you?" my mother repeated.

"There isn't a God," I said slowly, the tears welling.

I felt my father tense up behind his newspaper. I don't think that he was a man of any strong beliefs or passions, but he had been brought up a Methodist by his grandmother, and he probably didn't think to question the teachings that she had peddled.

My mother gave a short sarcastic bark – it was hardly a laugh.

"It's taken you long enough to find that out," she said. "I could have saved you the trouble. Now eat your breakfast. It's too cold today for you to go out without any food inside you. I don't want the welfare lady after me."

Bryony appraised me in a superior way from behind her virtuous table manners. She was fond of me, too, but that did not stop her excelling at being the good girl when I was in trouble.

As I think about that day now, I am left with two problems, one rooted in the past, the other in the present. The past problem actually has nothing to do with God: it relates to my father. For not quite the first time, but certainly the first time I have articulated it with any clarity to myself, I wonder what my relationship with Ronald Atkins might have been like if it had not been influenced, first, by my mother, and then by what Uncle Colin had told me. Would I have liked him better? Would we have been companions, as other men seemed to be with the boys in their care, and gone to cricket matches together or built things?

The second decidedly has to do with God. It also concerns Peter. How can I live under the same roof with him – he is an ardent Catholic – without his finding out that I do not believe? And what will be the effect on him when he does?

CHAPTER TWELVE

Policewoman Juliet Armstrong trudged up the short gravel drive of the shabby 1960s semi. She particularly hated the nature of her mission, though she had volunteered for it; it was her job, not Tim's, though he had offered to do it, and she would not shirk it.

Pausing, she quickly took stock of her surroundings. The house was at the further end of a cul-de-sac called Acacia Close. All of the houses in this street were identical, all obviously built by the same property developer at a time when complementing cheap brick with clapboard-style wooden panels was in vogue. Some of them were dilapidated, others cheerfully painted and recently embellished with additional amenities such as glass porches; some of the gardens even sported water features. Juliet guessed that this was because some were still occupied by people who had bought them when they were first built, and that others had more lately been purchased by young couples still full of optimism and energy, bringing new blood and lots of DIY as the original sixties occupants had grown too frail to live on their own and been forced to move out – or had, indeed, died.

Number 17 Acacia Close was in a particularly depressing state of disrepair. There were weeds growing up through the over-abundant gravel, and the borders on either side of it were choked with nettles and thistles. The privet hedge looked as if it had not been cut for many years, but instead of becoming a forest, some of its bushes had shot towards the sun like gangly youths, while others had died. The clap-board-style wood was almost bleached white with the sun and rain of many years, with no lick of varnish to stem the depredations of time. The doors and windows had last been painted long ago in a depressing shade of turquoise and this paintwork was now pealing.

Not everything was broken or run-down: the white plastic disk of the doorbell still glowed a faint orange. Juliet pressed it and waited for a minute or so, then pressed it again. She could hear the two-tone electronic chimes sounding within the house, but there was no responding bustle of movement. Juliet took a few paces backwards and looked at the upstairs windows. The transoms of what was probably the master bedroom were both open. She wondered whether Mrs. Sheppard was the sort of woman who would leave upstairs windows open when she was out shopping. Somehow, she doubted it.

She was startled by the sound of a bolt being shot, and real-ised that it was coming from a gate at the side of the house. A very small woman emerged. She was carrying a saucer in her hand which she was holding at arm's length. She was dressed entirely in brown: dark brown cardigan, pale brown blouse, brown polyester trousers and brown lace-up shoes. Apart from her hair, which was thick and bushy, a nascent white streaked with grey, and which was escaping from the rather inexpert bun into which it had been fashioned on the top of her head, she was extremely neat. She stopped in her tracks when she saw Juliet, her face stricken with alarm. It was a strange face: puffy and wrinkled at the same time, with surprisingly sharp pale brown eyes. Juliet guessed that Mrs. Sheppard must be in her mid to late seventies, but she looked older.

"Mrs. Sheppard? Juliet Armstrong, of the South Lin-colnshire Police." Juliet held out her identity card. "I'm very sorry if I startled you."

"What do you want?" The tone was peremptory, even abrupt. As she spoke, the woman turned away to place the saucer – which evidently contained milk – on the gravel on one side of the front door. "Whenever the police come to see me, it means trouble."

Juliet quailed inwardly. This occasion would be no exception. She looked up and down the street. The whole area seemed to be deserted. Even so, standing outside in full view of anyone who might happen to be watching from one of these banal houses was not an appropriate place to deliver the news that she had brought with her.

"Would you mind if we went inside? There is something that I need to tell you."

Mrs. Sheppard's worried expression turned into a scowl. "Aye, I suppose so. I hope you haven't frightened the cat: he's shy, and he might not come for his milk if you've scared him. He isn't my cat – he lives next door, but they don't look after him properly. You wait here while I open the front door."

"I can just as easily walk with you to the back door."

"I said, wait here," said Mrs. Sheppard very emphatically, her voice cracking with the effort. She disappeared through the side gate, and fastened the bolt again immediately.

Juliet waited for some minutes with growing unease. Eventually she heard the sound of another bolt and a chain being drawn back and saw Mrs. Sheppard's shape outlined against the frosted glass of the front door. The door opened.

"You can come in now."

Juliet stepped into a tiny hall, in which there was room only for the doormat and a potted plant in a black iron stand. The staircase led straight up from the doorway. Both the hall and the stairway were painted a very pale duck-egg blue. Mrs. Sheppard sidled past her and opened one of the two doors on either side of the stairs.

She gestured to Juliet to precede her. Juliet entered a long oblong room made light by the huge picture windows that dominated either end. This room was also painted pale blue

– a truer blue than the stairs, whose hue had a greenish tinge. The carpet and most of the furniture were mostly pale blue. There were two armchairs and a sofa covered in light blue cotton, with a darker blue throw on the sofa, a table with a pale blue linen runner and a dresser and cupboard coated in thick light blue paint. The lampshades were blue-white. There was a print of one of Picasso's cat paintings from his blue period over the fireplace and two photographs standing on the mantelpiece framed in silver-blue chrome. The only things that were not blue were a very small coffee table, which was probably made of pine, and the television. It was the most monochrome room that Juliet had ever seen. The effect should have been restful, but it wasn't: being there felt more like being held inside a fridge and unable to escape. It was a room that tried to be controlled, but in which the angst was almost banging round the walls, like a trapped bird trying to get out.

Mrs. Sheppard gestured to Juliet to take a seat. Juliet took one of the armchairs while she perched on the arm of the sofa, in what looked like a very temporary position, as if she soon expected to be escorting Juliet back to the door. Being inside her inner sanctum seemed to mellow her slightly, however. She attempted a smile, though her hands were convulsively twisting the edge of her brown cardigan.

"Would you like a cup of tea?" she ventured, before Juliet had had time to open the conversation.

"Thank you, that would be nice," said Juliet, thinking that she would try to achieve as much rapport as possible, and that Mrs. Sheppard herself would probably be in need of tea shortly.

She sat and waited while Mrs. Sheppard vanished into the kitchen. It was unnerving how soundlessly the woman moved. She had closed the door behind her as she went, and no sounds of kettles filling or other tea-making preparations could be heard. Juliet sat very still. There was nothing to do in this room: no books, no magazines, no music system, no evidence of any hobbies such as knitting. There was the television, of course. Surely Mrs. Sheppard didn't devote most of her time to watching it? Her eyes wandered around the room until her gaze fell on the two photographs. One was of a girl barely into her teens, wearing school uniform. Someone had managed to get the girl's whole figure and her bicycle into the frame, so the facial features were too small to be distinguished clearly. Juliet guessed that it was a picture of Kathryn. The other was a head and shoulders shot of a man in his mid-forties, grinning, his hair windswept, his casual shirt open at the neck. This photograph was in colour; the one of the schoolgirl was black-and-white.

Mrs. Sheppard returned, bearing a tin tray which held two china mugs, a bowl of sugar and a jug of milk. She placed it on the coffee table and proceeded to offload its cargo. Juliet noticed that the tray was decorated with a blue and white scene from Swan Lake.

"I didn't put the milk or sugar in, not knowing how you take it," said Mrs. Sheppard. "Help yourself."

"Thanks. I'd just like a bit of milk."

Mrs. Sheppard had settled herself more permanently on the sofa this time. She leaned back against the cushions, clutching her mug of tea. The atmosphere had thawed considerably. She was attempting another of her curious pudgy-faced smiles.

"Now," she said encouragingly, "that's better. What can I do for you?"

"Mrs. Sheppard, I'm afraid that your instinct was right: I haven't brought you good news. However, I hope that what I do have to tell you will bring you some comfort in time, even though it will be very painful at present."

The smile collapsed in ruins.

"It's Kathryn, isn't it? That skeleton that they've found?"

"Yes." Juliet paused. "I'm afraid it is – there can't be any doubt about it. We're lucky that you insisted on having those DNA samples analysed when you did."

The rubbery lips trembled, but only for a minute.

"I've always known that she was dead," she said. "I've known it from the first call we made to the police after she went missing. She just wouldn't have disappeared like that. She didn't live here any more, but she was always in touch. Even if she'd been running away from something and decided to emigrate, say, she would have told us. She wouldn't have put us through the agony of not knowing."

She paused for some moments. Juliet didn't interrupt.

"It was my idea to have the DNA tests done. I didn't need them for myself, but he needed them." She pointed to the second photograph. "Frank. It was eating him away, not knowing what had happened to her. He had a feeling that she was still alive and he would comb missing persons organisations for hours and go off on wild goose chases trying to find her. It was wearing him out. I suggested the DNA tests, thinking that when we got the results he would be calmer, because every time the police found a body they would try a match and then we would know that it wasn't her. But after the first few weeks, it didn't make any difference. Not really. What he wanted was an answer. He died five years ago, so I suppose he'll never have one now."

This time she did cry, soundlessly, her head bowed, her shoulders raised. After a while, she stopped as suddenly as she had begun, and said in a listless but matter-of-fact voice:

"There hasn't been much point to my life since then, except for the cat."

Juliet allowed another heavy minute to go by.

"Mrs. Sheppard, I do apologise for this, particularly as I know that you have helped the police with enquiries about Kathryn's disappearance on two previous occasions, but would you mind answering some questions?"

"Not if it makes you feel that you're doing your job better. You won't catch him, though, will you?"

"Catch who, Mrs. Sheppard?"

"The man who killed her. You won't catch him now."

"We don't have proof that she was murdered, or, if she was murdered, that the killer was a man. The pathologist has been unable to establish the cause of death."

"You don't have proof that she was murdered! What was she doing there by the side of the road, then? Tossed away like an empty crisp packet!" Her voice had risen almost to a shriek.

"I'm sorry, Mrs. Sheppard, that was insensitive of me. Of course, there is every likelihood that she was murdered. Do you have any particular reason for thinking that she was murdered by a man?"

Mrs. Sheppard shrugged. Her eyes were dull again.

"I'm just guessing: but what woman would want to kill a young girl?"

Juliet did not answer. She knew from experience that this type of speculation could be dangerous, for the police as well as the victim's family: it could lead to their making false assumptions which would actually hinder their investigation.

"As I said, I know you've answered questions like this before, but can you tell me exactly when you began to be worried about Kathryn? You said that she wasn't living here when she disappeared, so how long before you reported her missing did you last see her?"

"She was living in a flat in Little London. It wasn't a very nice flat: it was on the ground floor of one of those big Victorian mansion houses. The other flats were nice, but the ground floor was really half in the basement and it was damp and dark. I don't know why she wanted to live there, really. Originally she moved into the flat with a friend – Angela Jackson, someone she had known from school – but Angela didn't stay long. I think she went to live with her boyfriend. I thought that Kathryn might want her boyfriend to move in with her, but it didn't happen. In fact, she had two boyfriends during the time that she lived there, but neither of them moved in."

"Hedley Atkins and Charles Heward?"

"Yes. But she didn't go out with Hedley for long. I was pleased about that. He was a very strange young man. Of course, it turned out that it was no wonder he was strange, living in a household like that. But we didn't know anything about it at the time. Kathryn went to his house several times, and she said nothing about it being strange, either, except that she didn't like the old lady."

"You mean Hedley's mother?"

"No, his grandmother. Apparently she was a real old bitch – so Kathryn said. I never met her. Frank and I weren't invited to meet them; the relationship never got that far."

"By his grandmother, you mean Doris Atkins?"

"I suppose so, although Kathryn never mentioned her by name. Of course I remember the name because of what happened afterwards. It was splashed all over the newspapers for weeks. That's when the details of how weird that house was came out as well."

"Kathryn's next boyfriend – Charles Heward – did you meet him as well?"

"Yes, she brought him here on several occasions. Frank didn't like him – Frank didn't get on with that type of person." Mrs. Sheppard sniffed, and looked as if she were in agreement with her late husband. "But he didn't let Kathryn see it – she was his daughter, after all, and Charles was a much better choice than Hedley – or so we thought. Kathryn was absolutely head-over-heels with Charles, anyway. Nothing that we could have said could have dented her good opinion of him. We would just have ended up causing some kind of rift, which was the last thing that we wanted."

"You know that the police held Charles as a suspect for a short time?"

"Yes. We thought that was very strange, trying to pin a murder on someone when there was no body. Frank in particular was annoyed, because, as I've said, he never really believed that Kathryn was dead – or he wouldn't let himself believe it. Charles came to see us after the police released him. He said that he was really sorry about her disappearance, and asked if there was anything he could do. I must say that I had my doubts about him after that."

"What sort of doubts?"

Mrs. Sheppard shrugged again. "Nothing I can put my finger on. It was just that he didn't seem upset enough. After all, Kathryn was still his girlfriend – she wasn't his 'ex', like with Hedley. But it was almost as if Charles was already getting on with the next phase of his life, that coming to see us was part of the clearing-up process to give him a new start. And it did make me wonder if getting our approval was part of this as well, that perhaps he was throwing the police off the scent by courting us in this way. And in time I did begin to think that it may have been him, after all."

"You mean that you suspected that Charles Heward might be Kathryn's killer?"

"Yes. There was just something about his behaviour that didn't ring true: that and the fact that I could think of absolutely no-one else who might have wanted to harm Kathryn. But maybe I was just overwrought after she disappeared. That was what Frank thought, anyway. He didn't think that Charles could have killed her, even though he didn't like the man. But of course he never got as far as believing that *anyone* could have killed her."

"Do you ever hear from Charles now?"

" No. He sent Christmas cards for a couple of years and then stopped. My guess was that he had got married. If that was so and he was innocent, I certainly didn't begrudge him it. Better than living the kind of half-life that Frank and I had here."

"So, to go back to when Kathryn disappeared: she was living in the flat in Little London and going out with Charles, but not living with him. I think that Kathryn was reported as a missing person on a Monday?"

"That's right. Her father and I had called her several times

over the course of the weekend, and we couldn't get a reply.
We had a key to the flat, so Frank went round on Monday
morning – early, before she would have set off for work – to
check that she was all right. He said that he had knocked and
got no answer, so he let himself in. She didn't mind us going
in: we'd done it before. She wasn't there, but all her things
were: her uniform for the bank was hanging up, and her
handbag was lying on the table. He thought that she might
have gone out for a run – she was keen on keeping fit – so he
sat down and waited. She didn't come back, so he was still
waiting at the time she would have started work. He called
the bank and they said that she hadn't turned up for work,
although she didn't have the day booked as holiday. It turned
out that she hadn't been there on the previous Friday, either,
though she had left them a message saying that something
had come up unexpectedly and that she would like to take
the day as leave. All of this was quite unlike Kathryn: letting
people down, keeping them guessing in this way. The police
asked us to keep it secret that she had taken the day off on
the Friday. It wasn't reported in the papers."

"She had been at work as usual on the Thursday?"

"I believe so."

"Did you or Frank see Kathryn or hear from her at all over
the course of the preceding Friday or the weekend?"

"No."

"What about Charles?"

"Why would we have heard from him without Kathryn?"

"She could have been ill or upset about something. He
could have called to tell you."

"No. Nothing like that happened."

"When did you last see Kathryn?"

"The Monday before. She called in to drop off some information about bank cards that Frank had asked her for. She
stopped for a cup of tea."

"Did she seem quite normal?"

"Yes, though I wasn't expecting her not to be. She was a

sunny girl, Kathryn. Not often moody. But if there had been something troubling her and I had looked for it, I might have been able to tell. We were very close. The three of us, Frank as well. People always said what a close family we were."

Mrs. Sheppard seemed near to tears again. Juliet realised that she was unlikely to learn more about Kathryn on this occasion. She knew that she had pushed Mrs. Sheppard far enough already, given that the ostensible purpose of her visit had been to advise her of her daughter's death, not to interrogate her. She finished her tea and stood up.

"Thank you very much indeed, Mrs. Sheppard. Please allow me to say how sorry I am for your loss. I won't trouble you further today, but I promise to keep in touch with you as our investigation proceeds and I hope that you will let me contact you again if we think that you can give us any further help. Would you like me to request a visit from a bereavement counsellor?"

She understood but still flinched from the scornful look which distorted the woman's face.

CHAPTER THIRTEEN

"Are you there, darling?" It is Peter, tapping too discreetly on the glass panel of the flat door, as he always does before he enters. When I was still living on my own I had found it a charming gesture of good manners, but now I sense that there is something insolent about it: almost as if he were saying, "I know I'm here on sufferance; I know that the place is still yours, and I will observe all due decorum in order to spare your feelings (even though I am your superior), to prevent your taking offence." I have loved Peter from the start for his poshness, but sometimes my infatuation with it helps me to understand very clearly that what I feel for Peter is a masochistic kind of love. As far as Peter is concerned, I will always be his slightly grubby little working class friend.

"Of course I'm here," I say tersely. And of course Peter knows I am here. It is six-thirty in the evening, for one thing, and I am always home from work by five. The door has been left unlocked, for another – and we are both fastidious about security. Neither of us would have gone out without remembering to lock up.

"Good, good," says Peter brightly, entering the room. "I've brought you some flowers." With a flourish, he presents me with a bunch of hothouse blooms. They are quite exotic, the sort of flowers you see in contract displays in banks and offices. They include lilies and some of those peculiar half-thistle, half-flower things with green heads.

"Thank you," I say. I put them down on the coffee table.

"You aren't cross with me, darling, are you?" Peter darts me one of his lightning sideways looks. "Because if you are it would be very disappointing." He sits down opposite me, and looks at me in a rather strange, too-intense way. I think I have picked up a hint of menace in his tone. I could be mistaken, because the next moment he is his usual mercurial self, and launches into, first, an expression of empathy and, second, one of his anecdotes.

"I can see that you have had a disagreeable day. Poor you! It must be so hard to have to keep on grinding away in that drab little office day after day." He holds up his hand as I open my mouth to retaliate: it will not be the first argument we have had about the relative merits of my 'grubbing' for a living, as Peter is pleased to call it, while he lives on Daddy's legacy and Mummy's handouts, as befit his talents and refined personality.

"No, No! Please stop there. I assure you that I have no wish to provoke. I apologise if what I have just said has irritated you. It was meant merely as a prelude to my offering to prepare supper this evening. But first there is something that I simply have to tell you." He smiles conspiratorially. "Guess who I met when I was out today?"

I sigh. "I couldn't begin to guess," I say. "For a start, I have no idea where you go on your daytime forays. For another thing, I know virtually none of your friends and acquaintances."

"Jillian!" says Peter, ignoring all of this. "I bumped into my sister Jillian. Now, what do you think of that?"

"I had no idea that you had a sister, Peter," I say. "Now that you tell me that you do, I don't understand why your having met her by accident was such a big deal. It's a small town, after all."

"Oh, yes, but you see, she doesn't live here. No, no. She

lives in Birkenhead, close to Mummy. I don't think that she has ever been to Spalding before. So you see, she must have had a reason."

"Well, I assume that the reason must have been to see you. But if she came all the way from Birkenhead, I don't understand why she didn't tell you that she was coming. You might have been out, after all. In fact, you were out when you saw her."

"Oh, but you don't know Jillian. She understands me very well. She knows that I am a creature of habit; and also that I would avoid meeting her if I could. Not that I detest her or anything coarse like that, you understand. It's just that she takes a very superior moral stance where I am concerned; and she certainly frightens Mummy off whenever I ask the old girl for some money. So Jillian will have known that the chances of actually meeting me if we had prearranged it would have been very slender, because I would either have put her off, or more probably allowed her to come and then done a bunk for the day. I take my hat off to her for the tactic that she employed instead, which I guess was to follow me from the flat and then appear as if by accident when I was a safe distance away from it."

"This all sounds very paranoid to me. Did you ask her how she happened to be there?"

"Of course not. I simply took her to buy some tea. You don't understand sisters: you are in the fortunate position of not having had one. Jillian taught me all that I need to know about girls, especially that boys are infinitely to be preferred." I only recall much later that Peter gives me one of his sidelong looks as he says this. The superciliousness of his comment annoys me so much that I make a bad mistake. To this day I regret it. It sets in train a catastrophic sequence of events that might otherwise have been avoided.

"I know more about sisters than you think. I grew up with one."

Peter scrutinises me with his black button eyes.

"Really? You are a dark horse. What is her name?"

"Bryony." I swallow hard. One of the many beauties of my relationship with Peter is that he knows nothing of my family history – or so I believe. Now I know that it will take all of my strength and ingenuity to prevent him from poking and probing until he has wormed it all out of me.

"Bryony? What a ghastly name! What could your mother have been thinking of?"

"For Christ's sake, Peter, give it a rest, will you? For that matter, I don't think that Jillian's such a wonderful name, either."

"Well," says Peter, steepling his fingers, "I am in complete agreement with you there. But my view is coloured by association, no doubt. Where is Bryony, anyway? I presume that she lives away somewhere. Otherwise she would have called or telephoned on some occasion when I've been here, I'm sure. Does she live abroad?"

Something inside me snaps. I scream at Peter for the next five minutes. I don't know exactly what I am saying. It is as if I have lost consciousness and fallen into a bloody sea of anger. Gradually I find myself surfacing again and Peter's face emerges out of the red blur. I see that he is shocked, but also that something very important has happened. I realise immediately that I have probably told him other things that I will come to regret, apart from the fact of Bryony's having existed. Of course, I know with a sinking heart what they are likely to be about: myself and Tirzah.

Peter has been holding his hand up against the side of his face, as if to shield it. Now, as the vituperative torrent of words that I have dredged up from my subconscious slowly falters, he allows it to drop and pats my knee.

"Goodness me," he says, and I can detect no sarcasm now. "I have often congratulated myself upon my perspicacity at spotting from the start that you are a very interesting person. However, I could never have fathomed exactly *how* interesting. What a pedigree! It knocks Daddy's business dealings, which I have always suspected were a little shady, into a cocked hat. I really should love to meet your mother."

I do not ask Peter exactly what I have revealed to him, and in fact I am never to find out. Looking back later, I am convinced that even though this must have been be the occasion on which I revealed details about my mother's crime, Peter has known about Tirzah all along, though I doubt if he could have done his research diligently enough to have discovered Bryony as well. Actually, I have come to believe that Peter made his first overtures of friendship to me *because* of Tirzah.

"Anyway," he says airily, "to return to Jillian – a safer topic for us, even if I do regard her as a dangerously loose cannon per se. I should tell you that my sister is quite a little bitch. She seems to have spent her entire life scheming to make sure that I get as little from the parental pot of gold as possible. Mummy would be a darling without her. Mummy always appreciated me when I was small."

I am exhausted by my outburst. I am also feeling a little bit sick. It takes all of my strength to maintain the interest in Peter's own affairs that – especially after such a lapse – courtesy demands. I close my eyes and grip the arms of my chair.

"What did she want?"

"She wanted to talk about Mummy's money. I'm afraid that I skirted the subject and insisted that we talk about other things. Not that I'm not interested in it, as you know. In fact, one could say that it is my *passion* – next to you, of course, darling. But I will not have Jillian creeping up on me and trying to bounce me into new situations before I have had time to think about them. So I only allowed her to get so far. It would appear that she has a plan for putting Mummy permanently into the nursing home where she goes when Jillian wants a rest and selling the house. I have no objection to either of those things; but when Jillian started talking about what should happen to the money after the nursing home fees have been deducted, I shut her up."

"But why?"

"Because another of my sister's annoying traits is that once something has been discussed, she thinks – or professes to think – that it has been agreed. And it was very obvious to me by the way that she was leading up to it that a straightforward split between us, or even allowing each of us some of the money on account until the inevitable happens, is not what she has in mind. No, she will be thinking of tying it up in some way. No doubt she is indoctrinating Mummy to think along the same lines, as well. I therefore need to be one step ahead of her, ready both to say the right thing and to act pretty smartly, too."

"I don't see what kind of action you can take, short of having your mother certified."

Peter looks at me with intense distaste.

"Well, that isn't going to happen: I won't have my family name tarnished with that," he says pointedly. "Besides, you haven't met Mummy. When she tries, she is sanity and good sense personified."

"Peter, you are baffling me. And I'm very tired. Just tell me what you intend to do."

Peter cackles – a surprising sound, coming from his quarter.

"It is rather a question of what *we* are going to do, darling. And now I have had time to think – and in fact I was formulating my thoughts throughout your strange shouting episode, as well as on my way home – I have decided that we need to visit Liverpool with the utmost urgency. On Saturday, in fact, since I presume you are unable to take tomorrow away from your wretched place of work at short notice."

"I suppose that a visit would be useful for you, so that you can continue the conversation with Jillian. But I fail to see why you want me to go with you."

"Oh, but you are my very dear partner, darling, and I am devoted to you. It is high time that you met Mummy. Besides, you might be useful for keeping the old boot at bay while I talk to Jillian; and I am quite certain that you will be able to help if more drastic measures are needed."

I feel a sick pang of fear. "What do you mean?"

Peter thrusts his face much closer to mine than good manners dictate.

"I don't *mean* anything yet," he says, almost viciously. "We don't know what kind of turn events *will* take; and I'm sure I wouldn't want to pre-empt a superfluous action. But it is possible that needs must. No doubt your mother would understand perfectly."

The sick feeling grows worse. I am panicky.

"Just understand that I have no intention of doing anything illegal. That isn't the way in which I operate."

"Ah. I think it is, darling, when you care about the outcome sufficiently. You just need to give my affairs as much weight in your mind as you give to your own."

"I've got no idea what you are talking about." I am fighting hysteria now. Peter draws back a little, and the extra physical space helps to calm me, even though he says, very quietly so that I can only just hear him:

"So you say, Hedley. But I think you know exactly."

CHAPTER FOURTEEN

Detective Inspector Tim Yates was naturally a very cheerful man. He felt happy most of the time. Today, although it was still February and bitterly cold, he thought that he could feel some glimmerings of the spring: the light had changed, and the evenings were beginning to draw out at last. As he drove along the M42 in his battered BMW (he was a car snob, though half-ashamed of it, and would rather be seen in an elderly BMW than a chipper new Ford or Volkswagen) he was humming plain chant music to himself, and looking forward to the meeting ahead of him.

He was on his way to interview the psychiatrist who had examined Dorothy Atkins prior to her trial, and who had testified as an expert witness. When he had told his team that he would like them to find Dr. Bertolasso, he had thought it unlikely that they would succeed: the chances were that the psychiatrist had been middle-aged at the time of the trial, and would therefore now be very old or, in all probability, dead. However, it had not taken Detective Constable Juliet Armstrong long to locate the Professor, who was now an eminent criminal psychologist and held a personal chair at Birmingham University.

Tim flashed his police pass at the porter who was manning the impressive main gates of the redbrick and was directed to park in a multi-storey car park to the left of them. He had visited Birmingham University once before, when he was a student. Emma, his sixth-form girlfriend, had gone there to study Chemistry. At school they had been inseparable, but it had been on that first and only trip to Birmingham that he had realised that they had little in common. In the space of three weeks, she had acquired a coterie of dowdy conventional friends who had persuaded her to join the Junior Conservatives and take up going to church. She had immediately looked older and dressed more severely. He had described to her the much more raffish and exciting, though less scholarly, life that he was leading at the University of Leeds and she had responded with humourless contempt. They had agreed that trying to continue with their relationship would be pointless. He remembered running over a long stretch of grass after they had parted, exuberant to be free again, yet with one small secret part of him mourning the pretty and vivacious Emma that not only he, but the world at large, had lost.

Now he was walking more decorously on the path which abutted that same stretch of grass. He stopped a student with an Afro hairstyle to ask the way to the Department of Psychology. The directions that the student gave were somewhat garbled, so Tim had to ask again before he found the correct building and started to pace what seemed like miles of gloomy corridors. He wondered if Emma was still buried in here somewhere, delighting the rarefied world in which she moved with the audacity of her chemical experiments. The last time he had heard of her, she had been working for a PhD, and was obviously destined to take up an academic career. It would be strange – unnerving, even – to bump into her in this corridor.

Eventually he came to a secretary's office, and was asked to wait while she told Professor Bertolasso that he had arrived. The secretary was young, curvaceous and funky, dressed in a bright multicoloured calf-length skirt and little red buckled boots. She had a mass of dark curly hair which was escaping from the red bandana with which she had tried to tame it. She moved nimbly, and was back at her post in a trice.

"Professor Bertolasso is expecting you. He says please to go in when you are ready." There was the trace of an accent. Not English. Mediterranean? He returned her bright smile.

Professor Bertolasso was a tiny bald man who appeared to be seated on a velvet throne. He remained seated as Tim approached his desk, eventually extending a hand.

"Ah, Inspector Yates." His voice was another surprise: the thick lilting tones proclaimed him a native of Birmingham. "You'll have to excuse me for not standing," he continued, in his aggrieved-sounding sing-song. "I've hurt me back – which is why I'm sat on this ridiculous chair. No delusions of grandeur, I'm sure!" He nodded encouragingly towards a chair. "Do sit down. Would you like a coffee?"

"Not if it's too much trouble."

"Oh, no trouble at all – you see, I have this machine on the go all the time." He pointed at an electric coffee maker which was seething quietly on a glass-fronted cupboard. "Help yourself. There's biscuits in the jar."

Tim poured himself a cup of black coffee. He raised it: "Professor?"

"Oh, no thank you. I prefer tea. Rossella will bring some in for me later."

Tim re-seated himself, and took a sip. The coffee was surprisingly good: strong and nutty, and not bitter. Purchased by Rossella, no doubt.

"Thank you for agreeing to meet me, Professor. I believe that the detective constable who contacted you explained why I wish to talk to you."

The Professor's brown eyes stopped darting about, and fixed Tim's blue ones.

"I understand that you have come about Dorothy Atkins. A very strange woman. I gave evidence at her trial as an expert witness."

"On behalf of the Crown, I believe."

"On behalf of the truth," wailed the Professor in his best falsetto. "The evidence I gave was as much in her favour as against it. I didn't in fact suggest that she was insane – Dorothy is an unpleasant and devious woman, but she has a certain perverted magnificence, and she undoubtedly has her pride. I said that she was narcissistic, had borderline paranoia, and was suffering from undiagnosed depression. That did not mean she was a total basket case." His voice rose an octave as he uttered the last two words, surprising Tim with the slangy terminology. "It was the judge who decided that she should be sent to a secure mental unit. In his shoes, I would have sent her to a normal prison."

"But you did not challenge the sentence?"

"What do you think, Inspector? I was very young: Criminal Psychology was a discipline new to British universities at the time, hence my being offered the job despite my youth. There were no older and sager academics available to take it on. But it was not because I was cowed by the situation that I found myself in that I did not protest – not, I think, that protesting would have done me any good. I would have had a shot at it if I had believed that she was being treated too leniently. As it was, I thought that whatever sentence was passed on her, inevitable as it was, it would be unfair."

"I'm not sure that I follow you. You have said that she wasn't insane."

"Oh, I'm sure that she wasn't, though she was probably trying to convince me of the opposite. As I've said, she is an unpleasant person – devious, manipulative and self-inter-ested. But in one respect, and one respect only, she deserved my compassion."

"What do you mean? I'm not sure that I follow."

"It's quite simple, Inspector." His voice rose to soprano pitch. "Despite the circumstantial evidence, and the testi-monies of various witnesses – all relatives of Dorothy's, as I'm sure you will have noted – nothing ever convinced me that she was guilty of murder. In fact, rather the opposite."

Although this was a momentous statement, and judging from the swelling crescendo of his voice, the Professor intended it to be such, somehow Tim was not surprised.

"What makes you say that?"

"Well, for a start, Dorothy never confessed satisfactorily. I know that this is true of many, perhaps most, criminals, but you have to remember that Dorothy also entered a plea of guilty – or rather, she did not protest when her barrister entered the plea on her behalf. When I met Dorothy – as I did on many occasions before the trial, and they were long meetings – she would never talk directly about the murder. She would not describe the exact circumstances in which her mother-in-law had died – though I pressed her on this, because of course I wanted to understand the motive – nor exactly how she had died."

"From all I have heard and read, Dorothy is not exactly a co-operative person. Perhaps she was just trying to make life difficult for you."

"Of course you are right and of course I have thought of that. Alternatively, she may have blanked out the actual events from her memory, though she did not strike me as the sort of criminal who could not face up to the consequences of her actions. But there is another possible explanation – that she could not describe the murder to me in detail because she was not there. And then there is her one highly cryptic comment about the crime: that her mother-in-law died because she was 'too fond of gardening'. But it is my reading of her personality that I rely on most of all. I am convinced that if Dorothy had done it, she would have confessed. Not with bravado, but with a sort of defiant honesty. And she was a terrible liar."

"If you are correct, not so terrible that the jury did not believe her to be guilty and the judge was not convinced that she was sane."

"That also helped to convince me that my theory was correct. As I've said, Dorothy was not good at lying – although she had a good memory, she found it difficult to describe the events leading up to the killing and the killing itself consistently if she was asked about them repeatedly. I think that this was not only because she was fundamentally honest, but also – and this would be characteristic of her arrogance – because she had not rehearsed her story in her own mind. I doubt if she realised that a guilty plea had to be proven. She had given her version of events in a fairly ad hoc way when she was first arrested, and then realised belatedly that she would be asked for them again and again after that, both by the defence and the prosecution and of course by me. She knew that she was in a mess – unable to remember what she had said on the first occasion. If she wanted her guilty plea to be believed, there were two courses of action open to her: either to remain silent after giving the first account, or to appear to be confused. She tried a bit of each of these tactics: and it was the confusion, coupled with my psychiatric assessment – which I repeat did not indicate that she was insane – that determined the trial judge to send her to a secure unit. And you should take into account that this sentence was not necessarily in Dorothy's best interest. Sure, conditions at the unit were easier, and she had more time to cultivate the pursuits that she liked – she worked for an Open University degree while she was there – but she spent far longer incarcerated than she would have done for a single isolated crime, even a murder, if she had served a prison sentence and got time off for good behaviour."

"Can you explain why, if she was fundamentally rational, she would have behaved like this?"

"There are two possible explanations. One is that she did it to protect someone else. Based on many years of experience of dealing with such cases since, this would be the most commonplace and logical reason. The difficulty is that there is no immediate obvious candidate for her protection. The Atkins family was not close – in fact, it was as 'dysfunctional', to use the modern cliché, as any family could be whose members had not actually gone their separate ways at the time of which we speak – and Dorothy was not devoted to her children. As for her husband, she despised him; she would gladly have seen him put away. And it is highly unlikely that he would have killed his mother. He appeared to have been very fond of her."

"You don't think that she could have been protecting Hedley Atkins? Despite his mild manner, there seems to be something about him that doesn't quite fit. And he and Dorothy seem to circle each other from a distance, though they have not met for many years."

"It is a long time since I met him, and then only on one or two occasions. He seemed to be rather an effete young man, but he got on well with his sister, and I believe had also had a girlfriend. He was not your typical loner. I have to say that I quite liked him: he didn't give me any 'bad vibes', as they say. The sister was as 'normal' as can be."

"Oh, so you met Bryony Atkins as well?"

"I spoke to her on the phone, and as I say, she seemed quite normal, whatever that means. I suppose what I mean is that it is hard to believe that she grew up in that household and still turned into the girl that I interviewed. Have you met her?"

"No, we have just started trying to trace her. Apparently no-one has seen her since she was about to become a student. Somewhat surprisingly, the police did not call her as a witness at Dorothy's trial, although Hedley Atkins told me recently that she left home shortly before her grandmother's murder, which may explain why she was overlooked. Hedley claims that after the murder she cut herself off from her family, which I suppose would not have been surprising. She must have changed her identity as well: her national insurance number has not been used since that same year."

The Professor looked serious. He leant back in the velvet chair and shaded his brow with stubby splayed fingers.

"That is interesting – and seriously alarming. You should

also be aware that Dorothy's psychiatrist at the secure unit disagrees completely with my diagnosis of Dorothy; and naturally she has spent much longer analysing Dorothy's problems than I could, as well as offering extensive therapy. She believes that Dorothy committed the murder, and that the other behaviour that I have described demonstrates self-interest and a total lack of remorse. In short, her diagnosis is that Dorothy is a psychopath. Which brings me to the other possible explanation of which I spoke."

"Go on."

"If my assessment of Dorothy is wrong, then it is possible that she tacitly accepted responsibility for Doris Atkins' murder and displayed confusion because this was the only one of her crimes for which she had been caught, and that by focusing on it in this way she avoided having the police cast their net wider. This is Doctor Hemingway's view. If she is correct, then it means that Dorothy may have killed – in fact, has probably killed – on more than one occasion."

CHAPTER FIFTEEN

Dr. Hemingway had declined to see Tim at the secure unit at Bracknell where she worked. She had said that she was coming to London on the date that he had suggested, and had offered to meet at a café at Waterloo Station instead. Tim could have caught an early train from Peterborough to King's Cross, but instead he decided to take the opportunity to stay with his sister in Surbiton, and had bought her dinner on the previous evening.

The café chosen by Dr. Hemingway was in fact a rather down-at-heel pub which also served coffee. Although it was only 10.00 a.m., there were already several dishevelled characters propping up the bar and drinking what looked like brandy. Tim sat down at one of the steel tables which had been arranged outside the building, in a small square roped off from the main concourse. It was quite pleasant here, watching the pigeons swoop down on to discarded bits of pastry and the crowds hurrying past. None of the bar staff approached him, though he had not placed an order.

Tim liked watching people, in a professional way. He knew that it was one of the things that made him good at his job. He placed a bet with himself that he would spot Dr. Hemingway before she introduced herself. None of the people passing at that moment was a possible candidate. There were several men walking together, all with paunches and dressed in baggy suits, who were talking and laughing far too loudly; a couple of women in their twenties wearing tiny skirts over thick black tights; and a busker with straggling hair and day-glo panels sewn into his donkey-jacket, clearly looking for a pitch. His arrival precipitated some activity from the waiters: one of them darted out from behind the bar and asked the busker to move on – though politely, Tim noticed, and with the accompanying gift of a croissant and a carton of coffee. He applauded the tactic, and was sufficiently distracted by it not to notice the arrival of a slight middle-aged woman with crisply-cut short blonde hair. She sat down at his table with a poise and certainty which took him by surprise.

She waited for him to turn round, and then held out her hand.

"You must be Inspector Yates?"

Tim laughed. "Is it so obvious?"

"Well, there aren't too many candidates, are there?" she responded. Her voice was clipped and brisk. "But if you're asking whether I could spot that you are a policeman, the answer is yes; although you aren't as obvious as some."

Tim gave a slight bow. That will teach me, he thought.

Dr. Hemingway possessed the elegant angularity of a whippet, and her pale hair and finely-chiselled features served to reinforce the similarity. She was dressed in a biscuit-coloured wool suit with a very fine check and a tailored white shirt. Apart from an understated gold watch with a black leather strap, two tiny gold ear studs comprised her only jewellery. She wore no rings. Her shoes were highly-polished plain brown courts and, he guessed, expensive. She had no handbag, but one of those clever slimline briefcases that served as both attaché and handbag. She placed it carefully on the table. Tim could see at once that Dr. Hemingway and Professor Bertolasso were chalk and cheese, and he was not surprised that they had disagreed in their assessment of Dorothy Atkins.

"May I get you some breakfast, Dr. Hemingway?"

"Goodness, it's a little late for breakfast!" she exclaimed, consulting her watch as if to check that it was not earlier than she had thought. "But some coffee would be wonderful: a double espresso, please. And my name is Claudia."

Tim stood up. Immediately, the waiter who had shooed away the busker appeared at his side with an order pad. Tim was even more impressed than before: clearly the staff here knew when to intervene and when not to intrude. He reflected that they would make excellent witnesses, should a crime ever take place on this spot.

"First things first," Claudia Hemingway was saying. "May I see your credentials?"

Surprised again, Tim fished out his identity card.

"Thank you. You realise that I can't be too careful: Dorothy Atkins is a sensitive, not to say explosive, subject. There are some people, myself possibly included, who believe that she should never have been 'released into the community', as the government is pleased to put it."

"She was hardly released into the community at large. My understanding is that upon leaving Broadmoor, she immediately entered a local authority sheltered housing scheme for the elderly, and from that eventually progressed into full-time nursing-home care."

"And allowing a psychopath to bump off a few of the superfluous elderly is all right, I suppose."

Her tone was hard and ironic, but when he met her light blue eyes he thought he discerned a glint of amusement there.

"But surely there isn't any evidence that she . . ."

"No, none at all. And I don't think that she has attempted any violence while she has been there – not of the physical kind, anyway. I'm sure that she will have inflicted mental torture on some of the inmates; on some of the more vulnerable of the nursing staff, too, in all probability. But Dorothy has her head screwed on when it comes to looking after Dorothy. Hence she has co-operated and so helped to prove the wisdom of our country's wonderfully humane criminal care system: we have 'cured' Dorothy and are enabling her to live out a venerable and dignified old age."

This time the irony was harsh, the tone unequivocal.

The waiter arrived with two double espressos and a chocolate muffin. Tim took the opportunity to lead the conversation out of the rather rocky cul-de-sac into which it had strayed.

"Shall we start at the beginning? For how long did you treat Dorothy Atkins? I'm assuming that you weren't at Broadmoor when she was first admitted – you're clearly too young for that."

"You flatter me, Inspector Yates." ("Tim, please!"). Dr. Claudia Hemingway looked and sounded not only like a woman who was beyond flattery, but also one who was offended by those who were tempted to try it.

"On the contrary . . ."

"For your information, I was at Broadmoor for the duration of Dorothy's time there, but I was not always her psychiatrist. When she was first admitted, she came under the care of my old boss, Professor Theodore Rogers. I was his assistant and also working on a PhD thesis. Dorothy's was a complex case and Professor Rogers, who was always generous in his encouragement of the younger members of his team, allowed me to attend some of his sessions with her. He would have allowed me to attend all of them if Dorothy herself had not sometimes objected."

"She was allowed to object? Do you know why?"

"Patients in secure units and prisons have the same right to privacy and confidentiality as anyone else when it comes to medical or psychiatric care. He was her therapist, not me. There was no reason why she should agree to my being present in order to further my own understanding of my profession. It doesn't take a psychiatrist to understand why she sometimes agreed to my presence and sometimes would not tolerate it. The exercise of power was Dorothy's raison d'être.

She was a past mistress of her art, even within the confines of a secure institution."

"What was she like when you first met her?"

"She was quite withdrawn. Not sulky, exactly, but haughty. And totally without guilt. Whatever she had or had not done, she believed that it had been right. Her capacity for understanding the interests and feelings of others was limited, to say the least. If I did not have a deep suspicion of dealing in absolutes, I would say non-existent."

"Are these your own views, or those of Professor Rogers?"

"They are shared observations, my own conclusions. Professor Rogers made the same observations – her withdrawnness and arrogance could hardly be doubted – but he drew rather different conclusions. And of course you must remember that I did not make those conclusions at the time. They were based on years of working with Dorothy – if that is the correct way of describing our 'professional' relationship." That irony in her voice again. She paused as if to satisfy herself that he had picked it up.

"How did Professor Rogers treat her?"

"At first he spent many hours talking to her. He also asked her to complete various written tests, which she agreed to – anything that made Dorothy the centre of attention usually gained her co-operation. He diagnosed depression, and prescribed Librium. Of course, criminal psychiatry was a relatively young science then and we had fewer diagnoses – and far fewer drugs – at our disposal. I also felt . . ."

She broke off, and looked – wary?

"Please go on. I assure you that this is an entirely off-the-record conversation. I need to understand Dorothy Atkins as well as I can in order to solve another murder – and perhaps to prevent others."

Claudia Hemingway was still hesitant.

"It feels like professional disloyalty," she said slowly. "And I must emphasise that I had the greatest respect for Professor Rogers. He had a fine mind and in the years that I worked with him he taught me a great deal. Almost always I admired his work. But his assessment of Dorothy Atkins was an exception. I don't think he was ever really honest with himself about Dorothy. I understand perfectly how it happened. Rocco Bertolasso had been one of his students, and when Rocco was asked to give evidence as an expert witness, he consulted Theo. Theo suggested a range of possible disorders that might be relevant to Dorothy's case, and Rocco – who was very nervous about the role in which he found himself and, I have to say, entirely unsuited to it – he is cut out to be an academic rather than a practitioner – offered a professional opinion that incorporated all of them. I'm sure that this is not what Theo intended; and I'm equally certain that he did not give Rocco permission to mention his name in court. But Rocco did – probably with the most innocent of intentions. It is my guess that he was just trying to give authority to his own inexperience. I believe that the defence lawyer questioned him quite incisively. Anyway, my view is that when Dorothy became one of Theo's patients, he did not start with a clean slate. He started with a collection of hypotheses put forward by Rocco which Theo himself appeared to have endorsed. At the outset, therefore, he had not only forfeited the total objectivity that every psychiatrist has to try to preserve, but also the absolute integrity that goes with it. God knows, it's difficult enough to hang on to both of these once you have started working with the patient – especially a patient as intelligent and manipulative as Dorothy – but if you start by stacking the odds against yourself, you are lost."

Tim was not sure what to make of this. Was the analysis that Claudia Hemingway offered correct – was it truthful, even – or had he just been listening to a cleverly-couched piece of professional jealousy? He decided that he would try to encourage Claudia to focus on fact rather than opinion.

"I'm afraid that some of this is getting a bit deep for me. I'm sure that over time I shall learn to understand better by remaining under your tutelage – if indeed you are prepared to give me more time." He smiled engagingly, and managed to elicit a guarded smile in return. "Tell me, was Dorothy allowed visitors?"

"Of course. All the patients were, subject to the hospital's rules. Psychiatric patients are believed to benefit from contact with the outside world. Whether the visitors benefit is of course another matter." Her equilibrium and urbanity were evidently restored. Tim felt relief.

"Can you remember who visited her – or whether in fact anyone did?"

"She had quite a lot of visitors at first. Her solicitor, of course. Her husband came on a few occasions – I think primarily to settle the details of their divorce, which incidentally did not seem to worry Dorothy in the slightest. There was an elderly aunt – she had one of those old-fashioned Victorian names, which I can't quite recall at the moment. And her husband's Uncle Colin – he was a frequent visitor, for some reason, even though Dorothy had murdered his sister. And her son. Hedley. A strange young man – sometimes he came with Uncle Colin, sometimes without him. He would sit for hours without saying a word. Dorothy was obviously exasperated by his presence and I suppose that he understood that eventually. Anyway, he stopped coming. After a couple of years, no-one came to see her except Colin."

"Did you ever see the daughter?"

"No. As a matter of fact, I did not know of her existence until I had been treating Dorothy for many years. She was one of several people that Dorothy never spoke of."

"How did her name come up?"

"By accident. We had a new ward orderly called Bryony, and Dorothy was caught off guard. I heard her say to the woman that it was the name she had chosen for her own daughter. It was unlike Dorothy to give information away like that, but she was probably trying to get the woman onside for some reason. She had a habit of cultivating new staff."

"Did you try to talk to her about Bryony – the daughter, I mean?"

"Yes, in her next therapy session. But she just clammed up completely. It was only what I expected. She behaved in the same way when I tried to get her to talk about her mother-in-law, Doris – the woman that she murdered – or, for some reason, her own mother."

"Did she ever tell you anything about her father?"

"No, but I think that her reason for that was genuine enough. She didn't know who he was – her mother never told her – though she had her suspicions. Self-aggrandising ones, actually. She seemed to think that he was probably one of her mother's employers – her mother had worked as a house-keeper. Ronald Atkins told me that he had in fact been the chauffeur of one of them, though of course this information could not have been reliable, either. It was simply what he was told by one of the mother's sisters."

"There seem to have been a lot of things that Dorothy wouldn't talk about. What did you discuss in your therapy sessions?"

"As I've said, I shouldn't tell you: and although I'm pre-pared to give some indication, I won't divulge details. We talked about her childhood, her thwarted ambitions and her unsatisfactory relationship with Ronald. All the things, in short, that Dorothy believed had led her to where she found herself at that point in her life. She did not accept any respon-sibility for her status as a convicted murderer. She regarded herself as being entirely the victim of circumstance."

"What did this mean, from your professional viewpoint?"

"As far as I was concerned, it meant that none of the many hours of therapy which had been expended on Dorothy had worked. A first step towards rehabilitation for a crimi-nal offender is usually to get them to experience remorse, which logically means understanding the hurt that they have inflicted on their victims and those close to them. Dorothy never progressed beyond seeing herself as the injured party; and she certainly never displayed any empathy for either Doris Atkins or the other people whose lives had been affected by her death."

"If she was not 'cured' – I'm sure that is not the word you would use, but forgive me – you know what I mean – why was she allowed to leave Broadmoor and be released into the care of the old people's home?"

"As I've said before, Dorothy is manipulative, and she is very clever. Theo Rogers had treated her before I did, and his notes had said that she was making progress. At the first case meeting that was held to assess whether she should be released, my advice that this would be unsafe was upheld; but Dorothy appealed, citing Theo's notes and saying that her relationship with me was troubled by a clash of personalities. Through her solicitor, she asked for a second opinion, and two other psychiatrists were invited to examine her and make an assessment. They both said that they considered her to be harmless and recommended that she should be released into the community, on condition that she agreed to live in sheltered accommodation. Her medical doctor also testified that she was very frail and that in his view she could no longer be a risk to others. So that was that. It was my belief that a complex and devious character such as Dorothy's – and in my long career of dealing with deviant personalities, she is the trickiest person I have ever met – could not be accurately assessed by them in such a small snapshot of time; and that although she may not have posed a physical threat to anyone, she was still capable of imposing mental duress, especially on the elderly."

"Presumably you voiced these views?"

"Of course; but by this time there was an unspoken groundswell of opinion that I harboured some kind of personal resentment against her, and therefore that she was being victimised."

"Was there any truth at all in this? Forgive me for asking – as I have explained, I am just trying to understand."

Dr. Hemingway deliberated for a moment. "Perhaps," she said. "I admit that I was frustrated that I could not at all pierce the psychological armour that she put up. But unless my own professional integrity has been seriously impaired – and believe me, I scrutinise my motives every day – I think that this was a minor factor. That I could not penetrate Dorothy's psyche was the cause of my mistrust, not the result of a wound to my amour propre. I honestly believe that Dorothy was hiding something worse than the crime of which she had been convicted and that was why she was holding out on me."

"What do you mean by 'something worse'?"

"Given what I have just told you, of course you will realise that I cannot give a precise answer to that question. But I suspect very strongly that there is a clue in her refusal to speak about the three people that I have mentioned. I have no doubt that Dorothy blotted them out of her verbal recall, and possibly banished them from all her conscious thoughts, for a reason."

"My God! Are you suggesting . . ."

"I'm not suggesting anything, Inspector. I'm trying to be as factual and straightforward as possible. I am telling you that there was a logic to Dorothy's thought processes, and that eventually I discovered that she had blotted certain people from her mind. Cause and effect. That is all. I will not speculate further."

CHAPTER SIXTEEN

The journey in the Virgin Cross-Country train to Liverpool takes several hours. Peter has insisted on travelling First Class, and although I resent paying the extra money, I see as soon as we board why 'Standard Class' would never have done for him. There are far too many sticky-fingered children, matrons flanked by shopping bags and students butting into people with their rucksacks for him to have been able to cope.

We choose a table in the middle of the only first class carriage, each of us sitting by a window. Peter has bought a selection of newspapers and magazines at the station – the *Daily Telegraph*, *Ideal Home*, *The English Garden*, and somewhat bizarrely, *The Lady* – and for half an hour or so we sit reading them quietly, until the train stops at the next station and two men dressed in business suits come into our carriage and claim the two seats remaining at our table. Peter raises his eyebrows and scoops the magazines closer in to his quarter of the table. One of the men regards him with a certain hostility, but does not speak. Peter sighs.

"I probably shan't be able to read any more now," he says meaningfully. "Perhaps you'd like to chat instead."

I have in fact been quite happy reading *The English Garden* and do not see why the presence of an occupant in the adjacent seat inconveniences his own reading so much. However,

I nod meekly, anxious to avoid precipitating Peter into causing a scene.

"Have you ever been to Liverpool before?" he asks in his low-voiced confidential drawl.

"Only to catch the ferry to Dublin. I don't know the city at all."

"Hmm," says Peter. He regards me ironically, as if my not knowing Liverpool constitutes some social faux pas. "Of course, we aren't really from Liverpool: we're from Birkenhead. It is *quite* a different place. That's where Mummy's house is still; the house where Jillian and I grew up. I went to the Birkenhead Grammar School for Boys, you know, before Daddy sent me to Charterhouse. I was a very beautiful youth."

One of the businessmen glances across at him, and Peter rolls his eyes provocatively.

The tannoy crackles into life and the train guard launches into an announcement about carrying tickets at all times when moving about the train and not leaving luggage unattended. Then he adds:

"The buffet is now open. First Class passengers wishing to collect their complimentary refreshments can make their way to Coach D."

There is a small stampede for the door. The two businessmen get up and join the queue. Peter is glowering at the scene around him.

"How unspeakably vulgar!" he exclaims. "'Complimentary refreshments', indeed! Have you seen those lunchboxes, darling?", he adds, leaning forward and almost whispering. "They are made of cardboard – *cardboard!* – with plastic cutlery, and they contain the sort of food that common people might serve at a children's party. And who knows who prepared them! I daresay they come from one of those catering companies that employs illegal immigrants."

He tosses his head and flounces back against his seat, folding his hands neatly. I understand from this that we are not intending to partake of lunch. I think that this is to be regretted, partly because of the exorbitant cost of the ticket, but mostly because I am famished. However, I know that I will not have the courage to cross Peter.

The businessmen return, jovially noisy, and begin tearing open the plastic-wrapped packages that they take from inside the house-shaped boxes that they have carried back with them. Glancing at the food, I see that Peter has a point. He follows my gaze.

"I'm certain that we shall get something at Mummy's," he says consolingly. "Jillian will have filled up the fridge. Do you know, in her day Mummy was a very fine cook. She could make a meal out of anything – and I do mean *anything*. Daddy, of course, was a very hard man to please." He appears to be quite satisfied about this, as if being hard to please were a recommendation. He sits in tranquil reverie for a few moments and then says, as if he has been pursuing a train of thought and suddenly feels impelled to burst into speech:

"Of course, she is very old now. It is quite time for her to go. When I am there looking after her, I think to myself, 'Mummy, you've had a good innings, but it isn't seemly that you keep on lingering here so long.' I know that Jillian agrees with me, but as you would expect she is either too decorous or too crafty to say so. By the time the old girl takes herself off, we shall probably both be too decrepit to enjoy the proceeds."

Alarmed by his indiscretion, I look across at the businessmen, but they are deep into their food and a desultory conversation about painting windows.

"Now," says Peter, "wouldn't it be a splendid thing if we could effect a little serendipity? I know that it is quite impossible, of course – the timing is out and they belong to such different social classes that they would never consent to mix: but, if you will indulge my fancy for a moment, wouldn't it be wonderful if your mummy and Mummy could meet? We could then get yours to dispatch the old girl – for a consideration, of course. I hear that she made quite a good job of taking your grandmother out – so much so that one almost feels that she didn't deserve to get caught."

Peter shoots me a look of triumph. I know that I appear to be scandalised – I *am* scandalised – and it is apparent that he is enjoying my discomfort.

"Peter, that is outrageous, and you know it! Tirzah isn't some kind of random killer for hire. Although I've never fully understood her reasons for killing my grandmother, I'm sure that they existed – in her own mind, at least. She isn't a serial killer. And you know that you don't really wish your mother dead – you are just trying to shock me!"

Peter half-grins. "Are you quite sure about that?"

"About what? Tirzah not being a serial killer, or wishing your mother dead?"

"I can only quote Lady Bracknell. 'Both, if necessary'." He yawns, and looks out of the window. I no longer find it possible to read. The rest of the journey seems interminable, mainly because I am hungry and bored. I am also uneasy. Peter has managed to kindle something which disturbs me deeply, not just because, however much in jest, he is suggesting that we plot a murder, but because what he has said resonates with something just out of reach – something tucked away in the deeper recesses of my mind.

Liverpool strikes me as a dusty, untidy city that indubitably could have taken more care about how it presents itself. However, I only see it from the windows of a taxi, as Peter is keen to get to Birkenhead as soon as he can. Birkenhead is full of confusing streets and cul-de-sacs which look much like each other. There is mile upon mile of these. I wonder why there are so few shops here, until I understand the obtuseness of this observation: of course the no-doubt solid citizens that live here do not need too many shops of their own, with the great mercantile city of Liverpool on their doorstep. Birkenhead in fact represents the ultimate suburb.

Mummy's house is a substantial late Victorian red-brick dwelling. It falls short of being ugly, but it is not prepossessing. It stands foursquare in a large garden, and is overlooked by other houses just like it. In the gardens of some of these, smaller, modern houses have been built; but Peter's Mummy's garden is well-established, with mature trees and shrubs, and smooth lawns. I guess that the whole place is sacrosanct to the memory of her husband, and that time has stood still here for at least thirty years.

I am not entirely correct about this, for when Peter produces a key and lets us in through the front porch to a wide and gloomy red-tiled hall, I see that all of the furniture is utilitarian, and whilst it can hardly be described as 'modern' – which might conjure up images of edgy leather, glass and steel pieces that are certainly not of the style chosen here – these furnishings are not old. I doubt whether 'Daddy' had ever clapped eyes on them.

"Hello?" Peter calls out in the falsetto voice that he sometimes uses to greet me.

"Is that you, Jillian?" returns a surprisingly firm voice from beyond a door that is standing slightly open to the left of the hall.

"No, darling, it's me, Peter: I told you I would be coming today. And I've brought a friend!" Peter's voice rises with every word of the final sentence, which he utters with his head bent against the door, cooing into the opening like a pantomime dame playing partly to the inmate, but mostly to the audience.

"Come in, Peter," says the voice, I think with a hint of sternness. "What are you doing, fiddling about there in the passage?"

Peter turns and beckons to me theatrically over his shoulder, before giving the door a shove. He enters the room at a sprint, so that by the time I have followed him in, he is kissing Mummy on both cheeks and fondling her hand – which I notice is well-embellished with opulent-looking rings.

I stand uncertainly at the edge of the carpet, until Peter suddenly turns round and extends his arm towards me with a flourish. It has the useful effect of allowing Mummy to enter my range of view.

"And this," says Peter, keeping his arm outstretched like an impresario, "is Hedley. Isn't he just divine? Tell me truly if you would not like him for yourself, darling!"

The figure in the wheelchair brushes away his other hand, which he has placed on her arm.

"Don't be ridiculous, Peter," she says. "You can save your airs and graces for someone else." She peers across at me.

"You are welcome, Mr . . . ?" "Atkins," I say. "Oh, just call him Hedley," says Peter at the same time. "Atkins is rather a common name, isn't it?"

The old lady ignores this remark, and continues to peer at me with great concentration.

"Do take a seat," she says. "You are a little late for luncheon, but I am sure that there is something for tea. Jillian will have left something. Peter," she adds, raising her voice, "go into the kitchen and see what Jillian has left that you can eat."

"Now," says Mummy, when Peter has disappeared, "come and sit down and talk to me. I should like to understand why you are prepared to tolerate my son under your roof. Is it just masochism on your part, or does he have some kind of hold over you?" She smiles as she says this, her vermilion-lipsticked mouth stretching over long yellow teeth. I am not sure whether she means what she is saying as a joke or not.

"Peter and I have been friends for some time – and I . . . er . . . we're very close. I thought it would be nice if . . ."

"I do know that he's a bugger, you know. There is no need to spare my innocence!" She smiles her weird smile again, and leans closer to me.

"Something else with which I am quite au fait is that my son would like to get his hands on my money. In fact, since I refused to buy the lease on his flat, which would have left him homeless if you had not taken pity on him, I believe that he has thought of nothing else. And I am quite convinced that he would stop at nothing. Nothing!" she repeats the word with a high-pitched whinny, in a manner reminiscent of Peter himself. She also waves her hands like Peter does. "What I should like to know is, how far he has taken you into his confidence. Are you part of some kind of plot to swindle me – or worse?"

Again the curious smile. She rests her hands in her lap, which is covered with a pink cellular blanket. Her wrist joints protrude, huge beneath the stick-like arms that poke beyond the three-quarter length sleeves of her blouse. She is very emaciated. I noticed for the first time that she is wearing a blue felt hat on her head, as if she is just about to go out.

"Are you going somewhere?" I ask.

She looks ruffled.

"Of course I am not going anywhere! Where could I go? I see that you are changing the subject, however. Did my son bring you here for a particular reason?"

Peter returns at that moment, bearing a tray which holds a teapot, china cups, and a plateful of tiny coloured cakes.

"I brought him to see **you**, darling," says Peter, enunciating each word with care as if he were explaining something quite complicated to a not especially nimble-brained child. "Why would I not bring him to see you? He has invited me to live with him, as you know. I thought you would be interested to meet him, therefore. And besides, he is always nice to talk to." He puts the tray down carefully on a low table which stands next to the wheelchair.

"I have found that out for myself," says Mummy unexpectedly. "How long are you staying for?"

"Oh, we must go back today," says Peter airily. "Hedley has to work, unfortunately, and he needs Sundays for chores – a bore, but there it is. You aren't here on your own, though, are you darling? Jillian will come later."

"Does she know that you are here?" asks Mummy, narrowing her eyes at him. "She doesn't usually buy cakes for me. She says that they are bad for my diabetes."

"Nonsense," says Peter smoothly, "a little bit of what you fancy can't hurt you – especially at your great age." He has turned his back to me, so I cannot see his face. "And no, she doesn't know, because I rather hope she'll pop in before we leave – and she might not if she knows that we are here. I want to talk to her about something."

He hands his mother a plate with two of the small cakes on it, and pours tea. He clips a little tray to the side of her wheel-chair, and places a cup of tea on it for her, before handing one to me. "Help yourself to cakes," he says. "I expect you're hungry."

Mummy exchanges the plate with the cakes on it for the teacup and takes a few sips. She darts little glances at her two cakes, but leaves them where they are. Peter is not eating, but I see him pour a generous nip from his hipflask into his tea. Usually he carries gin around with him, but I guess that on this occasion it is probably whisky.

The room falls silent. Mummy continues to sip her tea. Peter is drinking his appreciatively. I inch forward to the low table and scoop up a handful of the cakes for myself, which I proceed to eat in as restrained a way as possible, given that my breakfast consisted of a single slice of toast at 6 a.m. this morning. It is now almost 3.30 p.m.

Outside, a car engine can be heard purring, before it stops. There is the slam of a car door, followed by a key turning in the front door lock and the rapid click of high heels in the hall.

"Cooee," shouts a plummy voice. "It's only me."

Mummy sits up straighter in her wheelchair. I cannot read her expression: is it apprehensive? Peter's face is as smooth and bland as a mask.

Jillian enters the room bearing a large bunch of flowers. She is a small immaculately presented woman with sculpted blonde hair. She has the same tailored slender poise that is Peter's most striking feature. She freezes when she sees Peter, although when he hurries forward to take her face in both hands and kiss it, she returns this with a perfunctory kiss of her own.

"Be careful, Peter, you are squashing the flowers. What brings you here?"

"Charming as ever, Jillian," says Peter, twirling on his heel slightly as he springs away from her. It could have been a question or an ironical statement. "I thought you'd be pleased to see me," he adds, daring her with his boot-button eyes. "Especially after your own surprise visit. I've brought a friend with me whom I'd like you to meet. This is Hedley." He looks across at me as he speaks, but there is none of the ceremony that he had conjured up when making the same announcement to Mummy.

Jillian passes the flowers to him, and moves across the carpet to shake my hand.

"Delighted," she says, her hand slim and cool in my hot sweaty one. "I have heard of you, of course. You must be a very brave man – or a rather reckless one."

"Nonsense," says Peter. "I know what you're up to: you're about to say something disparaging about me. But Hedley is quite aware of all my foibles, and he loves me just the same." He nods at me, smiling.

I grin back foolishly. "Just as I said," says Jillian. "Well, now that you're here, there are some papers that I need you to look over with me. Mummy's thinking of staying in the nursing home permanently from now on. It's not that she doesn't prefer it here, but these trips home are beginning to take their toll, and she is mindful also of the strain that it puts on you and me. ..."

"Mostly you," murmurs Mummy, evidently directing her remark to Jillian. No-one acknowledges it.

I scrutinise Peter's face. It is shiningly alert: there is not even a pretence of his usual sang-froid. "... so I've had Belkin draw up the papers to create a trust fund. Mummy is in complete agreement that this is the right thing to do, to protect our inheritance. We really should go through them together in private. I'm sure that Hedley won't mind entertaining Mummy for an hour or so?"

"Of course not."

"You see!" says Peter, twirling again. "He is an absolute little treasure!"

Jillian sighs, and is about to turn towards the door when she catches sight of the two cakes resting on Mummy's invalid tray. Her face freezes.

"Did you give her those?" she asks Peter fiercely. He shrugs and looks helpless.

"Oh, Peter, for goodness sake stop being so irresponsible," Jillian snaps. "You know that she can't eat cake. Do you want to put her into a coma, or something?"

"I didn't touch it," interjects Mummy. "I didn't eat any of it at all."

"Don't worry about it, Mummy. I'm sure you didn't." Jillian's rather angular features soften as she moves to her mother's side and kisses her on the forehead. "We're used to Peter, aren't we? We know that we can't trust him to use his common sense."

Mummy looks up at her guilelessly, and in that instant I realise that she is casting herself in the role in which Jillian wishes to see her. The sharp-edged irony that she had displayed to me during the brief time that we were alone has vanished.

Once the door has closed behind Jillian and Peter, some of this urbanity returns. She vouchsafes me that curious smile again, and says:

"Peter's a very naughty boy, you know. He certainly isn't to be trusted." She then rests her head against the rolled-up travelling rug that Jillian has placed at the back of her wheelchair, and closes her eyes. I doubt that she is sleeping, but she does not utter another word until they return.

In the train on the way home, Peter is half-jubilant, half-subdued.

"The old girl's loaded," he says. "She's got far more money than I realised – and the house is worth more than I thought, too. It's the trust fund that's the real fly in the ointment. Trust Jillian to think of that. It was so unfair of her not to have told me: and she stands to gain much more from it than I do, because she has two children."

He pauses and gives me one of his rare straight looks.

"You quite see the position, Hedley. I've got to get my hands on my share of the money. We've got to make sure that the old girl dies before Jillian has the trust fund set up."

CHAPTER SEVENTEEN

Tim Yates had a secret passion that no-one who worked for the police, except Katrin, knew about. He was an avid mountain-biker. Almost the only thing that he found unsatisfactory about his job with the South Lincolnshire police force was the flatness of the terrain. Even going off-road on his bike was difficult enough: the whole of the countryside in South Holland was parcelled up into neat farms and vast square fields with picture-perfect crops of wheat, potatoes and sugar-beet, and because the rich black alluvial soil had not been reclaimed until the eighteenth or nineteenth centuries, there were few ancient rights of way. "Trespassers will be prosecuted" signs bristled everywhere, and as a policeman he felt that if he chose to fail to observe them, it would have to be with circumspection. But even when he found a spinney or a piece of wasteland where he could take the bike, exhilarating opportunities to take foolish risks by going at breakneck speed were few. Sure, it was possible to get up a good speed, but there was little danger of coming off the bike, little of the challenge of toiling up steep hills, calf-muscles straining and heart pounding, to make the stomach-scooping descents that he had so loved during his student days in Yorkshire. There was, of course, plenty of opportunity to court danger on the narrow, windy roads on which everyone, farmers included, drove as if they were the last people in the world yet still in a hurry to get to their own funerals, but turning himself into road-kill held no appeal. You were hardly pitting your wits against the limitations of the bike and your own stamina and technical skill if you quarrelled with a juggernaut. Still, even in Lincolnshire he could go out on the bike to think; and now that the mornings were drawing out at last, it was possible to fit in a quick ride before work. Often he achieved this by putting the bike on the back of his car and driving out somewhere, but today was Saturday, so he had simply pedalled sedately out of the town until he reached Spalding Common, where it was possible to race across the fields without fear of reprimand.

Apart from his need for strenuous exertion after a week cooped up in the office or in various claustrophobic meetings with experts and potential witnesses, he wanted to think about the case. There was something about what they had found out so far which didn't quite hang together, but he couldn't put his finger on exactly what it was. He sensed that if he could only spot the anomaly in all the evidence that they had gathered, it would lead him to Kathryn Sheppard's murderer. Of course, he did not have, and would probably never have, conclusive evidence that she had been murdered, but murder enquiries had been based on much slenderer evidence. There could have been no innocent explanation for the dumping of her body by the roadside, for a start. He was confident that he was now conducting a murder enquiry and, as he thought it probable that Kathryn had known her killer, he also knew that it was likely to have been someone whom his predecessors or he himself had already questioned. So what had they all overlooked?

He had nearly reached the Common now. He stood on the pedals to get a bit more speed up. A couple of teenage girls standing on the pavement by Townend Manor wolf-whistled. He felt a childish surge of pride in the bike and his own appearance. Cycling didn't just help him to burn off energy: it also allowed him to indulge his taste for flamboyant clothes. He was wearing a shocking pink and green cycling shirt and skin-tight lycra shorts. His silver cycling helmet was set slightly back on his head. He grinned at the girls and pushed himself a little harder, rebuking himself inwardly for his display of juvenile exhibitionism as he did so.

Pondering the case, he felt a sudden pang of shame at his brusqueness over Juliet's methodical attempt to marshal facts, followed by a creeping intuition that she might have been on to something after all. As well as deflating her never very robust ego by implying that she had been wasting her time, he may have missed something of importance by being too sceptical. He made a mental note to apologise to her next time he saw her and again picked over the little pile of nuggets of information that she had assembled.

Juliet had established that the fragments of dress had been composed of a denim look-alike material widely imported in the nineteen seventies by several manufacturers who supplied chain stores. The metals rings that had once held together the straps of a bra had likewise been widely used at the time, and indeed were still used by some lingerie companies. He sighed. He may have been – he certainly had been – morally culpable to have belittled Juliet's efforts, but what of intelligence could be deduced from any of this, particularly when the DNA testing had proved without a shadow of a doubt that the remains were those of Kathryn Sheppard?

A rough idea of the date of her death would have been useful, of course: from the information that Mrs. Sheppard had given Juliet, and from the police reports that were filed at the time, he knew that she had disappeared in the late autumn of 1975, though it was possible – if unlikely – that she had not died until some time later. But knowing that at the time of her death she had been wearing a dress and a bra that could have been manufactured at any point between 1970 and 1980 was not going to yield a useful date; nor was the identification of a plastic Red Indian as having belonged to one of several batches supplied from a company operating from Hong Kong to a breakfast cereals manufacturer; nor that the friendship ring had been distributed by an East-End wholesaler to boutiques and ethnic shops just about everywhere in the country.

And then there was the whole Dorothy Atkins business. Aside from Juliet, who seemed to have no view, the other members of his team seemed to be convinced that Kathryn Sheppard had been murdered by Dorothy. But though this hypothesis, if proved correct, would offer a neat solution, and was obviously one that had occurred to him as well, was there any evidence to support it save that otherwise they would have been presented with the unlikely coincidence of two murderers operating in the same small town and moving in the same circles at roughly the same time? And would Dorothy even have had the opportunity to kill Kathryn? He knew by now that he would almost certainly have to obtain permission to question Dorothy Atkins in her nursing-home, and that this would need to be sooner rather than later; indeed he relished the prospect of such a meeting after all that he had read or been told about her. But he suspected that the whole Dorothy Atkins thing would prove to be a red herring as far as Kathryn Sheppard was concerned; and in any case, he needed more evidence before he could hope to extract anything of value from her.

What could help him to make some kind of progress? He was finding it unusually difficult to think outside the box in this case. He tried a different tack. If he had been writing a case study and presented these findings to junior colleagues as a textbook crime to solve, what else might he have added that would enable them to identify the culprit?

Timing. It all hung on timing. He did not realise this in a sudden burst of inspiration; rather it dawned on him slowly that it was the key factor, and that he should have thought of this earlier. The more he considered it, the more obvious it became: it caused him to switch from scepticism to a fervent hope that more evidence could be teased out of those modest scraps of artefact that had been dumped with Kathryn's corpse.

He had examined the plastic Red Indian carefully when it had first been found. Viewed objectively, it was a crude and simple toy, moulded in one piece from terra-cotta coloured plastic. It was a model of a Red Indian chief who had a feathered head-dress that stood out from his head. He was in the act of drawing his bow. Each individual feather had been scored into the plastic, as were his features and the folds of his loin-cloth. His feet, caught in mid-stride, were anchored to a small plastic rectangle which made it possible to stand him up on a flat surface. The words 'Hong Kong' and two or three Chinese characters appeared in tiny script on the underside of the rectangle. From the moment that it had been found Tim had been intrigued by it, though he knew that this was not because it had been found with Kathryn Sheppard's remains. There could be no proof that it had any connection with her, either in life or after death, unless some subsequent clue were to link the dead woman and the toy. It was because, as a boy, he had always loved promotional free gifts. There was something magical, almost talismanic, about them: the not knowing which particular model it would be, what colour, or when it would drop out of the packet. He remembered treasuring such toys, carrying them around in his pocket and scrutinising every detail of their features. That they were 'free' made them more special. Was it conceivable that the murderer had felt the same way? That the toy had been used as a kind of trophy in reverse? A gift to the dead of a treasured possession?

He remembered that Juliet had said that Nubisk, the cereals manufacturer that had imported the toys, had been quite helpful when she had contacted them. He hadn't listened properly to the details, but he did recollect that – somewhat amazingly – they seemed to have records of all their promotional initiatives, and had given Juliet the range of dates during which the Red Indians had been distributed, and with which products.

Dates! Could the discrepancy in this case that he couldn't quite fathom, the problem at the back of his mind which could not quite formulate itself into words, be associated in some way with dates and more particularly with the sequence of events leading up to and following the deaths of both Doris Atkins and Kathryn Sheppard? They – he – had certainly made some assumptions about both of these deaths. It was the lynchpin of the case that he and his team were constructing that both women had been murdered and that it was likely that they had been murdered by the same person; and therefore that Dorothy Atkins was the murderer. But did these hypotheses bear scrutiny?

That Doris Atkins had been murdered was certain. That Kathryn Sheppard had also been murdered was likely, even though no cause of death could be discovered because of the subsequent deterioration of the remains. If her death had been accidental, there would have been no reason for someone to have gone to such lengths to conceal her body, or indeed to have hidden the fact that she had died – unless they had a guilty secret which making it public would have exposed. Let us therefore assume, thought Tim, that Kathryn was indeed murdered. What leap of logic was required to suspect 'Tirzah' of the murder? None, if you were Claudia Hemingway, the prison psychiatrist, who was convinced that 'Tirzah' was capable of multiple killings and probably a psychopath; but Dr. Bertolasso would certainly have doubted her capacity to commit the second crime. If he was telling the truth and not just trying to bolster his reputation, he did not even believe that she had killed Doris.

As a policeman, Tim did not feel disposed to question that she had been guilty of the crime of which she had been convicted. He had read the many reports relating to the case, and he believed that she had been given a fair trial. The weight of evidence against her, although it was indeed circumstantial, had been overwhelming; and although it was not unheard of for innocent people to stay silent when charged with a serious crime, this was an expedient much more commonly used by the guilty.

That did not make her guilty of Kathryn Sheppard's murder, though. Her links to Kathryn were slender – the main one being that Kathryn was the former girlfriend of Dorothy's son Hedley – and if no-one had ever come up with a motive to inspire Dorothy to kill Doris, there could be even less reason for her to have killed Kathryn. Psychopaths did not need reasons, of course.

It was unlikely that he would be able to understand the workings of Dorothy's brain, either as it had functioned thirty years ago or as it was performing now. What he could try to do was to piece together accurately the timing of Kathryn's death.

He noticed that he had slowed his pace on the bike so much that it was wobbling into the centre of the road. He pulled it back towards the verge, and realised in the act of doing so that he had already reached the Common. He dismounted and took a swig of water from his CamelBack, feeling comforted by the familiar and not unpleasant, slightly astringent plastic aftertaste left by its nozzle.

He hesitated briefly and then drew his cellphone from the CamelBack's mesh pocket and pressed Juliet's number on the speed dial. She responded with disconcerting speed.

"Good morning, sir," she trilled, as if she had been waiting for his call for hours.

"Juliet? I'm sorry to bother you on a Saturday, but this shouldn't take long."

"It's OK, sir. I'm working this morning. Officially, I mean."

"What? Oh, good. I've been thinking about the Kathryn Sheppard case. You know all that information that you collected about the stuff that was found with the bones?"

"I understand why you were annoyed with me for spending so much time on it. I did get rather carried away . . ."

"No, no – on the contrary, I shouldn't have criticised you. It was obtuse of me not to see at the time how useful your work might prove to be – will prove to be, I am sure. It's the plastic Indian that I'm interested in at the moment. Can you cast your mind back to what Nubisk said about it? If I remember correctly, you said that they were very helpful."

"Yes – they were." She sounded surprised and almost elated.

"Can you remember what they told you about the consignment of the Red Indian toys? It's the date that I'm interested in. Not the date that they started putting them into cereals packets, but the date on which they actually received the shipment?"

"I'm not sure offhand whether they did tell me that, but I can look in the file. It won't take me more than a few minutes. I'll call you back."

He had propped his bike against a five-barred gate while he was talking. He decided that it would be best to wait there for Juliet's call, because the mobile signal had been a good one. He hoped she wouldn't be too long about it: he had worked up a sweat while he was pedalling and now he felt shivery as it cooled on his skin. It was a mild day for February, but still too raw to stand around for too long dressed in lycra cycling clothes. He took another swig from the CamelBack and contemplated the view. The sweeping flatness of the Fens held a certain beauty in the early spring, even if, as a cyclist, he found them less than challenging. They had challenged men in other ways in the past. He thought of Hereward the Wake, creeping through the treacherous marshland, in danger of being ambushed at any moment. It must have concentrated the mind, knowing that a wrong move could cost you your life.

His cellphone rang.

"Hello, Juliet."

"Hi." She sounded confident, even excited. "I've found the schedule that Nubisk sent me. The plastic Indians were imported towards the end of September 1975. Although as a foodstuffs manufacturer Nubisk did not specifically target the Christmas market, the models were intended as a kind of Christmas gift – a loyalty reward, you might say – for kids."

"Great – thanks. I don't suppose the schedule also gives the date at which they were first put into the cereal packets, does it?"

There was a brief pause. He envisaged Juliet earnestly working her way through the schedule as rapidly as she could, as always anxious to please.

"Yes and no," she said eventually.

"What does that mean?"

"They weren't actually put into the cereal packets. That had been the original intention, but there was a court case involving another food manufacturer earlier that year. Apparently a company that made powdered milk drinks had put toy plastic battleships directly into the product, and a child had almost choked when one stuck in its throat – or so the mother claimed. She also claimed not to have known that the packet contained the toy, and not to have noticed it floating in the glass."

"My God," Tim marvelled at her mastery of such detail. "How do you know all of this?"

Juliet laughed. "I didn't need to dig very deep. There's a whole sheet of information and instructions attached to the schedule; presumably it's a document that was circulated at the time."

"What did they do with the plastic Indians, then? I assume that since we've found one, they weren't just disposed of."

"You're right: they didn't waste them. The Indians were packed in individual cellophane wrappers and supplied to retailers by the bagful, instead of being put directly into the cartons."

"And this process didn't hold them up too much? The retailers still had them to give away with packets of cereal before Christmas 1975?"

"Yes, according to the schedule. There are some more notes to retailers about only giving away the Indians with packets marked 'free gift inside', dated the 6th of November. I suppose that this was to stop them using up old stock for the promotion. But what I don't understand is . . ."

"Go on," said Tim impatiently. His mind was already leaping ahead to other dates.

"But all this information about the plastic toy actually makes it a red herring, doesn't it, sir? We know that Dorothy Atkins was being held in custody by the middle of September 1975, and that the plastic Indians did not arrive in the UK until at least two weeks later. What we've just proved, therefore, is that the plastic Indian has no connection with Kathryn Sheppard's death – or with her killer."

"Maybe," said Tim. "But only if Dorothy Atkins was indeed Kathryn Sheppard's killer. If, on the other hand, the plastic Indian was dumped with Kathryn's body – which I admit we still can't prove – then we know that the killer couldn't have been Dorothy Atkins – unless she found time to dump Kathryn's body on one of the occasions when she had temporary bail. Unlikely, since she couldn't drive. Unfortunately, all the work that you have done doesn't lead to a clear-cut conclusion; but it casts a considerable amount of doubt on the notion that Dorothy was the killer. Which is why I'm grateful to you for doing such a meticulous job, and somewhat ashamed of myself for not having seen the value of it before."

There was a long silence. He imagined that Juliet was deeply embarrassed by this apology. After he felt that the pause had gone on for long enough, he said:

"Was there anything else you found when you were making these enquiries? I seem to remember that the scraps of garment failed to yield anything specific?"

"Yes, indeed, sir. But I did find out one or two things about the friendship ring."

"Anything that might help us further with the dates?"

"No. The rings have been around since the 1950s. They're

cheap imports from Asia and the silver that they're made of isn't pure enough to be hallmarked. The one found with the skeleton was actually silver-gilt, so of slightly better quality than the average, but there were still thousands of them made – still are being made, as far as I know. But there is one thing that we can learn from the ring."

"Go on."

"You will remember that it has a kind of wishbone design. The 'v' of the wishbone is asymmetrical. If it bends slightly to the right, the ring was intended to be either given by a man to a woman, or a woman to a man, though not usually to mark a sexual relationship; if it bends to the left, as this one does, it was given to the wearer by someone of the same sex."

"Also not usually to mark a sexual relationship?"

"Well, they're all called friendship rings, sir."

"Point taken. I mustn't jump to conclusions!"

"What we do know is that if Kathryn Sheppard received this ring when it was new, it was almost certainly given to her by a woman."

"Well done, Juliet. So it would probably help us if we could find out who this woman was?"

He could almost see her nodding.

"Yes, sir."

"Thank you. I think that we need to visit Kathryn's mother again.

CHAPTER EIGHTEEN

Once more, Juliet was making her way along the faded cul-de-sac of Acacia Close, this time with Tim by her side. Before they reached Mrs. Sheppard's gate, Juliet paused and turned to speak to him.

"I hope you don't mind my saying this, sir: I'd like you to be as gentle as possible with Mrs. Sheppard. She has precious little left to live for now that her daughter and husband are both dead, and she finds visits from the police alarming – often with good cause. We have nothing to offer her except kindness and courtesy: inadequate though these will be, because we'll probably be ripping the scabs off her wounds again."

"Do you think that I'm habitually insensitive, DC Armstrong?"

Juliet smiled carefully.

"Not habitually, sir. It's just that sometimes you can be over-enthusiastic in your pursuit of facts, that's all. And you are a little apt to forget that not everyone can follow the speed of your thinking. I'd say that there's a fair chance that this applies to elderly widows whose minds have been dimmed by years of tedious grief, as well as to me."

Tim made a mock grin of astonishment.

"You make me sound like an intellectual monster! I congratulate you on your eloquence, however. I have seldom heard a request for empathetic behaviour better put. I didn't realise that there was a poet lurking inside you."

Juliet flushed, suspecting that she was being teased. She decided not to probe any further and carried on walking. In a few moments they had arrived at Mrs. Sheppard's shabby wrought-iron gates. A scruffy ginger tom cat squeezed through the privet hedge and threaded itself around her legs, before looking up balefully at Tim.

"Hello, Kitty," he said. The cat turned his back on them and returned to the garden from which he had emerged.

"This is the house, sir," said Juliet, opening one of the squeaking gates. "The gravel is quite hard to walk on."

Tim looked down the drive. It was so thickly covered in small stones that it seemed as if someone had dumped a whole pebbled beach on to it. He held the gate for Juliet and gestured to her to go first.

On this occasion there was no prefatory game of hide-and-seek with Mrs. Sheppard. In fact, she seemed to be expecting them and had flung open the front door somewhat vigorously before they had even reached the porch. Once again, she appeared to be dressed entirely in brown, though Juliet could not tell whether she was wearing exactly the same clothes as on her previous visit, because this time Mrs. Sheppard was enveloped in a waist-to-ankle beige wrap-around apron of the type worn by waiters in pretentious restaurants.

It became apparent that despite her prompt door-keeping, she did not necessarily intend to invite them in. In fact, she had half-closed the door behind her, so that it was not possible to see beyond her into the house. She stood on guard, her arms folded across the top of the apron in a gesture which may or may not have been intentionally aggressive.

"I thought you'd be back," she said to Juliet in a tightly angry voice. "I'm not sure why, though. You've ruined my life as completely as you can. What else do you think you can do to me?"

Juliet cast down her eyes and did not answer. After a few

seconds, she looked sideways at Tim and she knew that she was silently warning him not to intellectualise Mrs. Sheppard's grief. Tim looked guilty – he had just been trying to recall what he knew about blame transference.

Juliet was exquisitely polite.

"Good afternoon, Mrs. Sheppard," she said. "I'm truly sorry to have to bother you again. May I introduce Detective Inspector Tim Yates? We would very much appreciate the opportunity to ask you for some more details about your daughter, if you can spare us the time."

Tim held out his hand. Mrs. Sheppard unfolded her arms and extended her right hand shakily. Tim clasped her fingertips and gave them a gentle squeeze. It was quite unlike his usual firm handshake. He looked into the dull, sad eyes, set deep in the shrivelled, nut-like little face in front of him, and felt profoundly sorry.

Mrs. Sheppard noted his compassion, and her face twisted up pathetically. Juliet wondered how long it had been since she had embraced another human being, or even held a meaningful conversation with one. Tim took advantage of the change in her demeanour.

"I am very pleased to meet you, Mrs. Sheppard. I am sorry that visits from the police have usually brought distressing news to you. You are right, of course, when you say that there is no more bad news that we can bring to hurt you further; please believe me when I say that I am glad of that. But I do believe that we might still be able to offer you some grain of comfort, however small."

Mrs. Sheppard withdrew her hand, and narrowed her eyes warily. Be careful, Tim, thought Juliet. Don't overdo it.

"I'm sure that you don't want revenge," Tim continued. "I can see that you have too much dignity for that. But it is my job to find your daughter's killer. It will be a very difficult task, as I'm sure you will appreciate, because we think that she was killed at around the time that she disappeared, more than thirty years ago. I need as much help as I can get, especially from you. If you are able to help me to catch the killer, I hope perhaps it may bring you a little bit of peace – what the Americans and indeed our own tabloid newspapers are pleased to call 'closure'." He screwed up his eyes in momentary disgust. Juliet could see that Mrs. Sheppard was with him here.

Tim watched her relax a little. He, too, could see that she appreciated the comment about closure and that she took it to mean, as he had intended her to, that in this at least they were allies, united in their superior understanding of how the English language should be used. He guessed that she might in the past have been a teacher.

"May we come in?" Juliet spoke after the little pause that ensued. Mrs. Sheppard at once stepped back into the house and held open the door.

A few minutes later they had been installed in the blue sitting-room with a tray of tea. Tim was perched awkwardly on one of the insubstantial fireside chairs, while Mrs. Sheppard sat in the other one and Juliet on the hard little sofa. Juliet was pouring the tea. She sensed that Tim felt as oppressed by the room as she had on her previous visit. She passed the teacups. Mrs. Sheppard stirred sugar into her tea and sipped it gingerly. She was clasping the cup with both hands.

"I'd like to help you," she said. "Truly I would. But I'm not sure how I can. Kathryn wasn't living here when she . . . went missing. I know no more than you do of her movements on the days leading up to her disappearance. There was a police reconstruction of them some years later – a film which appeared on *Crimewatch*, which I'm sure you've seen?"

Tim nodded.

"It isn't just her movements we're interested in, Mrs. Sheppard, though if we could plot the last week that she was definitely alive accurately day by day and hour by hour, that would of course be immensely helpful. The *Crimewatch* reconstruction was based on joining up the dots of a few known facts and supplementing the result with a great deal of intelligent guesswork. I am myself convinced that the actual time of Kathryn's disappearance is one of the crucial aspects of this case, and I am perfectly aware that you cannot help me with that. But you can certainly help me in a broader way, by telling me what sort of girl Kathryn was, who her friends were, and perhaps by giving us some more information about the objects that were found with her. I'm sorry to upset you," he added.

The tears were coursing down Mrs. Sheppard's cheeks. Juliet put out a hand to comfort her, and then withdrew it; she saw that Tim and Mrs. Sheppard were now inhabiting a fragile enclosed world devoted to remembrance of Kathryn Sheppard, which an intrusion from outside might destroy. Mrs. Sheppard wiped away the tears with the back of her hand, and began to speak.

"Kathryn was not perfect by any means. She belonged to that 'liberated' seventies generation that had such different values from those of us who had been through the war. Of course, Frank and I were considered to be quite elderly parents in any case, by the standards of our day, anyway; we were older than the parents of most of Kathryn's friends, and unable to have more children after her. In retrospect, I can see that she must have felt frustrated, and perhaps sometimes isolated, when she was living with us. Anyway, she moved out because I discovered that she was sleeping with her boyfriend and it was something I just couldn't condone under our roof. Her father and I quarrelled bitterly about it – and we never quarrelled as a rule – especially after she left. He said that I had driven her out." She sighed wearily. "It all seems so unimportant now. I'm sure that, to someone of your generation, my views are simply funny."

Tim did not respond to this last comment.

"Please go on," he said. "Which boyfriend was Kathryn sleeping with? Was it Hedley Atkins?"

"You will find this strange, but I never actually found out. I just found certain . . . things . . . in her room. She said that

I was snooping, there was a blazing row, and she left. I supposed that it was Hedley, although her father never believed it. He thought that Hedley was of quite a different persuasion – sexually, I mean." She flushed as she said the word. "Of course I'm sure that later she slept with Charles. But that was different. They were engaged."

"Did you like Charles?"

"I didn't get to know him very well. I suppose he was a . . . surprise. You realise that he was . . . coloured?" She flushed again.

Tim nodded.

"What about her friends? Was Kathryn an outgoing sort of girl? Did she make friends easily?"

"Kathryn was thoughtful. She wasn't one of those shallow people who like to boast that they have dozens of friends, but I think that she was loyal to those whom she grew close to. She stayed in touch with two or three friends from school, and at least one from university."

"Were they all girls?"

"Yes. I can give you their names if you like; though I expect that they are all married now, so their names will have changed."

Tim nodded again.

"Thank you. That could be useful." He produced two small plastic bags from his briefcase, and handed one of them to Mrs. Sheppard.

"Do you recognise this ring?"

"Of course," she said. "It's the silver ring that Kathryn wore on her right middle finger. Was it with the . . ."

"Yes," said Tim. "We believe it is a friendship ring, of the kind usually given by a woman to another woman. Do you know who gave it to Kathryn?"

"Of course," she said again. "It was a present from Bryony Atkins. I believe that Kathryn also gave one to her. I thought that it was rather a pointless exchange, as I said at the time." She laughed shortly.

Juliet tried and failed to stifle her exclamation of surprise, but she need not have worried. Mrs. Sheppard and Tim were by this time locked even deeper within the Kathryn memorial bubble that they had created.

"Kathryn knew Bryony Atkins?" asked Tim matter-of-factly. He did not mention that he had already been told this by Hedley Atkins.

"Of course," said Mrs Sheppard for a third time. "They met when Kathryn was going out with Hedley. I rather think that her relationship with Bryony survived better than the one with Hedley. That didn't last long." She spoke the last sentence with satisfaction. Tim wrote a brief note in his diary.

"Thank you. Finally," – he passed Mrs. Sheppard the other small plastic bag that he had taken from his briefcase – "this was also found with Kathryn's remains. Do you recognise it as having belonged to her?"

Just as she had turned over and scrutinised the bag with the ring, so Mrs. Sheppard now examined the contents of this second exhibit. This time, however, she seemed mystified.

"I can't make out what it is. May I take it out of the packet?"

Tim considered.

"I suppose that that would be OK: we've done all the tests on it that we can."

With thick fingers, she pulled apart the plastic griplock that sealed the bag, and extracted the object that it held. Evidently still puzzled, she held it up to the light and then set it down on the coffee table.

"It appears to be some kind of child's toy."

"That is correct. It is, in fact, a plastic Red Indian – one of a consignment of models given away with breakfast cereal at the time of Kathryn's disappearance. Would she have any reason for wanting to collect such figures?"

As precipitately as she had allowed Tim to beguile her with memories of Kathryn, Mrs. Sheppard snapped out of her reminiscences. She seemed to be irritated at the trivial turn that the conversation had taken.

"None that I can think of," she said, abrupt again. Juliet saw that the spell that Tim had succeeded in casting upon her for a while was breaking. They had had time enough, though, to get an answer to the most important question. "I can tell you one thing, though," added Mrs. Sheppard, "Kathryn did not buy the breakfast cereal herself. She was allergic to milk. She never touched the stuff."

"What did you make of that?" Tim asked Juliet as they crunched their way back down the gravel drive to the squeaking gate.

"I'm not sure that it told me much that I could rely on about Kathryn Sheppard's personality. All we got was a mother's recollection of how she felt about her daughter thirty years ago, filtered through the haze of years gone by, as well as sentimentality and remorse."

Tim nodded and grinned.

"Still in poetry mode, I see." He was suddenly serious again. "But we did get some information of value?"

"Yes. The most important thing that she told us was that Kathryn Sheppard and Bryony Atkins were friends."

"What do you deduce from that?"

"I think that it was a grave oversight of the original investigation that it failed to detect this relationship. I also think it likely that Bryony Atkins's disappearance was caused by something as disastrous as Kathryn Sheppard's."

"In short, that they were both murdered?"

Juliet nodded. "It seems probable, don't you agree?"

Tim nodded again.

"Tell me," he said, "where does the murder of Doris Atkins by her daughter-in-law fit into this?"

"I don't know," said Juliet. "Coincidence? Or perhaps that prison psychiatrist is correct, and Dorothy is a serial killer."

"I concede that it is possible that she is a serial killer; but Kathryn Sheppard was not one of her victims."

"How can you be so sure of that?"

"Timing," said Tim. "The timing is wrong."

"You keep on saying that!"

"Those plastic toys were imported about the time that Dorothy Atkins was jailed. And we now know that Kathryn Sheppard is unlikely to have acquired one of them by purchasing breakfast cereal. It is likely, therefore, that either someone gave the Red Indian to her while she was alive, or deliberately left it with her body when they dumped it."

Juliet nodded as she thought about what Tim was saying.

"What about Bryony?" she said slowly. "She can't have vanished into thin air. Yet no-one seems to have noticed that she'd disappeared, or exactly when she disappeared – no-one outside the family, that is. They must have noticed."

"Yes, they must have," said Tim. "My guess is that Bryony did not get very far away from home at all. In fact, I think that it's probable that she never left. What was Dorothy Atkins supposed to have said about her mother-in-law? That she was 'too fond of gardening'?"

"Something like that. Do you think that Bryony's buried in Doris's garden somewhere?"

"I think it's a possibility that we need to check out. And I also think that it's time we met Dorothy Atkins in the flesh."

CHAPTER NINETEEN

Recent events have made me quite determined: Peter will have to leave. I began to doubt that we were meant to be a couple when he insisted that I accompanied him to Liverpool and the more I have thought about it since, the more I know it is inevitable that we separate. I'm not sure what his comments about getting Tirzah to finish off 'Mummy' really meant, but I suspect that the whole thing – the visit, meeting the mother, meeting the sister, all that business about the will – was just an elaborate joke at my expense. He is merely running rings around me, parading me as his bit of rough. It is beginning to make me feel very angry indeed.

I have no idea where he is at the moment. I had let all of this boil up inside me until I thought I would explode and then, of course, it did erupt into the huge row that we had yesterday evening. Peter went storming out of the flat and I haven't seen him since. I know that he will be back, though. He didn't say that he was leaving, just that he was going out; and he didn't take anything at all with him, not even a toothbrush. I don't doubt that he spent the night with one of his louche boyfriends. Ugh! His promiscuity is something else that I can't stand. I thought that it didn't matter – he has certainly never tried to hide it – but I find that it does. It isn't so much the fidelity issue, though of course to have a faithful lover would be nice; no, it's something much more basic than that. To be frank, how do I know where these people have *been*?

It shouldn't be too hard to get rid of him; after all, we did say we would review the arrangement every month (his idea) and although he has barely been here for ten days, the cracks are beginning to show. Even he must agree that it isn't working out. Oh dear – I hope that he doesn't propose to stay the full month before he will consent to have the conversation.

All this is making me ill, with the same old desperate illness. If he only knew what he was doing.

There's someone banging about in the corridor outside: I can hear footsteps slipping and sliding. Odd, because we don't often get drunks in these flats. I supposed it could just be some kids, fooling around. There's someone scrabbling at the door now. I'll bet it's one of those kids from the flat downstairs. Little bastards! I'm going to give them a piece of my mind.

I stride to the door and fling it open. I am horrified when Peter stumbles inside and collapses on the hall floor. He is moaning.

"Hedley, darling boy, please help." He sounds like a child, helpless and frightened, and he is slurring his words. I cannot see his face, but assume that he is blind drunk. What a disgrace! It is the last thing I need; I have already stretched the terms of my tenancy agreement by having him here at all. I look up and down the corridor, but can see no-one about. I grab hold of Peter's legs, which are blocking the doorway, and drag him into the flat, turning them ninety degrees so that I can get the door shut. I drop his feet on to the floor without ceremony and slam the door, locking and bolting it for good measure. His trouser legs are torn and muddy, and his usually highly-polished shoes scuffed and spattered.

Peter groans again and remains lying on the floor tiles, face down. He is clearly too drunk to get up. He disgusts me, and I am about to tell him so, when I see a trickle of blood seeping out from under the hand on which his head is resting. A shock of fear runs through me and I kneel down to turn him over. I see that his face is a mass of blood and bruises.

"My God! Peter! What have you been doing?" To my horror he begins to cry.

"I haven't been doing anything. Can't you see that, you stupid fucker? I was on my way back when I was attacked. Is my face quite ruined? Tell me what it looks like!" He is crying horribly now, deep sobs which distort the bloody mess yet further. My anger dissolves. I take him in my arms.

"Don't cry!" I say. "Please don't cry! I'm going to get a cushion to make you comfortable and then I'll fetch some warm water to wash your face. It is probably not as bad as it seems."

He breaks away from me and lies in the foetal position, whimpering. "I can't live with a damaged face," he snivels. "My face is what I am. My face is my fortune!"

I feel both exasperated and amused by this and have to resist a very strong urge to laugh. Taking one of the cushions from the small sofa that stands in the hall, I shove it under his head and go to fetch water and towels without saying another word. When I return he is still lying in the same position, his shoulders heaving with sobs.

"Peter," I say, none too gently. "For God's sake stop it now. You're not making it any better by behaving like this. Try to pull yourself together. Sit up so that I can wash your face."

Meekly, and to my surprise, he does my bidding, in an exhausted kind of way, leaning his back against the sofa for support. I take the piece of muslin that I have brought from the first aid box, squeeze it through the warm water and very gently pass it over his face. Peter flinches, exclaims and tries to shy away.

"Hold still! You know I have to clean the wounds. The less you struggle, the sooner it will be over." Even to myself, I sound like his nanny. Yet he seems curiously comforted by my having taken charge, and once again tries to obey. I find myself enjoying his subservience!

After I have washed his face two or three times, I can see

the extent of his wounds. He has two black eyes, a split lip and a broken tooth. Nothing that won't heal or can't be fixed. But I am more perturbed by the rash of tiny pellet marks that I see against his temple. Shotgun pellets, if I'm not mistaken.

"Has someone been shooting at you?"

He shrugs and looks defensive.

"Peter, look at me. Tell me what happened. I can't help you unless I understand exactly. And if you've got some pellets lodged in your head, even superficially, you're going to have to go to the hospital, because I don't know how to get them out."

Peter lets his head loll, and closes his eyes.

"I can't and won't go to the hospital," he says, with some of his old petulance, though it seems to me that this is just a thin disguise to mask his fear.

"Why not?"

"I just can't, that's all. You wouldn't understand, so I can't explain it to you."

"You can try."

"No." Suddenly he opens his eyes, leans forward, and vomits on the floor.

"My God," I say. Peter regards his own vomit, horrified. We are both squeamish. I realise that I am going to have to clear it up. I wonder what to do about getting medical help for him. I can see that he needs more than the limited first aid that I can offer.

"Help me to bed," he says in a thick voice.

"No," I say. "You can't go to bed yet. It isn't safe for you to lie down until we're sure you aren't going to be sick again. Besides which, you need a bath. And if I'm going to look after you, you owe it to me to tell me what happened."

Peter looks sulky. Now that his face is cleaned of mud and blood, I see that, although it is horribly swollen, all of his injuries are superficial. It is only the pellets that worry me.

"All right. But you should take some of the blame for this, so there's no need to behave so damned self-righteously. If you hadn't kicked me out last night, it wouldn't have happened."

"I didn't kick you out. You flounced out."

Rather unexpectedly, he grins. "Ah, yes. I'm rather good at 'flouncing', aren't I?" Gripping the arm of the sofa, he raises himself shakily to his feet and then collapses back on to the sofa's seat after he catches a glimpse of himself in the gilt ormolu mirror that hangs above it.

"My God!" he says. "Just look at my face! You didn't tell me how bad it was." His mouth puckers. I think that he is going to cry again.

"Stop being so childish, Peter!" I say. "You will survive – and you'll even get your pretty face back again." His little button eyes dance malignantly, affronted at the jibe. "What you should be worried about are those pellet marks. I can't tell if they just grazed you, or whether you have some lead shot lodged in your head somewhere."

He shrugs, make-believe brave.

"And stop creating diversions," I add. "You were going to tell me what happened. So tell me."

Peter looks crafty. Although his knuckles are grazed and bloody and there is unaccustomed dirt under his fingernails, he steeples his fingers elegantly and regards me over the top of the pyramid that he has created.

"As you know, I have rather an extensive acquaintance in London," he says, watching me carefully. "Most of them don't know that I'm here. But on occasion, someone shows up. And it isn't always someone that I'm particularly rejoiced to see, if you understand me."

"If you're going to tell me some sordid tale about a rent boy, then I don't want to know."

Peter looks put out.

"Oh, but you said you did want to know. So which is it to be? Anyway, Hugo isn't a rent boy. I don't know how you'd describe him. I suppose he is a crook."

"What do you mean? What sort of crook?"

"Oh, come, now," Peter says, smiling a little lop-sidedly. "There's only one kind, isn't there? A dishonest one. A dishonest man. Someone who breaks the law. A felon."

He spells out all of these short definitions slowly and with exaggerated patience, as if I am an extremely slow schoolboy whom he is coaching.

"So how do you come to know him? And why does he want to beat you up?"

"To tell you the truth, I don't know why he beat me up, or who his friends were. I met him some years ago, when I was much more interested in horses than I am now. I believe that he and I placed a few bets together – we had a kind of little syndicate going."

"That doesn't make him a felon. In fact, from the way that you're telling this story, it sounds suspiciously as if you were the dishonest one. Did you swindle him out of some money – some winnings, perhaps? Is that why he decided to pop you one?"

"Oh, for God's sake, Hedley, stop being so vulgar. Of course I didn't swindle him – not of anything that was legally his, anyway. And I'm far from sure that he did 'pop me one', as you so crudely put it. I seemed to be talking to him perfectly amicably when this fist appeared from nowhere. The next thing I knew I was lying on the ground, and Hugo was nowhere to be seen. I'm convinced there was another person involved. I'd have noticed if Hugo had been about to assault me. Besides, he's *such* a nice boy."

"Really, Peter, I give up."

"Oh, but you don't really, do you, darling? I mean, I think you thought you *had* given up, temporarily, yesterday evening; but now I've returned to you in a *very* delicate state – wounded, no less – you have begun to realise the depth of your affections for me, haven't you – *darling*?"

He emphasises the last word with such heavy sarcasm that I feel forced to meet his eyes. They are two glinting little pieces of jet, malevolent and calculating.

"I understand," he says, in a light and genial voice. "I understand that you lost your temper yesterday. You're entitled to do that – no-one's perfect. You've been planning to kick me out, haven't you, Hedley, my sweet? But out of compassion, you're going to let me stay after all, aren't you? And if you don't quite feel sufficient compassion to agree, I have a little bartering counter up my sleeve. Would you like to know what it is?"

He keeps my frozen countenance in his gaze. My scalp crawls with fear. Peter leans forward and pats my hand.

"I've found out the truth, Hedley, my friend, my dear, dear lover. I won't spell it out in detail – I'm sure that you will agree that we can't be too circumspect. But I want you to know, nevertheless. I know everything. Everything!" he whinnies the last word, his falsetto voice returning for an instant.

"But don't worry, darling. Everything will be all right. I want to assure you that your secret's safe with me." The cliché cannot have been unintentional.

He withdraws his hand.

"Time that you cleared up this horrible mess now, don't you think?"

I remove my eyes from the grip of his, and look down at my fingers. A gory snail's trail of blood and mucus is working its way across them.

CHAPTER TWENTY

It was a long, narrow garden, confined by an old red brick wall on both sides. There was a heavy wooden gate at the end which was painted pale green and secured by a bolt and a large padlock. It appeared to lead nowhere more interesting than the yard of the adjacent tractor hire company. The wall on the right-hand side was covered in a profusion of old English roses. That on the left-hand side was bare, save for a few gooseberry bushes that straggled against its lower reaches. The wall itself was streaked with the silver of phosphorus; about ten feet in height, and at least four inches thick, it had been topped at some time in the past with pieces of broken bottle.

Inspector Tim Yates pointed to the jagged shards of glass.

"Not very neighbourly, is it? How long has that been there?"

Ronald Atkins fiddled nervously with his watch-strap.

"Oh, a long time – ever since I can remember, and I grew up here, you know. I think my uncle had it done because at one point there was a very large and rowdy family living next door. The Needhams. My uncle couldn't abide them."

"Hmm. I'm not sure that it's legal – it may have to be removed – but that's not why we're here today, as you know. Do you want someone to walk through the garden with you and take an inventory of the plants? You are entitled to have it restored to its original state as far as we can manage, after we've finished."

"I'll leave that to Doreen. She's more interested in it than I am."

Tim looked back towards the house. A tall, untidy-looking woman in her seventies was standing at the sash window, her arms folded across a beige-clad bosom. He could not read the look on her face.

"As you wish. Please tell her that if she wants to take the inventory, she needs to arrange it with one of my officers in the next hour. After that the digging team will arrive."

For all his deference, Ronald Atkins flushed deeply, evidently angry.

"Is this whole thing really necessary? Could you tell me exactly what you think you might find?"

Inspector Yates regarded him levelly.

"I don't know, Mr. Atkins. Perhaps you have more idea than I do."

"Why would I know? I have only just inherited the property."

"Yes. Why is that? I understand that it is many years since your uncle died."

Ronald Atkins shrugged. "There was a dispute about who had rightful ownership. My uncle's will was badly-phrased and ambiguous. I did not prove my case until early this year. Doreen and I only moved in a few months ago."

"You lived here as a child, though."

"Yes. But the house belonged to my uncle – and my grandmother. My mother and I lived here on sufferance. She acted as their skivvy, in return for a roof over our heads."

"You sound very bitter."

"Bitter? Not really. A little resentful, maybe, of the opportunities that were lost to me because of circumstances. But we were fortunate, really. At the time, many unmarried mothers were sent to mental institutions and their children put out for adoption. I think that my grandmother was unprepared to go that far: after all, my mother was her only daughter. But at the same time she wanted to make the point – in perpetuity, as it were – that my mother had forfeited her rights to equal treatment. My mother was trapped in a life of everlasting penance. My grandmother was a Methodist and had very black and white ideas about morals. Ironically, my mother only found out after her death that she had herself been almost four months pregnant at the time of her marriage. But of course the difference was that my grandfather had married her."

"It was your mother who looked after the garden?"

"She looked after most things. But she liked the garden. I think it gave her some kind of creative outlet – or maybe just the opportunity to get out of the house. The atmosphere in there could be very oppressive; and even when it wasn't, my grandmother and Uncle Colin would sit on either side of the fireplace, gazing into each other's eyes like two spaniels. It must have been galling for my mother, to have been so conspicuously the odd one out."

"I know I have asked you this before: but why would your first wife have commented that your mother had to die 'because she was too fond of gardening'?"

Ronald Atkins shrugged. His moment of expansiveness evaporated, and he was clearly on guard again.

"Who knows why Tirzah said or did things? I know you have read all the case-notes, Inspector, so you must be aware by now that I could neither influence her nor understand her. I had no control over her whatsoever. It was like being married to an alien."

"Did you think that she was insane?"

"The judge decided that the best place for her was in a secure mental unit."

"That doesn't answer my question."

"I realise that; and I hardly know how to answer it. I've thought about it, of course; and I've come to the conclusion that it depends on your definition of insane. My wife was examined by several psychiatrists and they each said that she had 'borderline' something – narcissism, psychosis, depression. I don't quite understand that term 'borderline' – does it mean she was almost normal, or almost mad? One thing of which I am certain is that she was not 'normal' in the sense that most people would understand the word. I'm not sure that that means she was insane, however."

Tim Yates nodded. Ronald's comments were unhelpful, except in so far as they confirmed the conclusions that he had himself drawn from the case notes, and from talking to the psychiatrists. Once again he determined to gain an opportunity to interview Tirzah properly himself. Her manipulative powers appeared to be very highly developed. He was sure that talking to her at length would be interesting, as well as perhaps leading to the crucial information that was eluding him.

Ronald Atkins shivered.

"I am sorry, Mr. Atkins, I am keeping you out in the cold. Do go back to the house: I will come and find you if I need you again. And please mention the inventory to your wife."

Ronald Atkins gave him the lop-sided smirk which passed for his smile, and turned his back. He walked swiftly back up the path, a quick, neat figure despite his age.

Tim carried on walking to the end of the garden. He examined the padlock on the gate. The padlock was rusted to the chain, and the small metal sleeve that protected the keyhole had corroded so much that it was immoveable. Clearly no-one had passed through this gate for a long time. He wondered why it had been kept locked. Answering his own question, he supposed that it had been to allow Ronald to play safely when he was a child; or perhaps to prevent snatch-thieves breaking into the shop via the back way. He made a mental note to have the chain removed, so that he could walk through the gate as Doris Atkins might have done when she was out tending her garden.

He turned and glanced up at the house next door – once the residence of the pestilential Needhams – and thought that he saw someone step quickly back from one of the bedroom windows.

He had intended to interview Doreen Atkins while he was waiting for the SOCOs to arrive, but upon reflection decided that he would leave the two Atkinses to stew for the time being. He was convinced that Ronald, at least, was keeping something secret that could have helped the police. Doreen was more of a known quantity. Not bright and prone to hysteria; he doubted if it would take long to persuade her to reveal everything that she knew under strict questioning and in due course he would put this to the test. He doubted that she knew very much, however. Even if Ronald trusted her, she was an outsider, not part of the unholy charmed circle that had been his original family. Doreen might even turn into an ally.

CHAPTER TWENTY-ONE

Tim had thought hard and long about the best way to introduce himself to Dorothy Atkins. Like all of the other inmates at Elmete Park, she was considered to be psychologically vulnerable and he did not wish to become the object of the wrath of a care worker, or, even worse, have some complaint about his treatment of Dorothy leaked out and plastered all over the newspapers. At the same time, he knew from everyone to whom he had spoken about Dorothy – the two psychiatrists he had met and a retired prison warder whom he had interviewed by telephone – that she was dangerously manipulative and probably far less 'emotionally fragile' than he was himself. And he considered his own mental faculties to be pretty robust.

He had now spoken to Mrs. Meredith, the matron at Elmete Park, and also arranged to meet her prior to visiting Dorothy. He had told the matron that he would take DC Juliet Armstrong with him and that at the meeting with Dorothy she would do most of the talking. Mrs Meredith had sent waves of approval down the telephone. He and Juliet would take advice from the matron on how best to approach Dorothy, and they would follow her recommendations exactly. The matron oozed concurrence.

Unsurprisingly, when Juliet was informed of this plan she was a little less enthusiastic. Never brimming with self-confidence, she expressed doubts about her own ability to obtain anything useful from an allegedly cunning elderly female psychopath. Tim tended to agree, though of course he did not tell Juliet this. He wondered if there was any possible way that he could take over the interview with Dorothy without either incurring the displeasure of the matron or hurting Juliet's feelings.

The first hurdle to leap, however, was to get Dorothy to agree to the meeting.

The matron, who by this time had decided that Tim was possibly the nicest young man she had ever met, offered to smooth the way. She did not tell Tim how she had achieved it, but she rang later the same day to offer him and Juliet an appointment to see Dorothy Atkins early the following afternoon.

Tim was slightly peeved that he was reduced to 'making appointments' to see a suspect, yet at the same time also intimidated by the prospect of meeting Dorothy. This in turn made him annoyed with himself: so far, his reaction to the woman's reputation had been little braver than Juliet's. He frowned as he swung the car into the gravel sweep of the mid-Victorian mansion that was Elmete Park. Of weather-darkened grey stone, it was typical of the houses built by Lincolnshire's wealthy gentlemen farmers when the newly-drained fens had reached the peak of their prosperity. He turned to Juliet, who sat, tense and silent, beside him.

"I wonder which shepherd with delusions of grandeur commissioned this particular horror," he said.

"I believe it was actually built by Anstruthers, the brewing family," she said. "They invented Green Giant – it's now quite a celebrated real ale. The house isn't so bad: the grounds are nice, and the rooms are probably spacious."

"Hmm, yes, but it reeks of institution, doesn't it?"

"Well, it **is** an institution," said Juliet, not unreasonably.

The matron was older than Tim had expected – probably in her late forties. She had a pleasant, careworn face. He could imagine that she would be good with difficult elderly people.

He noticed that when she spoke, she included both Tim and Juliet in every part of the conversation. Not many people had the skills or could be bothered to do that.

She did not beat about the bush, however, and launched straight into her account of Dorothy Atkins.

"Something you must understand straight away, Inspector, is that Dorothy Atkins was not brought here as a criminal. We took her after she had served her time. It was decided by the court that she was no longer a menace to society. Her mental state is, however, considered to be delicate. She receives some psychiatric care here, but not the same kind of rigorous treatment that they gave her in her later years in prison. Latterly, that was to assess her suitability for release into the community, and consequently was well-documented: some of the key psychiatrists' reports were published, with no permission from her required. Here the treatment that she receives is gently therapeutic and totally confidential. She is almost always called 'Tirzah', by the way."

"I had heard that was her nickname. Do you know why?"

"Dorothy is never very expansive when it comes to her personal details, but I understand from one of the notes that I've read that it was a pet name given to her by an old man that she knew when she was a child. She seems to have liked it and used it for her whole life, at least with those with whom she is familiar. I was going to say 'close', but I don't think that Tirzah is close to anyone. I wonder if she ever has been."

"What is she like as an inmate here?"

Mrs. Meredith laughed.

"The people that we care for are residents, Inspector, not 'inmates'. I would say that Tirzah is a model resident, at least on the face of it. She obeys all the rules, she doesn't cause disturbances, she behaves in a reasonably sociable manner – she will help others sometimes, and do them small favours, such as bringing the less mobile residents drinks or playing cards with the ones who are up to it. Beneath this veneer, however, she is – I hardly know the correct word to use – subversive? She has on occasion been believed by staff to have wound up some of the more vulnerable residents."

"What do you mean by 'believed to have wound up'? How do your staff define such an activity? By overhearing her conversations with the others?"

Mrs. Meredith laughed.

"That's a good question, and one to which I can't necessarily supply a good answer. Of course, if we had definitely caught Tirzah in the act of distressing another patient, we would have regarded it as a breach of the rules and addressed the problem. But it is not as clear-cut as that and Tirzah is clever. Therefore I can only tell you that some of the residents here are not in full possession of their mental faculties, and these are the ones that Tirzah often chooses to help or to talk to. All very laudable, you might think, especially as these are the people most in need of help, and also, often, the ones least likely to receive it. The staff are too busy, and the 'normal' residents don't get enough personal reward for bothering with people who can't interact with them properly. I and others have often sat with Tirzah and one of the residents that she is in the act of befriending, and witnessed nothing untoward. But sometimes the same people have become very agitated and upset quite soon afterwards. When asked what is distressing them, they have muttered garbled accounts about their fears. More often than not, these are totally incomprehensible, but on occasions some very disturbing words have been thrown up by a little gentle probing: words such as 'pain', 'death' and 'blame', for example. But of course words like this can come up in ordinary conversation, and when we have tried asking Tirzah what has gone wrong, she has professed complete innocence. When she left the person in question, they appeared happy, cheerful, tranquil, etc. De-da, de-da, de-da", she added, making her own scepticism clear.

"Why don't you keep her under permanent surveillance, or try to tape these conversations?"

Mrs. Meredith gave him a look that was half-quizzical, half-reproving.

"Really, Inspector, that would hardly be ethical, would it? As I've said, we aren't a penal institution. Besides, these episodes don't occur every time that Tirzah sits with someone. And, as she herself says, having her sit and talk to others is generally very beneficial, both for them and for the nursing staff – not to mention Tirzah herself."

Tim opened his mouth to speak, but she cut him off.

"Oh, I am quite aware that Tirzah is trying to manipulate me as well, Inspector, and she may even be succeeding. The real question as far as I am concerned is how best to respond. Don't forget that she is under my care, as all the residents are; and please don't make the mistake of thinking that she is the only tricky resident here. Anyone who has worked in an establishment like this will tell you that society's received notions of sweet little old ladies and benign altruistic old gentleman are largely mythical – and probably always have been. Don't forget that each of the residents here has fought and clawed and triumphed and suffered through seven, eight or nine decades of life. Some few may have achieved this with all their moral values intact and also have emerged with sunny dispositions; but most are just people of all the many hues of grey that I am sure that you encounter every day in your work, Inspector. Old age does not confer sainthood."

Tim inclined his head in agreement. Juliet Armstrong, sensing that he might be eroding the good opinion that he had won so effortlessly from Mrs. Meredith, decided to steer the conversation back to trying to elicit from her the more specific information about Dorothy Atkins which had been its original purpose.

"Tell us what kind of approach works best with Tirzah," she said, leaning forward so that she could make eye contact with Mrs. Meredith. "We should be really grateful for your help in understanding what we are up against."

Mrs. Meredith had visibly softened when Juliet started

speaking, but she sighed when she heard the policewoman's concluding words.

"As I've tried to explain, that is just the sort of attitude that won't work with her. If she thinks you are pitching yourselves 'up against' her, she will regard it as a competition: a battle of wills that she will be determined to win. And which she will win, I can promise you that."

Juliet dropped her eyes, and blushed.

"What I would advise," continued Mrs. Meredith more gently, "is to focus on Tirzah herself. Make it very clear that you are interested primarily in her. Tell her that you want to know more about Kathryn Sheppard because she is one of the few people alive who may be able to remember Kathryn clearly, and what she was like as a young woman. Ask Tirzah about herself, especially her own childhood and young womanhood. You can talk to her about her time in prison as well, if you must. But don't ask about her family, especially her former husband or his mother, the woman that she was convicted of killing, unless she raises the subject first. Sometimes she is willing to talk about her conviction and the events which led up to it – though not necessarily in terms which you will find either helpful or intelligible – and at other times any mention of them makes her hostile, withdrawn and silent for days. Whether or not Tirzah is a psychopath and a killer, please understand that she is indeed very damaged. If I were a psychologist, I would say that her manipulativeness is a form of self-protection against her own vulnerability."

"Thank you. That is very helpful," said Tim. "Your viewpoint also intrigues me – especially your comment about 'the woman that she was convicted of killing'. Can I ask if you are in some doubt about this? It is a totally off-the-record conversation, of course."

Mrs. Meredith regarded him archly.

"It is not my job to speculate about the residents, Inspector, and I am not properly qualified to comment on Tirzah's case in particular. I have not read the contemporary reports on her conviction, nor am I familiar with the details of the case itself. I have, of course, read the subsequent psychiatric reports and I know in broad terms, but not specifically, what the psychiatrist who visits her here thinks about her condition. I am not privy to the details of their conversations – as I have said, she is not a prisoner, and she has not given permission for anyone else to be told of them."

She paused, and looked at Juliet alone.

"But if we were to put all of this aside for a minute – and in the strictest confidence, of course – and always bearing in mind that Tirzah's exceptional skills as a manipulator – I don't think that murder is part of her make-up."

"Why do you say that?" It was Tim again.

"Because Tirzah is about two things: ongoing control and self-promotion. You cannot practise either of these two things if your target is dead; and you only have limited capacity to exercise them in a prison environment. On the other hand, the type of environment that we have here is ideal – as is being the stronger partner in an unequal marriage, especially if there are children."

"Thank you very much, Mrs. Meredith. You have prepared us well, even though some of the traits that you outline seem contradictory and, of course, hard to understand. Perhaps we can see Tirzah herself now?" He consulted the big round clock on the wall of Mrs. Meredith's office. "I believe that she is expecting us to keep our appointment in five minutes' time."

Mrs. Meredith smiled.

"You learn quickly, Inspector. Courtesy and consideration are important here, and 'an appointment' is the correct way of describing this meeting. Elmete Park is Tirzah's home."

Tim inclined his head in acknowledgement of the compliment.

"There is just one thing, though . . ." He picked up the edge to her tone, and looked up quickly again.

"You said that Detective Constable Armstrong would be

taking the lead, but she has only been given the opportunity to speak once so far. May I suggest that your conversation with Tirzah is at least three-way, rather than a dialogue? Otherwise Tirzah is likely to cast DC Armstrong in the role of eavesdropper."

"Of course," said Tim. "Good point."

"Thank you. There is more than one type of controlling behaviour, you know."

She smiled and stood up, adroitly indicating that the conversation was at an end before he could retort.

CHAPTER TWENTY-TWO

Peter has almost recovered from his beating now. He has no scars and his teeth have been expertly repaired. The bruises around his eyes have all but disappeared, leaving only dark hollows under his eyes that merely serve to make him look interestingly world-weary. His face is paler than it used to be, and perhaps not quite as tautly handsome. But his cherished good looks have weathered the experience and survived almost intact.

As for our relationship, things have actually been going quite well between us. He has persuaded me that we need a holiday, and says that he will pay for it because I have 'looked after him so well.' I don't know about this – my services have not been altogether ungrudging – and I am sceptical at first, fearing that my budget will not stretch to paying for the sort of holiday for both of us that Peter will expect. But I know that I ought to take some holiday soon, or forfeit my annual entitlement; and when I express my doubts about Peter's capacity to pay, he looks mock-hurt. He demonstrates that I am wrong and I see that he has certainly got the money, although he does not vouchsafe where from: wads of it. He has suggested that we go to a little hotel that he knows on the Solway Firth, and although I'm not a great lover of Scotland, I agree.

At present we are therefore on a train again, travelling First Class (on off-peak, advance tickets) and heading for the border. We have reached Berwick-upon-Tweed, and I am admiring the spectacular sweep of the coast and the wonderful old bridge that stretches across the mouth of the estuary, when I turn to Peter to make sure that he also is enjoying the view and notice for the first time what he is reading. Although he made his customary magazine purchases at the W.H. Smith's on the station concourse before we boarded the train, I see that they are all neatly stacked up, unread, against the window. Instead of perusing them, he is deeply engrossed in some papers that he has taken from a pink cardboard wallet. When I look more closely, I see that they are photocopies of newspaper clippings.

"What are you reading?" I say idly. "Whatever it is almost looks like work, the way you have it filed in that businesslike way."

I expect one of Peter's indignant ripostes about the grubbiness of work. Instead, he scrutinises me over the top of his rimless spectacles and looks severe.

"It *is* work, Hedley, no *almost* about it. Homework, to be a little more precise. I am finding out more about my nearest and dearest. History is a very fascinating thing."

"Are you interested in genealogy?" I ask, surprised. "I wouldn't have thought it of you. After all, you know that your family were in trade, not aristocrats; and who knows what you might dig up about them if you go back far enough? You might find a convict, or even, God help us, a farm-labourer!"

I intend my comment to be tinged with the type of humorous quasi-malice at which Peter himself excels. He flattens me effortlessly with one terse sentence.

"I am not the least interested in my antecedents, dear boy: only in yours."

"Just what have you got there?" I ask, suddenly both fearful and annoyed. I hear my voice rise an octave. An elderly woman who has been scribbling in biro on a newspaper looks up.

"Keep your voice down, darling, we don't want to bandy

our business about so that everyone can hear, do we? All I have here are a few newspaper clippings that my friend Marjorie obtained for me. She works in the BBC archives, you know." He nods affably at the elderly woman, who is still staring, and she looks away, burying herself in her crossword again. "There's nothing at all here that isn't in the public domain, and no reason on earth why you should get upset." He has gathered the papers into a sheaf as he speaks, and is now holding them aloft at arm's length away from me, as if I am a dog trying to pilfer the best fillet steak that he has bought for his supper. The gesture infuriates me. I keep my temper with some difficulty.

"All right," I say as evenly as I can. "I can see that they're newspaper clippings, as you say, and not private papers. Nevertheless, would you mind telling me what they're about?"

Peter sniggered. "Well, the trial, of course. What else would they be about? How often have members of your family got their names into the national press? What did you expect them to be about?"

"You mean Tirzah's trial?"

"Yes. Of course. You aren't going to surprise me now by telling me that you come from a family of many felons, and that I might have had the pick of half a dozen trials?"

"I won't say that you have no right to do this, because as you have just pointed out, technically speaking you have. But would you mind telling me *why* you are doing it? Of what possible interest can her trial be to you? And why have you brought all this stuff with you now, when we're supposed to be on holiday? Did you think that I would enjoy sitting here and watching you read it?"

"Well, I didn't expect you to be as upset as you clearly are, and I do apologise for that," Peter says smoothly and in a voice devoid of contrition. He is watching me carefully, his eyes viscous and very black. "I actually have your best interests at heart. There are too many mysteries attached to your grandmother's death and I intend to get to the bottom of it."

I flush. "I don't know what you mean by 'mysteries', or 'getting to the bottom of it'. It was all very straightforward at the time. Horrible, of course, but straightforward. There was no doubt that my mother committed the crime and she did not at any stage try to say that she was innocent."

"Yes, yes, I know that, my dear Hedley. Don't forget that I have been reading the accounts of the trial myself. In fact, she said neither that she was innocent, nor that she was guilty. She said very little. Other people said a great deal, though. For example, there were several witnesses who testified that she had had a good relationship with your grandmother, and that in fact she got on better with her than with her own mother. From your own recollections as a young man – delicious thought! – would you say that that was true?"

I shrug. "She certainly didn't have the kind of disagreements with my grandmother that she had with my father. In general, they seemed to get on – as far as my mother ever did get on with people. I wouldn't say that she and my grandmother were on intimate terms – I doubt if my mother would have confided in her – but I don't remember there being any friction between them. Why do you ask?"

"You read crime thrillers sometimes, don't you?"

"Yes – you know I do."

"So what is the Plod who's sent to solve the murder always on the look-out for?"

"It depends on the novel. Fingerprints. Incriminating evidence. Circumstantial evidence. Motive."

"Ah, motive! Quite right. What do you suppose your mother's motive was? Why would she have killed your grandmother?"

"The judge decided that she was a psychopath. Psychopaths do things like that."

"I know what the judge said; and I know what psychopaths do. It remains to be proved that your mother is one; opinion seems to be divided about that. But a bright psychopath – and I do your mother the honour of assuming that if she is a psychopath, she is an intelligent one – is usually quite cunning about not getting caught, at least not until he or she has a good few murders under his or her belt. He or she tends to kill people and get away with it, perhaps because they value their freedom, perhaps so that they can go on killing. In fact, from my study of the subject, I would say that they usually choose someone with whom they are only slenderly connected, with the express purpose of not getting caught. Killing one's own mother-in-law when one's family are gathered under the same roof would not seem to apply, would it?"

He eyes me narrowly. I feel my face flush and then grow pale. I don't answer him.

"So," he continues, "unless Tirzah is a stupid psychopath, which we have discounted, there are two possible explanations of the motive. One is that the murder of your grandmother was not a psychopathic act at all, but motivated by the extreme irritation that most of us feel when confronted with the company of our relatives for any period of time – in fact, one marvels that a domestic murder does not break out in every town on every day of the week. A crime of passion, in fact. Or indeed, a crime with some other motive – to keep Doris quiet, for example."

I nod. "But the evidence does not support that hypothesis." I manage to formulate the words, knowing that he expects something from me and hope that because I am echoing his own view I shall not be required to engage in debate.

"Precisely," he says. He is still watching me intently, gauging my reaction, evidently waiting for me to elaborate. I swallow.

"You said that there were two possible explanations. What is the other one – in your view?"

"The other one, darling, is that Doris Atkins was indeed killed by a psychopath – or just possibly a family member acting under extreme irritation or fear of being found out about something – but that that person was not Tirzah. Which would have three further consequences: the first, that Tirzah is innocent; the second, that the actual killer, if he or she is not dead, is still at large; and the third, that almost certainly it is someone that you know."

My brain scrambles to a mush. I think that I might pass out. I open my mouth again, but I have no idea what I can or should say. But Peter has relaxed his extreme scrutiny of my face as he gets carried away by the ingenuity of his own deductions. He holds up a finger.

"Ah, yes, I know what you are going to say: that there are sticking-points in my argument. The first and most obvious one is that Tirzah herself, not, I think you will agree, a woman known for her generosity of spirit or fellow feeling and therefore unlikely to be moved to take the rap for someone else, never asserted her innocence of the charge of murder. But she did not say that she was guilty, either. She simply refused to say anything that would establish that she was guilty or otherwise. The second is that everyone else involved – the other occupants of the house, the police, the shrinks – seemed to agree that Tirzah was the murderess. Even the character witnesses, friends or colleagues who could have testified in support of her, agreed that she had it in her to murder. So, if they were wrong, and assuming that they weren't all party to a giant conspiracy to victimise her, what were all of these people overlooking? It must have been something so obvious that it was staring them in the face, and yet they missed it. What could it have been?"

I feel the pressure on me relax. I even give a short laugh.

"I have no idea, Peter, but I am certain that you are going to tell me."

"Ah, that is where you are wrong, dear boy. I am afraid that this is as far as I have reached with my sleuthing. I am unable to draw any further conclusions: and, most disappointingly, there is also a piece in my jigsaw that I can't make to fit at all."

I grow wary again. "Oh?" I say, trying to indicate that I feel that the subject is becoming rather tedious now.

"It's that comment of Tirzah's. She made it two or three times, in her initial statement to the police, and later to her counsel. It was quoted in court and she was asked what she meant by it, but she did not answer."

"You mean the so-called 'garden excuse'?"

"Yes – I thought you would be with me there. It was so well-documented in the press that you could hardly have missed it – and of course, you may have heard it repeated yourself, at the trial – did you? Did you attend the trial?"

I don't answer. Peter darts me several looks, and then quotes thoughtfully:

"'She was too fond of gardening.' A gnomic utterance. A bit like 'she should have died hereafter'. But what do you suppose it could have meant? I'm assuming that it did mean something. As we've agreed, Tirzah was essentially truthful, and not given to flights of fancy. So why did she make this comment? Was it a mistake, a giveaway remark that she would later regret – hence her refusal to expand on it – or a clue, if people would only try to interpret it?"

I shrug.

"Do you know what I should really appreciate?" Peter is dangerously alert again. His gaze bores right through me. I shake my head and try to be flippant. But I have recovered enough to emulate Peter's own urbanity.

"You can't expect me to second-guess your desires, dearest. You are far too complex. Indulge me and tell me what it is. I will do my best to oblige."

Peter throws back his head and laughs his refined whinny.

"Excellent! That is what I like best about you, Hedley – your subservience. It becomes you well, just as accepting the dominant role becomes me even better. I should really like to hear your account of the day that your grandmother died. You were there, weren't you?"

"I – I wasn't in the house at the time. I didn't see her die. I only saw the body afterwards."

"That will do. Just your memory of it, your own observations as exactly as you can, with any hearsay or subsequent speculation removed, if your memory is acute enough."

"I will try. But I don't understand what use it will be. I wasn't a witness – not to the murder; and I wasn't called as a witness in court."

"I know. Odd, isn't it? Exceedingly odd that there were three people in the house at the time of Doris Atkins' death besides your mother – Doris's own mother and her brother Colin, your sister Bryony and, then, shortly after the event, yourself – and none of you was asked for a statement, let alone called as a witness. The main witness relied on by both the prosecution and the defence was your father – who, by his own account, did not arrive home until well after Doris was dead. Correct?"

I nod.

"Peculiar, isn't it? But you will indulge me?"

I make no sound or gesture; Peter interprets this as assent.

"Good. Excellent. But first of all we shall have lunch – a proper lunch, in the buffet car, where they serve proper meals with claret. This is a real train, dear boy, not a travesty of one that serves food in cardboard boxes. Come along, now. I have made a reservation for the buffet car and I see that we are five minutes late already."

CHAPTER TWENTY-THREE

It was inevitable when Tim and Juliet finally met Dorothy Atkins that they should feel a sense of anti-climax. Mrs. Meredith had suggested that they should first see her through the internal observation window before she introduced them. They peered through the clouded glass and saw an elderly woman seated in one of the curious stiff high-backed chairs that are an inescapable feature of residential homes. As she was sitting down, it was difficult to estimate her height, but Tim guessed that she was taller than average, which when she was young would have been exceptionally tall for a woman. She was stooping over a coffee table on which a newspaper had been spread. Her clothes were dowdy and unfashionable: she was wearing a crimplene skirt of a curious yellow ochre hue, and a lemon-yellow high-necked blouse with a ruffle. Her rather skimpy long grey hair had been caught with grips into an indifferent 'French roll'. The skirt was quite short – it had ridden up to show her knees – and her legs, which were encased in thickish tights, were lumpy, with fat calves and virtually no tapering to the ankles. Rather incongruously, her feet were shod in scarlet leather moccasins.

She riffled through her newspaper for a while, studiedly nonchalant, and then gave a quick sideways glance at their window. "She knows, or suspects, that you are watching," said Mrs. Meredith. "Time to meet her properly now."

She led the way across the polished parquet floor, the

crepe soles of her flat black lace-up shoes squeaking slightly as she went. Tim and Juliet followed in single file, and Tim saw that to an acute observer they would have presented rather a comic spectacle, trouping along as if they were part of a song-and-dance routine or some other frivolous activity. However, none of the old ladies whose chairs they passed, marooned like small islands in a brown parquet sea, bothered to look up and watch them. Most appeared to be dozing. There were no old gentlemen present, at least not in this part of the vast room.

As they approached Dorothy Atkins, she seemed to be entirely engrossed in the newspaper. Mrs. Meredith waited for Tim and Juliet to catch up with her, and then tapped Dorothy gently on the shoulder. She gave a little start. It was almost too theatrical.

"Hello, Matron," she said, emphasising the second syllable of the first word and looking up to smile beatifically into Mrs. Meredith's face. Her eyes were blank of emotion, however. Mrs. Meredith was clearly ill-at-ease.

"T-Tirzah," she said, almost stammering. "Here are your visitors."

Tirzah craned her neck so that she could look past Mrs. Meredith. Her hazel eyes met Tim's jade-coloured ones. She held out her hand.

"Pleased to meet you," she said. She did not ask his name. Her voice was characterised by its low monotone and flat Lincolnshire vowels.

"Pleased to meet you, too," he said, taking her hand and shaking it reverently. Her own was quite slender, but long-fingered and surprisingly rough to the touch. "My name is Tim Yates. I am an inspector from South Lincolnshire police."

"Tirzah." she said. She stared at him for a long minute. "That's the name I always go by now. My guess is that you are familiar with my history, so I won't take the trouble to retell it. Sit down, if you want to." She made an all-inclusive gesture at the other two chairs that had been pulled up to her table. Tim took the one immediately opposite her. She either did not see or deliberately ignored Juliet Armstrong, whom Tim also had forgotten until she slid noiselessly into the other chair. He hesitated and cleared his throat. He wondered why the woman made him so nervous: why she had evidently made Mrs. Meredith nervous, too. Glancing round, he saw that Mrs. Meredith had strayed away to talk to an old lady swaddled in tartan blankets who had been parked in a wheelchair on the other side of the room. Perhaps she had forgotten her promise – threat? – to stay with them.

"This is DC Juliet Armstrong," he said, after what seemed like a very long pause. Tirzah inclined her head graciously, but did not offer Juliet her hand.

While she was bowing to Juliet, Tim took the opportunity to inspect her profile more closely. On previous occasions when he had come face to face with a suspected or convicted killer, he had played a kind of game with himself, and he tried it again now. Was there anything in Dorothy Atkins' physiognomy that marked her out as a murderer, from his own experience of them?

Her face was long and sallow, the skin more brown than olive. It was an unattractive colour, but its texture was pretty good for a woman of her age, though her cheeks sagged and loose skin hung in a fold on her neck. Her hair was rather greasy, and combed straight back from her forehead in an unattractively severe style. She wore cameo earrings in ears that looked grubby, but that might just have been an effect of her sallowness. The hazel eyes were deep-set and small, topped by heavy untidy brows that made them seem yet smaller, but they were watchful. There was a large patch of darker brown skin on her high forehead. The residue of an old wound, perhaps? He realised that she had turned away from Juliet and was observing him with a look of amusement that could easily have turned into a sneer.

"It is a disorder of the skin pigmentation, Inspector. One

of the hazards of growing old." Embarrassed, Tim looked away.

She clapped her hand on his suddenly, so that he almost cried out in alarm.

"Aren't you going to tell me why you've come?"

"Yes, of course." He made himself refrain from recoiling. It was taking her a long time to remove her hand. Juliet leaned forward to help him out.

"Mrs. Atkins, do you remember that when you still lived at home your son Hedley was going for a while out with a girl called Kathryn Sheppard?"

She snatched the hand away, slightly grazing his skin with her thick talon of a thumbnail. She looked thoughtful. Was it an act?

"Tirzah", she said. "Please call me Tirzah. Now, what was the question?" She sounded confused, but shot Juliet a look of wicked alertness.

"Do you remember that your son once had a girlfriend called Kathryn Sheppard?"

There was a long pause.

"Not exactly," she said at length, and with studied caution. "I remember Kathryn Sheppard, but I don't think she was Hedley's friend. She was someone else's friend."

Tim didn't know how to respond to this cryptic utterance, but Juliet persevered.

"Whose friend? Can you remember?"

The swarthy brow clouded. She seemed to be struggling with her memory. She put her hand to her temple.

"I don't think I do remember, exactly. It was another girl. A pretty girl. She was very slender."

"Did you know this girl?"

"I'm sure I did." She put both hands to her forehead. "Now, who could it have been?"

"And this girl was a friend of Kathryn's?"

She nodded happily. "Yes. She was a very pretty girl. Kathryn was a pretty girl, too."

"And you're quite sure that you don't remember her with Hedley?"

"Hedley will have known her, of course. She came to the house. She must have done, otherwise I wouldn't have seen her. I don't go out much, you know. But Hedley doesn't like girls, does he?" She sniggered harshly.

"Hedley says that she was his girlfriend."

"Hedley would say that, wouldn't he? He doesn't want to get found out!"

"Found out about what, Mrs. Atkins?"

"Not found out about anything, found out for what he is."

"What is he?"

"Oh, you know!" She rolled her eyes and gave Tim's arm a playful little push. "I didn't much mind myself, but his father couldn't stand the idea. Neither could she."

"She? Do you mean Kathryn, Mrs. Atkins?"

"No, of course not. I mean her. Doris. Hedley's grand-mother. I had thought you'd come about her, you know. Whenever people talk to me, sooner or later they get on to her. I'd rather you didn't call me 'Mrs. Atkins', by the way. Atkins was her name, though she was always a 'Miss'. I'm Tirzah."

"Do you want to talk about Doris?" Tim butted in.

"If you like. But I don't really have anything to say. She shouldn't have liked gardening so much. Then it wouldn't have happened."

"We haven't come to upset you . . ." Tim began, aware that Mrs. Meredith had returned and was hovering in the background.

"Oh, I'm not upset. Doris made me famous. I can't think why. She was such an insignificant person herself. There was such a fuss about it all. And the irony of it was, I quite liked her. I had no reason not to get on with her. She was very clear-sighted about Ronald, for one thing."

Tim was aware of some movement behind Tirzah. He looked up to see Mrs. Meredith signalling to him quite ener-getically.

"Change the subject," she mouthed. He nodded.

"So you have no specific memories of Kathryn Sheppard that might help us, Mrs. . . . Tirzah?"

"I'm afraid not. Just another pretty girl. There are so many pretty girls, don't you find, Inspector?"

"Yes, indeed," said Tim, bewildered once more. He felt frustrated. It seemed impossible to lead this disjointed conversation into coherence. There was a prolonged silence. Then Dorothy spoke again. Her voice was harder now, her tone venomous.

"There is something you can do for me, if you would be so kind," she said.

"Of course, if we are able. What is it that you would like?"

"Since you are clearly in touch with him, you can tell that scapegrace son of mine to come and see me. He owes it to me. He knows that he does. He can't get away with hiding forever."

"What is he hiding from, Tirzah?"

"The same thing. The thing that I told you about before. But hiding doesn't work. He has to face up to it."

Once again Mrs. Meredith signalled frantically. She was shaking her head. This time Tim felt irritated. He supposed he must bow to her superior understanding of what Dorothy Atkins could take, and he certainly didn't wish to provoke an outburst of some kind; but if he were to be steered away from asking any really pertinent questions, the interview would simply be a waste of time.

"Such a ninny isn't she?" said Tirzah sardonically in a low, confidential voice.

"Who?" asked Tim, startled and a little disorientated. Was she speaking of the past as if it were the present? Did she mean Juliet? Or was she harking back to Doris Atkins, or even Kathryn Sheppard?

"That Meredith woman," said Tirzah, jerking her thumb behind her without looking round. "Always hanging around, trying to wrap us in cotton wool." She raised her voice. "It was a bit late for cotton wool, my dear, by the time I got myself in here."

Mrs. Meredith looked uncomfortable. Despite himself, Tim had to suppress a grin.

He thought it unlikely that he would manage to extract any more from Dorothy Atkins today.

"Well thank you very much, Tirzah," he said, rising and touching her hand, which was once again clutching a balled-up piece of her cardigan. "You've been very helpful. Perhaps you will not mind if I come to see you again?"

"You can if you like. I'm not sure what use it was, either to you or to me. But it is quite nice to have visitors." She nodded at Juliet, who had also got to her feet. "She doesn't say much, does she? What's the matter, dear, cat got your tongue?"

Mrs. Meredith had already slipped out of the room. Tim and Juliet followed her quietly, so they did not make the same spectacle of themselves as when they had entered it. When they reached the swing doors, Tim looked back at Dorothy. She had folded her newspaper neatly into four, and was looking at the crossword. She appeared to be absorbed, but he sensed that she was still acutely aware of their presence. He thought that a slight smile hovered on her thin lips, but he might have imagined it. The interview had left him feeling that he might have imagined anything – that anyone, in fact, might have imagined anything – about this woman, and would have had an equal chance of either getting close to the truth or straying a million miles from it.

He repeated this thought a couple of minutes later, when he and Juliet were back with Mrs. Meredith in her office.

"Well," he said, "what did you make of that? I'm absolutely none the wiser!"

She looked at him guardedly.

"What did you make of it?" she asked.

"She was much more confused than I had expected. Vague, somehow. As if she wasn't quite in control. I'm sure that you're right when you say that she can be very manipulative. It just didn't show itself today, that's all. Perhaps she has off days. She's quite old now, after all."

Mrs. Meredith looked amused.

"If that's what you think, Inspector. Personally I am convinced that she was stringing you along. Ars est celare artem where Tirzah is concerned. You might find it useful not to forget that."

"You think she was putting it on?" said Tim. "The confused little old lady act? If you're right, she was amazing."

"She is amazing, in her own way. Besides, she's a good observer. She has plenty of role models to show her how to play the confused elderly female. She'll do it again next time you see her now. You'll have to trick her into giving herself away."

"How will we do that?"

"The best way is to make her angry. But not so angry that she either loses her temper or withdraws into herself."

As Tim and Juliet were walking back to his car, he suddenly paused and turned to face her.

"She's given us one lead, anyway," he said. "Hedley Atkins. He's been co-operative so far, but no-one's put him under any pressure. He's simply been asked some routine stuff about Kathryn Sheppard. I think we need to press him a bit more about the past – and about his sister in particular. And we need to find out more about her, too."

CHAPTER TWENTY-FOUR

I know that I cannot put it off any longer. We have eaten an excellent lunch in the buffet car – tomato soup, sea bass with fennel and chocolate torte – and drunk a bottle of claret. Peter has drunk much less than usual – normally he would have been quite capable of downing a whole bottle of wine on his own, as well as a couple of gin-and-tonics – and it is clear that he wishes to remain sober. I understand that this is because he wants to be entirely alert when he is listening to my story; also that he will insist on hearing it now. I can tell by the businesslike way in which he is paying the bill that he will brook no further delays. We return to our seats. I note with relief that we seem to have almost the whole carriage to ourselves. The elderly lady and the woman with two small children have vanished, presumably absorbed back into their communities in the Scottish borders. The only other occupant of the carriage is a middle-aged man who is lying sprawled in one of the airline seats, his mouth open, his snores prodigious.

Peter hands me in to my seat as solicitously as if I were a girl on her first date, then settles in beside me. I have never really felt intimidated by him before – on the face of it, his slight figure and damson-fly personality hardly inspire fear, even when he is being spiteful – but now I find him threatening. There is a sternness about him, an implacable determination to be told all of the truth without nonsense, that I find very alarming. He takes my hand and I flinch.

"Do stop being so jumpy, Hedley," he says, still unsmilingly. "There is no need to be afraid. It is just an anecdote that I want – well, perhaps something a little longer – but nothing that should cause you distress. I'm sure that you recollect the events of that day and I want to hear you recite your memories. Nothing more nor less than that. No embroideries, no false amnesia. If you have genuinely forgotten some of the details, of course, you must say so. And rest assured that this is between you and me: no-one else will hear any version of your account, at least not from me."

I nod miserably.

"Let's start then, shall we? A bit of background first, I think. You got up that morning. Were you sleeping at the house in Westlode Street, or did you go there later on?"

"We were all sleeping there. I can't altogether remember why. I think that my father had been staying there off and on for some time, helping to look after my great-grandmother as she became more frail. Also Uncle Colin was not in the best of health. He had always had a hunchback, and the long pale face that seems to go with it. He had been born with his deformity and as far as I know no doctor had ever been asked to diagnose the cause of it. I suspect that he had a weak heart – perhaps had always had one. He had fallen in his room a couple of times, and my grandmother – Doris – no longer had the strength to get him into bed. Colin wasn't very tall, but he was quite solid and very unco-operative, I seem to remember."

"So why did your father want the rest of the family to stay there as well?"

"I honestly can't remember. More to the point, I can't remember why Tirzah agreed to it. As I've said, my father had been sleeping there for some weeks before we joined him. It wasn't like Tirzah to do what he wanted, especially when it involved her having to take on extra work. There was probably a reason for her having given in. A financial one, I'd say."

"You mean, your father bribed her?"

"Not necessarily my father. Colin was quite close to Tirzah. He may have offered to pay her to help with his mother."

"You were already working at the time, weren't you? Yet still living at home. Why was that?"

"I hadn't been working for very long. I didn't want to live with them. I was actually quite desperate to get away, although the terrible rows that they'd had in my childhood weren't happening as often by then. I just didn't have the funds to be able to move out."

I feel defensive about this. Peter nods, conciliatory.

"And Bryony? She was there, too?"

I have almost forgotten that he knows about Bryony.

"Yes. It was the summer before she was due to go to university."

"Tell me about the sleeping arrangements."

"Doris had the room that had until recently been her mother's – the master bedroom, I suppose you would call it. My great-grandmother could no longer climb the stairs. She now had a single bed in a tiny room off the kitchen which everyone still called the scullery. Colin's room was the same one that he had occupied as a child, next door to Doris's, I suppose because as a boy he had been cosseted by his mother, so she had put him in a room next to hers. It was a bleak little room. It didn't contain much more than a narrow single bed, a chest of drawers and a wardrobe. Tirzah and Bryony had the room that my grandmother called the 'guest room' – like her own, the bed had a deep homemade feather mattress – and my father was sleeping on the sofa in the upstairs sitting room that was never used for sitting in. It was a real Victorian 'best parlour', and much of the furniture in it was swathed in dust-sheets."

"What about you?"

"I had a camp-bed made up on the landing."

"Rather a curious set of arrangements, wasn't it? I could

think of more congenial ways of exploiting the facilities. For example, why didn't your parents occupy the guest room together and Bryony share a bed with your grandmother, thus leaving the sitting-room sofa free for you and removing the need for makeshift billets on the landing? Bedding outside the bedroom is always quite sordid, don't you think?" He wrinkles his nose.

I shrug. The sleeping arrangements had not bothered me then, and I have no intention of exercising myself over them now. I imagine that my father and Tirzah had been quite happy to sleep apart. They will have just made me fit in with whatever they preferred.

"So," continues Peter, "you all got up at the usual time?"

"I suppose so."

"When was that?"

"My father will have been up first. He was obsessive about his bathroom routine. He will have made sure that he got his fifteen minutes in before anyone else. I don't know exactly when he got up on that day; when we were at home it was at 6.45 a.m. on the dot."

Peter nods again.

"Let us assume that this day was no different. Who was next? You, presumably, if you were working?"

"I honestly can't remember, but I doubt it. Uncle Colin opened the shop every day at 8 a.m. My guess is that he will have claimed the bathroom after my father, and my grandmother will have got up with him. She still had a basin and ewer in her room from the days before the fourth bedroom was converted into a bathroom. She normally bathed the night before, then washed quickly in her room in the morning."

"So your father and his uncle and mother were almost certainly up before the rest of you. That left you, your mother and Bryony, and the old lady, of course, of whom only you and your father had to leave the house by a certain time because you each had a job to go to. Is that correct?"

"I'm not sure. Tirzah did have a job at that time, as a school secretary, but she didn't work in the school holidays. Bryony was about to go to university. She certainly worked that summer, in the canning factory, but I think she may have given the job up by then."

"What was your job? The same as it is now?"

"No. It was the same company, but I've changed jobs several times since. I was the shipping clerk for Maschler's, where I still work. Now, as you know, we produce precision implements of all kinds; but then it was just farming equipment. And I'm a director now."

"So you don't remember getting up on that day, or going to work?"

"No. I remember coming home for lunch. We were all there for lunch. I remember what we ate: it was chipolatas and mash, which was probably cooked by my grandmother, and for dessert we had treacle tart and custard, which was one of my mother's stock puddings. My grandmother and my mother seemed to be doing the work between them. I can't remember there being any friction. Uncle Colin wasn't there: he had decided to eat with my great-grandmother, and had taken his own lunch as well as hers into her room to be with her."

"What about Bryony?"

"I suppose that she must have been there, though I don't remember it specifically. I can't remember what she was wearing, or what she said. I don't think that any of us said very much, because there was a Test match on the television, and cricket was my father's passion. He won't have taken kindly to having the commentary interrupted by conversation."

"What sort of relationship did he have with your grandmother?"

"I think that it was OK. Doris was a very pragmatic person: she didn't expect too much of anyone. I suppose that the way her life had turned out had taught her to be tolerant.

She always seemed pleased to see him – but she was always pleased to see any of us – and they shared similar tastes in books. She would get the Sergeanne Golon *Angelique* books from the library and let him read them on her ticket before she took them back. She talked about her garden to him. She liked gardening."

"So your mother said, rather memorably."

I shrug. Peter is looking at me beadily again. My defences are raised, which he notices.

"So – then what?" he continues, "you and your father returned to work?"

"I suppose so – I really can't remember."

"Well, let us suppose that is what happened. So that lunchtime will have been the last time that you saw your grandmother alive. She was dead by the time you returned to the house. Is that correct?"

"Yes." I look down at my hands, resting on the train's table. My fingers are interlinked. I am clenching them until my knuckles are pale blue.

"Did you come home especially?"

"What?"

"Did you come home because you were summoned – did someone tell you that Doris was dead, or did you receive a message of some kind that you should return home because something had happened?"

"No. I just left work as usual. When I arrived at the house, the police were already there. My mother and father were in separate rooms. She was taken away by the police just after I arrived. They didn't let me speak to her. My father was giving a statement of some kind. My grandmother's body was lying in the corridor that ran the length of the shop, which Uncle Colin used as a storeroom. I wasn't allowed to look at it. It was covered over with a blanket."

"Did you ask to see it?"

" I – No. Why do you ask?"

"Just curious. People often do pay their respects to the

dead by taking a last look at them, don't they? But not necessarily when they are murder victims, I should imagine." He looks reflective for a minute, and then shoots out swiftly:

"And Bryony – where was she?"

"I – don't know. I don't remember either seeing her or talking to her."

"But she was there? She must have been there, somewhere."

"I really don't know. She could have been out visiting a friend."

"Oh, come now, Hedley, that's hardly likely, is it?"

"Why do you say that?"

"Because, my dear sweet disingenuous Hedley with the suddenly very faulty memory, an announcement about the murder had gone out on Radio Lincolnshire, on the four o'clock news. If Bryony had been out visiting someone, she would almost certainly have heard or been told about it after that; but as you know, the police are usually quite – I was going to say sensitive, but circumspect is probably a better word – when it comes to making sure that the relatives of suddenly deceased people don't get a nasty shock from the wrong quarter. And the Lincolnshire police were no exception, even then. They had rounded up all the members of the family and got them back at Westlode Street before any details were released to the media. Which leaves a few loose ends to be tied up in the story that you tell, as well as the many omissions that you claim not to be able to fill, doesn't it?"

I bridle.

"What exactly are you trying to say?"

"I'm not trying to say anything, dear boy. I am saying it. What I say is this: that the, by your own admission imperfect, story that you have just told me is actually just a load of fabricated bullshit. Now, would you care to sit quietly and work your way through this?" He hands me his folder of news clippings.

CHAPTER TWENTY-FIVE

Bryony Atkins had never been registered as a missing person, and Tim was well aware that he would be discouraged by his superiors from spending too much time on trying to trace her, when (they would argue) his main focus should be to track down Kathryn Sheppard's killer. Police resources were scarce, relatives needed results, there were other crimes that needed solving, etcetera, etcetera. There was only slender evidence to support his theory that Bryony and Kathryn had met similar fates: that Bryony was last heard of at around the same time as Kathryn, that they had known each other, and Dr. Hemingway's half-articulated suspicions. He would have to find some short-cuts if he was going to pursue this line of enquiry. Rather reluctantly, he picked up his phone and keyed in Ronald Atkins' number.

"Mr. Atkins? It is Inspector Yates again. I'm planning to carry out a few routine enquiries about your daughter."

"You're not thinking of digging up the garden again, presumably?"

Tim laughed reassuringly. "Certainly not. Nothing nearly as dramatic as that. I just want to know which school your daughter attended."

"St. Thomas's C of E Primary School." Was the man really so obtuse, or was he being deliberately obstructive?

"That's helpful," Tim said smoothly, "but what I'm really interested in is the secondary school that she attended: the school that she was going to when she applied for university."

"It was the Girls' High School, of course. It's still the only school in this town from which girls go to university."

"Of course – you're right. I should have thought of that. Although she could have taken her 'A' levels at an FE college."

"Is that all you want to know?"

"For the time being. Thank you very much for your help."

Was it Tim's imagination, or had Ronald put down the receiver rather precipitately?

He looked up the number of the school and called it. He introduced himself and asked to speak to the Headmistress, and found himself talking to a bossily efficient secretary.

"Mr. Cooper is our Headteacher," she said. "I believe that he is available at the moment. May I ask what it is about?"

"Just some routine enquiries – about an ex-pupil of the school."

"Oh – I see. Just a minute. I'll ask him if he will speak to you."

In a few seconds he had been put through. "Alex Cooper here," said a bright voice full of energy. "How may I help – Inspector Yates, is it?"

"Yes," said Tim. "I'm trying to gather some information about a girl who attended the school about thirty years ago. Her name was Bryony Atkins. Would you still have any records for her?"

There was a brief silence at the other end of the phone.

"It's possible that there are records," said Alex Cooper slowly, "but if they exist, they won't be here. The school was rebuilt ten years ago, and we started keeping all our records electronically then. There were files going back from the mid-1990s to the foundation of the school in the twenties, but we no longer had space to store them here. They were taken to County Hall, to be put in the archives there. The intention was certainly to archive them at the time, rather than destroy them, but of course I have no idea whether they have been destroyed since."

"Thank you, that is helpful. I will pursue this further as one of my lines of enquiry. I don't suppose that there is anyone still teaching at the school who was there in the early 1970s, is there? You didn't by any chance know Bryony Atkins yourself?"

Alex Cooper laughed. "I was barely out of nappies in 1972, Inspector. I came here as a head of department when the new school was built. I have certainly worked with colleagues who were here in the 1970s, but I'm pretty sure that they have all retired now. There was a little group who had taught here all their lives whom the education authority encouraged to retire together about three years ago. I think that they were the last ones from that period. Apart from Mr. Eggleton, of course."

"Who is Mr. Eggleton?"

"He also used to teach here, but he retired a long time ago. He is still with us in a voluntary capacity, though: he runs the Old Girls' Association. He is also writing a history of the school."

"Would it be possible for me to arrange to meet him?"

"I should think so. I'll give him a call, and ring you back. When would you like to come?"

"Would this afternoon be too short notice?"

"I don't know. I can ask."

It took Alex Cooper less than five minutes to return Tim's call. "He says he is free this afternoon. He'll be happy to meet you for tea, here at the school, if you would like to come at about 3.30 p.m. To tell you the truth, he likes nothing better than having an excuse to turn up here. The school has just about been his whole life and he's like a fish out of water when he's not doing something connected with it. His name is George, by the way."

George Eggleton turned out to be a large, untidy man with rheumy eyes and the dropped-down jowls of a bulldog. He was dressed in a green checked sports jacket and grey flannels, and wore tortoiseshell spectacles perched on the end of his nose. Tim thought that he had probably been dressed much like this for the whole of the four decades that he had worked at the school. From his appearance, his age was indeterminable, but he must have been in his seventies. He was already ensconced in the 'Headteacher's' office when Tim arrived, occupying the only easy chair. After introductions, the bossy secretary brought in tea. Alex Cooper, who was dapper and wiry with a shock of dark curly hair, declined when he was offered some, saying that he had other things to attend to, and excused himself.

George fixed his bulldog eyes on Tim, who saw intelligence twinkling there, despite their wateriness.

"Mr. Cooper tells me that you are interested in Bryony Atkins."

"That is correct. Do you remember her?"

"Of course I remember her: anyone who had been at the school when she was there would have remembered her, after the murder case. She was the girl whose mother killed her grandmother. But I assume that you are aware of this?"

"Yes I am. But what I'm more interested in at the moment is whether you have any recollections of Bryony. What was she like? What were her interests? Was there anything unusual about her?"

"You mean anything that made her stand out as the daughter of a killer?" George Eggleton's eyes twinkled again.

"Just any memories that you may have would be helpful."

George sat back in his seat and sipped at his tea, which had been served in the kind of sea-green thick-rimmed cups that Tim remembered from parents' evenings during his own school days.

"Of course I have some memories, though how helpful they might be I'm not sure. English and History were my subjects, and I taught her both during her time at the school. She wasn't outstanding at either, though she was always in the 'A' stream. But she was very good at Art. I used to produce the school plays, you know, and she always helped with designing and making the sets. She was good at that, too. Just a little bit shy, I seem to remember, and not good at taking criticism if anyone ventured any – but that is quite normal for girls of that age, or indeed people of any age, don't you think?"

"I agree. So there was nothing out of the ordinary about her?"

"No, nothing. Her brother, though – he was a different matter. Of course, he did not attend this school: he went to the Boys' Grammar School. There was none of that nonsense of sharing lessons in the sixth form that we have now. But he would come to wait for her sometimes when we were working on the sets. I thought that he was a very peculiar young man indeed."

"In what way?"

"He came to meet Bryony, but his attention was always focused on the other girls. I don't just mean that he fancied them – in fact, I don't think that he did. He seemed to be fixated with girls who were Bryony's friends. Not in a nice way, either. He would give them some very ugly looks. I really didn't like him, but I did not have sufficient reason to ask him to wait outside for her; for a start, I supposed I could have been imagining things. It was slightly odd for a brother to want to wait around for his sister at all, or so I thought. But then we're all odd in one way or another, aren't we?" He beamed at Tim, who almost forgot to return the smile because he was busy following a new train of thought.

"Mr. Eggleton, do you remember the Kathryn Sheppard case? She was a young woman of twenty-four who disappeared at around the same time that Bryony Atkins left school."

"I do remember it vaguely – they never found her, did they? Her disappearance didn't make such an impression on me as the Atkins murder, because she wasn't a pupil here. In fact, I don't think that originally she was a local girl at all."

"You're right, she wasn't. But she did go out with Hedley Atkins for a while. Then she met another man on a train, and broke it off with Hedley. But their relationship had been over for some time when she disappeared."

George Eggleton appeared to be losing interest. "Poor girl," he said. "I wonder what became of her? And what became of Bryony, for that matter, Inspector? Did she get into some kind of trouble? Is that why you are here?"

CHAPTER TWENTY-SIX

It was 4 p.m. on St. Valentine's Day and, as Tim looked out of the grimy window of the briefing room at Spalding Police Station, he noticed with satisfaction that the evenings were beginning to draw out at last. It would be light for at least another hour. He had just finished giving his team a briefing, or rather he had led their regular information-sharing session, backed up as usual by Juliet's painstaking work. Nothing of any great significance had been brought to light since the last meeting. There was a report from Andy Carstairs on what had been found during the excavations of the garden at Westlode Street, which was, precisely, nothing, unless you counted the long-buried skeletons of three dray horses. Ricky McFadyen was working with *Crimewatch* to rebroadcast the reconstruction of Kathryn Sheppard's last movements which had been filmed fifteen years earlier, with 'new evidence' – though there was precious little of that, except the details of the discovery of her skeleton and the decision to release the information that she had taken the Friday of the last week that she had been seen alive as holiday. Tim himself had tried and failed to interview Hedley Atkins again. He'd been told by Hedley's boss that he was taking a week's holiday in Scotland. It was a nuisance, but they didn't have sufficient evidence to take steps to trace Hedley and either demand his early return or travel to Scotland to interview him. They would have to wait until his holiday was over.

Following Tim's earlier praise, Juliet seemed to have got hung up on the textiles stuff again. He realised that she had taken her researches to the point where they could no longer produce anything useful: the problem was that although it might be possible to identify the actual roll of cloth from which a garment had been cut and therefore establish its exact date of manufacture, it was quite impossible to ascertain how long it had belonged to its owner, or indeed whether there had been more than one owner. The same went for the ring and the plastic Indian. He didn't like to discourage her, but tomorrow he would have to tell her not to spend any more time on such minutiae.

The whole team had now read the substantial police files on Dorothy Atkins' arrest and trial, as well as the slenderer ones covering Kathryn Sheppard's disappearance. He had encouraged them to do this, but he knew that there was a risk that they would find spurious links as well as real ones. He himself believed that the two murders of Doris Atkins and Kathryn Sheppard were linked in some way, but he continued to be sceptical about the nature of the link. He believed that it had yet to be proved that Dorothy had killed Doris and he was almost certain that she had not killed Kathryn. However, he was aware that his own brief account of his and Juliet's visit to the nursing-home did not cast Dorothy in a sympathetic light.

After the team had gone their separate ways, he had remained standing in front of the glass information panels for a while, contemplating Juliet's neat blue felt-tip handwriting and wondering if there really were any useful clues amongst all this welter of detail, or whether they were just collecting some elaborate and very expensive red herrings which would take them no further at all towards establishing the circumstances of Kathryn Sheppard's death.

There was a knock at the door, and one of the administrative staff came in. "There is a call for you, Inspector," she said. "It has come through on your direct line. Do you want me to transfer it to this room?"

It took him a while to register what he was saying. "Oh – no thank you – Sheila? – I will take it in my office." Immediately he knew about it, he had a feeling about this call. He even wondered if the caller might be Tirzah. He had deliberately ignored her since the meeting at the nursing home three days before, neither calling her nor asking for permission to see her again, hoping that his apparent indifference would precipitate the sort of productive anger that Mrs. Meredith had been talking about. He had been told that Tirzah hated to be slighted. For this reason he took his time now, ambling into his office and seating himself comfortably in his swivel chair before he picked up the receiver.

"This is Inspector Yates speaking."

The voice that replied was female, quietly modulated but obviously troubled. Not Tirzah, he knew that in an instant.

"Oh, hello, Inspector, this is Margaret Meredith. I thought you should know. Dorothy Atkins died earlier this afternoon."

"Died!" he exclaimed. "But how? She wasn't ill, was she?"

"Not as far as we know, Inspector, and as well as we can tell before we get the results of the autopsy, it wasn't suicide either. She seems simply to have slipped away."

"Indeed," said Tim, raising one eyebrow. She could not see this, of course, but it was clear that she caught his tone.

"Tirzah wasn't the suicidal type, Inspector. She may have driven other people to contemplate ending their lives, but she got too much enjoyment out of hers. Not necessarily innocent enjoyment, but I hardly need to tell you that."

"How did she die? Did she collapse? Was she already in bed?"

"Neither of those. In fact, she was sitting in the chair in the day room, where you last saw her. She fell out of the chair on to the floor. She was sitting with Irene – one of our more challenged guests – and according to Irene, she suddenly keeled over. The sister on duty heard a bump as she fell. We called our usual doctor, of course, but he said that she had been dead for some minutes when he arrived. He thought that her death had been instant. A massive heart attack, in all probability."

"Did Irene tell you anything else? Had she been talking to Tirzah?"

"Apparently she had. Tirzah went and sat with her and struck up a conversation. This was not unusual – I think I told you that sometimes she would befriend the guests, particularly the more confused ones; rarely the ones that were still mentally agile, for some reason. Irene can't remember much of what she said – I wouldn't expect her to be able to – but Natalia, one of the ward orderlies, overheard some of it. According to her, Tirzah was describing Doris Atkins' death."

"But you told me that that was a strictly taboo subject. You said never to question her about it."

"I did say that and I would give the same advice again, even now. I have seen several people approach Tirzah with the aim of finding out exactly how Doris died, and each time she has reacted either with near-hysteria or a stony silence. I don't think that she was simulating the hysteria, either. Something about Doris's death really freaked her out."

"That's hardly surprising, is it? Many women – many men, for that matter – may contemplate murdering their mothers-in-law, but few actually do it. Even a hard-bitten woman like Tirzah must have had difficulty in facing up to the fact that she was a killer."

"If you say so, Inspector." He remembered that she had used the same phrase once before. It was her way of telling him that she did not doubt that he was wrong.

"I don't suppose you are going to let me question Irene." He took her silence to indicate that his assumption was correct. "Is the ward orderly still there? I'm assuming that she is of sound mind, and reasonably coherent. Please tell me that she has not completed her shift and gone off home!"

"She has indeed completed her shift, but I have persuaded her to stay to talk to you. I had a feeling that that would be what you wanted to do."

"Thank you," said Tim, grabbing his coat. "I'll be there as soon as I can."

Tim arrived at the home barely thirty minutes later. He was shown straight to Mrs. Meredith's office. Margaret Meredith had moved her chair from behind her desk and had placed it next to the visitor's chair. She was seated on it, in close proximity to the occupant of the latter, and talking gently to a very small, very thin woman, who had a pasty complexion and mousy hair. The woman looked as if she had been crying. She was balancing a cup of tea precariously on her knee. As Tim entered the room, the tea-cup slid a few inches across her slippery pale blue nylon overall. She halted its glide and restored it to the centre of her lap. Tim noticed that her fingernails, which were bitten to the quick, had been varnished pillarbox red and that her hands were half-covered by the cuffs of the bulky long-sleeved grey sweater which she wore underneath the sleeveless overall.

"Inspector, this is Natalia Kopinsky. She overheard part of Dorothy Atkins' conversation with Irene Morris earlier today. She is one of our ward orderlies."

"Good afternoon," said Tim, extending his hand. Natalia did not take it. She gave Mrs. Meredith one fearful look and then rooted her gaze on the floor. He realised that she was much older than he had at first thought – nearer to forty than the twenty-five that he had originally supposed.

"May I sit down?"

"Of course. Bring that chair over for yourself," said Mrs. Meredith, indicating a dilapidated metal and canvas folding seat propped against one wall. "Would you like some tea?"

"Yes, please." He opened out the chair and moved it a few feet closer to Mrs. Meredith and the woman before sitting on it, but at the same time took care to preserve some distance between himself and them. He had divined straight away that this interview was going to require some care, if he were to get anything out of the woman at all.

He took the cup that Margaret Meredith passed to him.

"How long have you worked here, Natalia?" he asked gently.

"Six year," she said. Her voice was deep – almost guttural.

"Do you like it?"

"Yes," she said flatly, fixing her gaze on Mrs. Meredith.

"I understand you were working in the day-room this afternoon. Do you often work in there?"

"Not often, but there was a mess. Irene Morris she spill lemon barley water everywhere and the floor very sticky. That was earlier, before she sit with Tirzah. I had already mopped up, but supervisor say I should polish."

"So you had come back to polish after Irene started talking to Tirzah?"

"She not talk to Tirzah. Tirzah talk to her. Irene not talk much. I think she understand, though. I think she understand more than Tirzah realise."

"Can you remember what Tirzah was saying?"

"Yes, though it was hard to understand. But Irene seemed to understand perfect, the way she was looking at Tirzah. She was very upset. It was horrible. Tirzah say that her mother have to die because of what she knew. She said it several times. She said that everyone who knew secrets had to die if they couldn't be trustworthy. I think she was frightening Irene."

"Did she say anything else?"

"Yes. She said that when a young girl had her whole life in front of her, she deserved to be protected. That we owe it to young people to protect them. That she would do it again."

"And then what?"

"Irene was very afraid. She kept gasping, as if she couldn't get her breath. I went to get a nurse."

"The ward orderlies are instructed not to get directly

involved in the care of the residents, unless it is an emergency," said Mrs. Meredith. "Natalia did exactly the right thing by going to get help."

"Then what?"

"Natalia didn't go back with the nurse. Her supervisor wanted her to do something else. But the nurse reported that when she went to check on Irene Morris, she was sleeping peacefully in her wheelchair, and that Tirzah was seated at a table nearby, doing the crossword in today's paper. The nurse asked her if anything had happened to distress Irene, and Tirzah said that she had seemed agitated earlier, but that she (Tirzah) had just assumed that she was tired. One of the things that has always made Tirzah so difficult to deal with is that she sticks to the truth. You might not agree with her interpretation of the facts, but she always presents them accurately. Used to present them, I should say."

"I realise that she may not have anything useful to tell me, but may I speak to the nurse?"

"She's gone off-shift now. She's an agency nurse because we're rather short-staffed at the moment, so it was not possible for me to detain her beyond her contractual hours. She will be here again tomorrow, though."

"And Irene Morris?"

"I will show you Irene Morris, Inspector, but I would rather you did not try to question her. She is likely to become extremely agitated, even hysterical, and it is unlikely that she will tell you anything of value. She really is not capable of engaging in a dialogue – you will see what I mean. I'd be grateful if we could leave that until tomorrow, too. Do you need anything more from Natalia?" Natalia looked up as she heard her name. Tim wondered whether she had been following the rest of their conversation, or had just drifted off into a world of her own.

"Just one thing more," said Tim, addressing the orderly again. "You say that Tirzah said that her mother had to die. Are you sure that she said 'mother' and not 'mother-in-law'?"

"Yes. She say 'mother'. Just 'mother'."

"Thank you, Natalia. You have been extremely helpful."

She gave him a wan smile, and looked at Mrs. Meredith again.

"You can go home, now, Natalia. Thank you very much for staying to help."

When she had gone, Tim said "Why was she so upset? Did she like Tirzah?"

"Possibly. Tirzah tended to make friends of the ward orderlies – I think so that she could get them to fetch and carry for her, though officially it wasn't allowed. But I think that Natalia's really just upset by the fact of her death. Death is upsetting, isn't it, even when its cause is natural?"

CHAPTER TWENTY-SEVEN

She drifted in and out of consciousness; it did not feel like sleep. Someone was hovering over her; she sensed that it was not someone who wished her well, but she was too tired to care. She knew that she was in extremis and that perhaps this was the time for which she had been waiting for almost forty years.

Suddenly, she was back in that dark passageway again. She had not wanted to help Doris with her aged mother – although she had been shocked by her own mother's death, she was relieved that she had never had to care for her – and she had ignored Ronald's requests to oblige. Ronald never influenced her unless he wanted her to do something that she had herself already decided to do. But Colin was different. He was different because he owned the shop and the house, and, she knew, quite a lot of money, too. And doing what he wanted had come to be important for another reason entirely.

She had been surprised to see him on that Saturday, pedalling laboriously up the street on his grocer's bicycle, still wearing his shopman's coat – especially when Ronald and Doris had both said that he was ill – and even more surprised when he had dismounted at her gate. In the family it was well known that he ventured out only on Christmas Day and Good Friday, unless he was collecting some item that could not be delivered to the shop – such as cigarettes or bananas – or if the part-time schoolboy that he employed did not turn up to make deliveries. Besides, any reason that he might have had for wanting to see her alone had been suppressed many years before.

He had pushed open the wooden gate and clumsily steered the unwieldy bicycle through it. The pannier thing kept on dropping down and he had to hoist it up again. She had moved away from the net curtains in the front room window, and gone to open the back door for him. When he had not appeared, she had walked round the side of the house, and found him still fiddling with the bicycle, attempting to prop it up against the coal-shed.

"Uncle Colin!" she said. "This is a nice surprise. What brings you here?"

"Don't bother with trying to be pleasant, Tirzah. It doesn't suit you. And I'm not your Uncle. As you well know."

"No," she had agreed. She was uncertain what to do next, even embarrassed at his proximity after all this time. "Would you like a cup of tea?"

"I expect it would do me good. Since I've come all this way." The shop was barely a mile from Chestnut Avenue, but a mile was a long way for Colin to cycle.

He had unfastened the cycle clips which held the bottoms of his dark green corduroy trousers in the tight bunched cuffs that exposed the ends of his woollen long johns, and now he stumped into the house behind her. As usual, he was wearing heavy boots with hobnails – farmers' boots, really. She knew that they drove Doris mad because of the black scuffmarks they made on her red-tiled floors. There was not much fear of that sort of anger from Tirzah.

Colin had sat in one of the two fireside chairs in the dining-room, still wearing his grey trilby hat, while Tirzah had made tea in the kitchen. She had used the little brown teapot reserved for when she had a single visitor; nowadays, that usually only meant Doris. In the past there had also been Eliza. She had poured tea into one of her willow-pattern cups, using the strainer for once because she didn't want Colin to choke on tea-leaves. She had offered him a custard cream, which he had taken and mumbled with his almost toothless gums. They had sat in silence for some moments, the only sounds those of Colin slurping his tea and biscuits.

"I've come about Mother," he had suddenly said.

"Oh yes?" Dorothy had said brightly.

He had scrutinised her with his brown spaniel-dog eyes.

"Don't be thinking that I trust you, Dorothy: but I think we both know that you and I speak the same language. It's brass that interests us. And we share confidences too. Don't think I've forgotten."

She had opened her mouth to protest, but could think of nothing to say that at once conveyed her sense of outrage and still enabled her to maintain his 'loyalty', flawed though it was.

"Don't bother to squeak about it. It's a fact. I know you."

She had lowered her head and concentrated on her tea. She had never credited Colin with any powers of perception – no powers of anything very distinguished, actually, and certainly no morals, but she felt a sneaking admiration for the way that he had managed to prise their share of their father's inheritance from his two older brothers and Doris. He was not unaware of this.

"As I say, I don't trust you: but I can make it worth your while to work with me; and I can certainly put a spoke in your wheel if you don't. As you well know."

"What's the problem?" Dorothy had asked in a harsh voice which nevertheless wavered with fear. She was already weary of playing hostess to his curmudgeonliness. She deserved better from him, and he knew that she did. Yet she was terrified of what he might do, if pushed.

"Mother's not well and I don't trust Doris to look after her properly. Mother's been saying some strange things lately, about perhaps they were being hard on Doris when they decided not to leave her anything – her share being used up by taking in her bastard children – and all the rest of it. I don't know what started all of it. Mother and I have always been very close, and we agree about most things. But Mother's eighty-two now, and she gets confused. It's my guess that Doris has been working on her. Doris, and probably that spineless husband of yours, as well. I could never abide him, even when he was a little lad."

He had looked at Dorothy levelly. She had not known whether to agree with him. She had tried to look mildly insulted.

"Don't give me that prim housewife kind of a look. We both know that you agree with me." He had almost snarled the words. "I've had a lot to put up with in my time, I can tell you."

Dorothy had nodded, impatient for him to continue.

"I know Ronald's asked you to help with looking after Mother, and I know you've said no. I can't say as I blame you: there was nothing in it for you, was there? But I'm asking now. I'm asking you to come and help Doris with Mother, but more than that, to keep an eye on both Doris and Ronald. I don't want them getting rid of Mother before her time, though I don't think she can have long left with us now; and I certainly don't want them pushing her into doing something stupid about her will. I'll make it worth your while, don't worry about that."

"How do you mean, worth my while?"

Colin had looked crafty. "That would be telling, wouldn't it? Let's just say that I've got a bit put by and a sizeable piece of it will be yours straight away if you help. And I'll make sure that the shop goes to your bairns and not to Dick or Bob."

"That doesn't seem like a very sound promise. How do I know how much I'll get, or whether you will really change your will for the children?"

"You'll have to trust me. But I won't break my word. I think you know that. Besides," he had fixed her with the watery eyes again, "if you don't help, I'll tell everyone the truth about

Hedley. And I'll tell Ronald about that fancy man of yours. Unless you want him to find out? But I warn you that if you two separate, there'll be nowt for you or the kids from the Atkins family afterwards. That I do promise you."

Dorothy had felt as if he had suddenly gripped her by the neck and squeezed. How could he possibly have found out about Frank Needham? True, his mother was Colin's next-door neighbour; but Frank didn't even live in Spalding now. Colin was right about something else, too: eventually, she had intended to use Frank to escape from her marriage; but what really alarmed her was that Colin was implying that he would broadcast the truth about Hedley. Surely he would not really do that? She knew that she could not take the risk by calling his bluff. The Atkins family was strange: look at Doris. She had never made any pretence of having been married, unlike Dorothy's own mother. What Colin was saying was making her rethink, rapidly.

"If I come to help, the children will have to come, too," she said. "It will mean more or less closing down this house for a while."

"Hardly children now, are they? But that's all right. Doris will be pleased, if anything; and I quite like little Bryony. She cheers me up. I'm not so sure of that lad of yours, though. He's respectful enough; but he strikes me as being a bit of a big girl's blouse."

They had only been living at Westlode Street for a few days when Doris had died.

Tirzah was back in the gloomy passageway again. It smelt overpoweringly of fermenting apples, with an under-tow of Flash. Doris washed the floor in there every two or three weeks – a backbreaking job, moving all the boxes and putting them back again. She was scrupulous about hygiene because of the food safety inspector. She washed the floor in the shop every day, and wiped out the cupboard with glass doors in which Colin kept loaves of sliced bread and other baked goods from the Sunblest man. The food safety inspector would close Colin down if he found evidence of mice in the passageway. Doris worried about all the boxes of packets of biscuits and big containers of toffees stacked up there.

She kept her bicycle at the top end of the passage. There was a narrow door there which opened straight onto the street, for which she carried a key. Colin had a key as well, but he rarely used that door: deliveries to the shop that were to be stored were usually carried through it into the hallway, and then stowed in the passage from there.

Tirzah was entering the dark hallway from the dining-room, carrying a chamber-pot which she had just removed from the old lady's room in the scullery. It was a Victorian chamber pot made of china and decorated with red and blue birds, and it had a curious kind of hinged lid which offered some protection from the reek of its contents. She had just lit a cigarette to ward off the smell. She was taking the chamber pot to empty into the lavatory that Colin had recently had installed at the garden end of the passageway, to save him from having to make his way through the house to the outside privy when he was working. He was still loath to invest in proper toilet paper: there was a store of the squares of tissue in which oranges had been wrapped in both places. A further supply of these hung from a piece of string at the side of the old lady's bed. A commode had been installed so that she would not hurt herself by trying to get to the toilet in the night, and she had taken to using it during the day as well. The elaborate pot fitted snugly into the aperture beneath the seat.

Tirzah had heard a scuffle and then a thud, then more scuffling. It was an autumn afternoon and she had turned on the electric light on the landing, but there was no light on the stairs and none that she could see coming from the passage. The door of the passage stood ajar and she elbowed it open, cursing as a large wedge of grey ash dropped from her cigarette to the floor. It was so dark in the passage that she could not see anything at first, though she sensed that someone was in there. As her eyes grew accustomed to the darkness, she was able to pick out some of the details revealed by the weak ambient light. The first thing that she noticed was Doris's bicycle. It made a dark shape against the far door, its handlebars and the basket that was attached to them outlined by the dull light that managed to penetrate the stained-glass fanlight over the door. She could make out some of the stacked boxes as well. She thought she heard someone catch their breath, and stepped into the passageway to grope for the light switch; she knew that it was set in the wall to her left, at about shoulder height.

Her foot encountered something soft. She scrabbled for the light switch, but could not find it, so she crouched down carefully and laid down the chamberpot. She knelt and felt the soft thing with her hand, and thought that it was someone's arm. Touching it left a sticky trail on her fingers. She was suddenly very frightened.

"Who's there?" she said. She thought she could hear someone breathing.

"Who is it?" she said again. From the shop, she could hear Colin's radio droning out the news. As usual, he had it turned up almost as loud as it would go. She thought about screaming for him to come. But he might not hear; and if he did and there was nothing amiss she would have humiliated herself for no reason.

"Oh, it's you," said a voice. "Could be worse, I suppose."

The light was snapped on. It was a dingy little light – Colin was as mean with light-bulbs as he was with everything else – and she felt disorientated, as if she had suddenly stumbled into a film-set and was required to take part in an unknown plot. She looked down at her hand, and saw the blood. With dread, she allowed her eye to travel further, and saw that she was kneeling beside Doris's body. The blood on her hand was from a deep cut on Doris's arm. It was not the sort of wound that could kill. For a moment, Tirzah hoped against hope that her mother-in-law was not dead. But one look at that stricken face lolling at an impossible angle told her that this was naïve. She looked up at the now retreating form of her interlocutor.

"I didn't do it, but I'm not staying around here to prove it. You can do that. You'll be much better at it than me. Besides, it's all your fault really. All your fault. All your fault. All your fault..."

A doctor took hold of her wrist.

"You're a good woman," he said.

She smiled and slid away from him.

CHAPTER TWENTY-EIGHT

It was 9 a.m. on the day following Tirzah's death. Tim now had the perfect excuse to demand Hedley Atkins' return. No-one at Maschler's seemed to have been given an address in Scotland at which he could be reached, so he had announcements broadcast on the radio. *Will Mr. Hedley Atkins, of 12 Welland Villas, Spalding, Lincolnshire, who is believed to be on holiday in the Solway Firth Area, please contact Inspector Tim Yates of South Lincolnshire Police to receive urgent information regarding a close relative*. While he was waiting for this message to produce results, he decided that another visit to the house in Westlode Street would be worthwhile. He wanted to gauge Ronald's reaction to his former wife's death. He also wanted to look again at the passage in which Doris Atkins had died. This time he did not let Ronald know that he was coming.

For once, Westlode Street was not completely lined with parked vehicles on both sides of the road. The space in front of the shop itself was free. Tim wondered as he parked his battered BMW in the spot whether this meant that Ronald was out. In some ways it would be useful if he could see Doreen on her own – but if she wasn't there, either, the journey would have been wasted.

The house adjoining the shop – the one that Ronald had indicated had been the Needham residence – was narrower than its neighbour, and had no bay window. Its main front door was the twin of the door to the passageway which Colin had used as a storeroom for so many years, except that it was painted dingily in maroon. As Tim stepped out of his car, he became aware that the maroon door was shuddering. Eventually the person behind it succeeded in forcing it open. A tall, powerfully-built woman with frizzled grey hair stepped out and rushed swiftly across to him, with such urgent purposefulness that for a moment he was alarmed.

"Hello," he said. "Do I know you?"

"Morning. Probably not, but I think I know you: you're that copper who dug up the garden next door, aren't you? My name's Marjorie Needham. Miss. I heard the radio announcement for Hedley."

"Yes, I am indeed that copper," said Tim. Remembering the twitching curtains, he did not even show surprise. He remembered something else as well, and that set him thinking. Ronald Atkins had said, 'At one point there was a very large and rowdy family next door: the Needhams'. Why had he referred to them as if they were no longer living there?

"What were you looking for? In the garden, I mean?"

"I'm not quite sure. Evidence of some kind, I suppose. We didn't find anything, though, so I expect my hunch was wrong."

She wagged her finger at him, incongruously coquettish in her flowered house-dress and down-at-heel slippers. He saw that she was quite elderly, though he had not realised it at first because of her vigour and the way that she stood upright.

"A little bird told me that you were after Bryony Atkins' body. I wouldn't be surprised. You know no-one's seen her since around the time Doris died? She just vanished into thin air."

"Did you know Bryony?"

"Not well – she didn't live here, though she stayed over sometimes. Colin and his mother disapproved of my family, so we weren't really on speaking terms with the Atkins.

Except my brother Frank, that is: he carried a torch for Tirzah." She sniggered.

"For Tirzah? You mean for Dorothy Atkins?"

"There wasn't anyone else around here called Tirzah, was there? She was sweet on him, too. Had my mother in a fair old panic. Frank was engaged and Tirzah was married, see, and although people said that we were a bit rowdy as a family, we had our standards. Good Catholics, too. Mam needn't have worried, though. Frank lost interest in Tirzah after what she did. Well, anyone would, wouldn't they? That was when he started wondering about Bryony. He came up with the idea that she was in the garden, too."

"Why did he think that?"

"He saw something going on in the garden when he was here one day. In the early morning, it was. He said something to Tirzah about it, and he thought that she was – shifty, like – about it. He said that wasn't like her. Tell the truth and shame the devil, usually, she was. Besides, Bryony and Hedley were both staying in the house at the time, but only Hedley gave evidence at the trial."

"Frank may have been letting his imagination carry him away, even so. As you know, we've dug up the garden pretty thoroughly, and the only skeletons we've found were those of old dray horses."

She rolled her eyes at him. It occurred to Tim that she looked a bit like a mad dray horse herself.

"Ah, but you see, you didn't get all of it."

"I'm afraid I don't follow. Get all of what?"

"The garden, silly!" She nudged him in the ribs with her elbow. "You weren't to know, of course: though when I saw you, I did think of coming down to tell you. But Ronald wouldn't have liked it."

"Come to tell me what?"

"The garden was twice the size in those days. All of that land on the other side of the wall, where the inspection pits for the tractors are now, belonged to the Atkins then. It was mostly orchard – apples and pears. Ronald played there as a boy, and so did I, sometimes, when I was allowed – he was about my age, we were younger than Frank and Iris – and then his children played there too. Bryony and Hedley – funny names Tirzah chose, didn't she? That was where Frank saw the digging. Not in Doris Atkins's flower garden, which is where you were looking."

"Well, that is very interesting. Thank you, Miss Needham. Is he still alive – your brother, I mean?"

"He is, but he's not very – available, like."

"What do you mean?"

"He's in a home for old sailors, in Skegness – he spent some time in the merchant navy, you know. But he's partially deaf and almost blind; and his memory's not up to much, either."

"Even so, would it be possible for you to let me have his address? I promise you I won't distress him."

She laughed. "You'd have a job! I can let you have it if you like; but I don't think it will be much use. Oh Lord," she added, "here comes Ronald. Don't you go letting him know that I've been telling tales out of school. He won't be pleased; and Iris and I have enough trouble with them as neighbours as it is."

"Who's Iris?"

"She's my older sister: Frank's twin. We were the two unmarried girls, see, which is why we got the house. For looking after Mam, as much as anything. Iris is blind, too, but she's a lot sharper than Frank. It was Iris that Frank told about the garden. Close as could be, those two were. They told each other everything, right up until the time they took Frank away. Now I do have to go – Ronald'll be here in a minute. I'll leave the address tucked under your windscreen wipers."

Tim was about to suggest a safer arrangement, but she had already skipped away from him and was pushing at the door, trying to get it open again. Looking up the street, he saw Ronald Atkins approaching on foot. Ronald had his hands hunched in the pockets of his overcoat, and was looking down at the pavement. The soles of his shoes slapped the pavement heavily. Evidently he had not spotted either of them. Tim waited until Marjorie Needham had burst back into her house before turning to face Ronald, who was within five yards of him before he finally raised his eyes.

"Oh, it's you again."

His expression seemed to reveal some intense private misery, but he quickly reassembled his features into the half-suspicious, half-insolent smile that Tim remembered from their last meeting.

Tim extended his hand:

"Good morning, Mr. Atkins. May I express my condolences at the death of your former wife? Also, would you mind if I took up a little more of your time? There are one or two extra questions that I'd like to ask. I think you might be able to help me again."

"Forget about sympathy for Tirzah: you know what I thought about her. As for your questions: I don't suppose I have much choice really, do I?"

"It is your prerogative to refuse; but even if you don't co-operate, I can still ask you to come to the station; and I can get another search warrant, if I see the need."

"I see. Back to that again, are we? Well I hope that this time you'll leave the bloody garden alone. What's it to be now? Ripping out the chimneys?"

"Do you mind if I come in for a few minutes? Unless you prefer to conduct this conversation in public."

Tim looked meaningfully across at the Needhams' house. Ronald was just quick enough to see the lace nets shimmer as someone moved away from them.

"Probably best if you do come in," he said grudgingly. "They're a right pair of nosy bitches, those two." He fiddled with the bunch of keys that he drew from his pocket, and selected two large shiny Chubbs.

Ronald had closed the shop when Colin had become too

ill to run it, more than twelve years ago now, but the front of the house had never been returned to domestic use. From the outside, because of the frosted glass, it still looked like a shop: even down to the detail of someone's having hung a 'CLOSED' sign permanently in one of the windows. Inside, the floorboards were bare, and the worn Victorian shelves stood empty. Two ancient disused fridges were huddled in a corner. The high stool that Colin had sat on at the counter was still there. Otherwise, there was nothing but dust. It was a ghost room. It felt very cold.

It was Ronald who was shivering, however.

"Come through," he said peevishly. "There's no point in standing around in here."

Tim followed him into the Victorian dining-room that he had barely taken in on his first visit, preoccupied as he had been with getting Doreen Atkins on his side. He looked around him now, and saw a room decorated in dark cream and green, with two outsize stuffed chairs covered in dark green leather by the fireplace. There was a gilt ormolu mirror over the fireplace, and, on the other side of the room, a marble-topped chiffonière over which another heavy mirror was suspended. Above this was a reproduction of *The Thin Red Line*, so that the picture was repeated in an endless corridor of images between the two mirrors. The effect was unsettling. The centre of the room was dominated by an unwieldy square table with bulbous legs, on which a dark crimson red cloth had been placed. A heavy green curtain hung over the door that led into the shop. As well as the picture, the walls were decorated with sets of sepia photographs of the children of a large family, mounted in threes in oblong passé partout frames. Somewhat incongruously, a 1950s radiogram stood in the corner nearest the window. Only the curtains, made of some kind of light-coloured chintz patterned in pale green, relieved the gloom. Doreen's touch, Tim supposed. Aside from the radiogram, the rest of the stuff looked as if it had been there for a hundred years.

Where was Doreen?

"Is your wife out, Mr. Atkins?"

"Yes – No. Not out in the sense that you mean. She's away visiting her cousin for a few days."

"Indeed? When will she be back?"

"Oh, Saturday or Sunday, I should think."

"You don't sound very certain."

Ronald Atkins tore off his overcoat and threw it at one of the armchairs. He took off his jacket as well, and loosened his shirt collar, although the room was not noticeably warmer than the shop had been. He sat down heavily on one of the hard dining chairs.

"I'm not certain. Doreen's upset – very upset – and you lot don't help. At least she's not here to see that you've come back again. She says that this place gives her the creeps, that it's full of unsolved business. She's been talking to the neighbours, too, and they've put ideas into her head. That's why she's gone away. I don't know when she'll be back – or even if she will."

"What sort of ideas, Mr. Atkins? Have they been talking about your daughter Bryony, perhaps?"

Ronald Atkins blanched visibly. He looked at Tim unsteadily for a moment and then dropped his gaze to the red plush tablecloth and kept it there.

"Well, don't you have anything to say, Mr. Atkins? Can you tell me why Bryony is not mentioned in any of the statements or reports about your mother's death? Or where she went to after she left this house? She was staying here when your mother died, wasn't she? The whole family was. When did Bryony leave and where did she go? Or perhaps she didn't leave. Why is it that no-one has heard of her for more than thirty years? And even more to the point, why haven't you tried to find out where she is?"

Tim became conscious of the fact that he had raised his voice and, because he was still standing, that he was towering over Ronald, who had now folded his arms across the top of his head.

"I apologise," Tim said. "Let us take this calmly, one step at a time. May I sit down?"

Ronald nodded.

"Would you like a drink? A glass of water, perhaps?"

Ronald nodded again.

Tim opened the door that led into the bleak little kitchen, and found a blue and white striped pottery mug on the draining board. He gave it a cursory rinse, and filled it with water from the tap.

"There you are." Ronald Atkins lifted the mug to his lips in a perfunctory way, and put it down again.

"Are you ready to talk now?" Ronald nodded.

"First of all, can you confirm that your daughter Bryony was indeed staying in this house at the time of your mother's death?"

"Yes, she was."

"Why wasn't she mentioned in any of the police reports about the death, or called as a witness during the inquest and your former wife's trial?"

"I don't know. She'd gone away by then. Dorothy didn't want her to be involved."

"When did she go away, exactly?"

"I don't know. Some time before it happened. Very shortly before, I believe."

"By 'it', you mean your mother's death?"

"Yes."

"Where did Bryony go?"

"I'm not sure. Dorothy said that it was something to do with the university course that she was about to start. Bryony and I weren't close."

"Evidently. But I had understood that you and Dorothy weren't 'close', either. Am I now to understand that you and she worked together to orchestrate the evidence? In short, that you conspired together to present your own version of events?"

"Not exactly. Dorothy just said that as Bryony had not

been there, it was unnecessary to involve her in the court case, just when she was starting a new life. I saw no reason to disagree."

"You are aware that as well as the considerable notoriety that she achieved for herself, your wife was also famous for telling the truth?"

"Yes."

"You don't disagree that honesty was one of her positive attributes?"

"No."

"Mr. Atkins, you will forgive me for saying that I think it rather odd that you have come up with this explanation only after the death of the former Mrs. Atkins. Is that because she is no longer able to contradict your version of events?"

"I don't know what you mean."

"Let us return to Bryony. If what you say is true, she departed for university shortly before your mother's death, and did not return. She also did not attend either her grand-mother's inquest or her mother's trial and, as far as we know, she did not contact her mother – to whom you say she was 'close' – during all the years that she was in prison. In addition to this, her National Insurance number has not been used since she worked as a part-time waitress during that summer and there is no record of her having attended Reading University, although she did win a place there. If this sequence of facts were related to you as an impartial listener, about someone you did not know, what conclusion might you draw?"

"I don't know. Hedley thought that Bryony was ashamed of her family after the news came out and built a new life for herself, with a new identity."

"Does he have any evidence of this? Do you think it likely?"

"I don't know. Look, if you're going to keep on question-ing me like this, you should let me have a solicitor present."

"Fair point, Mr. Atkins. We'll leave it there. But I shall need you to accompany me to the station, so that I can repeat some of these questions formally, as you point out, with your solicitor present. I will tell you that I am also going to arrange for a warrant to search the works yard of the tractor company next door. I believe that your family owned the land at the time of your mother's murder?"

"Yes," said Ronald. Tim had hoped that this last statement would hit Ronald Atkins like a bombshell: but it seemed to cause no particular emotion in him. "Shall I call my solicitor now?"

"You can do that from the station."

Tim led Ronald Atkins back through the ghost shop again, holding tightly to his arm while he locked the door, though he doubted that the septuagenarian would try to make a run for it. He also doubted that his own safety was at risk while driving with Ronald in the car, though strictly speaking he knew that he should have called for a patrol car. When they reached his vehicle, he saw a scrap of paper tucked under the windscreen wiper. Lifting it out, he found that it had been painstakingly inscribed with an address in Skegness, spelt out in clear, childish capital letters by a hand unused to writing much. He tucked it into his pocket.

CHAPTER TWENTY-NINE

Peter hands me the file of newspaper clippings. I tell him, truthfully, that I have never read an account of the trial before and that I am likely to become emotional as I read it. I ask him to let me read it by myself. I grab the pink folder and take it into the vestibule at the end of the carriage. There are two little flip-down seats attached to the wall next to the lavatory. I sit down on one of these and start reading.

Peter's researcher friend has done a good job. The first clippings are from the *Spalding Guardian* and dated two days after my grandmother died: 4th September 1975. The Spalding Guardian is a weekly newspaper, which will explain the short delay that had taken place between my grandmother's death and the publication of the story. The story was plastered all over the front page, though the actual report was very short. Most of the space was taken up by several very grainy photographs of the shop and one of an ambulance parked outside it, though rather quaintly no individuals were named.

Police called to the premises of a local shopkeeper on Tuesday 2nd September confirm that they discovered there the body of a sixty-three-year-old woman in the residential part of the building, on the ground floor. Chief Inspector Richard Cushing, making a brief statement to the Press, said that the circumstances of the woman's death were suspicious, but that he could release no further details. It is understood that a forty-five-year-

old woman is helping with enquiries. The owner of the shop and his very elderly mother are being comforted by relatives.

Next door neighbour Miss Marjorie Needham said that she had heard shouting and sobbing coming from the house at approximately two-forty p.m. on Tuesday afternoon. This was unusual: her neighbours were very quiet people who kept themselves to themselves, when not working in the shop. However, she knew that they had visitors staying in the house and she had thought that the screams and other noises that she had heard must be some kind of game. She therefore hadn't attempted to visit her neighbours to enquire if all was well and she certainly did not think that what she heard warranted calling the police. When asked if she had considered that a burglary might have been taking place in the shop, she declined to comment.

The shop is a convenience store situated in Westlode Street, and has belonged to the same family for more than eighty years.

The next cutting, from *The Lincolnshire Free Press*, is even briefer. It describes Tirzah's appearance at Lincoln Assizes when she is charged with murder.

Mrs. Dorothy Mary Atkins was charged with the murder of Miss Doris Ann Atkins, which was alleged to have taken place on the afternoon of 2nd September at 36, Westlode Street, Spalding. Mrs. Atkins, who was wearing a purple suit and black blouse, did not speak except to confirm her name and address. No plea was entered. Mr. Justice Evans, presiding, said that the accused should be remanded in custody pending the preparation of psychiatric reports. Responding to a request for bail from the defendant's solicitor, Mr. Liam O'Donnell, the judge, said that bail could not be granted because he did not accept that if freed Mrs. Atkins was not likely to harm either herself or others.

After this come several clippings from different newspapers speculating on what had happened in the house and why 'Dorothy Mary Atkins' might have murdered her mother-in-law. Peter has folded all of these in half, presumably to remind himself to skip them because they are really only a record of journalistic water-treading, of keeping public interest alive until the case is heard in court. I riffle through them, nevertheless. One of them interests and annoys me in equal parts: a luridly sensational account from Ronald Atkins of his marriage to my mother, complete with his own analysis of her mental condition. This was published in a magazine called *People's Post*. It is followed by another short clipping which records that Ronald Atkins has been reprimanded by the judge following a complaint from the defence for divulging the information and opinions contained in this article, and has been forbidden to talk further to the media on pain of contempt of court. I wonder if it is because of the article that my mother became so notorious. I have never quite understood why the whole country became so obsessed with the murderess of one little old lady. After all, murders happen all the time.

There follows a substantial sheaf of clippings from several national newspapers describing the actual court case. Once more Peter's 'little researcher' has served him with assiduity; she has included stuff from the whole spectrum of news on the subject, from the lurid to the learned. She seems to have found more about the case in *The Times* than other publications, however, and I decide to read the articles from this newspaper in sequence.

Although the accounts stretch to many pages, the most striking thing about them is how little happens during the court hearings, and how slight is the amount of admissible evidence presented. My mother refuses to enter a plea. Uncle Colin is called but can recollect nothing – his mother, my great-grandmother, has died in the interim and clearly the surge of grief that he feels at her death far eclipses any thoughts or feelings he may harbour for Doris. My father is called as a witness, but says that he only arrived after Doris was dead. However, he is questioned at length about his marriage to my mother and provides chapter and verse about how difficult she is to live with, though in more restrained terms than were used in the magazine article. Miss Needham tells her story of strange noises that nevertheless did not strike her as alarming enough to interfere with her neighbour's privacy. And so on. No-one actually admits to having seen my mother kill my grandmother and all the evidence against her is circumstantial.

And then, since she still refuses to plead one way or the other, Liam O'Donnell offers a plea on her behalf: guilty.

After this, Dr. Bertolasso says that she had a ragbag of psychiatric problems, including depression, narcissism and borderline personality disorder. He is asked to elaborate particularly on what he means by 'narcissim' and how it might affect someone who has been accused of murder. Mr. O'Donnell objects to this on the ground that the narcissim and the charge of murder are two separate 'events' that should not be conflated. His objection is upheld.

CHAPTER THIRTY

Ronald Atkins's solicitor was a surprise. A tall, broad woman with a nest of ash-blonde hair, she arrived in a flurry of intense perfume and leopard-printed chiffon, announcing breathlessly that she had been delayed during her drive from Peterborough (so that was why he didn't recognise her, Tim thought: she wasn't a local) by cows on the road. Tim immediately marked her down as 'fluffy' and decided that she wouldn't cause him any problems. He was shortly to regret this snap judgment.

"Detective Inspector Yates," he said, holding out his hand. "Thank you for coming."

"Jean Rook," she replied. She extended her own hand, which was tipped with formidable red talons. "Where is my client?"

"I'll take you to him. Would you like some time alone with him before we start?"

"That would be helpful, Inspector," she said levelly, suddenly transformed into a professional woman, despite the tight black skirt that was slit on one side and the filmy leopardskin blouse. She followed Tim down the corridor, not teetering at all on her four-inch stiletto heels.

Ronald was sitting at the square white table in the incident room in much the same pose that he had adopted at the table at Westlode Street. He rose to greet Ms Rook. She shook his hand and nodded a firm dismissal at Tim.

"Five minutes," he said, as she closed the door on him.

He returned exactly five minutes later, with Juliet Armstrong. Ms Rook and Ronald Atkins were sitting bolt upright on the far side of the table. Ronald was looking, if not arrogant, much more confident. Ms Rook simply looked very stern.

"This is DC Juliet Armstrong," Tim said. "She will be responsible for recording the conversation." He gestured to Juliet to sit at the smaller table which had been placed near the door, upon which sat a tape recorder.

"Have you cautioned my client, Inspector Yates?"

"No," said Tim. "At the moment, there are no charges. I want to continue to ask Mr. Atkins some questions that I began to put to him at his home, but which he very properly said that he would only answer with a solicitor present."

"But he did answer some of your questions?"

"Yes."

"Did you take notes at the meeting?"

"No. It was an informal meeting."

"Then I suggest that you expunge it from the record completely – even from memory. As you know, there is no prospect of your being able to use it as evidence in a court of law. If you wish to ask those questions again, you may of course do so in my presence."

"Thank you," said Tim, giving a slight bow. "That is precisely what I intend to do."

Jean Rook placed her elbows on the table and listened intently as Tim began his interrogation.

"Let us start again. Mr. Atkins, why was your daughter Bryony not called as a witness at either the inquest into your mother's death or at your first wife's trial?"

"My client need not answer that question," said Jean Rook immediately. "The responsibility for calling witnesses on either of the occasions that you mention clearly did not devolve upon him."

"Very well. Point taken. May I ask you, Mr. Atkins, whether

your daughter Bryony was at the shop in Westlode Street at the time of your mother's death?"

"Mr. Atkins should not answer that question, either, Inspector. It is my understanding that he was not on the premises himself when his mother died. Therefore, any response that he could give would only be conjectural, and consequently misleading."

Tim inclined his head again. The woman was beginning to annoy him, though he was determined that she should not see it. Juliet, sitting at her small table alone, recognised the signs – the momentary clenching of his fingers against his palms, the setting of his jaw which he quickly transformed into a wry smile – and hoped that he would be able to maintain his normal detached and courteous manner. If he did not, she knew that the solicitor would be likely to score a victory.

Tim stood up and leaned against the main table in the interrogation room. He bent forward for a while, as if in thought, so that neither the solicitor nor Ronald Atkins could see his face. He stood like this for some time, until the room became very silent. Ronald Atkins began to look uncomfortable. Jean Rook did not move. She continued to stare at Tim, and tried to make him meet her eyes when eventually he did look up.

He outwitted her by raising his head suddenly and thrusting his face at Ronald Atkins so that he was forced to meet his gaze.

"When did you last see your daughter?" he rapped out. He realised that the question sounded almost comic, put that way, but Ronald was not laughing. His face was the colour of parchment.

"I don't know. At some point during the autumn in which my mother was killed."

"That was in 1975?"

"Yes."

"Was it before or after your mother's death?"

"I'm not sure . . ."

"Don't insult my intelligence, Mr. Atkins! Two things happened that autumn, two calamitous things as far as you were concerned, or at least so I should suppose: your daughter disappeared and your mother died a violent death, for which your wife was convicted of murder. Are you really trying to tell me that you can't remember which of these things happened first?"

"Inspector, you are behaving in an intimidating way. I must ask you to sit down." Jean Rook got her remark in quickly, while Ronald was still trying to decide what to say.

"I apologise," said Tim grimly, taking his seat once again. "Do you allow, Ms Rook, that the question is a fair one, and one that I may expect to get an answer to, if put in a civilised way?"

"On the face of it, yes," she said levelly, meeting his gaze. She put her hand on Ronald's wrist. This was clearly a signal that she had prearranged with him to warn him not to speak. He sat there mute as one minute stretched out into two. Eventually, Ms Rook spoke again.

"Well, Inspector? You offered to put your question in a civilised manner. We're waiting."

Juliet thought that Tim would explode. Instead, he took a deep breath and hung his arms down by his sides. She could see that he was trying to relax his shoulders.

"Mr. Atkins, would you mind telling us whether the last time you saw your daughter was before or after your mother's death?"

"It was before it."

"Was your daughter still staying in the house at Westlode Street when your mother died?"

"Yes, in the sense that my whole family had made their home there temporarily, so that my then wife could help my mother look after her mother. But I did not see Bryony on that day, and Tirzah – my wife – subsequently told me that she had gone to Reading University to make some arrangements prior to the start of term."

"She would have been a first year student at Reading?"

"Yes. She left school that summer."

"So the reason that she was not called as a witness was because she had not been in the house at the time?"

"Inspector, I have already . . ."

"Yes," said Ronald quietly.

Then why make a mystery of it, Tim thought. He did not say it aloud, because he knew Ms Rook would say that he was being antagonistic.

"As I've already mentioned, Mr. Atkins, there is no record of your daughter ever having attended Reading University, though it is true that she was awarded a place in the summer of 1975. Also, her National Insurance number was not used again after that summer. Did you have any contact with her after your mother's death?"

Ronald Atkins took a long time to answer.

"No," he said. The word seemed to choke him.

"Did you not think it odd that she didn't contact you – write or telephone? Did you perhaps know, or think, that she was in touch with your wife, or your son? Did either of them mention her to you?"

"No." The same strangled voice.

"What did you think had happened to her?"

Ronald cleared his throat.

"I thought that she had probably been traumatised by her grandmother's death and her mother's conviction for murder. I thought that she might have changed her identity. Hedley thought so. I think that it was him who first suggested it."

"Indeed. Did it never cross your mind that it might be a good idea to report her as a missing person?"

"No," said Ronald Atkins. Suddenly he seemed to have regained some of his confidence, as if he was back in a part of the script that he had rehearsed properly. "I was very shaken up by what had happened. I had to take some time off work to recover. It was only some months later that I really thought about what Bryony might be doing and then Hedley reassured me with the explanation that I have given you. I did not think that it was up to me to try to track her down if she had been able to make a happy life for herself without any of the bad publicity that was sticking to the rest of us." His voice was almost sanctimonious now.

"Thank you, Mr. Atkins. One last question."

Ronald Atkins met his eye tremulously.

"How do you feel about Bryony now? Do you feel sad that all these years have gone by without your knowing where she is or what she is doing? Would you like to see her again now?"

"I . . . no, I don't think that I would. All of that is past and buried. We are left with what we're left with. Nothing can change the past. Nothing can bring the Bryony that I knew back."

Tim was watching him closely as he spoke. He did not look sad, or even wistful. No, Tim thought, the expression stamped all over his face was one of fear: fear for himself, in all probability.

"Is that all, Inspector?" asked Jean Rook.

"Yes, thank you Ms. Rook. Thank you, Mr. Atkins."

"In that case, I assume that Mr. Atkins may go home now?"

Tim nodded his assent.

"But please don't go away from the town without telling us, Mr. Atkins. We may need your co-operation again in a day or so."

CHAPTER THIRTY-ONE

Tim Yates was not a man who was easily depressed, but he did not like seaside towns. He particularly disliked east coast seaside towns in the middle of winter. He was therefore in a bleak mood as he drove the forty-odd miles from Spalding to Skegness, particularly as he suspected that he had embarked upon a wild goose chase. He'd also had quite enough of old people's homes. He imagined that this one, a retreat for old sailors, would be even more depressing than Elmete Grange had been. Despite Marjorie Needham's warnings about her brother's current state of lucidity, however, he knew that he had to at least try to get some sense out of the old man, always supposing that he knew something that it was worth the effort of making sense of.

He parked his car in a park near the seafront, and shuddered as he stepped out of it to walk along the promenade. A cold North wind was whipping in off the sea. Far out, across the grey and choppy waves, he could see a ship – a tanker, probably – making its way stolidly along the coastline. A couple of teenagers were playing on the beach with a dog, which was making wet sand spray in their faces, and two or three solitary figures walking ahead of Tim were bending their heads into the wind. Otherwise, everywhere was deserted. All the vendors' stands were boarded up for the winter and the Ferris wheel stood still, its cars rocking crazily with each gust of wind. Even the cafés that Tim passed were closed.

Newton Court consisted of a row of long, low buildings that took up almost the entire length of Newton Road, which was a shortish street leading directly off the promenade. The buildings were made of red brick faced with pebbledash, and dated, Tim guessed, from the middle of the nineteenth century. Each was a separate small house, two storeys high, with two windows on either side of a door that was reached via a short path, and two above them. The houses were joined to each other by a series of archways, but they did not form a terrace as such. The roofs were apparently flat, since they could not be seen, but were obscured from view by fake battlements. The windows had shutters, which were painted a dull green and appeared to be permanently fastened back against the pebbledash. An alcove had been built into the wall between the two upper windows of the middle house. It contained a wooden sculpture of a sailor leaning against an anchor, holding some rope and netting in one hand and a fish in the other. It was brightly painted in primary colours. The whole enterprise had probably been the whimsical architectural brainchild of some wealthy Victorian philanthropist.

Since the residents each seemed to occupy a separate dwelling, Tim reasoned that it was probable that they were relatively self-sufficient. Therefore Newton Court might not be a 'home' in the Elmete Grange sense, but was more likely to consist of what local councils were pleased to call 'sheltered accommodation'. That this might be the case cheered him up a little, though he was puzzled as to how it might square with Marjorie Needham's description of her brother's blindness and mental confusion.

Tim had not contacted anyone to tell them of his visit, and supposed that first he had better try to find the matron of the place, or whatever was the title that the person who ran it went by. He climbed the steep steps that led up through the central archway – Mr. Philanthropist had had little thought for elderly legs and a sailor's imperfect sense of balance on land when he had designed these – and found himself standing in an enclosed grassy rectangle. There were seven of the almshouses on each side of it, making the whole complex much larger than he had at first thought.

Tim took his bearings. The place was not just quiet: it seemed to be deserted. Yet there were curtains at all the windows, and everywhere was neat and tidy. The windows looked polished, the doors were freshly painted, the gardens well-tended. He was walking along the gravel path which divided the lawn into two, uncertain whether to try knocking on one of the doors, when he saw an arrow painted in black paint on the wall next to the central archway of the far block of buildings, with a small wooden plaque above it. The word 'Warden' was inscribed on the plaque in capital letters.

He walked towards the archway, and saw a door set into the wall beneath it, with an illuminated bell to one side of it. He was about to ring the bell when the door opened, and two women dressed in nurses' uniforms came out. They were both young, and chattering noisily. The taller of the two saw him first, and stopped talking to her companion in mid-sentence. They viewed him warily.

"Can I help you?" the taller one asked, after a short silence. "If you've come to see one of the residents, visiting hours are from two 'til four in the afternoon."

Tim showed her his ID card.

"Detective Inspector Yates, South Lincolnshire Police. I've come to talk to the warden. Is she in?"

The women relaxed a little. The taller one laughed.

"The warden's name is Jack Denning. Captain Jack Denning. He's always here, except when he's on leave. If you'd like to wait in here, I'll ask him if he'll come out to see you. I think he's still in his office at the moment. He won't have started his rounds yet."

She held open the door for him, while her shorter colleague stepped to one side to allow him to pass. Tim discovered that he had been ushered in to a small anteroom, or waiting room. It was painted a dull cream. Two rows of three chairs faced each other across a small table and there was an electric fire mounted high on the wall. The walls were decorated with posters about hygiene and emergency first aid procedures. There was a green baize board bearing notices of visits from the mobile library and the occupational therapist and a calendar listing social events such as a concert and 'film night'.

The taller nurse disappeared through the other door in the room, which obviously led deeper into the house. The shorter nurse hovered, apparently not sure of whether or not to make conversation, but clearly determined not to leave Tim on his own. Tim stood under the electric fire reading the notices on the notice-board.

The taller nurse was gone for some time. When she returned, she was preceded by a powerfully-built man of about fifty-five. He was dressed in a naval uniform. He extended a large hand and, when Tim held out his own in response, crushed it for an unpleasantly long time in a fierce grip.

"Captain Denning," he said. The two nurses melted away.

"Detective Inspector Yates, South Lincolnshire Police."

"What can I do for you?" Tim realised that Captain Denning was some three inches taller than he was, and was looking down his nose as he spoke in a clipped, business-like voice. There was a slight burr to his speech; Tim thought that he might have come from the West Country. Evidently he was no great respecter of the police.

"I'm investigating a murder – that of Kathryn Sheppard, whose skeleton was discovered by the side of the A1 two weeks ago. You may have seen something about it in the news, or in the papers. I'm trying to trace people who may have come into contact with Kathryn in the last few months of her life. One of her friends was a young woman called Bryony Atkins. We think that Bryony stayed for a while in a house next door to the house which was occupied by the sisters of one of your residents."

"I see. A bit of a tenuous link, isn't it?"

"It would be, if that was all there was to it. But we have reason to believe that the resident had formed a relationship with Bryony's mother – in short, that they were having an affair."

"Very interesting." Captain Denning smiled sardonically. "Of course, all our residents are sailors. Not renowned for fidelity, you know. Love 'em and leave 'em. A girl in every port. I'm sure you know the stereotypes. Who is the resident, by the way?"

"His name is Frank Needham. It was his sister Marjorie who suggested that we should come and visit him – she still lives in the same house, in Westlode Street, in Spalding, where they were brought up. We know that Frank wasn't living there at the time of which I'm speaking; it was his childhood home, but he had moved out by then. But he came back frequently. I do understand, by the way, that Frank is blind and that his mind has become confused. Marjorie told us that as well. If you think that it would be inappropriate or futile to try to speak to him, of course I will accept your professional judgment and leave him in peace."

He noticed that while he was speaking Captain Denning's face had flushed an unattractive brick red.

"I know Marjorie Needham!" he barked. "Damned busybody of a woman. She comes here sometimes, though not as often as she should – thank God. Frank doesn't really want to see her. It is his other sister he misses – Iris, they're twins – but Marjorie never brings her here. She says that Iris can't make the trip, because she is blind. As you say, Frank's blind, too: obviously a weakness that the twins share. But apart from that, he's as fit as you'd expect for a man nearly ninety, and no more 'confused' than most people of his age. Many of the residents here are much frailer and more gaga than he is. Some have round-the-clock nursing care: self-sufficiency is not one of the conditions of living here. The woman's talking twaddle, which squares with my experience of her." Captain Denning paced the few steps between the two doors, his hands behind his back, his expression one of extreme annoyance.

"So do you think it would be all right for me to have a short conversation with Frank?" Tim ventured.

"I don't see why not. Have to ask him, of course. Wait here."

He returned in a remarkably short time, his face now alive with curiosity.

"Frank says that he'll see you. He says that he's surprised that the police didn't contact him before. He wasn't talking about Kathryn Sheppard, though, or at least I don't think so. The liaison that you told me of: it was with Dorothy Atkins, wasn't it?"

"Yes. Do you remember the case, sir?"

"Of course I remember it. I doubt if anyone who was old enough to read the newspapers at the time could forget it. The woman who killed her mother-in-law. Amazing to think that Frank had a fling with her."

Tim inclined his head in agreement. It was wonderful how notoriety opened doors.

He followed Captain Denning back across the lawn to the back door of one of the houses that faced the street. The warden knocked perfunctorily before entering, and motioned Tim to follow him. Tim found himself standing in a small square kitchen with an open fire. The room was spotlessly clean, but the air was rank with the smell of stale tobacco smoke. A rather heavy old man was sitting in front of the fire, his legs swathed in a blanket, a stick by his side. His resemblance to Marjorie Needham was striking: he had the same oblong face and shock of thick untidy grey hair. Instead of her quick, darting eyes, however, his rolled in the random, unsettling way peculiar to the sightless. He was wearing a hearing-aid. He grasped the stick when he heard Tim approach and made as if to stand.

"Please, Mr. Needham, don't trouble to get up for me," said Tim, moving quickly across the room to take his hand.

"I'm Detective Inspector Tim Yates, of the South Lincolnshire Police. Thank you for agreeing to see me. I think that Captain Denning has told you why I've come."

"Yes." Frank Needham spoke slowly, with a strong Lincolnshire accent. "I don't know no girl called Kathryn, though." His voice was peevish and he didn't sound bright, but he was quite lucid. Tim wished that Captain Denning had not described the reason for his visit in quite so much detail. How he had achieved this in the short space of time that he had spent alone with Frank Needham was a mystery.

"Don't worry about Kathryn for the moment, Mr. Needham. I'd like you to focus on your friendship with Dorothy Atkins, if you would."

The old man cackled.

"You mean Tirzah. I thought you'd get on to that. Friendship! That's a good word for it." He leered as much as it was possible to leer without the use of his eyes.

"When did your relationship with Tirzah start?"

Frank Needham paused to consider.

"It was a lot longer ago than folk realised. I was in the navy, you see, and not home much, so folk didn't pick up on it. And we was what you might call discreet. That was her word. She didn't want a scandal."

"So can you recollect when it began – about when, anyway?" Tim persisted.

"It was – let me see. Well, I can't tell you the year, but it was well before Hedley was born, because she tried to lay him at my door. Not publicly, of course, but in private, so that she had a sort of hold on me. But I wasn't having any of it."

Despite the fact that his favourite mantra as a policeman was 'never be shocked', Tim found it difficult to conceal his surprise.

"Can we just go over that again, Mr. Needham? Are you saying that Dorothy Atkins – Tirzah – suspected that you were the father of her son, Hedley?"

"That's it. And I'm also telling you that I wasn't having

any. Thought I was born yesterday. The dates didn't add up, see. By the time she fell pregnant, I'd been at sea a good two months, by my reckoning."

"So you think that Hedley was in fact Ronald Atkins' son, just as everyone would have assumed?"

He cackled again, and brought on a fit of coughing. His face was alarmingly red when it subsided, and Tim could see that the hand that held the cane was shaking.

"Have a care, Inspector," said Captain Denning warningly.

"Oh, don't worry about me, Jack," said Frank Needham. "I've not enjoyed myself so much in a twelvemonth. 'As everyone would have assumed'! Well everyone might have assumed, but I knew different. She hadn't slept with Ronald for a long time. Barely let him touch her after Bryony was born, so she said. And I believed her. Despised Ronald, she did."

There was a pause.

"Well?" said Frank. "Aren't you going to ask me?"

"Ask you what, Mr. Needham?"

"Who I think Hedley's father was. Not 'think', really – I'm positive, though I can't prove it." Without waiting for a reply, he continued with a flourish. "It was Colin Atkins – 'Uncle' Colin!"

He sat there, looking sightlessly up at Tim, beaming and triumphant. There was a protracted silence while Tim decided how best to react. Finally Captain Denning cleared his throat. When he spoke to Frank, his tone was gentle.

"You may be right, Frank, but it was all a long time ago, and I doubt if it could be proved who the father was now, because the man who you've mentioned is presumably dead."

Frank was unperturbed. He beamed at both of them. Tim could almost have believed that there was a glint in his empty gaze.

"As you say, Jack. But I know it. And something else I know, too." He lowered his voice.

"What's that, Mr. Needham?"

"I know that Tirzah didn't kill Ronald's ma. Of course I can't prove that either; but I knew Tirzah inside out." He cackled again. "And I can tell you that she didn't have it in her to kill no-one. Drive them round the bend, yes, but that was different. Besides, the police never got to the bottom of it, as I said to Iris at the time. It was staring them in the face and they didn't cotton on."

"I'm not sure that I follow you, Mr. Needham. What didn't the police cotton on to?"

Frank Needham sighed with mock impatience.

"The girl, of course. Bryony. She disappeared and it was before Doris died. A few days before, at least. I was home on leave and I said to Iris, there's something odd going on next door. It was after Tirzah and the kids come to stay. I saw them – Ronald and Hedley, and Colin was there, too – digging a hole in the old orchard. I was still seeing Tirzah then, but funnily enough it was harder to meet her when she was living next door than when she was on the estate. Because all the rest of them was hanging around all the time. We'd meet up by the fire station for a cigarette when it was getting dark, and once or twice we managed to sneak back to her house on the estate. I said to her, I said, 'What's going on in the orchard?' And she was normally open with me – I knew exactly how she felt about all of them – but this time she clammed up. Wouldn't speak to me about it at all. I was certain something bad had happened, but I was sure that she wasn't mixed up in it – at least not more than she had to be. I saw a helplessness in her then, that I'd never seen before."

"What did she say when you challenged her, Mr. Needham? Did she say anything at all?"

"She said that if I didn't mind my own business, we were finished. And I told her I was getting pretty fed up with the whole thing, anyway. I didn't mean it: she and I went deep. But we parted on bad terms. I went back to sea and she was arrested soon after. I was still away and it wasn't my business to go making things worse, but Mam used to send me the papers and I was surprised that they never noticed the girl was missing. So I kept out of it. I did write to Tirzah once in prison and I asked her about Bryony, but she returned the letter unopened. Then Mam had one of her tantrums and said that it was bad enough that I'd been carrying on with a married woman, but that, God forgive me, I should let up now that I knew she was a murderer as well. So I did. No point in trying to keep on with it, was there, when Tirzah didn't want it and my family didn't either and she likely to be in prison all of her life in any case?"

"So did you never see her or speak to her again, after the occasion that you've described?"

"No, never. Still carry a torch for her, though." The old man's gleeful mood had vanished. His face puckered. "I didn't marry, myself, in the end. If you see her, tell her that Frank was asking after her."

CHAPTER THIRTY-TWO

The men who worked at Bevelton's Tractors were somewhat bemused by the order to dig up their own yard. At first they thought that their boss, Henry Bevelton, was joking, but one look at his face told them that he found the situation far from funny. If they had not understood before, when two police-men turned up to watch the proceedings, they realised that it was no laughing matter.

Henry Bevelton, who was a wiry little man with a strangely plump face and bulbous nose, had decided that he had better be nice to the policemen – since he wanted his yard putting back in exactly the order that it had been in before this started, all costs borne by the constabulary, as he had been promised – and get Gloria, his accounts lady, to offer them some tea. They accepted, but declined his offer to drink it in the tiny cockloft of an office into which his own desk and Gloria's were crammed, explaining that they needed to watch the digging all of the time. Gloria was therefore tasked with carrying tea out to them.

After a considerable delay, they saw her approaching. She picked her way through the mud and debris of the yard, cursing every time one of her black patent stilettos got caught in the uneven tarmac, her ample bosoms tightly encased in a slippery red garment and heaving with the effort. She plonked down two scarlet mugs adorned with the logo of a tyre company on a workbench near where they were standing, and inelegantly stumped off back towards her office without saying a word.

"Thank you!" called out PC Gary Cooper (whose mother had had a sense of humour that he had not appreciated as a child). He elicited no response, and shrugged as he watched Gloria's black-clad bottom retreat. He picked up both mugs and handed the other one to PC Chakrabati.

"Put your hands round that," he said. "It's going to be cold, standing here."

A digger roared up to them and its driver brought it to a halt and jumped out. He was a stocky man with a jowly, grey-stubbled face. He wore a yellow hard hat which did nothing for his ashen complexion. He had a cigarette clamped between his lips and now removed it in order to talk to them.

"I'm Jason Beech, the foreman here," he announced. "I'm sorry to have to move you, but you can't stand there. It won't be safe once we've got started."

"We've got orders to watch the whole thing," said Gary.

"I can't help that. I don't want to get done for manslaughter. Why don't you go and stand over there, by that tree? We can't get the digger that far into the corner, so I know we won't hit you there."

There was a solitary apple tree standing in the furthest corner of the yard, with some dustbins in front of it. Behind it was a high brick wall. The yard was bounded on one side by this wall, which was made of rather garish cheap yellow bricks, and the more attractive mellowed Victorian brick wall which separated it from Ronald Atkins' garden.

The two PCs looked at each other. Gary Cooper shrugged again.

"All right," he said. They moved to the place that he had indicated. It was smelly near the dustbins, but here they were more sheltered from the early spring breeze which came whipping round the buildings, straight off the North Sea. They slurped the hot tea and watched as the foreman jumped back into his digger and use it to rough up the tarmac. Another, younger, man then took over from him, and started tearing jagged pieces out of it. It was slow work. The digger worked in a cumbersome way, scrabbling at the ground like an old lady who could not get a purchase on something that she was trying to pick up, before ripping out what seemed like agonisingly small scraps. Another digger then met it head on with a scoop, and the first digger rested while the debris was clawed up, again in a clumsy, hit-and-miss kind of way.

"We're in for a long day," said Giash Chakrabati, as he finished the tea. "Let's hope we don't have to come back tomorrow."

"Yeah," said Gary. "It all seems a bit far-fetched to me. Why do they think there might be a body hidden under all this tarmac and, if there is one, why do they think that these blokes might hide it?"

"I don't think it's these blokes they're worried about. It's the old geezer in the house next door."

"Oh?" He looked across at the house, but from where he was standing he could see only the upstairs windows, which were in darkness. "Think the old geezer did it then, do they? But they'll have to find a body first."

"Well, that's the whole point, isn't it?"

Gary fell silent. He wished that he could take a fag break, like the workmen were doing now, but knew that it would be too risky. Policemen complained about paperwork, about louts bad-mouthing them, and about not getting enough home life. None of these things troubled Gary over-much, but every so often a day like this came along, and all he was required to do was to watch or stand guard and get numbingly cold and mind-numbingly bored, with no prospect of being able to smoke a cigarette until he went off-duty. That was when he questioned his own sanity in choosing to become a policeman.

The day lurched on. Each of the policemen took a toilet break. Henry Bevelton had offered them the use of the inside toilet, which was situated in a corner of the workshop, but it was clear from the way that she had tossed her head and then pounded away on her keyboard that Gloria considered this to be a personal affront. They had in any case decided to use the Portaloo in the yard, in common with the workmen. When lunchtime came, Henry offered to send out for something for them. Gloria was despatched to forage for food–evidently she did not mind this, presumably because she would get some of the spoils – and returned with hot Cornish pasties from The Prior's Oven.

By mid-afternoon, the whole of the yard had been dug up, and the debris piled in a skip, which was taken away. Now they were looking out at a waste of packed-down earth, with the two inspection pits exposed like giant sarcophagi in the middle of it. Henry Bevelton came out to speak to them.

"What now, officers? How deep do you want us to dig into the earth?"

"At least six foot," said Gary. "But those'll have to come out, too." He indicated the inspection pits.

Henry Bevelton's patience was evidently wearing thin. "That's out of the question," he said flatly. "We use these pits every day. The smooth running of the business depends on them. If they're removed, the work of my company will be disrupted for weeks. "

"Out of the question, is it, sir? I realise that this is all very upsetting for you and is having a big effect on the operation of your firm, but we do have a warrant. We can get one especially for the inspection pits, if you like, but it would save a lot of time if you were to co-operate straight away. We'll make sure that you get some new ones in their place. These must have been here – what – about thirty years by now?"

Henry considered for a minute. If he played his cards right, he realised that he would get a good bit of refurbishment – some of it long in need of doing – free of charge, as well as compensation for loss of earnings. Besides, he had had a few brushes with the police in the past and he didn't want them to cut up rough – or take too great an interest in some of his more unusual day-to-day activities. He wasn't exactly breaking the law, at least not in his own book, but Bevelton's did sometimes carry out a few favours for their customers, such as turning the milometer back a bit on tractors that were for sale, or taking the best bits from two old tractors to make a new one; things that it was best to keep quiet about.

"All right, it's not out of the question, of course, if you say otherwise. But it is a major inconvenience and I want your assurance that the repair and replacement work will take place straight away, not months down the line. Otherwise I'll be suing the police for more than loss of earnings."

"I understand that Detective Inspector Yates has already made those promises, sir. He isn't a man not to keep his word."

Henry Bevelton walked across to where his men were gathered, watching, and spoke a few words to the foreman. He replied shortly, looking extremely annoyed. Henry outstretched both palms in a "What can I do about it?" gesture. Jason Beech stalked off, taking one of the younger men with him. They returned quickly, bearing several pick-axes, which they distributed. Then all five men began hacking at the concrete. Gary and Giash settled down once more, knowing that they were in for as tedious and cold an afternoon as the morning that they had just endured.

Two hours later, with the concrete fairly well broken up, the men brought the diggers in again. They had cleared away most of the concrete and lifted it into a skip by the time that darkness came. By now the temperature had dropped, and because they had been standing around all day, both policemen were very cold.

Jason Beech walked over to them, and spoke to them in a surprisingly friendly way.

"Time to call it a day, officers. That OK with you? We could start digging up the soil, but we can't see properly and we're all pretty knackered now. I expect you are too?"

Giash nodded. Gary didn't answer. He was busy looking across at the house next door.

"You all right with that, Gary?"

"Hmm? Oh, yes. Fine. Thank you," he said to the foreman belatedly.

"Got something on your mind?"

"No, not really. I was just looking at that house. There was a light on in one of the upstairs windows just now, and I could see the outline of a man standing there. I expect he's the old geezer that Inspector Yates was talking about."

Giash followed his gaze.

"No-one there now, is there?" he said.

"Not as far as we can tell. He's turned the light off, but he could still be standing there, I suppose."

"Why would he want to do that?"

"So that he can watch us without being seen, maybe."

"Nothing to watch now, is there? And no daylight to see by, either. Come on, let's go and get a cup of tea somewhere. I'm perished."

It rained all night. When the two constables turned up at the yard the next day, the rain was easing off, but there was a small lake sitting on the packed-down soil.

"It's clay, see," said Henry Bevelton, with a kind of morose I-told-you-so satisfaction. "Water doesn't seep through it easily. I've sent one of the lads to hire a pump."

There was more endless waiting, fortified with several cups of tea (Gloria had either come round, or she had had a talking-to), until the pump arrived, was assembled, hooked up to a generator and started sucking out the water. By the time they were able to bring the diggers in again, it was almost lunchtime. Gloria appeared. She favoured them with a fuschia-lipsticked smile.

"Same as yesterday, officers? Or would you rather have some soup and sandwiches?"

"The pasty was fine by me," said Gary. "And me," added Giash. They both watched Gloria sashay away. Today she was wearing boots, laced at the back. Her ample calves bulged a little over the top of them.

That afternoon, the men operating the diggers took off the soil foot by foot, as they had been instructed, with the policemen inspecting each layer, until six feet of soil had been removed. They had found nothing more interesting than some gnarled old tree roots.

Henry Bevelton descended from his office, looking pleased with himself and a little sanctimonious, just as DC Juliet Armstrong arrived. His face fell a little when he saw her – he had first met her two days ago, when she had visited him with Detective Inspector Yates to explain what needed to be done and why; he found her more of a challenge than the uniformed policemen. However, he did not allow himself to be deflected from giving her the little speech that he had just prepared in his head for the two coppers.

"Ah, good afternoon, Detective Constable. As you can see, my men have followed your instructions. As you can also see, we have found nothing. Is it all right if we put the soil back now? I'm anxious to get this yard to rights as soon as possible. There's someone from a construction company coming tomorrow, to advise about making some new inspection pits. It will cost a pretty penny, but I daresay you're ready for that."

Juliet regarded him levelly.

"I think we'd like to wait a little before we do anything else, sir. I'm just going to have a word with my colleagues; then I'll come back to you. I shan't be long. Should I come and find you in your office?"

"No, no, I'll wait here," said Henry. He was rubbing his hands together, though whether it was because he was anxious, full of glee in anticipation of the new yard that he was going to extract from the police force, or simply cold, it was difficult to say.

Juliet joined Gary and Giash under the apple tree.

"Have this lot been co-operating?"

"There were a few grumbles at first," said Giash, "but after that, they were fine."

"Is there anything funny about them?"

"No, I don't think so. Most of them don't have a clue what this is about, though I suppose the old guy's probably told them something, even though we asked him not to. He seems a bit jumpy, but it's probably because he's worried about the amount of time this is taking. Either that, or he's up to some petty dodges that he doesn't want us to find out about, is my guess. I don't think he knows any more about whether there's a body here or not than we do."

"You're sure that there's nothing in that heap of soil?"

"Well, we could sieve it I suppose." Giash had meant this as a joke, then instantly regretted saying it, as Juliet put her head on one side in reflection. "I think we've been pretty careful," he added quickly. "They've only been lifting the soil to the depth of a foot at a time, as we asked them, and we've turned over every layer. We've found a fair bit of debris – bits of old tools, shards of pottery, something that looks like part of a bicycle chain – quite small stuff, in fact, so if there had been any bones in there I think we would have spotted them. There are loads of tree roots, too."

"Well, it was an orchard. How long has the building been there? It doesn't look Victorian."

"No, it isn't, but it's pre-war. Henry Bevelton's grandfather founded the business in the 1930s, and the office and workshop were built then. The showroom at the front was added afterwards."

"How do you know?"

"I've been chatting to Henry, off and on. He's not a bad bloke, really."

"The land on which the showroom was built belonged to them right from the start, then?"

"I think so."

"I know that the orchard was bought from the Atkins family in the 1970s. Has every square foot of it been dug up now?"

"Most of it. There's just that little strip of path in front of the workshop. Henry said that there was a wooden fence there, dividing the properties, before he bought the land."

A gust of wind lashed the air around them suddenly. Juliet shivered, and looked up at the bare branches of the apple tree.

"How long has that tree been there?"

"Search me. Part of the old orchard, probably. In other words, for ages. One tree spared, or something. I could ask Henry."

"That tree's not old enough to have been part of the original orchard," said Gary. "Those trees would have been seventy or eighty years old at least, if they were still here. This tree's quite old for an apple tree, but you can see that it's still producing fruit" – he indicated some half-rotted apples lying on the ground. "My Dad used to grow apples. He used to reckon that the trees have outgrown their strength by the time they are thirty years old, or forty at most, and he said that they stop fruiting properly then. I'd say that this tree's somewhere between twenty and thirty years old."

"You're sure it could be as much as thirty years old?"

"I think so. But if it's important, we can ask Henry Bevelton."

"Good idea. Get him to come over here, will you?"

They turned round so that they could see Henry Bevelton, who was still hovering in the doorway of his workshop, his arms folded across his chest. He was slapping his shoulders gently, presumably in an attempt to warm himself up. He looked alarmed when they saw him watching them. Juliet smiled and lifted her hand in a fresh greeting. Gary walked across to Henry and asked him to join them.

"Well," he said when he caught them up, unnaturally hale and bright as he stood to face Juliet, "What now? Is there something else I can help you with?"

"Just some more information, if you please, Mr. Bevelton." Juliet regarded him coolly. She was taking a dislike to Henry because she suspected him of dishonesty of some kind. She could usually sniff it out. Otherwise she could think of no explanation for his nervousness.

"Fire away!"

"Was this apple tree here when you bought the yard from Colin Atkins, or has it been planted since?"

"Oh, it was here already. You don't have much use for fruit trees when you're running a heavy plant business." He said it with a chuckle. Juliet realised that although he was making a leaden attempt at humour, he was still extremely nervous.

"Indeed. I believe that there was a whole orchard of apple trees here when you made the purchase?"

"Yes, and pear trees. I think there may even have been a couple of cherry trees," he said expansively.

"All of which were cut down so that you could use the land as a tractor maintenance yard?"

"Yes – you know that was the case. Nothing wrong in doing that, was there? I consulted the council about planning permission, for the pits and for the petrol tank that we installed on the other side of the showroom."

"Nothing wrong with it at all, Mr. Bevelton. I'm sure you went through all the appropriate procedures. What we're curious to know is, why was this tree spared?"

"Oh, it was a very young tree at the time – little more than a sapling. And Mr. Atkins asked us particularly to leave it. He said that it had been planted in memory of his mother."

"Mr. Colin Atkins, this was?"

"No, it was actually Mr. Ronald Atkins: the present owner of the house next door."

"So the mother in question was Mrs. Doris Atkins, the lady who had met a violent death some time before."

"I guess so. I haven't really thought about it before. There was a very old lady living in that house, too – I went to see them several times in the space of four or five years, to try to buy the land. It took me all my powers of persuasion, I can tell you: for a long time, they wouldn't hear of it. I'd assumed that that old lady had died, and that was who he meant. But now I think about it, I suppose it could have been the one who was mur . . . died a violent death."

He's trying to sound casual, thought Juliet: as if he really hasn't given this much thought before. But he's still on edge. He's certainly hiding something from us.

"When did you finally succeed in buying the land, Mr. Bevelton?"

"It was in the spring of 1977. I can look up the date exactly, if you like."

"How did Mr. Atkins make his request about the tree? Did he accompany you and show it to you?"

"Yes. He was very particular that I should save the right tree. Well, there were a lot of trees to choose from!" He gave his uneasy chuckle again. "But that one was standing by itself – it wasn't part of the main orchard. So keeping it wasn't a problem. I thought that it might be nice for the lads to be able to help themselves to the apples when they came, too: but they were all cookers."

"How big was the tree when he showed it to you?"

"Not very big at all. As I've said, it was just a sapling."

"Would you personally have a problem if we were to uproot that tree?"

Henry Bevelton looked doubly uneasy.

"Not personally, no. But I did promise Ronald. Still I suppose that thirty years is a long time to have kept a promise – he couldn't in fairness expect more than that, could he?"

"Thank you," said Juliet. "Was it with Ronald Atkins you negotiated the sale, or with Colin Atkins?"

"With Colin Atkins, since you ask. Well, he was the owner of the house and the orchard. So I suppose Ronald had no right to ask for any favours anyway?"

"Anyone can ask a favour," said Juliet. "Whether it is granted, and for how long, depends of course on the person giving it – and their motivation."

Henry Bevelton looked down at his feet.

She turned to Gary and Giash. "Can you find someone who can cut that tree down? A tree surgeon, or whatever they're called?"

Three hours later, two men who had been requisitioned from Robertson's timber yard by Gary Cooper had cut down the tree. It was now after four o'clock in the afternoon, and as at the same time on the day before, darkness was now approaching.

"Best to call it a day," said Henry Bevelton. "They're going to have to dig that stump out manually: they can't get a digger into that corner without knocking the wall down; and I'm certain that your boss won't want the bill for that as well." He raised an eyebrow at Juliet.

"No," she agreed. "You're right. It's better if we all go home now. Thank you very much for all your help today, Mr. Bevelton. How early can we start tomorrow?"

Henry shouted across the yard to Jason Beech.

"Jason? Come here a minute, will you?"

The foreman arrived quickly, his hard hat pushed back off his forehead, the straps hanging loose.

"What's up, boss? I'd like to get off now, if no-one minds. It's Carol's birthday today, and I'm taking her to the pub for supper."

"We won't keep you for more than half a sec. Just tell us what time you can start tomorrow."

"Well, it won't be light until eight: but I guess we could start at 7.30, the same as usual, if we use one of the big floodlights that we hire out for the harvest. Then perhaps we can get the job finished tomorrow."

"Do that then, will you, Jase? And give Carol my love."

Jason Beech looked vaguely disgusted at the message.

Juliet wondered why. Perhaps Jason – or Carol – had their own private views about Henry? Or perhaps it was even because Henry had tried it on with Carol? Juliet had caught him leering at Gloria once or twice. But Henry Bevelton didn't seem to notice his foreman's reaction to his words. He clapped Jason on the back as walked away. Jason had the use of one of the company Land Rovers and he could be heard starting it up a few moments later.

"Well, I'd best be going home, too," said Henry quickly.

Juliet was gazing at the house next door. She thought that she saw an upstairs light flick on and then off again, quickly. The upstairs windows were glowing dully, but she could not make out whether that was because a light had been left on deeper in the house – on the stairs or landing perhaps – or whether they were just reflecting the last of the dying sunlight. The two PCs were flanking her. They were also both observing the house. She turned back to face Henry again. Once more she was struck by his air of unease.

"Just a couple more questions, Mr. Bevelton, if you don't mind. Then we'll let you go. It's been a long day for everyone."

"Of course," Henry said, bowing his head rather unctuously. "Would you like to come up to the office?"

"That isn't necessary. But perhaps we could just stand in the workshop for a few minutes."

"Of course," said Henry again. He pushed open the workshop door and flicked a switch. It illuminated the row of lights, fashioned in the style of Chinese coolie hats, which were suspended over the main workbench, a sinister-looking construction made out of huge railway sleepers, and blackened with use. "Come in, come in. I'm not sure that it's warmer in here: but of course it's very private. No-one to listen to us in here." Juliet thought that this was an odd comment to make, but she let it pass.

"Yes. That actually touches on what I wanted to ask you about. Do you see much of your neighbours?"

"You mean the Atkins, or the Needhams?"

"Either of them, but I particularly meant the Atkins. Your acquaintance with Ronald Atkins obviously goes back a long way. Do you meet him or talk to him regularly – or on any occasion, in fact?"

"You forget that Ronald did not actually live there until quite recently, except when he was a child. He was not living in that house when his mother died, just staying for a while. After his divorce – and all the other things that happened – I believe that he moved out of the council house that he had lived in with his first wife and rented a small property in Winsover Road. I don't know how long he lived there, but I imagine that he moved again when he married Doreen. I believe that they lived with her parents, who owned a house a few miles out of town, on the main road to Boston. It took Ronald a long time to get his hands on the property next door. They've only been living there for a few months. Colin Atkins died more than ten years ago, but there was some difficulty over the will. I think that Colin's brothers' descendants contested Ronald's right to inherit, or something like that."

"You seem to be very well-informed about Mr. Atkins, Mr. Bevelton; but you still have not answered my question. Do you speak to him much now that he does live next door to your property? Or the Needham ladies, since you mention them?"

"Pair of witches, they are," said Henry, grinning, perhaps to indicate that he was not being entirely serious. Juliet still sensed the same fidgety uneasiness that she had noticed before. "We do see them occasionally, but only when the younger one comes to complain about the noise."

"And Mr. Atkins?" Juliet persisted. Henry hesitated, and then came out pat with his story.

"Naturally, he came and made himself known to me again when he moved in. I've seen him in passing a couple of times. And I've said hello to his wife when she's walked past me in the street."

"You know his wife, then?"

"I know what she looks like. I don't think we've been properly introduced."

"Thank you, Mr. Bevelton. Have a good evening." He nodded, and disappeared up the stairs to his office.

Gary and Giash followed Juliet out to the street.

"I guess you'll be needing us again tomorrow?" asked Gary.

"Yes, please. It should be the last day you have to come here. We'll find out one way or the other whether there's anything buried under that yard. I've got a feeling about that apple tree. I'm going to ask Detective Inspector Yates if he can come here tomorrow, too. If he does come, he will brief you: see what he says, but I'm going to recommend that you keep an eye on the house next door as much as you can without being conspicuous. We'll want to know if we get any kind of reaction from Ronald Atkins when we start digging again."

Tim called Juliet on her mobile while she was still walking back to the station. She stood in the shelter of the doorway of Molson's the Chemist while she was speaking to him.

"Got something to tell me?"

"They haven't found anything yet. But I've got a hunch about a single apple tree that stands in the corner of the yard. It wasn't part of the original orchard, and we think it's much younger than the trees in the orchard would have been. Gary Cooper's one of the PCs who's been watching the work today, and apparently his Dad was a bit of an expert on apples. Gary says that he thinks that tree can't be much more than thirty years old, whereas the other trees would have been at least twice that. We've had the tree cut down now, but they need to dig out the stump before we can get to anything that might be underneath it. They should do that in an hour or two tomorrow morning: they've agreed to start work at seven-thirty. I think that this could be our breakthrough, sir. I really think you should be here, if you can."

"I'll be there. What about Henry Bevelton? Is he being co-operative?"

"Super co-operative with me, though apparently there were some grumbles yesterday when his inspection pits were dug up. They're going to cost quite a lot to replace, incidentally: Henry never wastes an opportunity to tell us. I don't like him, actually. There's something really shifty and nervy about him that I can't put my finger on."

"He's probably like a lot of people in the vehicle industry: seventy-five per cent businessman, twenty-five per cent crook. He's been done for a couple of things in the past, but he hasn't served time. Fines and warnings, that sort of thing. Of course, that doesn't mean he isn't hiding something bigger than that that he doesn't want us to know about."

"I suppose if he's a petty crook, that could explain it. But from the depth of his knowledge about the man and his affairs, I'm pretty sure that he was quite close to Ronald Atkins at the time of Doris's murder, though he is at pains to deny it, and he vehemently denies that he and Ronald are on more than nodding acquaintance now. I don't get it. There's no particular disgrace in being an associate of Ronald Atkins, is there? None that we know of, anyway."

"Not from Henry's point of view, I wouldn't have thought. I'm as certain about Ronald as you are about Henry that he's got something to hide, but in the eyes of his neighbours he is respectable enough. Perhaps that's what it is, though," said Tim, his voice rising in sudden inspiration. "Perhaps it is a shared secret that neither of them wants us to know about. In which case, it probably is something to do with Doris Atkins' murder or Bryony's disappearance, or both. Because I'm damn sure that Ronald hasn't told us all that he knows about either of them. Did you or the two PCs see Ronald while you were there?"

"Not exactly."

"Not exactly! What does that mean?"

"We've each seen lights in the upstairs windows of Ronald's house at different times, sometimes a light shining from deeper in the house. But often it has been in darkness. Some of the time it was so dark outside that if he had the lights off, Ronald could have been standing at one of the windows without our having seen him. I don't have any positive proof, but I wouldn't mind betting that he's watching what's going on."

"If Bryony's remains are under that tree, do you think he might do a runner?"

"Difficult to say. You've spent more time with him than I have. My guess is that he won't. I think that he'll say that Dorothy did it, or that he knew nothing about it, and that solicitor of his will back him up with a coherently pieced together story."

"It might be no more than the truth, of course. If there was another murder, maybe it was Dorothy who did it; or someone else altogether."

"Well, if it wasn't Dorothy and it wasn't Ronald, we're running out of suspects. Who do you think it might have been? The old granny? Or Uncle Colin?"

She could almost hear Tim shrugging.

"Anything's possible," he said. "Go home and soak in a hot bath. You must be frozen through. I'll see you tomorrow morning. Bright and early," he added ruefully. "I'll pick you up."

Hedley, Tim said to himself. It must have been Hedley. If we find Bryony under that apple tree, of course. There's not enough evidence to nail him without a body. Perhaps not even with one. But why? And why would they all have protected Hedley by keeping it a secret? They weren't a close-knit family, and neither Dorothy nor Ronald seemed to be particularly fond of him. And is there a connection with Kathryn Sheppard's disappearance, or not? I don't get it, he thought, echoing Juliet's earlier comment. But I'm not going to worry about it now. This is one evening when I do stand a real chance of getting home early enough to eat with Katrin.

CHAPTER THIRTY-THREE

It was the night of the *Crimewatch* appeal. The *Crimewatch* team had agreed to show again the 1990 reconstruction of Kathryn Sheppard's last known movements, and follow the clip with the new information about the discovery of the skeleton and the scraps of cloth, the ring and the plastic Red Indian. It was the first time that this information had been made public. Some new details were also revealed about the circumstances of Kathryn's disappearance, including the fact that she had called her office on that last Friday and asked to take the day as holiday.

The main programme had finished, and had precipitated a surprising number of calls. The *Crimewatch* researchers were trying to sift through all the responses they had received before the *Crimewatch Update* that followed the news. Despite requests made during the broadcast that people should not contact the police about where the friendship ring might have been purchased, or provide them with information about other owners of such a ring, many of the calls did relate to one or the other. Despite this, Andy's swift run through all of the calls that had come in while the programme was still on air with had yielded two possibly exciting results.

The first was from a woman who sounded frightened. She asked for her anonymity to be respected, but she rang off without giving her name. It might have been true, as she claimed, that she might have been identifiable by the man who might have been Kathryn's killer if all of the details that she had given were publicly disclosed. Despite her obvious fear, she said that she was unsure whether the information that she had would be valuable or whether it was just a red herring. She said that she had worked in Hedley Atkins' office at the time when Kathryn Sheppard had also worked there, about thirty years ago. She remembered that Kathryn had exchanged a friendship ring with Hedley Atkins' sister, Bryony, and wondered if that was significant. The *Crime-watch* broadcast had deliberately not mentioned Bryony, so Andy knew at this point that the woman's call was genuine. She also said that she had continued working in Hedley's office for some time after Kathryn had left, and that she was still there at the time of Doris Atkins' death. Shortly after Dorothy Atkins' arrest for Doris's murder, Hedley had asked a favour of her. She had been dubious about agreeing even at the time, but the explanation that he had given for requesting it was very plausible, and although she had never met Bryony Atkins, she had wanted to help her. Hedley had said that his sister had been traumatised by her grandmother's murder and the terrible invasion of privacy that the Atkins family had suffered. She had gone away to study at university under a false name, and could not face having anything to do with her family. There was a psychiatrist who wanted to interview Bryony about her mother's state of mind prior to the murder. He had agreed to conduct the interview by telephone in order not to put undue pressure on Bryony, but she still could not face going through with it, even though the psychiatrist had prepared most of the questions in advance. Hedley wondered whether this woman would take the psychiatrist's call instead, and pretend that she was Bryony. He would coach her in the answers to the questions. There would be no harm done, and it would help both Bryony and the rest of the Atkins family if she could smooth their path in this way. That was the exact expression he had used: 'smooth our path'. She had thought that it was an odd request, but she had seen no real reason for not helping out at the time and, besides, Hedley was her boss. So she had agreed to do it. Almost immediately after the call with the psychiatrist had taken place, however, she had begun to think that getting involved had been a mistake. This was mainly because Hedley, who had always been a decent boss who had treated her courteously, now began to pick on her and victimise her on every possible occasion, so that she had become quite afraid of him and had eventually found another job. She had not thought much about him since, but she could still recollect the unsettling sense of fear that she had felt at the time. She couldn't explain why she thought that the false call might have had something to do with Kathryn's disappearance, but because Kathryn and Bryony had been friends, she thought that the police might be interested.

The second call was also made by a woman, but this time one who identified herself with some stridency. Immediately, Andy's ears had pricked up, because the name was one that he recognised from conversations about the case that he had had with Tim and Juliet. The woman said that her name was Marjorie Needham. The call was a rambling one and at first the woman did not appear to be saying much, beyond that she had been trying to help the police with their enquiries and that it was a pity that they had not taken her into their confidence earlier, because then they would have found out how much she could help. It had been the same with the garden. You would have thought they would have learnt this time. Anyway, she was ringing about the plastic Red Indian. You would have thought that they would have put two and two together by now, but obviously they hadn't. Colin Atkins had kept shop at the house in Westlode Street and one of the things that he had sold had, of course, been breakfast cereals. He was a tight old skinflint and rarely, if ever, gave anything away. That was why she remembered, quite clearly, that in the closing months of 1974 he had received a consignment of plastic Red Indians. She knew it was 1974, because her nephew had come to visit and he had emigrated to Australia with his parents shortly afterwards. The Red Indians were intended to be given away with Nubisk breakfast cereal, but Colin had received a double consignment by mistake, and even he had not had the brazen cheek to try to sell the surplus ones. He had therefore given some of them to local children who went into the shop on errands, including some of her own nephews and nieces who lived round and about. The nephew bound for Australia had come to visit and gone into the shop to see if Colin would give him one as well; but, when Colin had looked for the rest of the surplus bag of the models, it had disappeared. Only the other bag, from which he was taking the toys to give to purchasers of the breakfast cereal, remained. Colin had been very annoyed about this – unreasonably so, she had thought, but that was Colin for you. Of course, anyone but an old skinflint like him would have given the kid a toy from the other bag, rather than see him disappointed. There would surely have been people coming into the shop for cereal who didn't want the gift. But that was typical of Colin, too. He had no sympathy or understanding for children. It was well-known that at Christmas all Bryony and Hedley ever received were packets of dolly mixtures past their sell-by date. Why, even Doris had had to pay for the biscuits that she ate with her elevenses. . . .

Andy barely listened to the rest of it. If she was right, Nubisk had actually distributed the Red Indians a year before they had said in the report that they had prepared for Juliet. If there had been a mistake on their part, it was likely to be genuine, but it was a crucially important mistake, nevertheless. He would go back to them and ask them to check their records again. There was something else about the appeal that nagged away at the back of his mind. He made up his mind to watch the reconstruction again.

CHAPTER THIRTY-FOUR

Jason Beech was behaving in quite a different way from yesterday. All his earlier surliness had melted away, and he had become assiduous in his desire to help the police as much as possible. He and his gang of tractor mechanics had assembled on the dot at 7.30 a.m. and by the time that Tim and Juliet arrived a few minutes later, they were already digging around the root with shovels and pick-axes. A huge floodlight had been rigged up on a makeshift platform against the far wall, and was bathing them in fierce white light. PCs Gary Cooper and Giash Chakrabati were also there. They had moved along a little from their station near the dustbins in order not to get in the way. Each of them looked across at the adjoining house every ten minutes or so, but it remained wrapped in darkness.

Tim went to speak to them straight away. Gary Cooper greeted him first.

"Good morning, sir. DC Armstrong said that you would want us to keep an eye on the house next door. Do you have any other instructions?"

"Just keep an eye on everything, will you? This place and that house as well, if you can." Tim spoke quietly. "I haven't got a feel yet for what you might call the dynamics of what is happening here." He frowned as he saw Henry Bevelton rounding the corner.

"Good Morning, Mr. Bevelton. I had not expected to see

you quite so early. It's before your usual opening time, isn't it?"

"A little before, but I'm often early. Besides, I thought I should show you a little hospitality, since you are on my premises. I shall put the kettle on for Gloria."

Juliet could not help smiling at the limited extent of his chivalry. He did not retreat to his office, however, but remained hovering at the entrance, his hands thrust deep into the pockets of his black woollen overcoat. Because he was standing behind Tim and herself, it was difficult for Juliet to keep turning round to look at him without attracting his attention; but on the two occasions on which she managed it, he was not looking at the tree root. His gaze was fixed anxiously on the house next door.

It took less than an hour to remove the root. It yielded itself up just as Gloria teetered around the corner in a pair of high-heeled red ankle-boots.

"Time for everyone to take a tea-break, I think," said Henry. He spoke with his usual unctuous urbanity, but there was a tautness in his tone.

Gloria rolled her eyes skywards, though she appeared to be in a good humour

"Let me get through the door, then," she said. "I've brought some biscuits today, too." She withdrew them from a green plastic shopping bag with *Harrod's* printed on it in gold, evidently expecting to be congratulated. "Your favourites," she said to Henry, when the gesture produced no reaction. He did not reply. Gloria tutted and headed for the stairs.

"Would you like to drink your tea in the office, Detective Inspector?" asked Henry Bevelton. Juliet thought that he seemed unduly keen to get Tim out of the way for a while. Before Tim could reply, she interceded.

"I don't think that there's room for everyone up there, is there, Mr. Bevelton? It would be nice if we could all take a tea break together. Could we use the workshop again?"

Henry's face registered an interesting combination of expressions. He seemed worried, annoyed, irascible and, at the same time, somehow contemptuous. He sighed in an exasperated way.

"Of course, if that is what you wish," he said. "I'll go and tell Gloria."

"What's the matter with him?" said Tim as they watched his retreating back. "He seems like a cat on hot bricks."

"I don't know; but I'm sure he's hiding something. He didn't take his eyes off the Atkins' house all the time we were standing here."

Despite Juliet's intention to gather everyone together for a tea-break, Jason Beech and Nick, Wayne and Karl had piled into the cabs of the two diggers with their thermos flasks. Their instinct that Gloria would not extend her hospitality to them appeared to be correct, for when she appeared with her tray of tea, it bore only five mugs, and ten chocolate ginger biscuits carefully set out in an overlapping circle on a plate.

"Thank you," said Tim. And, because he hated people to wait on him, he added, "won't you join us?"

Gloria wrinkled her nose.

"I aren't going in there, in all the muck and grease. Especially in these shoes. Besides, that place gives me the creeps."

"Why do you say that?" asked Tim.

"I don't know. It just does. There's never enough light in there for one thing – not proper light, anyway. And that old man hangs around it too much for my liking."

"Which old man?"

"I'm sure I don't know," said Henry Bevelton quickly. "Gloria, shut the door behind you when you go. There's one hell of a draught blowing through."

"I'd be grateful if you'd let her finish, Mr. Bevelton. Which old man?" Tim repeated.

Gloria gave Henry Bevelton a sheepish look. He stared

back at her, and forced a smile.

"The old man who lives next door now."

"You mean Ronald Atkins?"

"I don't know his name. The one who lives next door to Marjorie Needham. He only moved in a few months ago."

"Then you must mean Ronald Atkins. How often does he 'hang around'?

"Oh, I don't know. Once or twice a month, I suppose. More often, some months. He seems to do it in fits and starts. I won't see him for a while, and then he might be there two days on the trot."

"You say 'some months', but as you have also pointed out, he only moved into the house next door a short time ago. Are you saying that he used to loiter here before that?"

"I'm sure that Gloria doesn't . . ." Tim held up his hand.

"Could you let her answer for herself, please, Mr. Bevelton?"

"Much longer than that," said Gloria with a kind of quiet defiance, as if she sensed that she was probably getting herself into trouble, but also realised that it was too late to turn back. "I can't remember a time when he didn't do it. The first time I saw him, I thought he might be a flasher or a stalker or something. But no, he just stands there, and if the door's open, sometimes he goes in."

Tim deliberately caught Henry Bevelton's eye. Henry immediately looked away, blinking rapidly.

"Did you know about these visits, Mr. Bevelton?"

"I . . . no, of course not. If I or Jason had seen him there, we would have asked him what he wanted and told him to go about his business."

Gloria opened her mouth to say something, and then closed it again. She looked flushed. Tim realised that he would probably not get any more from her for the moment. She would not contradict her boss deliberately.

"Thank you very much for the tea, Gloria," Tim said.

She took it as a sign that she should go, as he had intended.

She almost scurried away. Tim closed the door behind her. Henry Bevelton's face had acquired a ghastly pallor which could not entirely be attributed to the strange yellow light cast by the Chinese coolie hat light fittings.

"Mr. Bevelton, I believe that you told DC Armstrong that your acquaintance with Ronald Atkins was limited to the brief period in the mid-1970s when you were negotiating with his uncle for the purchase of the orchard that became your works yard?"

"That is essentially correct. I also mentioned that there had been a few chance meetings since, both with him and with his wife."

"How long has your secretary worked here?"

"Gloria? About ten years, I suppose."

"She seems to imply that Ronald Atkins has been a frequent visitor here for much of that time, and she states with certainty that his visits pre-date his taking up residence at his uncle's former house."

"Gloria is possibly mistaken. I can assure you that . . ."

The heavy workshop door was flung open, and Jason Beech hurried in. He looked excited.

"Inspector, I think you should come back. We've just started digging and we've found a large package in the ground. It's only a couple of feet from the surface. We haven't lifted it out yet."

Tim hurried out of the workshop, closely followed by Juliet and Gary Cooper. Giash Chakrabati stayed behind. He was alarmed by the fact that Henry Bevelton was standing stock still by the workbench, his face set mask-like in a grimace. He grasped the older man by the arm.

"Are you all right, Mr. Bevelton?"

"I . . . yes, of course I'm all right. I just felt a slight pain in my chest, that's all. Must be something to do with the cold. Or perhaps I drank my tea while it was still too hot."

"Why don't you sit down, sir? There's no need for you to go out there again."

"I . . . yes, I think you're right. I'll just sit here," said Henry. He backed away from the workbench and propped himself on a large upturned plastic tub in one of the corners of the workshop. He leaned his back against the wall and closed his eyes. Giash left him there and went outside.

The floodlight had been trained directly on to the hole that Jason Beech and his team had just gouged out of the ground. Still in place, but exposed and wiped free of most of the soil that had covered it, could be seen a large expanse of dirty plastic. The workmen were standing back slightly from their handiwork. The two detectives and Gary Cooper were crouching over the plastic. Detective Inspector Yates was holding a small paintbrush, which he was using to brush off some of the earth that was clinging to it. The atmosphere was taut with almost palpable excitement and anxiety. Everyone watched in silence. Each was both fascinated at what was being exposed, and apprehensive of what horror might be discovered next.

"Can you see anything?" asked Juliet Armstrong.

"I think that the plastic was once clear, or at least only semi-opaque," said Tim. "It's several layers thick. There's something large under there: it feels quite soft. I'm not sure whether I should risk cutting into it, or just call SOCOs at once."

"What's that, sir?" said Gary Cooper, pointing to one side of the plastic.

"What's what?"

"There's something lying there. Something small. It's lodged at the side of the package."

Tim fished around gingerly. His fingers brushed something small and hard. He did not quite grasp it before it slipped further down the gap between the plastic and the edge of the hole.

"Lost it!" said Tim. "Turn the floodlight off." Jason Beech went to do his bidding. The small group stood there motionless as the powerful electric glare abruptly ceased, charcoal silhouettes set in relief against the paler grey sky of the early spring dawn.

"Has anyone got a torch?"

"Yes," said Juliet.

"Come and shine it here, will you? A bit further over. That's it. Got it!"

He pulled a peg-like object out of the ground, and held it under the beam of the torch, rubbing off as much of the dirt that was clinging to it as he could.

"Christ!" he said.

"What is it, sir?"

"It's a plastic toy Red Indian. Juliet, get SOCOs here as quickly as they can come. PC Cooper, have some posts put in the ground and cordon off this area as a crime scene. Cordon off the gate as well. Juliet, go to the house next door and detain Ronald Atkins. Just wait with him until we are ready to take him to the station. He will probably want to ring his solicitor. Allow him to do so. PC Chakrabati, make sure that Henry Bevelton does not leave the premises."

CHAPTER THIRTY-FIVE

As she had done many times over the past two days, Juliet scrutinised the windows of the Atkins' house. All were in total darkness. She thought that it was near impossible that Ronald had not been watching the excavation work at Bevelton's, and wondered whether he was in fact still resident. If he had some guilty secret connected with the apple tree, he would have realised that it would be exposed once he had seen it being cut down yesterday. That would have left him more than twelve hours to take whatever action he saw fit. Running was an obvious option, though somehow not one that she thought Ronald would choose. It was not just that he was too old, or that he gave the impression of not being very resourceful; it was because his whole life seemed to have been bound up with this house and what had happened there. She guessed that Ronald would be incapable of shaking off his past, however dire the consequences might be.

She debated whether to approach the house through the garden and then imagined Jean Rook standing up in court and representing such an action as unfairly intimidating to her client. It was true that if Ronald were completely innocent and unaware of the activities that had been taking place in the old orchard, he would be frightened by a knocking at the back door, because there was no public access to it. Besides, in the unlikely event of his trying to escape now, he would be less likely to make a successful getaway through Bevelton's yard than by simply walking out of his own front door and into the street.

Two minutes later, Juliet was therefore standing at the old shop door, knocking as loud as she could against the glass and rattling the letterbox. There was no response. She tried to peer through the windows, shielding her eyes with her hands to try to accustom them to the darkness inside the shop. As she did so, the street light that faced the Needham house went out, and she was left in semi-darkness. She shone her torch into the building, but could see nothing.

She rattled the letterbox again, and hammered as hard on the glass as she could.

"Mr. Atkins? Are you there? It's the police."

There was still no response. The house was silent. Eerily silent, she thought, though it would have been difficult to explain why. She had entered many unoccupied houses that were just uncomplicatedly empty; and some, like this one, that projected a different kind of ambience altogether.

The door of the adjoining house suddenly began to judder. Juliet heard a strange clawing and scuffling sound coming from behind it. It alarmed her sufficiently to abandon the task in hand temporarily and move closer to it.

"Hello?" she called. "Miss Needham, isn't it? Can you hear me? Are you all right?"

The response was a great deal of shoving and pulling from the other side of the door. Finally, it was yanked open far enough to expose a three-inch crack, through which Juliet could discern a considerable quantity of unruly grey hair and two sharp brown eyes.

"This bloody door!" said Marjorie Needham. "I heard you knocking at the shop. Is something wrong?" Her voice was cracking with the effort of trying not to display her curiosity too blatantly.

"There's nothing wrong as far as I know," said Juliet. "I just want to have a word with Mr. Atkins. Have you seen him today? Or heard him moving about?"

"Neither hide nor hair," said Marjorie Needham. Through the crack, Juliet could see the mane of grey hair bouncing as she shook her head. "But he can't have missed all that digging you've been doing for the past three days. It would be enough to put the wind up both of them, I should think."

"What do you mean? Has Mrs. Atkins returned?"

"Not as far as I know; and not if she's got any sense."

"Who do you mean by 'both of them', then?"

"Ronald and Hedley, of course." She said it slowly and distinctly and with great emphasis, as if Juliet were rather slow on the uptake."

"Miss Needham, can I come in for a moment? I don't want to stand here on the street talking to you like this."

"Sure, if you can get in. Give the door a good push. It's easier to get in from the outside, than out from in."

Juliet did as she was bidden. The door did not budge. Juliet remembered the training that she had received for breaking into houses when it was suspected that the person inside was ill or in danger. She took a short run at the door, and rammed it with her shoulder. It yielded suddenly, and she found herself skidding to a halt almost in the middle of Miss Needham's small, untidy, and manifestly none-too-clean sitting-room.

Marjorie Needham stood near the fireplace thoroughly enjoying the excitement of it. She was dressed in an ancient semi-threadbare rose pink candlewick dressing-gown with frayed and dirty cuffs and her stance, with both hands on her hips, was almost combative. Juliet held out her own hand.

"DC Juliet Armstrong," she said. "I'm sorry to have disturbed you so early. Is there any more that you can tell me about Ronald Atkins? You say that you've seen Hedley Atkins as well, but could you have been mistaken? It's my understanding that he's on holiday in Scotland at the moment."

"Not any more, he isn't. Hedley was here last night. Definitely. It's the first time he's come to see his Dad, to my knowledge, since Ronald moved in."

"You're quite sure it was Hedley?"

"Oh yes. I may not have seen him for a while, but I've known him since he was a little lad. He's put on some weight since I last saw him, but he still has the same peculiar expression on his face. I'd know it anywhere."

"Did you see him leave?"

"Yes. It was late – almost midnight. I'm not usually up at that time myself, but I just happened to . . . what with all the comings and goings in Bevelton's yard." Marjorie's account trailed off lamely. She had the grace to look a little sheepish about the fact that she had clearly been spying on her neighbours.

"It's a good thing you were," said Juliet briskly. "Was Hedley alone when he left?"

"Yes. Why?"

"You're quite sure?"

"That's the second time you've asked me that. I may be old, but I've got all my marbles, you know. Hedley was certainly on his own."

"Did you see Ronald yesterday? Did he come out to meet Hedley when he arrived, for example, or wave him goodbye when he left?"

"I didn't see him at all while Hedley was there, but I did catch a glimpse of him much earlier, coming back from somewhere. He was carrying a parcel of some kind. He used the side door –the one that leads to the corridor beside the shop – which was not like him. Why do you ask?"

"I'm just making routine enquiries, for the moment, Miss Needham. I would ask Mr. Atkins himself if I could make him hear me. I suppose he could have slipped out earlier this morning, before you got up?"

"He could have," Marjorie agreed, "though that wouldn't have been like him, either."

"Well, if what you say is correct, which I'm sure it will be, he did a number of things that weren't part of his regular routine yesterday. I'll go to see if I can raise him again.

Thank you very much for being so helpful, Miss Needham."

"That's all right," said Marjorie Needham. She felt a sense of anti-climax as Juliet prepared for her departure by wrestling with the door again. "Any time. You know where I am."

Standing out on the street once more, Juliet noticed that the neighbourhood had started to stir. She consulted her watch. It was almost nine o'clock. She decided to have one last try at raising Ronald. She seized the letterbox doorknocker and rapped it continuously for about a minute. Then she bent to shout through the letterbox itself.

"Open up, Mr. Atkins. Police!"

The house remained totally silent and in darkness. In the street behind her, daylight was rapidly replacing the early morning gloom. The interior of the empty shop loomed at her spookily through the plate glass window. If Ronald was inside the house, he would surely have been up by now, or at least sufficiently roused from sleep to hear her knocking. There were three possible explanations: either he was inside and did not want to answer the door, he was there and could not answer the door, or he had gone somewhere else. If it was the last of these reasons, it was almost certainly because he had done a runner. "Put the wind up him," mused Juliet to herself. "Of course we have, if he had anything to hide. But we couldn't arrest him before – we didn't have anything to arrest him for – may still not have, in fact."

She debated what to do next. The shop door would be difficult to break open, because it was made almost entirely of toughened glass, and Tim had told her that it was fastened with a paranoid number of Chubb locks. Trying to force it would also attract an unwelcome amount of attention from passers-by. Already the two or three people who had walked past on the pavement had loitered as long as they could, curious to see whether they were about to witness some kind of scene. She decided that the best thing to do would be to go back to the tractor yard and force an entry via the back door.

The crime scene tapes had already been put in place when

she returned to Bevelton's. PC Cooper was standing in front of them, keeping guard. She ducked under them and saw Tim standing outside the workshop. His expression was stern, but he gave her a brief smile.

"What's the matter? Can't you find him?"

"No. He's not answering the door. I don't know for certain that he isn't inside the house. I thought that it would be better to force the back door than the front one, if it becomes necessary. I did see Marjorie Needham, though, or at any rate she saw me. She said that Hedley Atkins came here to visit his father last night. She's quite sure that it was him. She's also certain that when he left again he was on his own."

"Really?" Tim frowned, trying to piece together the logic of what he was hearing. "Yet you say that Ronald isn't answering. We'd better get in there pretty quick. I'll come with you. I want PC Chakrabati to stay with Henry Bevelton. PC Cooper can brief the SOCOs if they get here before we come back."

Juliet saw that the padlock and chain of the garden door that separated Bevelton's yard from the garden of the old shop had now been sawn through. Tim must have asked one of the Bevelton's men to cut it for him. Jason Beech and his workmen were gathered now at the opposite end of the yard. There was nothing for them to do until the SOCOs arrived, and they couldn't go home because Tim had forbidden any of them to leave the premises. They hung around, alternately resting one leg and then the other against the far wall. Some of them were smoking. They seemed apprehensive rather than disconsolate. Juliet thought that their mood might reflect their loyalty to Henry Bevelton, but it was as likely that they just dreaded finding a corpse. Most members of the public were curious about crime scenes, but few liked to witness the actual retrieval of human remains.

She hurried after Tim. He had wrenched open the gate and was walking briskly to the house. Juliet was afraid of running, because the path was almost obscured with slippery mud, a legacy from when the police had dug up the garden a few weeks before. This was the garden that long ago had been Doris Atkins' pride and main source of recreation – the garden that had 'killed' her. It was a sorry sight now.

Tim showed none of her compunction about knocking at Ronald Atkins' back door, and was hammering on it when she caught up with him. He paused at tried to peer through the kitchen window, which was mainly obscured by a heavy lace curtain.

"Can you see anything through the dining-room window?" he asked Juliet.

She pressed her face against the glass, and held her hands against the sides of her head to shut out the light from the garden.

"I can see a table and chairs – that's all. If there's someone in that room, they must be standing alongside this wall. But I don't think that there's anyone there. I've just got a feeling that the house isn't unoccupied, though."

"Funny thing – so have I, though I don't have a reason for it. We'll knock again, and if no-one answers, we'll force an entry."

He pounded on the door again, and rattled the handle, which did not budge. There was no response from inside the house, though Juliet thought that she heard a door opening very quietly on the Needham's side of the garden wall.

"Right," said Tim. "Stand back- I'm going to force it. I'll tell you if I need your help."

She moved a few steps back down the path, so that she was standing level with what appeared to be a covered wood-store. She noticed that there were some embossed brass plates hanging just below its roof. They'd probably been slung out years before, but she knew that they were eminently collectible now. There was something wedged behind one of them. She looked up as she heard Tim's shoulder thud against the door. There was the sound of splintering, but the door held firm. Tim was rubbing his shoulder.

"Juliet?" Tim called. "Can you give me a hand? The door's

beginning to give, but it probably needs a bit more oomph than I can manage now that I've bruised myself."

"Of course, sir," she said. She lined up beside him, thinking that this mode of entry was becoming a habit, and they charged the door together. It gave way suddenly, with a sharp rending noise. The momentum propelled them both into the middle of the kitchen floor. Juliet almost lost her balance, but Tim caught her by the arm.

"Steady!" he said.

They had each been in that house before and had some idea of the layout, though neither of them had visited the upstairs rooms. The kitchen had the same sour, slightly fungoid smell that they recognised from their previous visits. There were two plates propped on two upturned mugs on the draining board. The door that led to the dining-room was closed.

Tim yanked it open.

"Hello?" he called. "Mr. Atkins? It's Tim Yates of South Lincolnshire Police. Are you there? Can you hear me?"

He stepped into the dining-room. Juliet followed him.

The room was empty and cold. There was no fire in the grate. It was tidy and unremarkable, except for a newspaper, some of the sheets of which had been spread out across the table. The thin red line performed its perpetual trompe l'oeil. The grass-coloured curtain of thick, felt-like wool that masked the door that led to the passageway and the shop was drawn right across.

"Look, sir," said Juliet, pointing at the curtain.

Tim nodded.

"Whoever drew that curtain must have entered by the front door and gone straight upstairs without coming in here, or left by the back door," he said. "Let's hope it was Ronald."

"Why do you say that?" asked Juliet. "I thought we wanted to find Ronald . . ."

"We do," said Tim shortly. "Alive, preferably. I'm going

through to the rest of the house. I want you to stay here until I call you. Call me if you hear anything, or, obviously, if you see anyone in the garden. Got your mobile ready?"

"Yes, sir. I . . ."

Tim placed his finger on his lips.

"Quiet, now," he said. He thrust back the curtain, and then opened the door suddenly. A further obstacle blocked his view: it was the door with the stained glass panels which led into the passage. It had been bent back on its hinges as far as it would go. It took him aback momentarily, before he realised what it was and pushed it shut.

The hall and stairs were in darkness. Tim turned on neither the lights nor the torch that he was carrying. Juliet was right in the doorway, watching.

"Stay there!" he hissed at her. "Go back into the room."

She did as she was bidden, leaving the dining-room door slightly ajar. She heard Tim ascend the stairs slowly – each step creaked. The creaks stopped when he reached the landing.

"Jesus Christ," he said softly.

Juliet opened the door a little further and called out to him.

"Are you all right, sir?"

"Call an ambulance, Juliet," he said. "Now!"

She heard a sawing sound, then a dull thud. Later she realised that she had been listening to Tim cutting down the body of Ronald Atkins, which had been swinging from a rafter in the ceiling of the stairwell.

CHAPTER THIRTY-SIX

I've repeatedly tried to say that pushing me too far will be dangerous and Peter has taken no notice. Well, I've been pushed beyond reason now. My home no longer seems safe – I no longer feel as if I have control of it. When we came back from Scotland, I realised that Peter has made me hate the flat. He has made me hate my life and all that I am. My friend has turned into my enemy. My ghoulish family has risen up to strike out at me again. I shall strike back; *have* struck back. Who can blame me? I know that my liberty is at stake. The comfortable life that I have dredged out of my horrible childhood is all but destroyed.

I feel homeless, friendless, bereft of all peace of mind, as I plunge into the night. I have a final straw to clutch at. I have agreed to do Peter's bidding one last time and in return he has agreed to leave my flat and never to get in touch with me again. And never to tell anyone what he knows about me. I know that I shall be able to trust him to keep his word, not because of his sense of honour – I know that he has none – but because what he has asked of me makes him my accomplice. Once it's done, one word from me and Peter will lose not only all that he stands to gain from the deed, but life itself. One step out of line after it is over and he knows that I will not shrink from killing him. This is where I hold the trump card; this is my great virtue. In this I know myself to be truly formidable; in this I tower above him. I can and will kill. I will take a life if it gets in my way. Peter does not dare. He hasn't got the bottle. He is just a gadfly. I despise him now that I understand. But I fear him, too. I fear the intelligence that could work out all the details of the past with such cruel accuracy. No-one else could do that; even Tirzah did not get it right.

It is dark, and I am seated on the bus that goes to Peterborough. I need to catch the 20.21 train for Liverpool, and I keep looking at my watch. The bus arrives in Peterborough shortly after the hour, which gives me only a few minutes to reach the station and buy my ticket. I know that I will miss the train if the bus is not on time. It is my fault that I have cut it so fine. I've spent the day in a kind of waking nightmare, drained of all energy. Peter had to work out the travel details; I could not concentrate enough to do it myself. I glance at my watch again. The bus trundles on through the fens, maddeningly slow. I look out of the window into the darkness, and see my own reflection thrown back at me. I look like a man haunted, beleaguered. I try to smile, but my lips freeze into a rictus, a cruel parody of humour. I feel affronted. I feel outraged. I was just getting on with my life, harming no-one. I do not deserve this. The ever-present mingled panic and despair of the hunted. This anguish that has been imposed on me. It makes me full of rage. It fills me with the fight-back of the hunter.

I am being made to act recklessly now, I who have always shunned risk. And I can't predict the outcome of what has already happened. How do I know that the police will believe that Ronald Atkins killed himself? He'd already bought the rope. I didn't encourage him, but I didn't try to stop him either. I just stood and watched. My dear 'father'. Father. Father and Mother. Ronald and Tirzah. Dorothy and Colin. Mother.

I would have guessed if Colin hadn't told me, though perhaps not the exact truth. I knew that I was different. Not like Bryony. Not like my father. An Atkins, for sure, unlike

Tirzah; but still not like them.

There were always things about Colin that were difficult to understand. His relationship with my grandmother, for example. I don't mean in the actual sense: everyone of course knew that they were brother and sister, the two siblings left at the shop which had been in the family for seventy years. What was hard to fathom was the nature of their feelings for each other – or the lack of them. Why did she choose to stay in that house, where she was so shabbily treated? It was easier to work out why Colin did not drive her away: he needed a housekeeper and he was too mean to pay for one. But Doris? She could have left years before, when Ronald first started work. Perhaps it was already too late. Perhaps the shame and the routine were too ingrained.

Colin with his long nose, his deep brown eyes, his hunched back and stocky frame. He looked quite unlike anyone else in the family. Whereas Doris and her other brothers were slender, with round, blue-eyed Saxon faces.

Colin would sometimes talk to me about his childhood when there were no customers and he was sitting in the shop on his high stool. He was Eliza Atkins' youngest child, born six years after Robert, and three after Doris, when Eliza was well into her forties. Colin was the apple of her eye. Her explanation for his deformity was that he had been 'soured in the womb' by his father's brutish behaviour. She insisted that the family always referred to his condition as 'curvature of the spine'. The children in the street simply called him a 'hunchback'. Colin was not encouraged to mix with other children and he had started at the Board School a year late, when he was six. From his first day there, Doris was assigned the task of chief nursemaid and bodyguard. Her mission was to protect Colin from every possible harm. Doris was often impatient with Colin and sceptical about his many ills. Colin would tell Eliza if Doris was unkind to him, or if she abandoned him to the other kids.

Colin was always the golden boy. Later on Doris, who

had already weakened her relationship with her mother by not adoring Colin, became the mother of the bastard child Ronald and was disgraced. Perhaps that was why she had continued to look after her mother in her long decline, and then had still stayed to keep house for Colin after that: she was continuing to atone for her sins with the penance that Eliza had imposed. Perhaps it was just too late to escape. Doris would hear no ill spoken of Colin, though it was clear that she bore him little affection. There was a lot of poison trapped in the house at Westlode Street. A lot of poison in my (titular) parents' house, too.

Titular indeed. I couldn't credit it when first Colin told me, but then when I thought about it I came to see how it might just be the truth. My mother couldn't possibly have loved Colin, or have even been attracted to him. Even if he hadn't cut the sort of shambling figure that he did, I don't think that in any case she thought in such terms. But she did respect property; she did respect wealth, even if of a modest kind; and I think that she had a sneaking admiration for the material success that had grown out of Colin's grasping nature. Added to that, of course, was her plainly-stated belief that marriage was a form of business transaction. The transaction between herself and Ronald had broken down, though the shell that had housed it remained. I doubt that she would have had the slightest compunction about replacing it with another, on the same exchange-of-goods basis.

My impending arrival must have given her a jolt, nevertheless. I wonder if she deliberately allowed it to happen, or whether it was a mistake? What did she tell Ronald? Was the fact of my existence the reason behind all those hideous night-time rows? There was one thing of which I could be certain: that everyone, including Tirzah, had loved Bryony best, even if with the very imperfect love which was all my family was capable of.

You'd think that that would have struck a chord with Doris, because Colin had always received more of her mother's love than she did. You'd think that she would have noticed the same injustice being done to me. But she showed just as much favour to Bryony as everyone else did.

As for Colin: apart from telling me the secret, which I supposed passed for a sort of intimacy, he barely took more notice of me than of the other children in the neighbourhood. Less, if they had been sent on errands by their mothers, and had money to spend. But telling me was actually an act of supreme selfishness, because it turned me into a freak, an outcast with an unpleasant secret coursing through my blood. And he didn't balance it up with anything good that could help me. No affection, no generosity. He wouldn't even give me one of those cheap plastic Red Indians, to put on my desk at work. I took the whole bag, to annoy him.

I didn't care much about Colin, though, and I never saw eye to eye with Ronald, even during my childhood, when I still believed that he was my father. It was Tirzah that I cared for, Tirzah whom I wanted to impress. And I loved Bryony, too, in spite of myself. Bryony's death was an accident. Truly, it was an accident.

When I was little, Tirzah always hated it when my grandmothers visited. She particularly minded her own mother's visits. Her mother was called Eliza, the same name as my great-grandmother's, Colin's mother. Since I knew the secret, I've often thought what a strange coincidence this was. I was nine years old when Tirzah's Eliza died. I remember the day of her last visit. Tirzah and Ronald had been up half the night before, having one of their terrible rows. It was some time after I realised that sending up a prayer-funnel was not going to have any effect. I lay quivering under the sheets as I always did during their fights, unable to sleep in case something dreadful happened before I woke up again.

The next morning I found myself listening to something very unusual when I was getting dressed: Tirzah was apologising to Ronald. She said that the row had been her fault, and it was because she was always tense and upset before Eliza's visits. I think that they may even have embraced.

I knew then that Eliza was the cause of all the rows, and I reasoned that if I could put a stop to Eliza's visits, it would not only end the arguments between my parents, but also make Tirzah love me more than anyone. It was simple logic, really. I didn't bear Eliza any ill-will – she was nice enough to me, even if, like most of Tirzah's family, she seemed to prefer girls to boys – but her life had got in the way of the smooth running of my family, and therefore I had to take it. I didn't put it in quite those terms at the time, of course, but that was what I meant.

When I came home from school on the day of her last visit, I went straight up to my room to wait for tea. Bryony and I had walked home from school together that day, but she stayed in the dining-room, talking to Tirzah and Eliza. I knew that Eliza would come upstairs herself just before tea-time, to powder her nose and wash her hands. It was what she always did. I waited in my room, listening, until she went into the bathroom, and then I stretched one of the French skipping ropes that Bryony had plaited out of rubber bands across the top of the stairs, fastening it on the wainscotting on either side of the staircase with drawing-pins. I went back into my room. I heard my grandmother come out of the bathroom, take a couple of steps, and then there was a crash and a cry and a series of bumps as she fell down the whole flight. A soon as the bumping stopped, I came out of my room and knelt at the top of the stairs to unpin the French skipping. I worked at it as quickly as I could, but the rubber broke away from the drawing-pin, leaving some strands trapped behind it on the skirting-board. I was still trying to prise the drawing-pin free when Tirzah came through the door from the kitchen into the hall. I looked up and met her eye, and I knew that she knew. She didn't say a word. She was looking past me. I became aware of Bryony, standing behind me. She must have just come out of my parents' room, dressed up in my grandmother's scarf. She and my grandmother must have come upstairs together. It was not until afterwards that I realised that Bryony had pushed her. I yanked the drawing-pin free and scooped up the pieces of rubber, and put them in my pocket.

Tirzah found her voice then. She told me and Bryony to come down the stairs and go to watch television in the din-ing-room. We did as she said, taking the hall door that led into the kitchen and then the kitchen door into the dining-room, because the hall door to the dining-room was blocked by the body. We had to step over our grandmother's legs on our way through.

As a family, we never discussed what had happened. Like the prayer-funnels, though, it didn't work. The arguments continued. My relationship with Tirzah didn't improve, either: in fact, I sometimes saw something close to dread flicker across her face when she looked at me. Her attitude to Bryony was changed, too.

The circumstances of Bryony's death were quite different, although paradoxically the way in which she died was very similar. I knew, of course, that after our split Kathryn had remained friends with Bryony. . . .

Shit. The bus is standing at some temporary traffic lights and I haven't notice that it has stopped. I look at my watch. It is already almost eight o'clock and we haven't reached the outskirts of Peterborough yet. I am on tenterhooks now. I hear the engine of the bus judder into life again and we rumble on, far too sedately to ease my nerves. I fidget with my watch strap and make myself count sixty between each time check. The driver is getting up speed now and I think that perhaps we might make it, when some hideous crone stands and presses the button. She is a fat old woman with several baskets and packages and it takes her an age to haul herself up the aisle of the bus and out on to the pavement. I feel faint with worry, overwhelmed with an exhausting mixture of frustration and anger.

At last the bus stops at the Queensgate shopping centre. This is where almost everyone wants to get off it and I have to force my way through. An old man sticks his elbow out and tells me to mind my manners. I brush him away, jump off the bus, and sprint to the railway station. I hear indignant voices calling after me, but I can't hear what they are saying and in any case I don't care. It is not far to the station, but I am weak with anxiety. My mouth is dry and I can't breathe properly. I can see that it has begun to rain, but I can't feel the rain on my skin, which is burning as if with a fever. As I reach the station, I get a stitch in my side and have to rest against a wall for some moments. Then I forge on. I run into the station and make for the departures board. It says 20.19. My train is already standing at Platform 3. I see that there is only one man in the ticket office, serving a queue of three people. I know that it is impossible for me to buy a ticket in time, and decide to board the train without one. There are no platform barriers to hinder me. I can explain my predicament once I'm on board, offer to buy a ticket then and if necessary pay a fine. I run onto the platform. I'm about to board the train, when I'm intercepted by one of those female railway officials dressed in long red coats who seem to spend their lives standing on platforms waving miniature tennis bats. She demands to see my ticket. I'm about to explain how important that it is that I catch the train when its doors close. I lunge towards the one nearest to me, intending to push the button to open it again, but the female with the bat holds me back. It takes all my self-discipline not to knock her down, as together we watch the train glide out of the station.

CHAPTER THIRTY-SEVEN

Tim Yates decided to wait until after the forensic pathologist had made an initial assessment of Ronald Atkins' likely cause of death and the time at which he had died, before he authorised a return to work on the raising of the package buried in Bevelton's yard. The pathologist, Professor Stuart Salkeld, would have to travel from Leicester University, so there would be a two-hour wait until he arrived. Giash Chakrabati was detailed to stand guard with the body. In the meantime, Tim called Andy Carstairs and asked him to apprehend Hedley Atkins and take him to the police station for questioning. The SOCOs arrived while he was doing this. Juliet Armstrong remained with Henry Bevelton, who seemed to have recovered both his health and his composure. He had been informed of Ronald Atkins' death, but asked to keep the information to himself until told otherwise. He did not appear to be unduly distressed by the news of Ronald's demise. It occurred to Juliet that possibly he was relieved: any shady dealings they may have had had or whatever bargains might have been struck between them could now only be disclosed according to Henry Bevelton's own version of what they had hatched.

Professor Salkeld examined the body meticulously before he pronounced that the cause of death was strangulation by hanging from a ligature placed around the neck. The ligature itself was made of reinforced plastic rope, of the kind commonly used for washing-lines. Asked by Tim whether he thought that Ronald Atkins' death had been a suicide, Professor Salkeld was cautious.

"It could have been," he said. "As you see, there is an over-turned chair on the landing. Did you find it like that, or was it disturbed when you cut the body down?"

"It was like that," said Tim. "I stood on one of the other chairs on the landing to cut down the body, so that that one shouldn't be disturbed. I'll have it checked for prints. Am I right in thinking that you are not ruling murder out as a possibility?"

"I'm not ruling it out," said Professor Salkeld, "but a death by hanging is much more likely to be suicide than murder. If you think about it, it is quite difficult to string someone up against their will, and I see no signs of struggle on the corpse. However, he was an old man, and someone stronger and younger than he was could have overpowered him without injuring him."

"Or he could have chosen not to resist," said Tim.

"Quite. Whether it was suicide or not, the act itself was carried out very professionally. Someone knew exactly what they were doing. It looks as if he died quickly and relatively painlessly. It's quite easy to botch a hanging, you know. Worth researching properly if that's how you're intending to finish things." He gave a wry smile. "Of course, you can probably find out how to do it on the Internet these days."

"And the time of death, Professor?"

"I'd say less than twelve hours ago. He's certainly not been dead for more than fifteen hours."

Tim looked at his watch. It was just after 2 p.m.

"So at midnight or in the early hours of this morning?"

"In all probability, yes. I'd like to do some more checks on the body, though. Examine the stomach contents, check for signs of alcohol or barbiturates, that kind of thing. I'll have it removed to my laboratory at the university, if that's OK with you?"

"Of course," said Tim. "Thank you. If you don't have a pressing need to return to Leicester immediately, I'd be grateful if you could stay here this afternoon. We're in the process of digging up something which could turn out to be human remains in the works yard which adjoins this property."

"Indeed?" Professor Salkeld raised one black and bushy eyebrow. "Is this a coincidence, or do you think that the two events might be connected?"

"I think that there's every likelihood that they are connected. In fact, I think that Ronald Atkins' death was precipitated by the police excavations that have been taking place next door."

"I see. No doubt you will explain it all to me in your own good time. Thank you for telling me, though. It will make me extra vigilant when I'm looking for any signs that his death was a murder. And of course I will stay. Otherwise, you'll only be dragging me back here again tomorrow, won't you? Is there any prospect of a cup of tea?"

The SOCOs had erected a tent over the place where the package had been semi-unearthed. Two of them were kneeling inside the tent. They were carefully loosening the earth around the package, and digging deep holes on either side of it in order to try to insert ropes underneath it and lever it out gently. Henry Bevelton's men were standing around a little distance away, uncertain of whether or not their help was still required, trying to peer into the tent from time to time. Jason Beech was standing a little apart from them, looking slightly aggrieved. Tim realised that he probably felt that it was unfair that the Bevelton's gang had been ousted by the SOCOs, just when things were getting interesting. He went across to talk to Jason.

"Your men can go home now, if you wish, Mr. Beech. I don't think we'll be needing them here again today. I'm not sure when they'll be able to work in this yard again – almost certainly not tomorrow. I'll keep in touch with you about it – and Mr. Bevelton, of course. I'd like to thank you and your team for the help that you've given us here. I'd also like you to ask everyone to be discreet about what you've seen. Please don't talk to anyone about it, particularly the press."

Jason nodded and moved back to his mates. They stood in a huddle, talking, and then gradually dispersed. Only Jason himself was left.

"Is it all right if I stay?" he asked.

"Not here, if you don't mind," said Tim levelly. "Perhaps you'd like to join Mr. Bevelton in the office?"

Jason Beech scowled, but nodded. Strange bloke, thought Tim.

He turned back to the tent. The SOCOs had levered out the package now, and were placing it on a tarpaulin. Stuart Salkeld had squeezed into the tent with them, and was giving them instructions, his words blurred slightly by the cotton mask that he had placed over his nose and mouth. Like the SOCOs, he was wearing a white paper suit as well as the mask. They all wore surgical rubber gloves.

"Don't pierce it – don't tilt it, if you can help it. Easy now. That's it. Well done."

The package was about five feet long, and sausage-shaped. It was quite thick. The outer covering was of opaque plastic sheeting, which had become brittle and faded with the passing of time, but which had once been blue. It was wrapped around at intervals with thick bands of tape, and also tied in several places with rope.

The two SOCOs came out for a breather, allowing Tim the space to crawl into the tent.

"What now?" he asked Professor Salkeld.

"I'm going to make a small incision in the plastic," he said. "I'll have to drill into it to quite a depth, because I think that the plastic has been wrapped around whatever it contains many times. If your guess is correct, and it contains human remains, there will probably be a thick soupy fluid trapped in this parcel. Decomposed human tissue. If the body had been buried in the open ground for the thirty-odd years that you're suggesting, all that would have remained by now, besides the bones and teeth, and possibly some hair, would have been black stains in the surrounding soil. But if there's a body in there, the fluids resulting from decomposition will have been trapped in the plastic, and are probably still there. Put on a face mask," he added. "If I'm right, this won't be pleasant."

Tim noticed for the first time that Patti Gardner was one of the SOCOs. She was standing nearest to the entrance of the tent, smoking a cigarette. Tim poked out his head.

"Hey, Patti," he said, grinning. "Pass us a face mask, will you?"

She turned to face him, then turned away again to exhale the smoke from her lungs. She walked over to the police van which she had driven there earlier that day and rummaged in the back of it, returning with a mask, latex gloves and a full protective suit, all of which she passed to Tim, stooping so that he could reach them easily.

"Thanks," he said, still grinning. She regarded him levelly.

"My pleasure," she said. He didn't miss the hurt in her eyes. He felt guilty about Patti sometimes. He knew that he hadn't treated her well. He scrambled into the suit and pulled on the gloves and mask.

Stuart Salkeld had affixed a slender bit to his drill, and was testing it on a piece of cardboard.

"Perfect," he said. "Lean back."

Tim squashed himself against the tent wall, sitting back on his heels. Stuart Salkeld held the drill above the plastic for a moment, then applied it deftly. The drill whirred efficiently. It only took a few seconds to produce a result. Tim had smelt death before, on many occasions, but he had never before experienced a stench like this. The tent was filled with the evil reek of remains that had been trapped in a synthetic shroud for decades. Black tar-like fluid was bubbling up through the plastic, trying to escape through the drill-hole. Stuart Salked produced a syringe, and poked it through the hole, suctioning up some of the vile liquid.

"I'm going to try to seal the plastic again, and have the whole thing moved as it is to the lab," he said. "But just in case that doesn't work, I'll remove some of this stuff now, for DNA testing and so on."

"It is a body, then?" said Tim.

Stuart Salkeld regarded him with cool amusement.

"What do you think?" he replied. "This parcel contains animal remains for sure, and from the shape and size of the parcel – and the very fact that they're in a parcel, as well as the distinctive smell – I'd guess that they are human. What we need to find out now is how long they've been here and, even more to the point as far as you're concerned, whose they were. Of course, we think we know the answer, which gives us a bit of a head start, doesn't it?"

Tim nodded. But by the time that Professor Salkeld had finished speaking, he was barely listening. He scrambled out of the tent, ripping off the mask and the gloves, and rummaged under the overall for his mobile phone. He pressed one of the speed dials.

"Andy?" he said. "Have you managed to get hold of Hedley Atkins yet?"

"Hello, sir. I'm at his flat now. He's not at work – technically speaking he's still on holiday – and he's not here, but his flat-mate is. A man called Peter Prance. I can't get any sense out of him. He won't tell me where Hedley is, or when he'll be back."

"Take him to the station, will you? I'm coming to join you. I'll be there as soon as I can."

He looked at his watch. It was almost six o'clock in the evening.

CHAPTER THIRTY-EIGHT

When Tim entered the interview room at Spalding police station, he found Andy Carstairs sitting at the table opposite a slight, finely-boned man with short white hair thinning on top. His face was narrow, his eyes black and beady, and his complexion bore the red-brick tinge peculiar to the incipient alcoholic. He was wearing a very offended expression.

"You cannot expect me to drink tea out of *that*!" the slight man was saying, making a small moue of disgust and pointing derisively with a manicured index-finger at a white polystyrene cup. "And before you suggest pouring it into a mug, I must tell you that I never use them. I need a tea-cup. And some fresh tea, now, in all probability. That has been *stewing* there for at least ten minutes now." During this last sentence his voice had risen by an octave.

Andy's reply was such a model of strained politeness that his words almost became a parody of what they were saying. Tim remembered that Andy had already spent most of the afternoon in this man's company and reflected that he himself would probably have lost his temper by this stage. The man was in any case so arrogant that he did not suspect that Andy was taking the piss.

"Well, I'm sorry, but I can't help you there, sir," Andy was saying. "The girls in the typing pool might have some cups, but they've all gone home now. I suggest that you try to drink it anyway. It looks as if we've got a long night ahead of us."

By now, Andy's interviewee had turned to focus his attention on Tim. He evidently sensed that Tim was the more senior officer, and sprang to his feet, holding out his hand.

"Peter Prance," he said in clipped tones.

Tim took the outstretched hand.

"Detective Inspector Tim Yates. Do sit down again, Mr. Prance. Am I to understand that you are Mr. Hedley Atkins' lodger?"

The small man immediately became very agitated. He had begun to retake his seat, but now he jumped up again.

"Lodger!" he squealed. "I hardly think that that is the appropriate term. Hedley and I are partners." He rolled his eyes. "Lovers, if you will."

"Indeed," said Tim. "Then perhaps you accompanied him on his recent holiday? It was to Scotland, I believe?"

"Yes," said Peter Prance. He tilted his chin at Tim. "It was my treat, if you must know."

"Oh?" said Tim. "How very nice of you. Do sit down, sir. I understand from Mr. Atkins' colleagues that the holiday was not due to finish until Saturday. It's only Thursday today. Was there a reason for cutting it short?"

Peter Prance swatted the air with a curved hand.

"Oh, Inspector, now you're playing games. You know very well that you sent out a radio broadcast suggesting that Hedley should return home."

"Yes, I did send out a broadcast: but what I specifically asked him to do was to get in touch with the police here. He hasn't done that yet, and there is something of great urgency that I want to discuss with him. I therefore need to know where he is. I understand that you haven't been willing to give that information to DC Carstairs. I must warn you, Mr. Prance, that if you know of Mr. Atkins' whereabouts and refuse to disclose it to us, we can charge you with obstructing the police."

"Oh, well if you're going to get rough, I must insist on

having a solicitor present. And some more tea while we're waiting, in a *cup*, if you please."

Tim sighed. It was indeed going to be a long night. He got up to leave the interview room, motioning Andy Carstairs to follow him.

"I'm going to send one of the coppers on the desk in with some more tea," he said. "It'll give you a bit of a breather from him. I'll go and call the duty solicitor. Let's hope we get someone reasonable. In the meantime, can you check to see if he's got form? The way he's behaving, I'm pretty certain it's not the first time he's seen the inside of a police station."

"You may be right," said Andy. "On the other hand, he may just be an arrogant little fucker."

Tim grinned. "Maybe we're both right. It's worth finding out, anyway."

The duty solicitor turned out to be Chris McGill. Tim was pleased. Mr. McGill was conscientious enough, but not over-zealous when it came to expostulating about his client's rights. He arrived less than an half an hour after he received Tim's call, still wearing a dinner jacket. He was carrying a canvas holdall.

"Is there somewhere I can change? I've come straight from the rotary dinner. It was just about to start. I don't feel like exposing myself to the ridicule of our man by appearing dressed like this."

"Actually, this particular client would probably respect you a great deal more if he did see you dressed like that, but I take your point. Please use my office to change in. You know where it is, I think? I'm sorry I dragged you away from the dinner."

"Don't be. I'd almost rather be here. My wife is none too pleased, though."

Ten minutes later, Tim and Chris McGill joined Peter Prance in the interview room. He was sitting ramrod straight in his chair, drinking tea from a china cup. Tim recognised it as the cup that Molly, who ran the station canteen, kept on the counter as a receptacle for tips. He smiled inwardly.

Knowing Sergeant Jackson as he did, he doubted if he'd given it more than a cursory wash out. He hoped that Peter Prance was enjoying his tea.

Tim turned on a hand-held tape recorder. "Detective Inspector Yates interviewing Mr. Peter Prance. Mr. Chris McGill, solicitor, is present, to advise Mr. Prance. Date: Thursday 24th February. Time: 20.08 hours."

He placed the tape recorder on the desk between them.

"Now, Mr. Prance," he said. "I want to make it clear that you are not here under suspicion of any crime and I have no wish to keep you for a minute longer than is necessary. I do, however, have the power to detain you for up to twenty-four hours without making a charge and I shall certainly exercise that power if you do not co-operate. Do I make myself clear?"

Peter Prance glanced across at the solicitor, who nodded.

"Perfectly clear," he said in an aggrieved voice, "though I can think of nicer ways of putting it."

"How much do you know of Hedley Atkins' background?"

"I know that his mother was Dorothy Atkins, if that's what you mean. The woman who killed her mother-in-law."

"That is correct. Did he talk about her much?"

"Hardly ever, Inspector. May I ask why you're using the past tense?"

"Because I'm talking about the past, Mr. Prance. The present is now. Since he is not here, you are clearly not able to say what Hedley Atkins is talking about at this moment, and I am assuming that you don't claim to know what he will say in the future?" Tim paused for a moment. Peter Prance lowered at him, then dropped his eyes. Tim continued. "When I was trying to locate Hedley Atkins while you were both in Scotland this week, it was because I wanted to let him know that his mother had died suddenly."

"Really? What a thing!"

"You don't sound very surprised, Mr. Prance."

"We did know she had died, but I didn't know the lady. Her death is of little consequence to me."

"Can you tell me what effect the news had on Hedley?"

Peter shot Chris McGill a mischievous look.

"Should I answer that?"

Chris McGill sighed.

"Strictly speaking, Inspector, that question is not answerable, since you cannot expect my client to be able to read Hedley Atkins' mind. However, it would be perfectly all right to ask him what *impression* he had of Mr. Atkins' feelings when he heard the news."

Peter Prance cocked his head expectantly.

"Well?" he said.

"Your *impression* of his feelings, then, Mr. Prance, if you don't mind recollecting them."

"Not at all. I'd say that he was agitated. And a little upset. Quite a normal response to such news."

"Indeed. And can you explain how he came to hear the news? The radio announcement simply asked him to contact me for news about his family. It did not say what it was."

Peter Prance glared furiously. He realised immediately that he had fallen into a trap.

"Very clever, Detective Inspector. Touché."

"I'm not playing a game, Peter. I am gravely concerned about Hedley Atkins' state of mind at present, and I want to know his whereabouts. Now answer the question, *if* you please."

Peter Prance looked at the solicitor again. Chris McGill nodded encouragement.

"He made a phone call."

"To whom did he make the call?"

"I really don't know," said Peter Prance slyly. "He made the call from one of those hooded contraptions in the foyer of our hotel. He didn't want to use the telephone in our room, for some reason."

"Was he calling Ronald Atkins, his father?"

"I've told you that I don't know . . ."

"Mr. Prance, aside from myself and the members of my

team, there were only two people to whom he could have spoken who could have known of his mother's death. One was his father, and the other was Margaret Meredith, the Matron of the home in which his mother lived. Now, I can easily call Mrs. Meredith and ask her if she received a call from Hedley; or you can tell me who he called. Which is it to be?"

"Now I think about it, he did say something about checking with his father," Peter muttered.

"Thank you."

Peter Prance looked up at the clock on the wall. It suddenly dawned on Tim that he was stalling for time, not just for the sake of it, but until a specific moment known only to himself had passed.

Andy Carstairs re-entered the room at that moment.

"Could I have a word?" he said.

"Of course. Detective Inspector Yates, leaving the interview room in the company of DC Carstairs. Time: 7.45 p.m. Mr. Chris McGill of McGill & Son, Solicitors, remains in the room with Mr. Peter Prance."

"What is it?" asked Tim irritably. "I was just beginning to rattle him. I must find out where Hedley Atkins is. I'm convinced that he's doing something this evening that Peter Prance knows about, very possibly something illegal, or something that he doesn't want us to find out about – or at least not until it's too late. If what I'm thinking is correct, Hedley is already responsible for two, possibly three, murders, and may be contemplating another. If so, he'll be desperate to do it before we can locate him. Catching him tonight may be vital."

For answer, Andy handed over a computer print-out.

"This might help then, sir. You were right when you guessed that Prance's got form. The list of convictions is fairly short, but I wouldn't mind betting that there are others that have been expunged from the record because he was fly enough to get acquitted. Fraud charges, mostly, associated with gambling swindles – not the sorts of offences for which juries tend to sympathise with the victims, because they're usually guilty as well as the perpetrators. It's all a question of degree. He's mostly been fined or sentenced to community service, but he did do time for one stretch. Three years ago, he served eight months of a fourteen-month sentence for embezzlement, at HMP Liverpool. He got beaten up while he was in there, too. Officially it was just the kind of routine beating often dished out by the inmates to nancy-boys when they're inside, but the prison governor thought there was probably more to it. He thought that Prance's crime might just be the tip of an iceberg, part of some bigger fraud, and that he was being warned to keep his mouth shut. The governor suspected that a local racketeer called Whitey Coonan was at the back of it. Whoever it was, the beating left Prance terrified, and it served its purpose. He clammed up completely. His sentence was reduced by more than the usual period of remission for good behaviour, because arguably he should have been better protected by the prison authorities, so he was let out shortly afterwards, on probation. He asked if he could move to London immediately and register with a probation officer there. After that, as far as his criminal record goes, there is nothing until now."

"Thanks, Andy. Well done," said Tim. "Are you coming back in there with me?"

"Let's take it in turns, shall we? You carry on now you've started to get to him, and I'll come back if you aren't getting anywhere. We'll keep Chris McGill sweet that way: his idea of fair play is likely to be better satisfied by one cop against one witness."

"True," said Tim, "you're probably right – especially as Prance isn't a suspect. Yet."

Tim returned to the interview room. Peter Prance was expatiating on the merits of professionally-starched collars and cuffs. Chris McGill was listening, his arms folded, an affable smile on his lips.

"Right," said Tim. "I'm sorry about the interruption." He picked up the tape-recorder again. "Detective Inspector Tim

Yates, returning to the interview room, 7.58 p.m. Now, Mr. Prance, when did you arrive home from your holiday?"

"Yesterday evening."

"What sort of time?"

"It was about eight o'clock. I remember saying that we would have to send out for something for supper, because there was no food in the flat, but Hedley said that he wasn't hungry. He said that I should go round to the Punch Bowl and get something to eat there."

"And did you?"

"Yes. I unpacked my suitcase and left after that. I was in quite a hurry, because they stop serving food at 8.30."

"Bit of a rough pub, the Punch Bowl, isn't it?"

Peter Prance rolled his eyes heavenwards.

"Needs must, Inspector, on occasion. Besides, I'm not averse to a little bit of roughness, sometimes." He giggled. "To tell you the truth, I was gagging for a drink. By some oversight, there was no alcohol in the flat and we'd had none on the train, either."

"I see. At what time did you return?"

"Oh, it was quite late. After 11 p.m., I should think."

"Was Hedley Atkins in the flat when you returned?"

"Yes – no. I'm not sure."

"Come on, Peter, you can do better than that. Was he there, or not?"

Peter Prance's eyes flickered and were drawn to the clock again.

"I don't think that he was. I'd had a few drinks, you understand. I didn't see him, certainly."

"Thank you. And when did you see him again? Definitely see him, that is."

"This morning. He was already up when I got up."

"Did he say anything to you? Did he tell you where he went last night?"

"No."

"Did you ask him?"

"No."

"Mr. Prance, may I reiterate my previous statement about being obstructive? If you waste police time or try to pervert the course of justice, you might just end up with another custodial sentence. You wouldn't want to find yourself back at HMP Liverpool, would you?"

"That's a threat!" screeched Peter Prance, looking accusingly at the solicitor. "You tell him! That was a threat!" He was clearly scared.

"It might possibly be construed as a threat," said Chris McGill mildly. "On the other hand, it might just have been intended as a friendly warning."

Peter Prance looked at the clock again.

"You seem to be very interested in that clock. Have an appointment this evening, do you? If so, you're not going the right way about keeping it. Let's try again. What did Hedley Atkins talk to you about this morning?"

"His mother's death. And the funeral arrangements."

"Had he made progress with them?"

"I believe some progress, yes."

"Then he'd been to see his father?"

"I very much doubt it. He never went to see his father, in my experience."

"Then he couldn't have made progress with the funeral arrangements. Hedley Atkins was his mother's next of kin, but his father was the executor of her will. Either by an oversight or by her own design, she hadn't changed her will at the time of her divorce, so Ronald Atkins was responsible for organising her funeral. And before you decide that I am forgetting my grammar again, I say 'was' because that is the correct tense in this instance. Ronald Atkins also died last night."

Peter Prance's look of astonishment could not have been fabricated. It was quickly replaced by an expression of intense fear.

"May I have a glass of water?"

"Of course. Let's take a short break, shall we?"

CHAPTER THIRTY-NINE

I feel calmer when I've boarded the next train, even though it means a long wait in Birmingham. I will still arrive in Liverpool before 8 a.m., well before she has left her house. I get off this train at New Street Station just before 11 p.m. and head for the waiting-room. There is an electric fire mounted on the wall in there, and a heater suspended over the door, giving out waves of heat. At the moment there are still a few people sitting half-asleep on the plastic chairs, waiting for the last ride home, but I think that they'll disappear soon enough, and leave me in peace. I think I'll probably be able to get some sleep in here before I catch my connection, which is due to depart at 4.03 a.m. tomorrow. The place is squalid with discarded sandwich wrappings and empty cardboard coffee cups. I've seen a cleaner further up the platform, clearing up debris with a huge brush. I hope that he won't want to come in here and disturb me.

The station lights dim just as the last person leaves the waiting-room and I stretch myself across four of the plastic chairs, as near to the wall-heater as I can get. I've set the alarm on my mobile phone and am just falling asleep when the lights in the waiting-room are snapped on again and a fat person enters, all of a bustle with his own importance. He talks to me civilly, however.

"Now then, sir, missed your train, have you?"

"No," I say, "it isn't due for several hours yet."

"Well, I'm about to close up the waiting-room. I'll be opening it again at 6 a.m. tomorrow, before I go off duty. I'm afraid you'll have to find somewhere else to wait meantime. We can't let people stay in here overnight. It's against the rules."

"Are you saying you're going to kick me out?"

"Sorry, I've no option. The waiting-rooms are closed at night. Security."

I swing my legs round, and plant my feet on the ground. I don't like him, and I'm taking my time. I stand up slowly.

"I suppose I'll have to wait on the platform, then."

"I'm sorry, sir, that's not allowed, either. There are no more passenger trains now for almost four hours, and our instructions are always to clear the station overnight. We'll be opening it up again about ten minutes before the first train is due in, tomorrow. You'll be able to see when that is if you look at the board."

I see red. I'd like to punch him, but I'm conscious of the need not to make myself conspicuous. I have to get to Liverpool without anyone taking too much notice of me.

"That's quite outrageous," I say half-heartedly. "You mean to say that you're turning me adrift into a city I don't know, with nowhere to sleep?"

"I wouldn't say that, sir. If you come back with me to the office, I can give you some lists of hotels and boarding houses where they'll accept you this late. Quite reasonably priced, some of them. You'll be more comfortable in one of them."

I shrug, and walk away. When I reach the ticket barrier, I see that it has been left open. There is another railway official standing beside it, but he barely looks at me. I shoulder the small rucksack that I am carrying and walk out of the station and into the night.

CHAPTER FORTY

Peter Prance was sitting with his head bowed, staring list-lessly at his hands, when Tim Yates decided to re-start the interview. It was some ten minutes after his announcement of Ronald Atkins' death. Chris McGill was still sitting next to Peter, looking tired to death. Tim guessed that he would be a more than willing ally in coaxing Peter to speak if he persisted with his prevarications.

When Tim entered the interview room, Peter Prance clutched at the plastic cup of water that he had been given, and started taking tiny anxious sips from it. All of his former chutzpah had vanished. He looked worried, bent and old. Just a few minutes before, he had seemed wiry and sinewy, but now he appeared to be gaunt to the point of emacia-tion. He shivered and his hand shook, causing him to spill a dollop of the water on to the table. Tim mopped at it with a paper towel.

"Are you all right, Mr. Prance? Are you feeling well?"

"Quite well, quite well," he muttered. "It's just a bit of a shock, that's all."

"What is a shock, sir? The news that Ronald Atkins is dead? Did you know Ronald Atkins?"

"No. I never met him. I've told you, Hedley didn't see him."

"Why has his death had such an effect on you, then? As you pointed out when we were discussing Dorothy Atkins' death, you weren't upset because you weren't acquainted with her. Why doesn't the same apply to your feelings for her former husband?"

"It's not the man himself I care about," said Peter, a ghost of his testiness returning, "it's the fact that he is dead."

"You have me there, sir, I'm afraid. Either you're talking in riddles, or I'm more obtuse than I thought I was." He leant across the table at Peter and thrust his face as close to the small man's as he dared without being reprimanded by the solicitor.

"Let's stop this nonsense now, Peter, shall we? I need to find Hedley Atkins, and I need to find him tonight. I have good reason to believe that he is behaving in an unbalanced way and that he may be dangerous, to himself as well as to others. I've no idea where he is or what he is up to, but I think that you do. I'm asking you once last time to give me what information you have. If you don't . . ."

Chris McGill jerked himself into alertness and held up his hand.

"Detective Inspector Yates, I must protest . . ."

"It's all right," said Peter Prance. "I will tell you what I know. I never thought that Hedley really was capable of murder, you see. But two deaths in twenty-four hours is too much of a coincidence."

CHAPTER FORTY-ONE

It is 3.30 a.m. I have paced the streets of this grim city for many hours. I feel exhausted, yet still pierced by shards of anxiety which propel me ever onwards. If I don't walk and walk and continue to walk yet more, I think that my brain will implode. Many years ago, I recognised in myself an infirmity, a kind of weakness of mind which did not have its origin in sloth or cowardice. It was as if a very thin skin, a fragile veneer of good qualities, were stretched over a black abyss of hate inside me. I think that is why I have allowed so much of my life to be governed by inertia. It is because I have also yielded to this hatred on occasions. The worst of it is that it is the only thing that truly makes me feel alive. Yet it is a strange kind of aliveness and once it has passed I can't remember it. I can't remember what I said or did while it was with me, or, sometimes, even who else might have been present while I was in its lethal grip. It creates a veritable hell of uncertainty within me. I no longer know what is real and what my mind is inventing. I don't, in truth, know whether I have killed or not, though I have told Peter that I have; or whether I will kill again. If I do, Peter has ordained that it shall be today.

I walk past dark doorways. Some are inhabited by filthy dossers whose shadowy forms, cloaked in shapeless rags, loom out at me as I pass. They curse and mutter. They seem real, but there are so many of them, and they seem so alike – a huge incontrollable army eking a living on the fringes of civilisation, yet uniform, somehow – that after a while I begin to suspect that they are not really there. They have been created by me: they are extensions of my mind. I am in another waking nightmare.

Twice I have been accosted by young men. I did not understand what they wanted. I put up my hand to shield myself from them and instead of attacking me, they just melted away. When cautiously I lowered my arm, so that I could face up to them, they had gone. Would they have done that if they had been made of real flesh and blood?

I am so afraid of the dossers that I hasten to where the street lights are brighter. This must be the centre of the city: it is a place of shops and offices, and massive civic buildings. It, too, is a place of grinning revenge. I see fat girls prowling the streets, dressed tartily. Each when she raises her head shows me Kathryn's face; or Bryony's face. Terrible, bloated faces, half-destroyed with decay. There are drunks brawling and vomiting. When I get close, each one looks like Ronald, his face purple, his eyes bulging, the rope around his neck.

The streets are crawling with policemen. They walk in pairs and patrol in vans. I shy away from them when I see them coming – they may have photographs of me and I cannot bear the way their hideous yellow-green jackets gleam under the street lights. Yet I want to scream out to them, to ask them to rescue me. I want them to rescue me from the nightmare, to forcibly remove me from the crime I have yet to commit. I try to accost one who approaches me on his own, but when I get close to him, I see that he has a gibbering monkey's face. I don't know whether he is my pursuer or my friend; or just another weird beast that I have invented. I wish to God that I had not missed that train.

I'm heading back towards the station now. I'm fearful and I look over my shoulder repeatedly. I don't know what I'm expecting to see; I don't think it is a tramp or a policeman. I feel that something worse is dogging me, something nameless, without being. Some horrible reproachful thing flits just beyond my reach. I can sense it there in the darkness. I'm certain I've seen it throw its shadow ahead of me, even though I'm convinced that it lurks behind. It is playing an evil game. I know what it is now: it is Bryony's ghost.

I am within sight of the station. It looks cheerful: it casts a block of yellow light on to the damp and dingy streets that surround it. I feel the shadow hang back. I look back over my shoulder, and can see nothing. But now I hear her. "Peter is right," she says. "He is right. He is right. Do what he says."

I ignore her. I'm standing inside the station now. The doors have been opened and there is a sleepy black attendant at the barrier. I'm standing beside the shutters of the closed-down shops that are clustered beyond the concourse. I crane my neck, trying to see if there is anyone beyond the barriers. Another railway official is leaning against the information kiosk, which is not yet lit up. That is all. There are no policemen, no strange young women, no-one who might try to trap me. I look at the black attendant. His peaked hat is pulled down over his eyes, as if he is trying to continue the sleep from which he has recently had to drag himself. Unless he is a good actor, he is showing no interest in me. I know that I must keep my nerve. I resist the urge to hurry through the barrier as quickly as I can. Instead, I saunter to it as nonchalantly as I'm able, carefully pulling my wallet from my pocket as I go. I extract my ticket with care. I hold it against the slit in the barrier, which snatches it from my grasp. The barrier springs open. The ticket reappears suddenly, and I retrieve it and walk through as slowly as I can make myself. The man standing at the barrier shows no awareness of my presence. I walk on.

The information kiosk is completely deserted: the man who was leaning on it has disappeared. This makes me nervous. I wonder if he has gone to report me, to fetch help. I decide that this is unlikely. I look at the digital information board. It is easy to understand, because few trains are running yet. I locate the train to Liverpool and see that it is on time. It will arrive in ten minutes, on Platform 8b. I descend the long flight of steps to the platform. Once there, I am totally alone. The platform is only dimly lit, and smells unpleasant. It is an industrial smell, a pungent mixture of oil and dirt.

Suddenly I realise that I am shaking with cold. I am hungry, too. I cannot remember when I last ate. I need a warm drink. There is a vending machine tucked in the corner at the bottom of the staircase, but I don't have the right change. I cannot risk retracing my footsteps to use the change machine that I know is located outside the lavatories. I put my hands in my pockets, and huddle my shoulder-blades together against the cold. I wait.

The train glides into the station a little before it is due. I board it. Of course I have no seat reservation, but this is clearly not important: the carriage that I have entered is deserted. I collapse, exhausted, on to the seat nearest to the door and close my eyes. I seem to be waiting, fearful, nerves pitched, for a very long time before the train judders into movement again. I open my eyes cautiously and see that I am moving beyond the station to the scrubby industrial hinterland that lies beyond. I fall into a fitful sleep.

I am woken by someone gently shaking my shoulder.

"I'm sorry to disturb you, sir. Could I see your ticket please?" It is a female train guard. She is plump, with curly fair hair. She is smiling at me and I try to smile back. produce the ticket. I feel my lips trembling, displaying the same paralysed rictus of yesterday. She gives me an odd look as she returns it to me. Looking around me, I see that there are now several other people occupying the carriage. A woman is approaching with a drinks trolley.

"Any drinks? Refreshments?" she calls in a sing-song voice. One by one, I covertly examine my fellow-travellers. All of them appear to be sleeping, but I can't be sure. I can't see their faces clearly; perhaps their sleep is feigned. They may be pretending to show no interest in me. I know that appearances are often deceptive; only too well, in fact.

shrink back into my seat and turn my face to the window. There is nothing but blackness outside. The woman with the trolley draws level with my seat.

"Any drinks? Refreshments?" she says again.

I am gasping for a cup of tea, but I decide that to buy one would be too risky. I keep my face pressed close against the window. I don't acknowledge her and she passes on.

I do not sleep again. I remain facing out into the pitch black night for all that remains of the journey. Almost two hours later, I see the first stirrings of a dawn breaking over an endless mosaic of lights. I realise that we must be approaching Liverpool. My neck is so stiff that I can hardly move it. Painfully, I twist it round so that I am facing forwards again. The tannoy crackles into life.

"Ladies and Gentlemen, we shall shortly be arriving at Liverpool Lime Street. When leaving the train, please remember to take all your belongings with you. Mind the gap when alighting on to the platform."

I am about to commit a murder. Afterwards I shall be caught by the police, or give myself up to them. It will be the first murder for which I can be charged under UK law, but no-one – probably not even Peter, now – will believe that this is the truth.

CHAPTER FORTY-TWO

Peter Prance's collapse was sudden. In an instant he had dropped his veneer of insolent urbanity. After his promise to help, he fell forward on to the table, apparently distraught. He burst into a paroxysm of tears, his chest and shoulders heaving.

"Are you all right, Mr. Prance?" Chris McGill had stood up and was bending over him almost panic-stricken. Tim's own reaction was more measured, not to say sceptical. He knew the man was a consummate actor. Peter Prance lay with his head buried in his arms, which he had folded on the table top, for what seemed like several minutes. Tim motioned to Chris McGill to leave him, and, somewhat reluctantly, he took his seat again. Finally Peter Prance raised a tear-stained face. Tim could see that the tears were genuine, but he believed that the little round dark eyes that peered through them were as calculating as ever.

"Are you all right?" Chris McGill said again. Then, turning to Tim, "Perhaps we should leave it for this evening. We are all exhausted."

"Certainly not," said Tim, quickly. "If this were a routine enquiry, I would agree with you. But it is imperative that we find Hedley Atkins tonight. I am afraid that someone's life may be in danger."

For the first time he sensed that Chris McGill was not onside.

"Whose life?" he asked guardedly.

"I wish I knew," said Tim. "All I can say is that I believe that currently his state of mind is dangerously unstable and that in a fit of panic or rage he may injure or even kill someone."

"Really, Inspector, I . . ."

Peter Prance sat up.

"No," he said. "Don't." He turned a tear-smudged face towards Tim. "I agree with you," he said, "but I'm afraid that it may be too late already. He was only meant to frighten them. I may have suggested that he should kill her, but I never for a moment believed that he would be capable of such a deed."

CHAPTER FORTY-THREE

The telephone calls had been made. Now all they could do was sit and wait and hope that Peter Prance was right. He had been allowed a short rest in one of the cells. Chris McGill had also taken the opportunity to get a couple of hours' sleep in Tim's office. Tim himself, bursting with a kind of fevered energy, had meantime been briefing members of his team by phone.

"You say that you want to help us now, Mr. Prance. Perhaps you might care to tell us what you know."

It was 6.45 on Friday morning. Chris McGill, who a few hours previously had seemed almost comatose with fatigue was bright and alert now. Peter Prance himself had also regained some of his former ebullience. Tim was on an adrenalin high, determined to power on.

"I'm not going to tell you anything that you couldn't have worked out for yourself," said Peter Prance, chipper and combative once more.

"That may be. I'm assuming, however, that you may not only have outwitted us, but also got Hedley Atkins to endorse your version of events?"

"Yes, indeed."

"I congratulate you. Please continue."

Peter Prance looked at Chris McGill.

"You don't have to co-operate, Mr. Prance, but given what you've just told us, I strongly suggest that you do. Detective

Inspector Yates may be better disposed to discover some mitigating circumstances."

Peter Prance shot Tim a malicious glance.

"Indeed." He steepled his fingers.

"I am quite prepared to admit that I cultivated Hedley, for a number of reasons. One of these was undoubtedly that I thought that he would be likely to offer me a home if my mother refused to renew the lease on the flat where I was living. Another was that I had discovered who his mother was and I was intrigued. I'd very much like to have met her."

"Why is that?"

"Oh, one meets so few people of distinction – and notoriety is a form of distinction, or at least of distinctiveness, don't you think? Almost everyone of a certain age can tell you that Dorothy Atkins was the woman who murdered her mother-in-law, even now.

"Anyway, at first I didn't tell Hedley that I knew who his mother was, mainly because he hadn't mentioned her to me. It was obvious that he was sensitive about her. But I did take a profound interest in the murder case. When Hedley was out at *work*," – he rolled his eyes, and stressed the word with distaste – "I made it my business to research it as thoroughly as I could. I'm quite a keen amateur sleuth, you know," – he batted his eyelids at Tim – "and as I gathered more and more information, I made a list of the things which puzzled me. Allow me to enumerate them now." He shot back his cuffs and held up one slender immaculately manicured hand. He ticked off the points that he was making on his fingers, striking them lightly with the index finger of the other hand.

"Number One, Tirzah – I will call her Tirzah, since Hedley always does – had no motive for murdering her mother-in-law. Number Two, no-one managed to get to the bottom of the cryptic comment about Doris Atkins being 'too fond' of gardening. Number Three, Tirzah did not admit to the murder, but she did not deny it either. She must have had a reason for this. Number Four, all of these previous points could be explained if Tirzah were insane at the time, but I have found absolutely no convincing evidence to suggest that she was, and a great deal to the contrary. Number Five, some of the inmates of the shop at Westlode Street appeared never to have been questioned, even routinely, about Doris Atkins' death – especially Bryony, her grand-daughter. In fact," Peter Prance added, looking up at Tim with his black eyes snapping, "Tirzah's daughter's existence was so well-concealed that I have to confess that I did not find out about it during the course of my researches. No, no, it was Hedley who told me about her. Inadvertently he gave away some information about her, and one or two other things as well, during the course of the most terrible tantrum. I was quite frightened by it, I can tell you."

Peter Prance nodded his head vigorously several times.

"Now," he said, "this tantrum of Hedley's was very important, because it helped me to make sense of some of these strange details – made the stranger, I have to say, by the fact that the police of the time did not pick up on them either." He shot Tim a look of defiance. Tim returned his gaze steadily.

"The Atkins family – both Atkins families, the ones who lived at the shop and the ones who lived in Chestnut Avenue – were not close, as I think you will agree. Individuals within each family weren't close, either, with the exception of Colin Atkins and his mother, who idolised each other. The first thing you may ask yourself, therefore," – he steepled his fingers, and shot Tim another of his sidelong looks: Tim wondered if he was consciously parodying the typical language of a judge's instructions to a jury – "is what persuaded the younger Atkins family, by which I mean the Chestnut Avenue branch, to move in, even temporarily, with the older branch, by which I mean the residents of Westlode Street."

"Dorothy Atkins said that it was to help Colin look after his aged mother."

"Yes, indeed: I know that she *said* that; and I also believe it to have been true. As I think we are both aware, Tirzah usually told the truth. But I'm not talking about Colin's reason for their taking up residence in his house: I'm talking about Tirzah's reason. Why did she agree to it? What possible reason could she have had for humouring her husband's uncle?"

"Ronald Atkins thought that it was because she wanted to ingratiate herself with Colin, so that he would leave Ronald the house – as in fact he did in the end, though because it was not entirely his to leave – it had never formally been given to him by his brothers after their father died – it took rather a long time for him to get probate."

"Yes, yes, but now you're giving me Ronald Atkins's reason. I don't doubt that is correct, too. And also more or less proven is Tirzah's acquisitiveness. I'm sure that she would have loved to get her hands on that property. But consider again: there is evidence that she was thinking of leaving Ronald. Presumably she would have stood to gain nothing from her husband's relatives if she and he were separated or divorced."

He paused to see what effect his words would have, and was evidently disappointed when Tim replied:

"If you're talking about her affair with Frank Needham, I have met Mr. Needham now, and he tells me that the affair more or less fizzled out after Doris Atkins' death."

Peter Prance recovered his composure quickly.

"Yes, yes," he said again, rather testily this time. "But that was with hindsight: for some reason she did not want to continue the affair with Mr. Needham after the calamitous events that happened to her in the autumn of 1975. According to Mr. Needham, whose recollections you have evidently gathered and whom presumably we have no reason to doubt. That is all part of the mystery, don't you think? At least one of the people in that household – I mean the Westlode Street household – had some kind of hold over Tirzah. Whatever it was, it prompted her to do three things: to make the temporary move to Westlode Street to assist with the care of her husband's grandmother; to break off the relationship with Frank Needham; and to take the blame for a murder which she didn't commit." Peter Prance allowed his voice to crescendo, then tossed his head back with a little laugh. He could see that this time he had both surprised and intrigued his listener.

"Oh, yes, Inspector. I realise that I can't prove it conclusively, but I am absolutely persuaded that Tirzah was innocent of murder. Not only did she have no motive, but there was someone else in that house who had a very strong reason for killing Doris."

"I suppose that you are going to tell me that it was Hedley? Ironical, isn't it, that you seem to be exerting a hold over him in the same way that you say that someone was also threatening Dorothy Atkins?"

"Oh, I wouldn't say I was *threatening* Hedley. That is a very ugly word indeed! One has ultimately to face up to one's heritage, a fact that Hedley appears to be able to confront with only the most extreme reluctance. But you are wrong about the irony – or shall we say, what you perceive to be a coincidence? Because actually it isn't a coincidence at all, but the self-same thing. Hedley is afraid of the same thing that also terrified Tirzah. Would you like me to continue?"

Tim felt a very strong urge to slap Peter Prance's malicious little face.

"Let's have less beating about the bush, shall we? I know that there is an art to the building up of suspense, but you've had your bit of fun now. Tell us what this fucking 'secret' was that in your opinion seems to have haunted the Atkins' family, and I'll tell you whether I think that there is an ounce of credibility in it, or whether I just think that you've been wasting police time."

"Oh dear, that isn't very nice, is it? I shall have to . . ."

Andy Carstairs burst into the room.

"You're wanted on the phone, sir, immediately. It is Chief Inspector Collins of the Liverpool Police."

CHAPTER FORTY-FOUR

I see the wheelchair as soon as I step on to the platform. Someone has parked it against the wall of the station, facing towards the exit, perhaps because a chill wind is sweeping through the draughty outside waiting areas. I can therefore only see her in profile, and that not clearly, because her face is half-hidden by a scarf and most of her body is obscured by the same cellular blanket that she was swathed in when first I met her. I know that it is she, nevertheless. She is wearing her navy-blue felt hat, for one thing, but even if she were not, the outline of her face itself would have enabled me to recognise her instantly and without doubt. There is no mistaking those fine, bird-like features, so exactly like Peter's.

I know that she cannot be here alone. Someone must have accompanied her, must have helped her manoeuvre herself and the wheelchair into a taxi and out again, must have pushed the wheelchair containing her on to the platform. I scan the crowd of two dozen or so people who are waiting, trying to catch sight of a familiar face; trying to glimpse Jillian, in fact. Jillian must be here, somewhere. Peter has told me to watch out for her, above all.

I wonder why they are not at home. What can have impelled them to come to the station so early, on such a raw day? Perhaps they are planning a holiday. Perhaps the old lady is ill, and needs to see a doctor. Perhaps Jillian has a sixth sense, some inner warning mechanism that has told her of my impending visit.

Suddenly I am very angry. I realise that, but for this lucky chance sighting, my journey might have been in vain. I might have reached the house and found no-one there. As it is, I am going to have to act swiftly, and in a public place, too. I shall have to change my plan of execution completely. I shall have to improvise.

The obvious method would be to push her on to the track in front of a train. But I quail at the barbarity of it. I'm also not certain that I can pull it off: I imagine it is much more difficult to shove someone in a wheelchair on to the tracks than someone who is merely standing on the platform. Besides, the ostentatiousness of such a move repels me.

I scan the platform again. There seems to be an area beyond the building that is deserted. It would be possible to push her out of sight of onlookers and then strangle her. I contemplate the practicalities. I've never strangled anyone before. How difficult will it be? Will she scream, or put up a struggle? Will she make a fuss before I can remove her from view? I look across at her again. She is completely inert, though not, I think, asleep. I may be imagining it, but I'm sure that I see the gleam of a boot-button eye beneath the hat.

I decide to approach her. I'll have to be quick, before Jillian returns. I decide that I will have more chance of abducting her if I creep up on her from behind. I walk past her on the platform, keeping as close to the edge as I can so that I am as far away as possible when I pass her. I turn on my heel, walk fast towards the building and position myself just a few yards from the rear of the wheelchair. She moves her head slightly, but does not turn round. I can smell her now, her old-lady smell, overlaid with the lavender toilet water that she uses.

I'm suddenly beset by doubt. How will I cope with taking a life, even a life as old and compromised as hers? Bryony and I took an old life when we were children and it has haunted me for more than forty years. I remember my promise to Peter, and stiffen my resolve. I edge closer to the wheelchair. I am within three feet of it now.

Two young girls are walking towards me, their arms linked. I dread to see their faces, but feel an irresistible compulsion to look. It is as I had feared: they are Kathryn and Bryony. They are giggling. They pass within a foot of me, without greeting me, without pausing in their chatter. They are closely followed by a spry older woman. This time I will not look. I refuse to meet her eye. I stare at the station building. "Aren't you going to say hello, Hedley? After all these years?" I raise my head, again unable to resist. She has Doris's face, but while I am still trying to meet her eye, it ripples, changes, and turns into Tirzah's. I feel panic now. They are closing in on me. Closing in. My family.

I see with a sudden marvellous clarity that it is all about my family. Peter and his family are an irrelevance, they are nothing to do with me. If Peter needs to alter the situation within his family, he must do it himself. He has no business asking me. I have my own family to attend to. Besides, it would not be right.

I am shaken, and shaking. I might have done this poor woman in the wheelchair a great wrong. And I like her, as well. She has done nothing to deserve harm by my hand. I must ask her forgiveness.

I hasten to stand before her and drop to the ground. I feel for her hands beneath the covers, and fall sobbing on to her knees. She is alarmed, and tries to snatch away her hands, but I reassure her.

"I'm sorry," I cry. "I am so, so sorry. Forgive me. Forgive me, please."

She is shouting for help. A man is running towards us. He is carrying a plastic cup of coffee, which he is spilling as he runs. When he reaches us, he yanks me to my feet.

"Who are you?" he shouts. "What are you trying to do to my wife?"

Two policemen appear. They are wearing lime-green

waistcoats – gilets, I believe they are called. They are labelled: British Transport Police. They haven't tried to pass themselves off as Ronald or Colin. I am suspicious.

"You've not played fair with me," I say, the tears coursing down my cheeks. "You can't get away with a straight bat now. I shall report you for deceiving me by wearing other people's faces."

CHAPTER FORTY-FIVE

Hedley Atkins had been apprehended, not, as had been planned, outside Mrs. Prance's house in Birkenhead, so that he could be charged with her intended assault, perhaps with intent to murder her, but on the platform at Liverpool Lime Street Station. He was now being held in custody in a secure mental unit. He appeared to have suffered a complete mental breakdown, according to Chief Inspector Collins, but Tim Yates was sceptical. Having met Hedley's mother, he suspected that he might have inherited the same formidable gift of dissimulation. He would wait until he saw Hedley, and judge for himself.

Tim decided not to tell Peter Prance of Hedley's arrest, because he wanted him to finish the narrative that he had begun in the early hours of that morning, and he was afraid that he might change his story if he knew that Hedley was no longer at large. There was no guarantee that Peter would tell the truth in any case, but it was worth giving it a try. If Peter could give Tim a logical explanation for the events that had happened in the Atkins family over the past forty years, he might be persuaded to believe that it was the truth.

Tim looked at his watch. It was almost 9 a.m. Earlier, Peter Prance had asked permission to wash, and Chris McGill had used the opportunity to go home and take a shower himself. Peter Prance had also been provided with breakfast. Tim himself felt grimy. His adrenalin high was beginning to wear off and he had drunk so many cups of coffee during the night that there was a dull ache in his stomach. He ran his tongue over his teeth. They felt as if they were coated with a thick film of something unpleasant; something gluey and industrial. He resolved that he himself would go home to shower and change after this next, and, he hoped, final interview with Peter.

They had agreed to reconvene at nine o'clock. Peter Prance was escorted to the interview room punctually by Andy Carstairs. Peter regarded Tim with a kind of wary triumph. He no longer seemed afraid, or even remorseful.

"It's disgusting, having to get dressed again in the clothes that I was wearing yesterday," he observed.

"I'm sorry for that, Mr. Prance. I understand that you were offered some fresh clothes."

"You don't think that I would have contemplated even touching those rags, do you, let alone put them next to my *skin*? Goodness knows where they have been, or what kinds of person have worn them already."

"They may not match your usual standards, but they have been laundered, sir. That was the point of offering them to you: they are clean."

"How much longer do you intend to keep me here?"

"That rather depends on you, sir."

"You're bluffing," said Peter Prance, rather nastily. "As you said yesterday – and, as it happens, I knew it already – you have to bring me before a judge or a magistrate within twenty-four hours. Or let me go."

Tim looked at his watch.

"I see you're an expert on the law. If you're correct, we've still got a good few hours left, then, sir."

Chris McGill entered the room at that point. He looked from one to the other of its inmates, evidently picking up the tension in the atmosphere.

"I'm sorry I'm late," he said. "Shall we sit down?"

"Would anyone like coffee?" asked Andy Carstairs. Tim

waved him away for answer, but Peter Prance said unctuously:

"I should like a cup." Andy left the room.

"We don't have to wait until he comes back," said Tim. "If you're ready, Mr. Prance, I should like to pick up where we left off earlier. You were about to tell me what it was you thought was haunting the Atkins family, and to offer me your version of the events that took place in the house at Westlode Street in 1975."

"Was I really about to do that? It seems a long time ago, now." Peter Prance narrowed his eyes. "Why did you halt the meeting earlier, Inspector? I heard the comment about the policeman in Liverpool. Have they found Hedley?"

"I'll answer your questions later, if I may, sir. If you don't mind, I'd like you to answer my questions first. Please remember that, by your own admission, you could still be charged with conspiracy to commit murder."

"I very much doubt that you could make that stick. I've told you already, I just wanted him to frighten Mummy. Besides, if you have found Hedley, as I suspect, it was because of the information that I provided, wasn't it?"

Tim sighed. Chris McGill intervened.

"I suggest that you answer the questions, Mr. Prance. The information that the Detective Inspector is asking for can't incriminate you, and, as I mentioned last night, if you are co-operative it is likely to benefit you later."

"Oh, very well."

"I'd like you to continue from where you broke off earlier, Mr. Prance. You were about to tell us why you thought Tirzah agreed to take up temporary residence at the house in Westlode Street."

Peter Prance settled himself back in his chair, and prolonged the pause, for effect.

"Fear of scandal," he said, steepling his fingers again and observing Tim over the pyramid that he had constructed. "Colin wanted everyone under the same roof for his own purposes. He wanted as many people to be in the house as possible if the need arose to take drastic action before his mother could change her will, so that he could dilute suspicion. He blackmailed Tirzah into agreeing to come to help his sister look after his mother, knowing that she would arrive accompanied by Hedley and Bryony."

"Leaving aside that this sounds very far-fetched, you haven't explained how he managed to blackmail her."

"It's quite simple. Colin was Hedley's father."

Peter Prance made this announcement with a kind of nasal fanfare. He almost took a bow after he had uttered his bombshell, and stared Tim squarely in the eye. He was clearly disappointed by the low-key response that he elicited.

"Yes, I have heard that that might have been a possibility; but I don't understand how it could have led to Doris Atkins' death."

"Tirzah would have done anything to avoid a scandal – just as her own mother had managed to do after her birth, by moving to a different part of the country and passing herself off as a married woman. Respectability counted for everything in Tirzah's world – everything except material gain, that is. I'm persuaded that she agreed to have an affair with Colin in the first place because of his comparative wealth. She had not only trapped herself in a loveless marriage, but – what was worse from her point of view – a poverty-stricken one."

"OK, so Tirzah agreed to help Doris Atkins look after her aged mother because Colin wanted her to, and because – presumably –otherwise he threatened to expose their shameful secret. Assuming that Colin did not care whether or not he himself became engulfed in a scandal, I still don't understand his motive. Why was he so desperate to have Tirzah help with his mother? Tirzah was not renowned for her caring qualities."

"Colin adored his mother, and he was also a little tiny bit twisted. He had come to believe that Doris was going to persuade his mother to alter her will, and make Doris an equal beneficiary with himself, in recognition for having taken care of her for so many years. In other words, she had decided at last to forgive Doris for the shame that she had brought on the family by giving birth to Ronald out of wedlock. Oh, thank you so much." This last comment was directed at Andy Carstairs, who had returned bearing a tray set out with three coffees in cardboard cups and a fourth in the canteen's single china cup. Peter Prance quickly removed the latter, and sipped at it delicately.

"But if the old lady had altered her will, the ultimate beneficiary would still have been Ronald – the heir that Colin himself named in his own will."

"Correct. But there was a difference between Ronald inheriting eventually and Doris inheriting almost immediately. Colin would have had to share everything with Doris; more to the point, he would have lost his sense of control over her. And," – Peter Prance lowered his voice here, and looked very grave – "there is a further important point which I have myself deduced, although it is the one thing on which Hedley simply refuses to agree with me, so you may, if you wish, take it as conjecture . . ."

Tim nodded encouragement.

"It is my own view that Colin may also have been Ronald's own father." There was no flourish this time. Just a simple statement. Against Tim's better judgment, perhaps because this time Peter Prance had not embellished what he said in any way, he almost made Tim believe that he may have stumbled upon the truth. With some effort, Tim chose not to offer an opinion.

"Let me get this straight. By threatening to tell the truth about who Hedley's father was, Colin blackmailed Tirzah into going to stay at his house to help look after his mother, so that she could spy on Doris and report back if there were any indication that Doris was trying to influence the old lady to alter her will. Doris herself had stayed all her life in a house where she was treated like a servant, because she had borne

323

a child by Colin (one assumes that her mother did not know or would not believe that Colin was the father), and she could not afford to live anywhere else unless she married: but marriage for her was out of the question, because then she would probably have to tell her future husband who Ronald's father was. Assuming that you are absolutely correct about all of this, I still don't see how it led to the deaths of two women, Bryony Atkins and Doris Atkins. Especially as circumstantial evidence suggests that Bryony died before Doris."

Peter Prance's boot-button eyes became very black.

"Oh, so you have found Bryony's body, then? Or is it merely your conjecture that she died at about the same time as Doris?"

"We have found some remains which we believe to have been Bryony's."

"Let me guess: they were buried in the garden?"

"Why do you say that?"

"It explains Tirzah's rather gnomic remark at the time of her trial, that her mother-in-law had been too fond of gardening."

"Indeed – and if your deduction is correct, it also suggests, as I said, that Bryony died before Doris did. Can you offer any explanation for that?"

"As a matter of fact I can. I did not 'deduce', as you put it, the facts of what I am about to tell you. Hedley told them to me during an extraordinary outburst, during which he seemed to lose not only his temper, but every vestige of his reason. I therefore have no doubt that what I am about to say is the truth."

Tim nodded again, reigning in his scepticism.

"When Bryony and Hedley were children, they, and Hedley in particular, realised that their parents' marriage was a very unhappy one. For whatever reason, Hedley attributed the cause of their unhappiness to the visits of Tirzah's mother, Eliza Drake. He was nine and Bryony was ten when together they arranged for Eliza to have an 'accident' when she visited their house. They caused her to trip and fall down the stairs. It killed her. Despite her honest nature, Tirzah was obliged to suppress the truth about the fall and present it as a true accident, because she knew that, at the age of ten, Bryony had reached the age of criminal responsibility. She believed that Hedley, who had been nine at the time and therefore not criminally responsible, was the main culprit, and this had an effect on their relationship ever afterwards, although after the inquest Eliza Drake was never mentioned by the family again. No-one knew about the exact circumstances of Eliza's death except Hedley and Bryony. Tirzah did not see it happen, and Ronald had been out of the house."

"What does this have to do with Bryony's death?"

"I'm coming to that – give me time, Detective Inspector. Soon after Tirzah and her family moved into the house at Westlode Street, Bryony went out for a drink with Kathryn Sheppard, with whom she had kept in touch after Kathryn's relationship with Hedley had ended. Hedley, apparently, although he says he no longer entertained any particular feelings for Kathryn, was jealous of all of Bryony's friends. He doesn't explain why, but my guess is that he was haunted by his maternal grandmother's death, for which he felt he had taken an unfair share of the blame, and therefore he believed that Bryony owed him her undivided friendship in return. She was much more popular with everyone than Hedley was. Whatever the reason, when Bryony returned to the house that night to find the house in darkness and Hedley sleeping in his made-up bed on the landing, he awoke and got up, and they had a violent disagreement. Triggered by his resentment of her night out with Kathryn, he accused her of refusing to take some of the blame for Eliza's death, and therefore of turning Tirzah against her. Apparently she gave him a shove and he pushed her back, and she fell down the stairs, in a ghastly parody of Eliza's own death. Like Eliza's, her neck was broken. But this time it really was an accident."

"If that was the case, why didn't Hedley report it to the police?"

"For a number of reasons, chief among which was that Colin and Ronald emerged from their respective rooms, and persuaded Hedley that because of the earlier incident with Eliza, the police would not believe that Bryony's death had been an accident. Hedley is vague about why they were so insistent about this, but he certainly believed them. And, of course, they had a point, though not on the face of it one that was as compelling for them as it was for Hedley. So why were they so insistent? For what it's worth, my own opinion is that now that Bryony was dead, if Hedley had been sent to prison, Tirzah would have had no reason left to co-operate with Colin's plans, which I'm sure Ronald must also have been party to. Colin would have found it very hard to stop Doris from influencing her mother's will, if that was indeed what she intended to do, and impossible to get rid of her if he saw the need, had there already been one suspicious death reported at the house. And then of course there is the additional reason that I believe in but Hedley won't acknowledge: Ronald's possible parentage. Ronald and Colin had always seemed to get on. If Ronald thought that Colin was his father, he was not appalled by it in the same way that Hedley was. They worked together."

"If all this is true, where were Doris and Tirzah while this was going on, and how did Colin and Ronald get them to agree to be accomplices as well?"

"They didn't agree: or Doris didn't, at any rate. As it happened, neither Doris nor Tirzah had gone to bed when Bryony died, because the old lady had had one of her episodes. I'm not sure exactly what form these took: Hedley seems to think that she had fits, though it's equally possible that she invented some malady when she wanted attention. Anyway, both were with the old girl in her improvised bedroom in the scullery during the drama with Bryony. Doris in fact stayed with her mother all night. By the time that Tirzah retired to bed at some point after Bryony's fall, Colin and Ronald had concealed the body in the passageway that ran the length of the house, which Colin used as a storeroom. All three of them – Colin, Ronald and Hedley – then got up early next morning and buried the body. Hedley did not actually tell me where it was buried, so I had to work it out for myself, which I must admit I was slow to do. That cryptic remark of Tirzah's had me puzzled for far too long. Far too long." Peter Prance repeated the phrase with emphasis, waving his hands.

"So at some point they told Tirzah what had happened, and what they had done?"

"They had to. Although she wasn't particularly maternal, Tirzah was closer to Bryony than to any of them. It was true, of course, that Bryony was about to leave for university, but she wouldn't have gone without saying goodbye to Tirzah, and indeed involving her in her preparations."

"But surely if Tirzah was close to Bryony, which is my own impression, too, she would have been angry and upset about her death, and refused to co-operate with them?"

"I'm sure that she was quite devastated by it: but a moment's reflection would have told her that she had no choice. She had supped with the devil, and reaped her reward. If she were to retrieve anything from the situation, it would be the freedom of her only living child, and the promise of reasonable prosperity for herself and Ronald when Colin died. And, of course, being allowed to maintain her 'respectability' intact. There was still every likelihood that Colin would betray her if he didn't get his own way exactly. She was a cold and self-interested woman, as you know, or became one, but he was even more calculating."

"So Tirzah was party to the interment of Bryony's body, but Doris wasn't?"

"Yes. Doris remained the only threat – and she was a double threat, now. Not only might she persuade her mother to change her will, but she would be very likely to report all of them to the police if she had the slightest suspicion that something untoward had happened to Bryony. And she was suspicious. She had not gone to bed the following day until Tirzah came downstairs to sit with the old lady again. When Doris awoke, it was almost lunchtime, and Bryony was not there. Tirzah explained Bryony's absence by saying that she had mistaken the dates of some preparatory meetings that she had to attend at the University of Reading, and had had to leave in a hurry. Doris accepted this at first, but when Bryony failed to return after a couple of days, she began to say how odd it was not to have heard from her. No doubt the replies that she received from the other residents of the house failed to convince her that all was well: as you know, Tirzah in particular was a clumsy liar, and Hedley and Ronald were undoubtedly consumed with guilt by what they had done. Whether or not Doris actually went as far as thinking that Bryony might be dead, I don't know. I surmise that she may have been taking an undue interest in the wet patch of earth in the orchard – the garden was her province, after all – but of course I don't know that."

"Are you saying that Doris became so troublesome in voicing her worries about Bryony that Tirzah was forced to kill her? Because I have to say that I don't find that argument very convincing."

"My dear Inspector, I don't find it convincing, either: moreover, I'm pretty certain that that was not the case. I should tell you that I began my investigations into Tirzah and her crimes because I was interested in what made her tick, and therefore in what made Hedley tick. I later came to the conclusion that in all probability she did not murder her mother-in-law, and I must admit that, for a brief time, I thought that Hedley himself might have been the murderer. In view of the recent deaths of both Tirzah and Ronald, which, as you are aware, shocked me very considerably, and which seemed to have followed too close on each other not to be attributable to foul play, I may have to revise my opinion again. Nevertheless, at this moment I pronounce myself at least ninety-five per cent convinced that it was Colin Atkins who killed his sister."

"Why do you say that?"

"Because he had both the motive and the opportunity. Because Tirzah could never describe in detail exactly how Doris died. Because Hedley is either shifty and evasive – not to say mendacious – or downright aggressive, when I bring the subject up, but we know that he and Ronald were both at work at the time of her death. And finally, because of all the possible culprits – Tirzah, Ronald, Hedley and Colin himself – the only plausible murder scenario that my fertile but, if I may say so, extremely logical imagination can paint is one that puts Colin firmly in the role of protagonist."

"Really, Mr. Prance, I don't think that the Inspector wants . . ." It was Chris McGill, speaking for the first time in almost an hour.

"I agree that I don't usually listen to conjecture," said Tim quietly. "But on this occasion, I should be quite interested to hear an account of Mr. Prance's 'scenario'. Although it will be inadmissible as evidence in any future trial that may take place, of course."

Peter Prance gave a gracious little bow.

"I don't actually think that Doris died because of her obsession with the garden, though Tirzah may have believed this or been told it. Doris was a very conscientious housewife. She kept the house and the shop immaculate. She had been upset some years previously when a health and safety inspector had discovered evidence of rodents in the passage that Colin used as a storeroom, and threatened to close the shop down if it happened again. Colin had not allowed her into the storeroom until then, probably because of his extreme miserliness. He made her pay for any goods that she took for herself from the shop, and despite her sterling honesty he probably harboured groundless worries that she would have a better opportunity for appropriating goods from the storeroom undetected. Anyway, after the incident with the health and safety man, she insisted on cleaning the passage thoroughly every fortnight, herself moving the boxes around as she worked until every area of the floor had been scrubbed. It's my guess that she set out to clean the storeroom again a few days after Bryony's death, and found some evidence that her body had been lying there. A shoe or an article of clothing, perhaps, or even something more unpleasant." He wrinkled his nose in distaste. "Colin either followed her, afraid that she might discover something, or was already there by chance – there was a lavatory at the far end of the passage, and he may have just been using it. Either way, she confronted him, and he killed her. Tirzah came in shortly afterwards, perhaps alerted by a noise of some kind, and he made her agree to take the blame for Doris's death, probably by using his old threat of otherwise exposing Hedley's parentage, and by making the additional point that she was already an accessory after the fact of concealing her daughter's body, and could easily be charged with Bryony's murder, too."

"And Ronald?"

"He certainly wasn't there when the murder took place. Either he believed Colin's version of events, or he was party to making Tirzah take the blame. As you know, there was little love lost between them. I think that Hedley may have known the truth – or at least guessed it. He certainly lied to me when I first asked him for his recollections of the day that Doris Atkins died. But Hedley was afraid of being charged with Bryony's murder, and he would have kept his mouth shut for that reason. How is Hedley, by the way? I do hope that the dear boy has managed to regain his equilibrium."

"Why do you say that?"

Peter Prance shrugged. His black eyes glinted.

"No particular reason. But you have chosen to keep me in the dark about what is happening with him; and I must say that recently his behaviour has been somewhat erratic. He is very highly strung, you know. Capable of having quite a serious breakdown, I should say."

CHAPTER FORTY-SIX

Peter Prance was charged with conspiracy to cause grievous bodily harm, and released on bail, on condition that he tried neither to leave Spalding, nor to contact his family. After his release, Tim went home for a shower, and was now returning, still more tired than refreshed, to the police station. He had asked Juliet Armstrong to gather the murder team together in the interview room during his absence. He walked through the door at 12 noon precisely, just in time to listen to Andy Carstairs' final sentences as he retailed Peter Prance's story to Juliet and Ricky MacFadyen.

"The whole rigmarole sounds totally unbelievable to me," said Ricky.

"I agree that it is a very strange tale, and no doubt made the stranger by Peter Prance's various embellishments," said Tim. "And of course we have no reason to trust Prance: on the contrary, we know that he has been convicted of fraud several times, and is probably an expert liar. Nevertheless, I can pinpoint no glaring inconsistencies in his story; nor can I think of any other version which could incorporate without contradiction all the evidence that we have. What he has told us may be an approximation of the truth, or as near to it as we are ever likely to get."

"But it doesn't account for all the evidence, does it, sir?", said Juliet. "For example, we don't have an explanation for the plastic Red Indians. We don't know if either Dorothy

Atkins or Ronald Atkins – or both – were murdered; and if they were, as Peter Prance suspected, Hedley was almost certainly the murderer, which would make him, not Dorothy Atkins, a serial killer. And we haven't solved the murder which we set out to solve in the first place: that of Kathryn Sheppard. If Hedley did kill Dorothy and Ronald, then I'd say that it was likely that he killed Bryony, Doris and Kathryn as well."

Tim nodded.

"I agree that there are many loose ends to tidy up. As far as the Red Indians are concerned, once we found out that they were issued the year before the murders of Doris and Bryony, they ceased to be important. Hedley probably took the extra bag from the shop and gave the Red Indians to people that he knew, as mascots or even as a sort of joke against Colin. There was no Red Indian found with Doris Atkins' body and none with either Tirzah or Ronald, for that matter. And despite Peter Prance's panic when he learned that Tirzah and Ronald had both died this week and therefore concluded that the coincidence was too great and that Hedley must have been responsible, there is absolutely no evidence that Hedley had visited Tirzah at Elmete Court on the day that she died or at any time in the recent past. Conversely, although we know that Hedley did visit Ronald Atkins on the night of his death, this does not prove that Hedley murdered him: the circumstantial evidence rather points to the opposite, in fact. We know that Ronald bought a new washing-line earlier in the day; that his wife had probably left him; and that he knew that Bryony's body was certain to be found the following day. He had every reason to kill himself and little cause to want to carry on living. As you know, Professor Salkeld said that very few hangings turn out to be murders."

"What about Henry Bevelton?"

"I'm not sure whether Henry Bevelton was accessory after the fact when Bryony was buried or not. We can question him and try to charge him, but I doubt that we shall make anything stick. He has behaved in a shifty way, as you know, and some of the things that he has said don't bear close scrutiny. My guess is that Henry is just a petty crook who agreed to do the Atkins a favour in return for keeping quiet about something that they knew about him – or alternatively he had heard the neighbours talking, and suspected that Bryony was buried under the apple tree, but kept it to himself, because he wanted to buy the orchard. Even if he is guilty, he has one inestimable advantage: all the Atkins family are now dead except Hedley, so there is only one person left who could betray him; and I'm pretty certain that Hedley is in such a state that although the CPS may decide to press charges, no judge will pronounce him fit either to testify or to stand trial. The whole thing has turned full circle, in other words: he is in practically the same position that Tirzah was in more than thirty years ago. Whatever the truth of all of it is, they have succeeded in keeping it in the family. Only Peter Prance has come anywhere close to piercing their conspiracy of silence."

"If Peter Prance was right and two incestuous liaisons with Colin Atkins were at the root of all that followed, wouldn't it be possible to check this out by getting some DNA tests done?" asked Ricky.

"Perhaps," said Tim. "It would be worth a try, if only to satisfy our curiosity. I doubt if the results could be used to convict Hedley of murder, or to exonerate him, for that matter. The problem is that we shall only be able to obtain specimens from Tirzah and Ronald and Bryony – and Hedley himself, of course. Doris Atkins and Colin Atkins were both cremated."

"From the previous work I've done with DNA testing, I think that specimens from the immediate family should be enough," said Juliet. "Enough, at least, to prove whether or not Ronald was Hedley's father, whether he and Bryony were full brother and sister, and probably whether there is any sign of inbreeding in Ronald, and, even more to the point, in Hedley."

"Call Professor Salkeld and arrange it, then," said Tim. "He is carrying out the post mortems on Ronald and Bryony, in any case. I'm sure that he'll be happy to add Tirzah to his list and to take a few swabs from Hedley."

"I still can't think where Kathryn Sheppard fits into all this," said Juliet. "With all these deaths going on in the Atkins family, it seems to defy logic that her murder did not tie in with them somehow. Yet, if Peter Prance's story is to be accepted, the only Atkins actually to have been murdered in 1975 was Doris. If Colin Atkins was her murderer, I cannot see why he would also have killed Kathryn Sheppard. If he knew Kathryn at all, it could only have been as a passing acquaintance when she was going out with Hedley. We don't think that Colin was a psychopath, do we?"

Andy Carstairs rose suddenly from his chair.

"I've got it at last!", he said. "Something's been nagging at the back of my mind for weeks, now, and I've just realised what it is."

CHAPTER FORTY-SEVEN

Delicate spring flowers were just beginning to bloom in the flowerbeds at Gray's Inn when Andy Carstairs returned, accompanied this time by Inspector Tim Yates. It was early in the morning and still chilly. Mr. Charles Heward, QC, MP, was expecting them. Andy had spoken to him on the telephone the day before. It had been a friendly conversation, in which Andy said that something else had come up with regard to the Kathryn Sheppard case and he thought that Charles Heward might be able to help. He had taken care to make this further investigation sound routine, and he appeared to have succeeded in this. If Charles was disconcerted or alarmed by being contacted again, his voice did not betray it. He said that he would be in court for the whole of the next day, but that he appreciated that police time was valuable and that holding up investigations cost money. He would therefore make himself available for one hour from 8.30 a.m. onwards, if that was acceptable to Andy. Andy thanked him and said that he would be there. He did not mention that he would be accompanied by his boss. This conversation was taped and the tape was afterwards played in court.

Tim met Andy at King's Cross Station – Tim had elected to spend the night with his sister in Surbiton, rather than catching an early train from Peterborough – and they made their way to Gray's Inn together, both preferring to walk the distance of a mile or so rather than braving the tube or a taxi during the rush hour. Tim appeared to be amused rather than intimidated by the air of ancient privilege that emanated from the cloistered buildings. He was smiling – perhaps somewhat ironically – as he followed Andy up the corkscrew staircase to Charles Heward's office. He drew level with Andy as the latter tapped on the closed door and, taking the lead, entered as soon as Andy had knocked. He did not wait for the imperious 'Come!' that Andy had described from his previous visit.

Tim saw a bulky figure sitting behind a partner's desk that was absolutely denuded of papers. Fleetingly, he thought that this was a strange state of affairs for a barrister who professed to be working in court for the whole of the day. The bulky man rose slowly from his seat and extended his hand across the broad extent of the desk.

Charles Heward may have sounded his usual confident, slightly overbearing, self on the phone, but as soon as Andy saw him, he was struck by the change in his physical appearance. Although still thick-set, he appeared to have lost weight: his face was no longer so rounded and his jacket seemed to be a size too big. His face, which had been flawless and deep mahogany in colour, seemed paler, somehow less full of rude health than before; if there had been wrinkles there before, they were not as noticeable as they were now; and his black hair was certainly more grizzled. Once he had shaken hands with both Tim and Andy and motioned them to take the two chairs that he had placed in front of his desk, he sat down rather heavily and regarded them warily across the wide expanse of furniture. Tim's instinct was not to put him at ease, but to force him to take the lead in the conversation.

"So," Charles Heward said at length, "since I can only offer you a little time, perhaps we had better get started." He addressed Andy. "You say that you have some new leads in your investigation into Kathryn's death?"

Andy nodded.

"One lead in particular, actually," he said. "Do you remember that when we last spoke, you said that you had seen Kathryn Sheppard on the Thursday before she was reported missing, with the intention of breaking off your engagement?"

"Certainly I remember it: I told you that it was something that had been troubling my own conscience and my wife's ever since and I thought that the time had come to make a clean breast of it."

"Can you remember what you said next, sir?"

"I . . . in what context? Which part of our conversation are you referring to?"

"The part when you said that, after you broke off your engagement to Kathryn, on the last Thursday that we know she was alive, she had not turned up for work on the following day, which was, obviously, a Friday. How did you know that?"

"Well, it wasn't a secret, was it? I think that it even featured on the recent *Crimewatch* programme, which of course I watched, out of curiosity, after your last visit."

"What you say is partly correct, sir. The *Crimewatch* programme that was broadcast a few days ago did mention that Kathryn had phoned her office that Friday morning and asked to take the day as holiday, at very short notice. But that piece of information was never made public at the time, or in the subsequent investigation that took place about fifteen years ago. It was one of several facts about the case that were revealed for the first time during last week's programme. In 1975, when Kathryn disappeared, and again in 1990, when the case was reopened, the police decided not to tell the public that Kathryn had taken that day as holiday, because they realised that only her parents and her employer – who were asked to keep quiet about it – were in possession of that piece of information. And in all probability her killer, of course."

Tim was watching Charles Heward closely. He half expected him to make a run for it. He was a big man and could possibly have overpowered both himself and Andy if he were determined enough. What happened next was more unexpected. Charles Heward removed his heavy gold wedding ring and laid it carefully on his desk. The he opened his hands in a gesture of surrender. He suddenly looked very tired indeed.

"All right," he said. "I will tell you exactly what happened. I realise that I am entitled to have a lawyer present before I say any more, but I will tell you what happened now, both as a gesture of goodwill and to demonstrate that, essentially, I am innocent. You should know that I shall fight any charge of murder tooth and nail and take it to the highest court in the land, if necessary. I don't even admit to manslaughter. Kathryn's death was an accident."

Charles Heward picked up the gold ring, and rolled it in the palm of his hand. He took a deep breath.

"Go on, sir," said Tim steadily.

"When I told DC Carstairs that Veronica knew that I had not broken off my engagement to Kathryn until shortly before her disappearance, I was not telling the exact truth. In fact, Veronica thought that Kathryn herself had broken it off some time before. Veronica would not have consented to resume our relationship if she had known that I was still seeing Kathryn; and it would probably have been the last straw if she had found out that I had been deceiving her again. For a short time, I led a double life, but it was getting more and more difficult to maintain. It was only possible at all because Veronica insisted on keeping the fact that we were seeing each other again a secret – partly through pride, partly because she did not wish either of us to stretch her father's patience to breaking-point. At first I was confused: I really did not know whether it was Kathryn or Veronica whom I wished to marry. Over time, however, I realised that Veronica and I had much more in common: we moved in the same circles, shared the same interests. And I don't deny that the fact that her father was who he was had some bearing on my final decision. Being with Kathryn, on the other hand, was becoming more and more tedious. She lived in a backwater that was far removed from my everyday life and she could not understand how a young lawyer's career unfolds, or what kind of effort he has to put into it in order to make it do so. Of course, not all lawyers are married to other lawyers: many make happy marriages to women – or, nowadays, men – who are content with keeping house for them and entertaining their colleagues. But I could not see Kathryn in this role, either. She wanted her own career. In the end I recognised that we were incompatible and arranged to see her on that Thursday evening in order to tell her. But I had to work quite late that afternoon and, by the time I reached King's Cross, there had been a fatality on the line and there were no more trains running to Peter-borough that evening. I called Kathryn and told her that I would return home to fetch my car and that I would drive to Spalding, but that it would be late when I arrived. It wasn't long after I'd put the phone down that Veronica turned up at my office as a surprise and suggested that we went out to dinner. Of course, I had no good reason for refusing and this made it impossible for me to travel to Spalding until the next day. I called Kathryn early the following morning and said that I would be with her by about 10.00 a.m. I asked her to take the day off work."

"I see," said Tim. "Why do you suppose that she didn't tell her boss the reason why she wanted the day off when she called him? After all, it would have made her behaviour seem more responsible: her colleagues knew that she had a fiancé who lived in London, and that your time for being together was therefore somewhat limited."

"I don't know why, but my guess is that she knew what I was going to say. As I've explained, we had been meeting less and less regularly over the previous few months and our relationship was becoming strained. I think that pride will have prevented her from indicating to colleagues that something was wrong until the inevitable happened – in her mind, of course, it was not yet inevitable – and that at the same time she was safeguarding herself against questions about her day off the following week, if the worst came to the worst."

"I see," said Tim again. "So you arrived at Kathryn's flat at around 10.00 a.m. as you promised." Charles Heward nodded. "Then what happened?"

"It was a nice day, and I suggested that we went for a drive. She was fond of Bourne Woods and there was a pub close by them where we used to go for lunch sometimes. I wasn't thinking very clearly, but I suppose I had some kind of farewell lunch in mind."

"Or a cynic might say that you chose not to enter her flat, because you knew there was every danger you might leave some forensic evidence behind." Tim said this with a smile.

"I assure you that that was not the case," Charles Heward replied, rather stiffly. "We drove to the woods, chatting. The conversation was rather laboured – at least, I thought so – but it was amicable enough. I was dreading having to break the news to her. When we reached the woods, I decided to go ahead with the walk, rather than tell her straight away. We were actually walking back towards the car before I realised that there was no more time left and that I would have to tell her that it was over."

"How did she take it?"

"Far worse than I had imagined. She became quite hysterical. She beat me about the head with her hands – ineffectual little blows, they were pathetic – and screamed and shouted. Then she burst into tears, and begged me to change my mind. I was afraid that someone would hear all the commotion, as we were very close to the car park by this time, but we didn't see a soul. Finally, she took a knife from her bag – it was a kitchen knife with a fairly long, curved blade, a sort of fruit knife, I would guess – and threatened to kill herself with it. I tried to grab her wrist, to make her drop the knife, but somehow she jerked away from me, and fell on it. There was nothing that I could do to save her. It must have gone straight through her heart. She was dead within minutes."

"Why didn't you call the police?"

"For the reasons that I have already given DC Carstairs. I didn't want to jeopardise either my career, or what was becoming the likelihood that Veronica would once again agree to marry me."

"What did you do then?"

"I hid the body under some bushes and ran to the car park, to make sure that no-one else was there. I took a travel rug from the car, went back to the bushes, and wrapped Kathryn in it. I put her body in the boot. Then I . . . I removed the knife, and cleaned it on the grass, then threw it into the wastebin at the edge of the car park. I went into Bourne and bought a trowel from a supermarket – I daren't go to a proper tool-shop to buy a spade, in case someone recognised me – and then drove around until dark. I dug a shallow grave by the slip-road on the A1, put her body in it, and covered it with earth. I then drove back to London. I took the travel rug with me, and burnt it. I stayed up all night preparing some case notes, so that when the police asked me what I had been doing on that day, I had the evidence of a day's work to show them."

"Did you place the plastic Red Indian with her body?"

"No. I didn't know she had it on her: it must have been in her pocket. I know where it came from, though: it was some kind of in-joke that she and Hedley Atkins and Bryony all shared. They each had one, and were playing some kind of silly game with them on the occasion on which I met Hedley."

"Your car was thoroughly searched and tested for forensic evidence when you were briefly under suspicion for Kathryn's murder. Why do you suppose that none was found? Was it just luck?"

"I wasn't driving my own car when I went to see Kathryn.

I had borrowed Veronica's, because she brought it with her when she came to meet me on the Thursday evening. I told her that I needed to go home to fetch my car, because I had to drive to see a client the following day, and she lent me hers. I spent the night at her flat – I had spare clothes there. It did strike me as odd that Kathryn did not ask me why I wasn't driving my own car. I think that she must have known for sure that I was going to break off with her when she saw the car. She probably put the knife into her bag while I was walking up the path. I returned Veronica's car to her on the Saturday and told her that I had been too busy to use it, after all. Of course she was never a suspect, so the police did not impound her vehicle. What I told DC Carstairs about Veronica standing by me when I lied about still being engaged to Kathryn was true, although it nearly ruined our relationship again. But Veronica had no inkling that I had actually witnessed Kathryn's death."

"Very ingenious," said Tim. "Thank you for telling us your story, sir. And now I think you do need to appoint a lawyer, as you suggested. I'm sure that you have plenty of acquaintance to choose from."

"What do you mean?"

"Charles Heward, I am arresting you for the murder of Kathryn Elaine Sheppard on or about October 15th 1975. You do not have to say anything . . ."

EPILOGUE

Charles Heward, QC, MP, was charged with the murder of Kathryn Sheppard. He assembled an expert team of lawyers to defend him, including Sir Cecil Petrie, one of the UK's foremost barristers. Sir Cecil argued that the version of events that Mr. Heward had recounted to Detective Inspector Tim Yates and Detective Constable Andy Carstairs had been scrupulously truthful; that he had demonstrated his willingness to help the police clear up the mystery of Kathryn Sheppard's death in an almost selflessly honourable way; and that he had finally confessed because he wanted the truth to be known, despite the detrimental effect that going public might have on both his career and his marriage. His only crime had been his foolish concealment of Kathryn Sheppard's body after she had – probably unintentionally – killed herself with a knife which she had hidden in her bag in order to create a scene. Concealing a body was, of course, a serious offence, and Mr. Heward was fully aware of the gravity of this crime, but it was a much lesser crime than murder. He was willing to face the consequences for the ill-judged course of action he had taken more than thirty years before; but Sir Cecil asked the jury to bear in mind the fact that at the time he had been a young lawyer in the process of building his career who had managed to get himself tangled up in a love triangle. His had been the action of a confused man, rather than an evil one.

The judge directed the jury to return a verdict of not guilty to the charge of murder, because of lack of evidence and Charles Heward's otherwise impeccable record of good character, and asked them to consider only whether he was guilty of the charge of unlawfully concealing a body. He was found guilty of this latter charge and given a suspended sentence. He did not get off entirely scot free, however: his wife Veronica left him shortly afterwards and subsequently sued him for what turned out to be (for him) a very expensive divorce. He also lost his seat in the next general election.

No evidence was found to suggest that either Dorothy Atkins or Ronald Atkins was murdered. The coroner recorded a verdict of death by natural causes for Dorothy. An open verdict was lodged on Ronald's death.

Testifying in court, Professor Salkeld said that DNA tests confirmed that Ronald Atkins was indeed Hedley's father, though when cross-examined, he agreed that recent research carried out in the Netherlands indicated that DNA from close relatives could be so similar as sometimes to give misleading results. When questioned further, he confirmed that this would especially be the case if one or more instances of incestuous births had occurred within a family.

Hedley Atkins was charged with the murder of his sister Bryony. It was stated that his father, Ronald Atkins, and his uncle, Colin Atkins, had probably been involved, but that it was impossible to determine to what extent so long after the event, particularly as both had since died. After reading psychiatric reports and listening to expert witnesses, the trial judge decided that Hedley was unfit to plead and he was committed to a secure mental unit, just as his mother had been more than thirty years before.

The case of the murder of Doris Atkins was not reopened, and Dorothy Atkins was not posthumously exonerated of her conviction for murder.

Peter Prance's account of how the deaths of Eliza Drake, Doris Atkins and Bryony Atkins had occurred was ruled inadmissible in court, partly because it was largely based on hearsay and therefore conjectural, partly because Prance was deemed an unreliable witness. For the latter reason he was also unable to testify on Hedley Atkins' behalf. Prance retracted the confession made during his night at Spalding police station on the grounds that it had been given under duress. He was acquitted of the charge of conspiracy to cause actual bodily harm, on the grounds that Hedley Atkins was not fit to testify against him. He moved back to London, where he appeared in court on yet another charge of fraud less than twelve months later. He was released on bail, and disappeared before his trial could take place. There was some concern that he had been abducted rather than that he had absconded of his own free will, but police resources were stretched at the time and neither he nor the reason for his disappearance were to be discovered.

The coroner's report on the death of Eliza Drake was examined, and yielded no evidence that her death had been anything but an unfortunate accident.

Henry Bevelton retired, and led a pious life in old age, becoming one of the churchwardens of Spalding Parish Church.

The house in Westlode Street became the property of Hedley Atkins, and consequently was destined to stand empty again for very many more years.

One day, after Hedley had been sent to Broadmoor, and Tim and Juliet were working on another case together, she turned from writing some information on the glass screens on which the story of their latest murder investigation was unfolding, and said to him:

"I hope that this one turns out more satisfactorily than the Kathryn Sheppard case. I always felt unhappy about that. Two friends who died at almost the same time, their deaths apparently unrelated, one of them murdered, the other dead as the result of an accident. It didn't ring true, somehow."

"No," Tim agreed. "It didn't. But I don't think that the deaths *were* related; and it's my guess that they were indeed

a murder and an accident. But I'd bet my life, or almost, tha
it was the other way around. And now Hedley Atkins is lan
guishing in a mental home, just as his mother did; and in al
probability, she was always as innocent as I believe that h
now is. Innocent in the eyes of the law, anyway. Some fami
lies have their own morality. Both Tirzah and Hedley pai
dearly for keeping what they knew in the family."